CAST IN PERIL

MICHELLE SAGARA

CAST IN PERIL

ISBN-13: 978-0-373-80350-7

This edition published by arrangement with Harlequin Books S.A.

For questions and comments about the quality of this book, please contact us at CustomerService@Harlequin.com.

www.Harlequin.com

Printed in U.S.A.

For Tobin,
who escaped to the west coast,
but has since discovered that being a brother is a life sentence.

CHAPTER 1

The worst thing about having a roommate, in Kaylin's opinion—and admittedly after only two weeks—was morning. The fact that this particular roommate was a Dragon didn't help. Bellusdeo was clean, tidy, and ate very little. She didn't actually require sleep, and for the first couple of nights, that had seemed like a good thing because Kaylin's apartment only had one bed. It only had one room.

But around morning number four, which had come on the heels of an urgent mirror message from the Guild of Midwives and a hideously touch-and-go birth, the "good thing" developed the preceding words "too damn much of a..."

Ten days—which included three more emergency calls—later, Kaylin struggled out of bed when the shadows in the room were far too short, and came face-to-face with someone who looked refreshed and annoyingly cheerful. She always looked refreshed and cheerful, but the annoying part had grown with time and familiarity.

It was far too late for breakfast, in part because Kaylin hadn't managed to get to the market the previous day and there was no food in the apartment. So she scrounged for clean clothing, taking what little time she had to tend to the large unhatched egg she slept wrapped around.

"Kaylin, I think the egg has changed color," Bellusdeo said. She stared at the egg but didn't actually touch it. She did, however, help Kaylin gather the cloth she kept wrapped around it when she left it for the day.

Kaylin, who was still bleary from sleep and fatigued by the work of the previous night, squinted. "Maybe. Do you think—do you think that means it's going to hatch?"

"I don't know. I don't recognize the species of egg."

Kaylin pressed her ear against the shell. She could almost hear something moving within it—but the sound was so faint it might have been due to hopeful imagination. She considered taking the egg into the office with her, remembered that it was magic-lesson day, and decided to take the risk of leaving it untended for the afternoon. It was afternoon by this point, so it would be a shorter absence than usual.

Bellusdeo then accompanied Kaylin into work.

Kaylin accepted the barrage of amused mockery her hour of arrival caused with less than her usual grace. She had managed to go almost three weeks without being late. Admittedly on two of those days she'd perambulated around the office like someone doing a good imitation of the walking dead—but she'd been timely walking dead, damn it.

"If you dislike the mockery," Bellusdeo told her as she walked gracefully by Kaylin's side, "why don't you just arrive on time?"

"I need to sleep."

"You don't have to go to the midwives' guildhall."

"If I miss a few hours here in the morning, Marcus snarls at me and I expose my throat for a few minutes. I also win someone some money in the betting pool. If I miss an emergency call from the midwives' guild, someone dies. Guess which is more important?"

Bellusdeo nodded. "We have an etiquette lesson this evening," the Dragon added. It was true. It was also a subtle reminder that Bellusdeo did make Kaylin's life a little easier, because while Lord Diarmat pretty much despised Kaylin, he couldn't openly treat Bellusdeo with contempt, and Bellusdeo had an uncanny knack for asking the direct questions that would have caused mortal offense had they come from Kaylin's mouth. In this case, mortal was accurate.

Kaylin grimaced and straightened up. "I have a magic lesson in half an hour."

"With Sanabalis?"

"The same." Kaylin hesitated and then added, "Do you think you could call him Lord Sanabalis?"

"Why? You don't. If you don't, I can hardly see that it will make much difference if I fail to do so."

"It won't make much difference to you. It'll get me in less trouble." She headed toward the reception desk, where Caitlin was watching their progress down the hall. The mirror dutifully announced the time the minute Kaylin's foot had crossed the threshold. At least it hadn't called her by name.

"Good afternoon, dear," Caitlin said, rising from her chair. "The midwives called you in last night?"

Kaylin nodded. "Marya woke me at two in the morning."

"It was bad?"

"It was very bad; I almost didn't make it in time."

"Did you eat anything before you came here?"

"Yes."

Bellusdeo lifted a lovely golden brow but said nothing. Not that words actually had to be spoken around Caitlin, who pursed her lips.

"Lord Sanabalis is waiting for you."

"Of course he is."

Bellusdeo didn't actually join her for magic lessons; as a member of the Dragon Court—albeit on a technicality—she didn't require them. She did, however, go to Elantran language lessons in the East Room for the duration; the Imperial Palace had ordered two linguists to work with her during that time. What the linguists made of Bellusdeo, Kaylin didn't know; she was just grateful for the few moments in which Bellusdeo was someone else's problem.

"I admit I'm surprised to see you on time, Private," Sanabalis said as she cringed her way through contact with the room's door ward and entered.

"Oh?"

"Given the time at which you left your dwelling last evening, I assumed you would be at least an hour late."

Kaylin sat and folded her arms across her chest. "You're having my apartment watched at two in the morning?"

Sanabalis didn't answer the question. Instead he said, "How is Bellusdeo adapting to life in the City?"

"She hasn't changed much since I spoke to you about it two days ago."

"And have you reconsidered the Emperor's offer to house you in a more suitable location?"

Sadly, she had. On offer was a much, much larger apartment. It was, however, farther from the office, and Kaylin still held on to the faint hope that Bellusdeo would get tired of living in a run-down, single-room apartment with no privacy and choose to move out on her own.

So far, Dragon stubbornness was running neck and neck with human stubbornness. It seemed unfair that only the human was suffering. If they had a larger dwelling, Kaylin could have an entire room to herself, and they would have room for Bellusdeo's Ascendant, a Norannir who would only barely fit through Kaylin's current door—if he crouched. Maggaron could keep an eye on Bellusdeo, and Kaylin might actually have a day—at work—in which she didn't have the Dragon as her constant companion. As it was, that Ascendant, Maggaron, had been exiled to the Tower in the fief of Tiamaris, and he was very, very glum about the separation.

What she said, however, was "No. We're doing fine." Kaylin's biggest fear was that she would move, lose her small—but affordable—apartment, and have nowhere else to go when Bellusdeo finally decided to move out. Severn had suggested that she pay her rent while staying in the Imperial building, but it galled Kaylin to spend that much money on something she wasn't even using.

She glared at her nemesis, the candle.

Sanabalis folded his hands on the table's surface; it had been newly oiled and waxed, and the Dragon's reflection stared back up at him. "Your etiquette lesson is tonight."

"I know."

"You seem to have survived the previous lessons."

"Yes. So did Diarmat and Bellusdeo."

Sanabalis winced, but he chuckled, as well. "I believe Lord Diarmat is on the edge of repenting his decision to teach you; he may well ask the Arkon to undertake that duty instead."

"But he won't fall over that edge until we've suffered at least as much as he has?"

"Ah, no. I believe he would be more than willing to continue to teach you, but he feels that Bellusdeo is an impediment to your effective absorption of necessary knowledge." Sanabalis nodded at the candle. "Begin."

* * *

The entire department heard her shriek.

Only half of them left their desks to see what had caused it—or at least only half of them were visible when Kaylin threw the door open and tried to run through them into the office. She was bouncing.

"Teela! Tain! I did it!"

"Whatever you did, kitling," Teela replied, "you broke the silence spell that usually protects us from your cursing during class." She glanced pointedly at the warded door. "What do you think you did?"

Kaylin spun and pointed.

The candle's wick was actually burning. She'd been staring at it every class for what felt like years—but couldn't have been more than a couple of months in objective time—and had even cut it in half in a foul mood. Not once in all those months had the damn thing done what it was supposed to do.

But today?

Today she'd almost felt the warmth of fire; she'd grasped and visualized its name. It had taken the better part of an hour to accomplish that much, because it was a large name and parts of it kept sliding out of her grip. It didn't matter; this was the first class she'd had with Sanabalis that hadn't ended in total, frustrating failure.

Lord Sanabalis rose, and Kaylin hesitated, losing a little of her bounce. "You didn't do it, did you? It was me?"

"It was you, Private Neya. And because you've succeeded—once—I will consider today's lesson complete. If you will accompany me?"

"Pardon?"

"I believe Lord Grammayre and Sergeant Kassan would like a few words with you. They did want to speak with you earlier, but I felt the matter could wait until after your lesson."

Yes, because Lord Sanabalis was a Dragon and Lord Grammayre and Sergeant Kassan were only the men responsible for signing off on her pay chit.

Lord Grammayre and Marcus were waiting in the Hawklord's Tower. Kaylin, torn between panic at the length of time they'd been made to wait and worry about the topic of discussion, went up the stairs at a brisk clip, as if rushing to her doom. Dragon knowledge of the effective chain of command in the Halls of Law was pretty simple: the Dragon Court's desires took precedence over everything. It was hard to get that wrong. Their knowledge of the finer details, on the other hand—and in particular Kaylin's place in the food chain as a private—left a lot to be desired, especially since their pay and their rank weren't ever going to be at risk. She tried not to resent this as Sanabalis, curse him, practically crawled.

The Tower doors were open, which was a small mercy. Kaylin approached them, the sound of her steps on stone drawing two pairs of distinctive eyes—Leontine and Aerian. Marcus's facial fur was standing on end, and his eyes were orange. The Hawklord's wings were slightly extended, and his eyes were a gray-blue. Had she been a flower, she'd've instantly wilted under that much dry heat. Angry Leontine Sergeant, angry Aerian Commander in Chief, slightly bored Dragon, and panicked human—you could practically call it a racial congress, with humans in their usual position.

Marcus was in such a bad mood that he didn't even mention how late she was; he wasn't in a bad enough mood not to growl when she hesitated in the doorway. She crossed the threshold quickly and offered Lord Grammayre a salute. It was as perfect as she could make it—and if two weeks under the Draconic Lord Diarmat had given her nothing else, it had certainly improved the quality of necessary gestures of respect, not that she was required to salute a member of the Dragon Court.

Lord Sanabalis, as a member of said court, wasn't required to offer a salute to anyone in the Halls of Law. Kaylin wasn't certain what formal gestures of respect he offered the Eternal Emperor, because thankfully she'd never seen the Eternal Emperor—at least not yet. She'd seen the rest of the Dragons interact with each other, and while they were polite and formal when nothing important was being discussed, they didn't spend all day bowing, saluting, or speaking full titles. She now even knew what their full titles were.

"At ease, Private." If an order could be guaranteed to make her feel less at ease, she didn't want to hear it. The Hawklord's tone of voice had enough edge to draw blood. She nodded stiffly and dropped her arms to her sides.

"Lord Sanabalis," the Hawklord continued, "we have news of some import to relay to the Imperial Court."

"Good. Does it involve the current investigation into the Exchequer?"

"It does. We have an unexpected lead. Our subsequent investigations have given us reason to believe it is extremely relevant."

Sanabalis raised a brow. "May I ask the source of that information?"

"You may; it is the only reason Private Neya is currently present."

"I will assume that the lead did not come through the Private."

"No. Not directly. She has been involved as your attaché in the fief of Tiamaris for much of the investigation; as she has not yet been released from those duties, she has had no direct involvement in the Exchequer affair."

Lord Sanabalis nodded.

"Even if she is no longer required as frequently in the fief, she appears to be the unofficial minder for the newly arrived Lady Bellusdeo."

Kaylin cringed.

"Private?" Marcus growled.

Kaylin cleared her throat. "She doesn't like to be referred to as Lady Bellusdeo."

"And given her position at the moment, that is understandable. I will endeavor not to cause her the hardship of appropriate Elantran title in future," Lord Grammayre said. "However."

Sanabalis's eyes had shaded to a pale copper. Kaylin wasn't certain what color her eyes would be if human eye color shifted at the whim of mood; given that she was standing near an angry Leontine, an annoyed Dragon, and an unhappy Aerian, it probably wouldn't be good.

"What is Private Neya's involvement?"

The Leontine glared at the Hawklord. The Hawklord pretended not to notice either the glare or the question. "The usual method of paying in Imperial currency for information was rejected; the information, however, was deemed necessary."

"And?"

"The information offered to us came via Lord Nightshade of the fief of Nightshade."

Copper shaded toward orange in the Dragon Lord's eyes. "He offered the information first?"

"Of course not. But he offered some of the information to indicate the importance of the offer."

"And the information he did offer was not sufficient for our investigators?"

"No; if we attempted to investigate thoroughly, we would

almost certainly be detected, and any proof of criminal activity would vanish."

"What was the tidbit he dangled?"

"The Office of the Exchequer has been working in conjunction with two highly placed Arcanists. Both," he added, "are Barrani, and both might be in possession of some of the embezzled funds."

Kaylin did not, through dint of will, whistle. She did sneak a glance at Sanabalis; his eyes hadn't gotten any redder, which was a positive sign. On the other hand, Marcus's hadn't gotten any less orange, which was not, given that Marcus now turned the full force of his glare on her. She felt this a tad unfair, given that she'd already warned him what Nightshade would demand in return for the information; she was not, however, feeling suicidal enough to point this out.

"Were you aware, Private, that the leave of absence requested in return for this information would be extensive?"

"...How extensive?"

"The fieflord is asking for a minimum of six weeks if we provide the transport, and a minimum of eight weeks if we do not."

She blinked. After a moment, she said, "Eight weeks?" thinking, as she did, of her rent.

"Eight weeks."

"I can't take eight weeks off!"

For some reason, this seemed to improve Marcus's mood. "When you agreed to Teela's offer of aid during your leave of absence, did it ever occur to you to look up a map of the Empire?"

"...No."

Sanabalis lifted a hand. "Why is a leave of eight weeks required?"

"She's to travel to the West March."

"A map wouldn't have done you any good, Private," Sanabalis now told Kaylin. "The West March is not technically part of the Empire. It is a remote stretch of forest of some significant size. It is not, however, the size of the forest that makes it worthy of note."

This was not exactly a comfort. "What makes it noteworthy?"

"The trees contained in the heart of that forest are not considered…entirely safe."

"What does that mean? They don't burn when you breathe on them?"

Sanabalis's answering silence was glacial.

"Given Teela's offer, she will also be missing for eight weeks. It's a good damn thing Nightshade specifically demanded that you go without any other Hawks, or we'd probably have to do without Corporal Handred, as well."

Kaylin was still stuck on the eight weeks. "Minimum?" she finally managed to say.

"Minimum. There is the possibility of poor weather and impassable roads, and Lord Nightshade wished to make clear that eight weeks might not suffice."

She shook herself. "The information was useful?"

"The information," Lord Grammayre replied, before Marcus could, "may finally crack the case for us. It is more than simply useful, but we wasted some time in negotiations for your release, and we are only now in dialogue with the Lord of Wolves."

The Wolves.

"How bad is this going to be?"

No one answered, which was answer enough.

"You agreed to the leave of absence?"

The Hawklord nodded. Kaylin desperately wanted to ask

if this absence involved pay, because she'd have nowhere to live if it didn't. On the other hand, the right person to ask was Caitlin, not Marcus, and certainly not Marcus in this mood.

"When does this leave start?"

"Teela will be able to better inform you of the actual dates of import; I suggest you speak with her, because she'll also be able to inform you of expected dress, weather, and, apparently, colorful wildlife. Lord Nightshade, however, is likely to be in touch with you shortly; you are to leave in five days if we are not to provide the transport he's asking for."

"And if you do?"

"We're not."

"But—"

"Yes?"

"The midwives. And the Foundling Hall. And the—the etiquette lessons—"

"Lord Sanabalis will, of course, evaluate the information once you've left, and discuss it with the Imperial Court. In a strict currency evaluation, eight weeks of your time is far less than we might be expected to pay for information of this nature; it will save money at a time when finances are—"

Sanabalis coughed loudly.

"Now," Marcus growled, "get lost."

Teela was loitering at the bottom of the stairs, her hands behind her back, her shoulders at a slant against the slight curve of the wall. She glanced up when she heard Kaylin's steps. Given that Kaylin wasn't exactly attempting to move silently, this wasn't hard.

"You've heard the news?" she said as Kaylin took the last step and drew level with her, in a manner of speaking. Teela, like all Barrani, was tall; she probably had seven inches on

Kaylin when Kaylin was standing at her straightest. Teela wasn't even trying at the moment.

"Yes."

"Don't look so glum. Have you ever been outside the City?"

"No."

Teela whistled. "Well, this will be an adventure for you, then. It's a useful experience; you can't stay cooped up behind the City walls for all your life."

"Why exactly not?"

"In this case? Because Nightshade had a very important piece of information and you happened to mention his offer to Marcus."

"I didn't think I'd be gone for eight weeks!"

"Eight is, in my opinion, optimistic."

Kaylin's jaw momentarily unhinged. Teela reached out and pushed it shut. "Don't fret. It'll be fun."

"That's not making me feel a whole lot better, Teela. I know what your definition of fun is."

Severn was waiting for Kaylin in the office when she at last reached her desk; she knew this because he was sitting in her chair. He looked up when she tapped his shoulder.

"Bad news?" he asked as he moved to let her sit. He reached into the pack at his feet and pulled out the bracer that prevented her from using magic. She'd thrown it over her shoulder on the run, because she knew it would return to Severn. It always did. "Midwives?"

She took the bracer, slid it over her wrist, and closed it. "Two in the morning."

"And I heard that I should offer congratulations on the candle."

The triumph of a lit candle had evaporated. She sat and folded her arms across her desk in a type of lean that implied her spine was melting. "They took Nightshade up on his offer," she said, speaking to the wood grain and the interior of her elbows.

"Did you expect them to do anything else?"

"...No."

"Then?"

"...I'll be absent for eight weeks. Teela thinks it'll actually be longer." She lifted her head and turned to look at Severn. "You're not coming, either."

He shrugged; it was a fief shrug, and it was a tense one.

"So you'll be out patrolling with some other Hawk, not me, and gods know if they won't decide that you're more effective working with someone else. Marcus might give my beat away."

"Marcus won't—"

"And the midwives won't be able to call me. They've had four emergencies in the last two weeks. If those had been part of the eight, at least four people would have died."

"At least?"

"I think they could have saved two of the babies."

"But Nightshade's information may well crack the Exchequer case."

"May well? It had better tie it up in expensive cloth with bows on top." She lowered her chin to the desk again. "But putting the Exchequer in prison—or under the ground—wouldn't save the lives of those mothers. I'm hard put to see which lives it would save. Besides the Hawks."

Severn tactfully steered the topic away from her visions of mortality. "Teela's going with you?"

"Yeah. She's a Lord of the Barrani Court, and apparently whatever this jaunt to the West March is about, it's ceremonial. She's got an invitation to go."

"Well, keep an eye on her."

Kaylin almost laughed. "Me and what army? You know Teela."

Severn didn't have a chance to answer. Bellusdeo appeared at his elbow. "They've finally let me out," she said in accented but reasonable Elantran. She frowned. "You don't look very happy. The magic lesson didn't go well?"

"No, the lesson went very well."

"This is how you react to a good lesson?"

Kaylin snorted but pushed herself off her desk and out of the chair. "No. It's how I react to bad news."

When Bellusdeo's brows rose, Kaylin could almost hear them snap. "What bad news?" she asked in almost entirely the wrong tone of voice.

"The Barrani have some sort of ceremony out in the West March, and I'm obliged to attend it."

"Why? You're not Barrani."

Kaylin's mouth stopped flapping as her brain caught up with it. She glanced at Severn for help, but he had nothing to offer. "I can't really talk about it," she finally said. "Not without having my throat ripped out."

Bellusdeo, however, knew that this wasn't literal. It had taken her a couple of days to figure that out, because Marcus was still his usual suspicious and unfriendly self when dealing with Dragons. "I almost think I will apply for a job in the Halls," she said, her voice cool. "I've heard that the Hawks are very multiracial, and they've even had a Dragon as a member before."

"Marcus would be your boss," Kaylin replied quickly.

"Yes. I'll admit that is a deterrent. Are you ready to go home?"

Kaylin had been ready to go home an hour ago, which would have been during the meeting with the Hawklord, Sanabalis, and Marcus. She nodded, looking out the window, which was silent for the moment. "We have time to grab something to eat—and get changed—before we head to the palace and the charming Lord Diarmat for tonight's personal torture session."

The streets wouldn't be empty for hours yet, but they weren't quite as crowded as they had been on the way in, and Kaylin couldn't be late, in a career-detrimental way, to enter her own apartment. She could, however, miss the few remaining farmers in the market, so she hurried to that destination, Bellusdeo in tow. Bellusdeo had a few questions about food acquisition, but in the main, the worst of them had been answered on their first foray into the market, much to Kaylin's frustration and the bemusement of the farmers.

It was helpful to have Bellusdeo here, on the other hand, because the baskets in which food was generally carried home were still in said home. They made their way back to the apartment; by this point, Bellusdeo had no difficulty finding it.

The Dragon practiced her Elantran in the market, and she practiced it in the street. Kaylin tried—very hard—to elide all swearing from her commentary and her answers to Bellusdeo's questions, and only in part because it was slightly embarrassing to have to explain what the rude words meant.

But she was hungry and slightly discouraged as she made her way to the apartment, her thoughts mostly on the midwives, Tiamaris, and the total lack of privacy one room afforded.

She unlocked the door, entered her room, and made a beeline for the mirror; when it showed a total lack of calls, she relaxed. She let her hair down, literally, and tried to put the stick where she could easily find it in the morning. She then went to the kitchen for a couple of plates. There was still water that was potable, and the food she'd bought for the evening didn't require anything as complicated as cooking.

Bellusdeo took a seat on the bed, which was fair; the chair was a clothing repository at the moment, and Kaylin wasn't so exhausted that she needed to fall over and sleep. The bed, however, creaked ominously as it received Dragon weight, and while it hadn't yet collapsed beneath Bellusdeo, the sound reminded Kaylin of the unhatched egg that now resided beneath her. She quickly shoved the remainder of a hard, smooth cheese into her mouth and tried not to look as if she was diving in a panic for the box that contained the egg.

Bellusdeo snorted. Kaylin had the grace to look a little embarrassed as she unwound the various bits and pieces of cloth that served as poor insulation for the egg during her absence.

The egg was a pale shade of purple in her hands.

"It wasn't that color earlier," Bellusdeo observed, leaning back on her hands and stretching.

"No, it wasn't. Tomorrow, if it hasn't hatched, I'm going to bring it with me to the office."

"Oh, your Sergeant will love that, I'm certain." She frowned and looked up at the shutters of the window as they popped open.

Kaylin, still holding the egg, winced and rose. "Sorry about that," she said, because the shutter had narrowly avoided the back of Bellusdeo's head. "They're warped. I keep meaning to see about getting them replaced—"

"When you say 'replaced,' do you mean you intend to build new ones?"

"Hells, no. I couldn't make new shutters that would be half as good as these, and these are no good. Let me tie them together."

Bellusdeo, however, was looking at something in her lap. She rose, her expression freezing solid. It wasn't her expression that was the problem: it was the color of her eyes. They'd shifted from lazy gold to a deep, deep red without stopping for anything else in between. "Kaylin," she said, moving toward her and toward the door, as well. "The shutters—"

But Kaylin didn't need to hear more, because something flew in through the open window.

CHAPTER 2

Kaylin's first instinct was to ram the shutters shut, but she was carrying the egg, and she'd have to set it down—or drop it. "Get down, Bellusdeo." Her voice was sharp, harsh.

Bellusdeo caught Kaylin by the shoulders and dragged her from the window as Kaylin ducked out of any line of sight that wasn't at a severe angle and tried to see where the crossbow bolt had landed. She didn't find it.

"Kaylin, we have to leave."

"If there's more than one assassin," Kaylin countered, "running out the door in a panic is playing into their hands." She grabbed for the egg's carton as a second bolt flew through the open window.

Except it wasn't a bolt. Kaylin felt the hair on her neck instantly stand at attention, which was bad; the marks on her body began to burn, which was worse. She couldn't see what she'd clearly heard land on the floor of her apartment, but she didn't need to see it to know—suddenly and completely—what it was. Her eyes widened.

"Gods—Bellusdeo—it's an Arcane bomb—"

The room exploded.

Wood flew out in a wide circle: shutters, parts of the wall, wooden floor slats, and the soft wood that formed their base. Her mattress sent feathers into the air, and the feathers were caught in a blue, blue sizzle, becoming a miniature lightning storm. There was so damn much magic in the room, Kaylin's entire body was screaming in pain on the way to total numbness.

Which was better than being dead.

Bellusdeo had her arms around Kaylin and her back toward the window; her body was pressed against the egg that Kaylin still held between almost nerveless palms. The world expanded around them; shards of mirror flew past Kaylin's cheek and lodged in the Dragon's hair. The floor beneath their feet cracked and gave; the joists above their heads did the same, bending up toward someone else's floor. Wind whipped whatever wasn't nailed down through the air—which would, in this apartment, be everything.

Everything except the two women who stood at what had once been its center. Kaylin could see a sphere surrounding them; it was a soft, pale gold, like the color of a living word—but there were no words to shed it.

"Are you all right?" she shouted.

Bellusdeo nodded. Her eyes were still bloodred, and her hands were like bruising pincers.

"I didn't know you were so powerful—"

Bellusdeo's brows rose into her very disheveled hair. "I'm not. This isn't me."

"It's not me, either." Kaylin looked at the bracer on her wrist; its gems' lights were flashing so quickly they looked like chaos embedded in gold. Somewhere above, below, and to the right, people began to shout and scream as Kaylin looked at her hands.

For once, Kaylin was barely aware of the civilians.

The egg's shell had cracked, and bits of it were flying in the unnatural wind the Arcane bomb had caused. It didn't matter. What was in—what had been surrounded by—that shell stared up at her. It was small and pale; it was also, like slightly smoky glass, translucent. Everything except its eyes. Its eyes were disturbing; they had no irises, no pupils, no whites. They would have been gray or silver, except for the constant, moving flecks of color that seemed to all but swim across their surface. Like opals, she thought.

Or, remembering the effects of the Shadow that had destroyed the watchtowers in the fief formerly known as Barren, like malignant storms.

Bellusdeo looked down, as well. She tried to move out of the way, but since she didn't actually let go of Kaylin's shoulders, it was awkward. Dragons weren't known for their flexibility. She hissed, a wordless sibilant. "Kaylin, your arm."

"The bracer does that some of the time. Ignore it."

"I wasn't talking about your bracer. Your—your marks, Chosen."

Kaylin frowned. She couldn't take her eyes off the small creature—and only in part because she didn't want to. It had the form and shape of something reptilian, but not the actual scales. A long neck, a long tail, and a delicate head with a tapered jaw, the beast now sat in her palms.

"Kaylin."

It opened its mouth, revealing translucent teeth, translucent tongue, and some hint of translucent upper palate. "I think—I think it's yawning."

"I think you're crazy," Bellusdeo snapped in Elantran. In Barrani, she added, "Is that the right word? It means *insane*."

"Yes." But when it stretched its neck, its tongue flickering like a snake's tongue might, she saw the last little bit of its body as it slowly unfurled wings. For something that fit more or less in the palm of her hand—well, a little less—it had long wings. Long wings; eyes like opals.

"Kaylin—"

Kaylin shook herself. "I'm sorry," she said, looking at the spot where the floor wasn't anymore. It happened to be far beneath her feet, but she hadn't yet fallen. Neither had the weightier Bellusdeo. "What about the marks?"

"If you can manage to divert your gaze by a few degrees, you'll see for yourself."

Kaylin looked slightly over the small creature's head. "Oh."

"Oh, you say."

One of the marks from Kaylin's arm was floating in the air above the small creature's head, hovering, in miniature, the way the spoken True Words did. "Bellusdeo, can you read it? Can you tell me what it means?"

Bellusdeo shook her head. "I was taught very little of the ancient tongue."

"But you're as old as the Arkon—"

"Yes. I was not, however, considered adult in my Aerie, because I wasn't. What I learned, I learned by subterfuge and charm. Mostly charm."

"It wouldn't kill you to try that on Diarmat. It might, at this point, kill him."

The rune began to thin as Kaylin watched it. No, not thin—compress. Three horizontal strokes began to shift their position, making a jumble of a pattern that had, for a moment, looked tantalizingly familiar. There was a short, fat dot in the center of the pattern, and slender, vertical squiggles to the left; those were pulled in as well, until there was something the shape of a very odd funnel just above the hatchling's delicate head.

It flicked its tongue and then roared. Which came out as a pretty pathetic squawk. As it inhaled to try again, the funnel above its head began to descend; the creature opened its mouth and…began to eat it. Or drink from it.

"Bellusdeo, pinch me. Oh, never mind—you already are."

Bellusdeo, however, was staring at the creature. "Do you understand what you have in your hands?" she finally asked in a hushed voice.

"A baby Dragon?"

"Remind me to speak to the Emperor about the standards of your biological education," was the scathing reply. "Anything that small and delicate that hatched in the Aerie would be crushed or suffocated before it got out of its shell."

"Well, it looks like a Dragon, except for the color."

"It looks nothing like a Dragon!"

Kaylin decided not to press the point.

"And if it were, we'd both be dead."

"What do you mean?"

"It's a familiar," Bellusdeo replied. "They're almost legendary creatures. No, let me rephrase that: they *are* legendary creatures. I've never seen one before."

"Then how do you know what it is?"

"Familiars, according to legend, are born in magical conflagration."

"From eggs?"

"Funnily enough, the legends didn't specify. This one, though, was."

"What can you tell me about familiars? From legend, I mean," she added hastily.

"Very little. They were the creatures of sorcerers, and in

one particular story, the sorcerer who sought to summon a familiar destroyed half a world in the attempt."

"Half a world?" Kaylin looked around the wreckage. "This doesn't even qualify, if that's the level of magic you're talking about."

Bellusdeo shrugged. "Legends are neither scientific nor historical. Arcane bomb? Is that what you called it?"

"Yes." She frowned. "I didn't see it; I could feel it. But I can see the sphere that absorbed most of the impact. On us," she hastily added, looking at the debris.

The Dragon looked around the ruins of what had once been Kaylin's apartment. Or rather, her building, since the one above and the one below weren't going to be suitable living quarters for anything but desperate mice.

"Is this," Kaylin nodded at the small dragon, "the source of the sphere?"

"Pardon?"

"The sphere. The one surrounding us."

Bellusdeo closed her eyes. When she opened them again, Kaylin was happy to see that they were orange. "You are correct," she said softly in Barrani. "There is a sphere surrounding us. You can see that without casting?"

Kaylin nodded. "It doesn't seem like a strong spell."

Bellusdeo's eyes rounded fully. Apparently this was idiocy beyond even her expectations of mortals. "In what way?"

Kaylin was now looking, eyes narrowed, at every standing surface in the surrounding apartment. "No signature," she replied, still examining the walls.

The small dragon turned its head toward the large one; its tongue flicked air, and Kaylin saw that its tongue was now the same color as its eyes. The rune was gone.

Kaylin was almost afraid to move, but she did—slowly—the small dragon cupped in her hands, the large Dragon attached to her shoulders. She didn't tell Bellusdeo to let go, because she had a hunch that the sphere was generated somehow by the creature Bellusdeo had called a familiar, and it was the sphere that seemed to be allowing her the slow, timid steps she was taking through what was essentially air with splinters thrown in. She didn't want Bellusdeo to fall.

But she looked at what remained of the floor where the Arcane bomb had exploded, and she could see the harsh illumination of a sigil against the broken floorboards; it was huge and splashed up against what remained of the walls.

"What are you looking for? The device?"

"No, that's gone. I'm looking for the signature of the mage who created it. Arcane bombs are usually designed to have up to three different magical signatures, and none of those signatures is guaranteed to correspond to an actual criminal." She frowned.

Bellusdeo looked shocked. Outraged. It instantly made Kaylin feel better. "What do you mean, an actual criminal? Isn't the creation of a magical item of that nature criminal enough?"

Since it was more or less an annual rant on Kaylin's part—if she was being generous—Kaylin had no arguments to offer in response. "This one's different."

"How?"

"I can only see two, and frankly, they seem a bit on the small size."

"Maybe it wasn't what you thought it was?"

"Or maybe the whole egg-hatching-in-conflagration thing did something with most of the magic the item contained." She glanced at the creature, who had curled up so that his head was practically under one of his wings. He appeared to be sleeping. "He's really, really cute," she whispered.

"Kaylin, please. Focus."

"Yes, Bellusdeo," she said in exactly the same meek tone she sometimes used to ward off Marcus-level irritation.

Kaylin was wondering how in the hells they were supposed to leave the apartment and make their way down to the presumed safety of the street below, because the floors between here and the door—which had incidentally been blown clear off its admittedly flimsy hinges and probably lay in pieces on the stairs below—were nonexistent.

Bellusdeo, however, didn't appear concerned. Enough of the wall was missing that she could probably go Dragon for a few minutes and jump out; the fall wasn't likely to harm her in her Dragon form. Going Dragon was technically illegal, and even if Kaylin was certain there would be dispensation granted for the act—and she was—Bellusdeo hesitated.

They were saved by the beat of frantic—and familiar—wings. "Kaylin!"

Clint had come. And if Clint was here, so were other Aerians. He shouted her name again, the tenor of the two syllables laced with fear so visceral it was painful. Kaylin shouted back, "We're here, Clint. We're alive. We're all right. There's no floor, though, so we're not sure how to get out."

"You're alive?"

She rolled her eyes and lifted her voice again. "No, I was lying. I'm dead and I'm here to haunt you and pull at your flight feathers for the rest of your natural existence!"

There was a pause and then a harsh bark of laughter; not just Clint's, either.

"Glad you think it's funny, Clint. Now can you fly your butt in here and carry us out?"

Kaylin Neya, Private, and a Hawk of long standing even if she hadn't technically been on the payroll as a Hawk for much of that tenure, loved her job. It was a defining responsibility, and it actually helped people. Or at least hindered frauds like the ones on Elani street. But at the end of a long day at work, what she usually wanted was to go home, eat—when there was food in the house—and curl up in bed.

The workday had ended, and she'd gone home for the last time. She just hadn't realized it.

From the cobbled stones of the street, she looked up at the very impressive hole in the wall of the building that had previously contained that home. She also looked at the debris on the streets and at the radius of its scatter. Clint was breathing heavily by the time he'd landed with Kaylin, because she'd insisted he take Bellusdeo out first.

"Kaylin?"

She glanced up at Clint. His wings were high; they weren't extended, but they made clear he was ready to fight if necessary. The skies were alive with Hawks. At this time of night, the Halls weren't exactly fully staffed; someone had sent out almost everyone they could get their hands on with short notice. She'd always loved to watch Aerians fly.

"Kaylin."

She looked at Clint again. "Sorry," she said. "I'm a little distracted." She lifted the small creature cupped in her palms. He was warm, and he was the only thing, at the moment, that seemed to be providing any heat. Her clothing, or the clothing she'd been wearing—and at least she hadn't stripped it off and settled into bed before the bomb had come sailing through the damn window—was covered in small shards of silvered glass and splinters. It was now the only clothing she had. That and whatever she'd shoved into the bottom of her locker in the Halls.

"Kaylin," Clint said again. This time, he accompanied the words with action: he lifted her in his arms. She wanted to tell him she was fine, she really did—but she was cold, and she was trying very hard to think like a Hawk and not like an upset civilian. Clint turned to Bellusdeo. "There's an escort just above your head. The two to your left and right in the sky will be flying at window height; the third will fly down to shield you if there's any perceived danger. We're under orders to get you both back to the Halls of Law immediately."

"Whose orders?" Bellusdeo asked. If she was shaken at all by what had happened, it didn't show; Kaylin envied her the composure. She also felt more ashamed of her own lack.

"The Lord of Hawks," Clint replied. "But expect there to be an Imperial Dragon or two at the Halls by the time you get there."

Clint had been slightly optimistic—or pessimistic, depending on your viewpoint; there were no Imperial Dragons waiting for them at the office. The office, however, was fully staffed, mostly by Barrani Hawks. Caitlin was still at her desk, because Caitlin had been working long hours for the past several weeks; the Exchequer investigation had caused a second shift replete with its attendant paperwork and bureaucracy.

Marcus, eyes pretty much red, fur standing up everywhere it was visible, and claws fully extended, was at his desk. His lips were drawn up over his teeth; all he needed was foam or spittle and he'd look entirely rabid. Teela and Tain intercepted Kaylin as she made her way to said desk, her hands still cupping the only thing, besides Bellusdeo and the clothing on their backs, that she'd managed to save.

Marcus, however, didn't appear to notice what she held in her hands. Given his fury, she was hoping he'd at least recognize her. The good thing about the Barrani—and good was entirely subjective—was that when they were seething in fury, their eyes shifted color. To blue. To midnight-blue, which in this light looked suspiciously like black. She knew this because Teela's and Tain's eyes were that color. But they hadn't suddenly sprouted claws and they weren't bristling with weapons; they looked decidedly less friendly, that was all.

Of course, she could only think something as inane as this because they weren't angry at her. Even furious, however, Teela noted that she was carrying something small in her hands. "What is that? A glass dragon?"

Bellusdeo snorted smoke.

Kaylin, however, understood the question. "No," she said quietly. "It's alive."

Teela's eyes lightened to a more familiar blue; Tain's, however, didn't budge. "What is it, and where did you find it at a time like this?"

"It hatched from a very large egg."

"An egg? The one in your apartment?"

Remembering that Teela had not only seen the egg but by all reports burned her hand when trying to touch it, Kaylin chose a nod as the safest bet. When Teela's stare wandered into glare territory, she added more words.

"It's a— I don't know what it is. Bellusdeo thinks it's a familiar."

The silence was like a knife: long and sharp.

Tain turned to Teela. "Please tell me I did not hear what she just said."

Teela was staring at Kaylin's hands. "I think," Teela told her, "we'll need to hear the longer version of that answer." She glanced at Marcus's desk. "It will, unfortunately, have to wait."

Taking a deep breath, Kaylin headed to Marcus's desk. She couldn't really stand at attention, and the usual at-ease posture wasn't going to work, either, unless she wanted to drop the sleeping dragon on the ground. Marcus actually looked at her hands. He didn't, however, ask her what she was carrying. More important, he didn't tell her to get rid of it. He left his chair and she saw deep scores in both the armrests. She winced. Marcus had to replace his desk on a relatively frequent basis. He seldom had to replace his chair.

He walked around the desk toward Kaylin, who instantly lifted her chin to expose her throat. His mood was bad enough that he even reached for it, although he lowered his hands before he touched skin. "Did you destroy your apartment?" he asked in a rumbling growl of a voice.

"No, sir."

"Then why are you exposing your throat?"

Because you're in the worst mood I think I've ever seen you in? She thought it massively unfair that she was the one who'd almost been killed and everyone was more than happy to vent their rage and fury at that fact on her. Kaylin, still aware that no one had yet denied her the promotion she desperately wanted, kept that one on the right side of her mouth. He was in a bad enough mood that he didn't wait for an answer, which was good, because she was too tired to come up with one. She was also still very cold—except for her hands.

As if she could hear the thought from across the office, Caitlin appeared with a blanket. She wrapped it around Kaylin's shoulders and knotted two corners just under her chin. She also paused to look at the small, translucent creature in Kaylin's hands. "He is adorable, dear," she said.

Bellusdeo, silent and unassailed by Marcus in a fury, snorted.

"I'll get you something warm to drink. The Hawklord should be down— Ah, there he is."

The entire office was like a living catalog of racial foul moods. The Hawklord's eyes were as dark as Teela's, and his wings were high, the arches poised as if to strike. "Private," he said in a much friendlier voice than the Sergeant had used. "You're alive."

"Yes, sir."

He looked at her hands. "If the item you are carrying is not essential, I suggest you set it down somewhere safe."

She swallowed. "It's essential."

"I see. Perhaps, at a later point in time, you can tell me where, in the regulations, carrying glass is considered essential for performance of your duties."

"Yes, sir."

"What happened?"

"We went home to change for the etiquette lessons. While we were there—" She took a deep breath, held it, and continued. "While we were there, something was thrown or shot into the apartment through the window."

"The window was open?"

"No, sir. The shutters were closed, but they're really warped, so they're only tied shut. Sometimes they pop loose—"

He lifted a hand. "Continue."

"I think an Arcane bomb landed in the room."

His brows rose. "Impossible."

She swallowed. "Sir—"

Clint cleared his throat; she'd forgotten he was even there. "It's not impossible, sir."

"You have a damage report?"

"We have Hawks working with a portable mirror now, but I did see the building."

"And?"

"It's sustained severe structural damage. Very little remains of the walls, floor, or ceiling in the room in which the suspected bomb exploded."

"And you, Private, were somehow not in the room when it did explode?"

"I was."

He looked over her head to Bellusdeo, who was standing and looking vaguely regal. Although Dragons were not Barrani, and therefore lacked some of their innate grace and cold beauty, they certainly weren't mortal. They could, on the other hand, hide it better when they chose to do so. "We were both in the room."

"You are unharmed?"

"Yes."

"Did you shield yourself?"

Bellusdeo's brow rose a fraction. "I did not."

"Can you explain how you are both alive?"

"Not definitively, but I have some suspicion."

"And that?"

"The necessary item in Private Neya's hands."

Every set of eyes in the office that were close enough to Kaylin now turned their attention to what she was carrying. The Hawklord's eyes were already losing the sapphire edge of their blue. Tain and Marcus still looked enraged, however.

"Private, explain."

"When we had the problem with the magical surges a few weeks ago, the midwives had some problems with some of the deliveries."

"Yes. I read the reports." It was hard to tell from his tone of voice whether or not he was being sarcastic.

"This came from one of those problems." She lifted her hands, extending her arms to enable her commander to get a closer look. The translucent dragon lifted its wings and then raised its delicate head, elongating its neck in the process.

Kaylin hurriedly drew her arms back in, because she wasn't entirely certain what the little creature would do—and biting the Hawklord's nose appeared to be a distinct possibility.

"I...see." To Bellusdeo he said, "How did this small dragon preserve your lives?"

"He is not a Dragon," she replied as she approached Kaylin's side. "But I believe he is a familiar."

The Hawklord and the Sergeant exchanged a glance. Kaylin was willing to bet a large amount of money—and given her finances, large was relative—that the Sergeant, at least, had never heard the term.

"What is a familiar?" Score. His fur was slowly sinking, but his ears would probably be standing on end for an hour.

"Theoretically?" Bellusdeo asked.

"It doesn't look very theoretical to me."

"A familiar is theoretically the companion of a Sorcerer."

Marcus glanced at the Hawklord again. On the other hand, Kaylin was pretty sure he knew that word. He growled. Kaylin winced. The small creature spread its wings.

"Sergeant," Bellusdeo said in an entirely different tone of voice, "I suggest you approach—and speak—respectfully. If we are correct, the small creature in front of you absorbed the brunt of the magical explosion and converted some of that power into a protective barrier."

"What? Something with a brain that size?"

The creature opened its little mouth and tried to roar. It squeaked.

"I think he might be hungry," Kaylin said.

Marcus's eyes had actually cooled to a more workable burnt-orange by this point. Irritation and fury clearly couldn't occupy the same turf in his mind for long. The creature squeaked again, and Marcus covered his eyes, briefly, with his pads. "I-do-not-believe-I-am-having-this-day," he said. "Private!"

She stiffened. "Sir!"

"Do you know why the office is so crowded tonight?"

"No, sir."

"Because we are about to move into three important areas with the aid of the Wolves. Do you know why we haven't left yet?"

"No, sir."

"Because your apartment exploded."

"Sir—"

"We are under orders to secure Lady Bellusdeo until representatives of the Dragon Court arrive."

"And me?" she asked, feeling a little of the cold recede. "Since she's safe and I don't have anywhere else to be, can I go with Teela and Tain?"

"Absolutely not," a new voice said. A familiar new voice, and not one she particularly wanted to hear in her own office. "I believe the Private and Lady Bellusdeo are otherwise occupied this evening."

Standing in the doors that served as either entrance or exit was the familiar and detestable Lord Diarmat. In his Dragon armor.

Caitlin returned to the office with a steaming mug of what Kaylin privately suspected was milk filched from the mess hall. She had to maneuver herself and the milk around Lord Diarmat's stiff body, because he didn't appear to notice her.

"Lord Diarmat," Bellusdeo said sweetly. She bowed.

"Lady Bellusdeo," he replied far less sweetly. He did, however, also bow. "You are to return, with escort, to the Palace."

"Oh?"

"The Emperor is concerned; he feels it likely that you were the target of the attempted assassination."

Kaylin was relieved for just as long as it took her to remember that even if Bellusdeo weren't here, she would still have no privacy because she didn't have a home.

"However, since Private Neya is also somewhat unusual, he considers it not impossible that she was the target and you would merely have been collateral damage." The Imperial Dragon turned to the Hawklord. "Lord Grammayre."

"Lord Diarmat." The Hawklord bowed; the Dragon didn't. Kaylin watched, memorizing the details of the Hawklord's bow and hating the fact that it was necessary. "You are prepared?"

"I am. I have a dozen of my own men waiting; three of the mages of the Imperial Order are also in position. Lord Emmerian will meet us there."

Kaylin shook her head. Caitlin brought the milk and set it carefully on the edge of Marcus's desk. "Do you think you can hold your little friend in one hand?"

Kaylin nodded but didn't move. "Teela, what is he talking about? He's not here to take Bellusdeo to the Palace?"

"No," she replied.

"That is correct. I am here on more martial, but not more necessary, business. Lord Sanabalis, however, is waiting in an Imperial Carriage in the yard. He will be your escort. Lady Bellusdeo, should there be any threat of magic or physical attack, the Emperor will excuse any transformation you deem necessary."

Bellusdeo said nothing at all—and given her expression, which was glacial, that was a good thing.

CHAPTER 3

"Does this mean that we're off the lesson hook?" Kaylin asked Bellusdeo as they walked to the yard. They were shadowed by Clint, whose wings still hadn't come down and whose eyes were still blue. She particularly hated to see Clint's eyes go blue, because, among other things, he had the laugh she loved best in the entire department, and when his eyes were that color, there was no chance of hearing it.

"I have no idea. Given the time, and given Lord Diarmat's current disposition, I would guess that we are, indeed, excused from a few hours of his pompous and unfortunate cultural babble."

Clint actually choked slightly, and his eyes did clear a bit. Lord Diarmat was the captain, and therefore commander, of the Imperial Guard, and the Imperial Guard wasn't generally beloved by the Halls of Law; the Imperial Guard had a very high opinion of themselves and a less than respectful opinion of anyone else in a uniform who also served at the Emperor's command.

The small dragon was now sitting half in her hand; the

other half extended up her arm so that his neck could more or less rest against it.

"I wish that creature could make himself invisible," Bellusdeo said quietly.

"Why?"

"Because I worry about the attention he'll attract."

"Could it be any worse than an Arcane bomb that destroys his entire home?"

"Oh, I don't think his life—if it even is a he—is in any danger. I think yours, on the other hand—"

"Let's pretend I just repeated that question."

Bellusdeo lifted a brow and then just shook her head. "Do you honestly think that the bomb was meant for you?"

"Does it matter? If it was meant for you, it still destroyed my home and everything in it that wasn't attached to something breathing." She took a deep breath, expelled it, and shook her head. "Sorry. You don't deserve that."

"You're certain?"

"No. I was trying to be polite. If someone's trying to kill you—" which, in Kaylin's opinion, was the most likely option "—it's probably not fun for you, either. But that's been my home since I crossed the bridge from the fiefs. Caitlin helped me find it. Caitlin let me choose it. It's the only place I've ever been certain was mine."

"…And if someone was trying to kill me, it's indirectly my fault that it's gone?"

"You're sure you're not a Tha'alani in disguise?"

"Relatively."

Kaylin muttered a few Leontine words and wished she could just sew her own mouth shut for the next hour or two. Because part of her did feel exactly that, and she wasn't proud of it. She just couldn't figure out how to squelch it. It would be different if she'd begged Bellusdeo to live with her; she hadn't. She'd practically done the opposite. And if Bellusdeo had been living in Tiamaris or the Imperial Palace—which had been Kaylin's first and second choices—Kaylin would still have a home.

The small dragon sank claws into her arm and dragged itself up to her shoulder, where it perched to bite her ear. She cursed in louder Leontine and then swiveled her neck to glare. The opal eyes of the small creature regarded her, unblinking, for a long moment.

"I guess I deserved that," she said in a quiet voice as some of the tension began to leave her jaw and neck.

"Why?" Bellusdeo asked in the same cool, practical voice.

"Because if you're right—and given my luck, you probably are—he's trying to tell me that he wouldn't have hatched at all if someone with a crapload of magical power hadn't been trying to kill you."

Sanabalis was enraged. If he'd opened his mouth and foot-long fangs had sprouted, it would have looked completely natural. Kaylin, who'd been following on Bellusdeo's heels, almost backed out of the carriage. She managed not to, but only barely. "I—I have another place to stay," she began.

"Get. In."

She did. To Kaylin's surprise, given his mood, Sanabalis did not slam the carriage door.

They traveled halfway to the Palace in silence. Sanabalis broke it, because he was the only one who dared—or cared to; Bellusdeo didn't seem overly concerned with his mood. "What is sitting on your shoulder?"

"The—the hatchling," Kaylin replied, managing to stop the words *small dragon* from leaving her mouth.

"Hatchling?"

"I— Yes. From an egg."

He raised a brow, and the color of his eyes began to brighten into a much safer orange. On the usual bad day, orange wasn't a safe color; funny how context was everything. "Generally the word *hatch* implies *egg*. What egg?"

"I don't suppose we can wait until we get to the Palace? The Arkon's going to ask the same questions."

A white brow rose as Sanabalis snorted smoke into the enclosed space.

When the carriage pulled into the Imperial drive, the road was swarming with guards. This was impressive, because Diarmat implied he'd taken a few dozen with him; she wondered if any of the Imperial Guard was off duty tonight. More impressive, for a value of impressive Kaylin often found annoying, were the half-dozen older men in the robes of the Imperial Order of Mages. If they resented being dragooned into guard duty, they very carefully kept it off their faces as Sanabalis and Bellusdeo disembarked. They even managed to do so when Kaylin did.

They were less impressively poker-faced when they caught sight of the glass dragon perched on her shoulder, but only one man was foolish enough to ask, and he didn't get more of an answer than Sanabalis's curt dismissal.

"Private," the Dragon Lord said to Kaylin as the mages who were technically junior to him in every conceivable way did the polite version of scattering, "you will spend the evening in the Palace in our most secure chambers."

"How much magic is in your secure chambers?" Kaylin asked, trying not to cringe.

"Not enough, I'm certain, to be unbearably uncomfortable."

"Meaning I can live with the discomfort."

"If you feel any, yes. I do not require that you do this in

silence; I require that you do it where no Dragon—except Lady Bellusdeo—is in danger of hearing you."

Sanabalis led them into the Palace, where a by-now familiar man in a perfectly tailored suit was waiting. He bowed to Sanabalis, bowed far more deeply to Bellusdeo, and then led them to a part of the Palace that Kaylin vaguely recognized: it was where Marcus's wives had briefly stayed.

"These will be your rooms," he told both Kaylin and Bellusdeo. "If you prefer separate quarters—"

"We don't," Bellusdeo replied before Kaylin could gratefully accept the offer.

"Very good." He bowed, making clear by this gesture that Kaylin's preferences counted for the usual nothing. "Food will be provided at the usual mealtimes. If you require specific food or desire it on a different schedule, that can be accommodated. If there are any specific likes or dislikes—"

Kaylin opened her mouth; Bellusdeo lifted her hand. Clearly her hand was also more important. "We are satisfied. Thank you."

The man then bowed and left them alone—with Sanabalis.

"He was just getting to the good part," Kaylin told Bellusdeo.

"Which part would that be?"

"The part where I get to choose whatever it is I'm being fed."

"Given the quality of what you do eat, I believe you'll survive your silence." She turned to Sanabalis. "Please don't let us detain you."

Sanabalis, whose eyes were still orange, met her dismissal impassively; he also folded his arms across his chest.

"Yes?"

"The Emperor requests a moment of your time."

Kaylin froze.

"Not yours, Private. He merely wishes to ascertain that Bellusdeo is, in fact, unharmed. He was…most upset…when word of the attack reached the Palace."

"He must have been if he mobilized half the Dragon Court so quickly."

"That mobilization was not a response to the attack," was the curt reply. "And no, before you ask, I'm not at liberty to discuss it. Lady Bellusdeo?"

"I would of course be both honored and delighted to speak with the Eternal Emperor. I do, however, have one request."

"And that?"

"I believe Kaylin should speak with the Arkon, unless the moment of time the Emperor requests also involves the Arkon's presence."

"It does not, and I believe your request can easily be accommodated. We will escort the Private to the Library before you speak with the Emperor, if that will suffice. Corporal, if you would care to accompany us?"

"I wouldn't dream of missing it." There were whole days when Kaylin hated Dragons.

The Arkon was not, in fact, in a red-eyed, raging fury. He was only barely bronze-eyed, and given any other Immortal she'd seen this evening, that was a blessing; it wasn't as if the Arkon ever looked happy to see her. He did, however, say, "I see the reports of your demise were exaggerated."

Kaylin's eyes rounded. "Someone told you I was dead?"

"It was rumored that you were, in fact, dead."

"You didn't believe it."

"I believe there is a phrase that is in common usage among your kind: 'Only the good die young.'" The Arkon was seated at a table in the main Library, surrounded by books, scrolls, and a handful of very expensive crystals, none of which were activated. He had a mirror to the left, buttressed by books; it, too, was inactive. Seeing the direction of Kaylin's glance, the Arkon said, "Yes, I was about to resume my work." Frowning, he added, "What exactly are you carrying?"

"Sanabalis, did you want to stay for this part?"

The Arkon cleared his throat loudly.

"Lord Sanabalis, sorry." The small dragon sat up in her hands but spread his translucent wings as he did. "This is a—hatchling."

"It looks remarkably like a tiny, glass dragon."

Bellusdeo rolled her eyes; she did not, however, snort. "Lannagaros, your eyesight is clearly failing."

The Arkon winced. "Bellusdeo, I would appreciate it if you would observe correct form; I am the Arkon."

She raised a pale brow but said nothing.

"Private Neya?"

"You remember there was a lot of trouble caused by the magical flux of the portal that eventually opened in Elani?"

"Indeed."

"It affected a number of different things. Among them, deliveries—of babies," she added, because from the Arkon's expression, the distinction needed to be made. "Not, apparently, pregnancies; any baby born in the area after the portal had opened was normal."

He nodded.

"One of the births produced an egg, rather than a normal infant. The father wasn't interested in keeping the egg, and it was handed to me. I was going to give it to Evanton, but I never had the chance; Elani still hasn't been fully opened to normal pedestrian traffic, and Evanton's been—busy."

"So you kept the egg."

"I did."

"She took care of it," Bellusdeo interjected, "as if she'd laid it herself."

"Bellusdeo, don't you have somewhere else you have to be?" Kaylin asked sharply.

"Apparently, yes, but I'm certain that the question of my survival—and possibly yours by extension—will arise, and any information the Arkon can provide lessens the chance that you will personally be called to the audience chamber."

Wincing, Kaylin apologized.

"How did you incubate the egg?"

"In a totally inadequate way," Bellusdeo replied. "It does not appear to have suffered."

The small dragon stretched before climbing up Kaylin's arm, where it sort of clung to her left shoulder; it draped the rest of its body across the back of her neck; its head, it perched on her right. It wuffled in her ear.

The Arkon frowned. "Records," he said, and the mirror's surface shivered. The room's reflection faded from view. "Lizards. Winged lizards. Translucent lizards." He turned and readjusted the mirror so that it faced Kaylin full-on. "Capture information and attempt to match." He paused and then added, "All archives." Turning back to Kaylin, he said, "I will not dispute Bellusdeo's comment on the adequacy of your incubation decisions, but the egg clearly hatched, and its occupant is clearly alive." He glanced at Bellusdeo before returning his attention to Kaylin; given that Bellusdeo had answered most of his questions before Kaylin could finish taking a breath, this wasn't surprising. "When did the egg hatch?"

"Well, that's the strange thing."

Bellusdeo snorted. For an Immortal she was really short on patience; Kaylin tried to imagine her as the Queen of anything and gave up—although, admittedly, the idea of Bellusdeo being Queen had one appeal: she wasn't likely to chew the heads off her Court for their lack of appropriate etiquette.

"The egg didn't hatch until the bomb exploded in the center of the apartment."

The Arkon froze. Sanabalis lifted a hand to the bridge of his nose; his eyes, however, were now about the same bronze as the Arkon's.

"Let me be clear. You are telling me that the egg's hatching was contingent on the explosion of an Arcane bomb?"

"No. I'm telling you the egg hatched when the bomb exploded. It may have cracked the shell."

The Arkon turned to glare at Bellusdeo. "I trust you are enjoying yourself, Lady Bellusdeo?"

"I feel a small amount of self-indulgence, given the events of the day, is not unreasonable, yes."

"I see that your definition of small amounts of self-indulgence has remained a constant." He turned to Kaylin. "Forgive the interruption, Private. Was there anything unusual that occurred when the egg hatched?"

"Define 'unusual.'"

"Honestly, Sanabalis," the Arkon said in a much lower voice, "I feel that Bellusdeo is not the correct companion for the Private. Some of her influence is bound to manifest itself at inconvenient times." He also lifted a hand to the bridge of his nose. "Anything out of the ordinary. Anything magical."

Kaylin nodded crisply. "A barrier of some kind appeared. It protected both Bellusdeo and me from the debris and the possibility of injury."

"Anything else?"

Kaylin hesitated.

"Private."

"It ate one of my marks right after it hatched."

* * *

After a very long pause, the Arkon rose from his desk and approached Kaylin. The small dragon lifted its head, bumping the side of Kaylin's cheek as it did. The Arkon examined the dragon from a safe distance, during which time he was uncomfortably silent. "Given the current status of the Hawks, it is probably too much to ask for a full Records capture of your marks tonight. I will expect a full capture to be arranged for tomorrow, and all records are to be transferred to the Imperial Archives for my perusal. Is that clear?"

"As glass, sir."

"Good." He held out a hand. "Please give me the creature."

Kaylin hesitated, and the Arkon's eyes narrowed. She tried to disengage the small dragon; he dug in. Literally. "I don't think he wants to leave," she said, pulling at four small, clawed appendages. He responded by biting her hair.

The Arkon lowered his hand. "Has the creature spoken at all?"

"Pardon?"

"Spoken. Communicated."

"Uh, no."

"Has it separated itself from you at all, for any length of time?"

"Separated itself?"

"Left. You. Alone."

"No, Arkon."

"Have you attempted to put it down at all?"

"Not until now, Arkon." She winced; she'd had burrs that were easier to remove from her hair. "Can I ask where this line of questioning is leading?"

"Did Bellusdeo say anything about the creature prior to your arrival here?"

Kaylin glanced nervously at Bellusdeo, who conversely didn't appear to be nervous at all.

"I told her, Lannagaros, that I thought she was in possession of a familiar."

"I…see."

"Do you disagree?"

"Given that I have never seen what I would consider to be a genuine familiar, or at least the type of familiar about which legends arise, I am not in a position to either agree or disagree." He turned to the mirror. "Records."

Since Records was already searching for whatever he'd last asked for, Kaylin thought this a bit unfair—but then again, it wasn't as if the Records were overworked mortals.

"Information, myths, or stories about familiars. This may," he added, "take some time, if the Emperor is waiting."

Bellusdeo nodded, fixed a firm and not terribly friendly smile to her face, and gestured at Sanabalis. Sanabalis bowed. "We may possibly revisit this discussion," he told Kaylin as they headed toward the door.

Only when they were gone did the Arkon resume his seat; he also, however, indicated that Kaylin could grab a chair and join him—at a reasonable distance from the table that contained his work.

To her surprise, the first question he asked when the doors had closed on the two departing Dragons was "You are well?"

The small dragon had settled back onto her neck like a scarf with talons. She blinked. "Pardon?"

"While I have often heard various members of my Court and your Halls threaten you with bodily harm, strangulation, or dismemberment, you have seldom been a victim of an attack within the confines of your own home. If I understand the nature of the attack correctly, you now no longer have a home, and I am therefore attempting to ascertain your state of mind. Are you well?"

She told him she was fine. Except the words she used were "No. I'm not." Closing her eyes, she said, "It's the only real home I've had since my mother died. Every other place I've lived belonged to someone else, either before I moved in or after." In the fiefs, there were no laws of ownership. At least not in the fief of Nightshade. It wasn't that hard to eject a handful of children from the space in which they were squatting so that you could squat there instead.

She opened her eyes. "I'm happy to be alive. I am. But—it doesn't feel real."

"Being alive?"

"Being homeless. When I leave the Library, I don't get to leave the Palace."

"You are a guest, Private, not a prisoner."

"Tell that to the Emperor." The small dragon lifted its head and rubbed its nose along the side of her cheek. "Yes, yes," she whispered. "I'm getting to that part."

The Arkon raised a brow, and she reddened.

"Bellusdeo believes that the egg wouldn't have hatched without the bomb, so—I have the hatchling." She hesitated. "Would someone really kill me over it?"

"Not if they understood its nature."

"What about its nature?"

"It is, in its entirety, yours."

The small dragon's eyes widened; it swiveled its head in the Arkon's direction and opened its delicate, translucent mouth. There was a lot of squawking.

"Umm, did you understand any of that?" Kaylin asked as the Arkon stared at the dragonlet.

"No."

Kaylin had, in her youth, engaged in staring contests with

cats—she'd always lost. She had a suspicion that the Arkon in his age was beginning to engage in a similar contest with the small dragon—and given large Dragons, and the inability to pry the small one off her shoulder, she could see a long, sleepless night in the very near future. She therefore reached up and covered the small dragon's eyes with her hand—something only the very young or the very suicidal would ever try with the large one.

"Can we get back to the *entirely mine* part?"

The small dragon reared up and bit her hand—but not quite hard enough to draw blood.

"Fine. Can we get back to the part where I'm entirely its?"

The Arkon snorted.

"And also the stories where Sorcerers destroyed half a world in order to somehow create or summon one?"

"Yes. Understand that those stories are exactly that: stories. They are not reliable or factual. There may be some particulars that suit the current situation, but many more will not." He turned and readjusted the mirror, which made Kaylin wince; in general it wasn't considered safe to move active mirrors, although Kaylin had never understood why. Angry Leontine was more than enough incentive.

"By the way, what is a Sorcerer?"

"For all intents and purposes? Think of a Sorcerer as an Arcanist but with actual power."

Since her apartment was now mostly a pile of smoldering splinters, Kaylin thought his definition of "actual power" needed fine-tuning. "Any less arrogant?"

"There was purportedly one extant in my youth, but there was never confirmation of his—or her—existence. Given that people who possess power frequently decide what qualifies as humility or arrogance in a way that allows little dissent, I will offer a qualified no."

"Fine. Arrogant and very powerful." She looked pointedly at her shoulder. "How, exactly, is a small dragon of great use to an arrogant and very powerful Arcanist?"

"Bellusdeo implied that the 'small dragon,' as you call it, shielded both of you from the brunt of the damage the Arcane bomb would have otherwise caused. It is almost a certainty that you would not have survived otherwise. Further study is warranted, but it is clear to me that Bellusdeo would have been, at the very least, gravely injured. She was not."

"If a Sorcerer is actually more powerful than the Arcanists, I don't think some form of impressive magical defense would be beyond him—or her. I understand why the familiar might be helpful to someone like me, but I didn't exactly destroy half a world to get one."

"Ah, I think I see the difficulty. If you are referring to this story," he said, tapping the mirror so that the image immediately shifted, "the Sorcerer didn't destroy the world to, as you put it, 'get' a familiar; he destroyed half a world as a by-product of his attempt to produce—or summon—one. I'm afraid the original word could mean either, so the meaning is not precise. It was what you would consider collateral damage. And if you fail to understand how that damage could occur—"

She lifted a hand. "Not stupid," she said curtly. "I know why the egg happened. I know what kind of magical disturbance produced it. Given the total lack of predictability of the effects of that magic, I can understand the how. I'm just stuck on the why."

The Arkon nodded in apparent sympathy. "Dragons were not, to my knowledge, Sorcerers."

"Meaning?"

"It makes no clear sense to me, either; the stories that we have are fragmentary and somewhat conflicting. The story that I am currently considering—and you may look at the mirror images if you like, but you won't be able to read the words—doesn't reference the practical use of the creature. It does, however, make reference to its astonishing beauty." He lifted a brow. "This story implies that the familiar was winged, but of a much more substantial size."

"Oh?"

"Yes, apparently its owner could ride on its back, and did. On the other hand, the use of the word *summon* is more distinct and implies something demonic in nature."

"Demonic?"

"It's a religious story."

"Do any of the stories imply the familiars were a danger to their owners?"

The Arkon took minutes to answer the question. "...Yes."

"Figures. Does it say how?"

The Arkon's frown deepened. "I'm afraid," he finally said, "that this is also a very dead language, and I'm uncertain. I will have to consult with the Royal linguists when time permits. You said that he ate one of your marks?"

She nodded. She didn't, however, point out that the Devourer had also eaten some of her marks; her testimony was in Records, and if he failed to recall it on the spot, she wasn't going to remind him. Why, she wasn't certain.

"And that would be—" The rest of her sentence was lost to the sudden roaring that filled the Library. It wasn't the Arkon's voice. He lifted a brow and then shook his head. "Bellusdeo hasn't really changed very much."

"That was Bellusdeo?"

"Ah, no. That was the Emperor. I believe Sanabalis is at the doors." The doors swung open—and shut—very quickly as Sanabalis entered the Library.

"I consider it a very good thing that Lord Diarmat is with

the Hawks," Sanabalis said when normal speech could actually be heard in the room.

"You didn't stay for their discussion?"

"No. If the Emperor is to lose his composure, it is best for all concerned that there be no witnesses." The last half of the last word was lost to the sound of more roaring.

"That," the Arkon pointed out while distant breath was being drawn, "was Bellusdeo."

The Arkon decided, during the small breaks between roaring—which frequently overlapped—that it was safe to leave the small dragon with Kaylin. By "safe," he meant that she was allowed to leave the room with the dragon attached. He was aware that keeping the dragon, at this point, also meant caging the Private, and declined to, as he put it, subject himself to the endless interruption and resentment that would entail.

Sanabalis therefore escorted her from the Library. "Do you know the way to your rooms?" he asked when the doors were closed and there was another break in the roaring.

She looked at him.

"Very well, let me escort you. Attempt to pay attention, because this will no doubt be the first of many forays between the Arkon and those rooms. You will, of course, be expected to perform your regular duties during your transitional stay in the Palace." He turned to face her as she regarded the door ward with dislike. "You will not, however, be in residence for long if the raid conducted this evening bears fruit."

Kaylin wilted. "Nightshade?" she asked, too tired to pretend she didn't understand what he was talking about.

Sanabalis nodded. "I am not entirely comfortable with the exchange of information for your time; the information, however, was crucial. Bellusdeo will be staying in the Palace while you discharge your obligation to the fieflord."

"Was that part of the discussion with the Emperor?"

"It was—and is."

"Then it's not decided?"

"It is. The Emperor has been willing to grant leeway in all of Bellusdeo's irregular demands for autonomy, but he will not allow her to leave the City—or the Palace—at this time. She intended to accompany you. He has pointed out one thing for which Bellusdeo has no reply."

"What?"

"She endangered your life."

It was true, but Kaylin felt it was also unfair. "Neither of us knew that someone would try to kill her."

"It has always been an Imperial concern."

"She probably thought you were being paranoid."

"Yes. She made that clear. Her second thoughts will therefore occur in the Palace, and in your absence. I would suggest that you attempt to make the best of your status as guest here; you will depart for the West March in five days."

CHAPTER 4

When Kaylin headed to the Halls of Law the next day, she went on foot. Bellusdeo wasn't terribly happy about it, because Bellusdeo had been asked not to accompany her. The fact that she was willing to accede to a request that she clearly detested confirmed what Sanabalis had said about the almost deafening and totally incomprehensible Dragon conversation.

"You're taking the familiar with you?"

"I wasn't going to," Kaylin replied, which was only a half lie. "But I can't keep it off my shoulders for more than five minutes." This wasn't entirely true; it was willing to sit on the top of her head or be gathered in the palms of her hands, but neither of these were as convenient.

"You're going to have to come up with a name for it sometime; if I hear it referred to as the 'small dragon' or 'glass dragon' again, I'll scream."

"That's what the Arkon—"

"He's ancient and probably half-blind."

"Dragons don't go blind with age."

For some reason, this completely factual statement didn't meet with Bellusdeo's approval.

When she exited the Palace, Severn was waiting. He fell in beside her in a stiffer-than-usual silence.

"I'm sorry," she said without looking at him. "I—"

"I heard about it this morning."

"How?"

"Teela mirrored me; she thought I'd like to know before I hit the office."

"I—"

"You had better things to worry about."

"You're angry anyway."

"I'm angry, yes, but I'm not angry at you." He stopped walking. "I should have been there."

"You didn't know."

"Why didn't you mirror when you hit the office?"

"Everyone was so pissed off, I didn't think about it." She hesitated and then added, "I'm still not thinking about it very clearly. At all. I know what happened—I was there—but part of me still thinks I can take the normal route home."

"You could stay with me."

She hesitated. "I would," she said, because it was true. "But I can't leave Bellusdeo. The Emperor won't give permission for her to live with you—not that you'd enjoy it—and I'm betting he won't give his blessing if I move out on my own, unless she requests it."

He glanced at the small dragon on her shoulder but made no comment; Kaylin guessed that Teela had also mentioned its appearance, and didn't ask. Mention of her home had dampened a mood that hadn't been that cheery to begin with.

Kaylin made it to the Halls with a few minutes to spare and found Tanner and Kelmar on the doors. Getting into the Halls took a little longer than usual, because both of the Hawks wanted to take a look at the glass dragon, and the glass dragon seemed lazily inclined to allow their inspection. While they looked, Kaylin asked if they'd had any word, and their nonanswer was incentive enough to jog through the Halls to the office.

There, she headed straight to the duty board. She read it with care, grinding her teeth as she noticed the address of her apartment and the fact that it wasn't anywhere near her name.

She then headed straight for Caitlin. "Why am I not being pulled in on the investigation into my own apartment?"

"Think about what you just said, dear."

"But it's my—"

"Exactly. Your judgment would not be considered impartial or objective enough." Caitlin frowned slightly. "I realize you're upset—"

"I think I'm allowed!"

"—but you shouldn't be so upset that you forget one of the more significant rules governing investigative assignments. If it helps, the Imperial Order has been working since—"

"Have they found anything?"

"Not conclusively."

Kaylin perked up. "What was inconclusive?"

"There was, as far as the mages could tell, only one signature left at the site."

"That's unusual." Kaylin hesitated and then added, "It's also inaccurate."

Caitlin winced. "I think you should talk to Marcus, dear. But he's been dealing with Dragons and mages, so he's not in the best of moods."

"This had better be important," Marcus said as she approached his desk. He didn't even bother to look up. He was elbow deep in reports. This would have been unusual, but as it was not the most unusual thing about Marcus at this very moment, Kaylin barely noticed. His left arm—or the fur on it—had been either seared or singed off. "What are you staring at, Private?"

"Nothing. Sir."

"Good. Why are you gaping at nothing in front of my desk?"

She took a deep breath and lifted her chin slightly. "It's about my apartment."

"No."

"It's not about the investigation," she said quickly. "But the Imperial mages apparently only found one magical signature at the detonation site. I saw two."

Marcus dug a runnel into the desk. "When exactly did you see these?"

"Just after the bomb destroyed my home."

"Good. I'd hate to have to demote or discipline the Hawks on duty there today; you are not supposed to be on-site. At all." He gave up on the report he was writing—for a value of write that involved reading and a signature that was shaky to begin with—and lifted his head to stare at her. After a significant pause, he pulled a report from one of the piles. "Here."

Kaylin had learned love of reports from Marcus but took it anyway.

"I'm up to my armpits in Imperial Concern," he continued before she could ask about its contents. "The Imperial Order will be interested in what you have to say about a second signature. They're also likely to feel insulted. I suggest you go directly to Lord Sanabalis; I've come this close to relieving one mage of his throat this morning already."

"Yes, sir."

"Read that report. You can give me a précis of what it actually says later. And, Private, I mean it: you go anywhere near our investigators at your former address, and you'll be suspended without pay until you leave the City."

Reading reports wasn't nearly as onerous as writing them—unless you happened to be the Sergeant. Kaylin retired to her cramped, small desk, discovered that someone had commandeered her chair, and sat on the desk's nearly pristine surface instead of going to find it. Bellusdeo was not in the office, and her mood was not Kaylin's problem, but she felt guilty enjoying the Dragon's absence. The report helped with that, but not in a good way.

She was uncertain as to why the report was even on Marcus's desk, because in theory, it involved the fiefs. The Hawks kept an eye on the bridges between the fiefs and the rest of the City, but it was cursory; they couldn't stop traffic from entering the fiefs, and they couldn't stop traffic from leaving them, either, although admittedly questions were asked in either case. There was, with the exception of Tiamaris, very little of either.

Oh, wait. There it was: the small tendril that led to the large, omnipresent web. A boy, Miccha Jannoson, had, on a dare from his friends—Kaylin snorted at the word—crossed the bridge from the City into the fiefs. He was lucky, in that the fief in question was Tiamaris; there was enough traffic over that bridge, and most of it seemed to return in the other direction at the end of the day.

He was unlucky, in that he didn't appear to be one of the returnees. His grandmother had filed a report with Missing Persons the following morning. Which would be yesterday.

Tiamaris was both fieflord and Dragon Lord, and he was willing to cooperate with the Halls of Law in their search.

She read through to the end; there, transcribed, was a brief message from Tiamaris: the boy was not the only person to disappear within his fief in the past two weeks. In other fiefs, such disappearances might not be noticed, noted, or of concern; in Tiamaris, they were apparently personal, Tiamaris being a Dragon. He requested, at the Halls' leisure, a check for possible similar disappearances within Elantra, but asked that the check be broader: not teenage boys, but people, period. Mortals.

Kaylin glanced at the small dragon draped across her shoulders. She had four days before her departure. Four days wasn't a lot of time for an investigation of something big—and the fact that Tiamaris had made an all but official request meant he considered it significant. Maybe it was time to visit the fief and speak to Tara.

Teela dropped by her desk as she was planning. Kaylin almost fell over when she saw the Barrani officer's face; it was bruised. Her eyes, however, were green. Mostly.

"Kitling," Teela said, sounding as tired as she looked.

Kaylin felt her jaw hanging open, and shut it.

"Why are you staring? I don't recall ever saying I was impervious to harm."

"What the hells were you fighting? Barrani?"

"A dozen."

Report forgotten, Kaylin swiveled in her chair. "What happened last night?"

"We met some resistance."

"You didn't go on a raid with two bloody Dragons expecting no resistance."

"Sit down. I didn't come here to deliver bad news; I came here to extend an invitation to the High Halls."

Kaylin's brows disappeared into her hairline; if they hadn't been attached to the rest of her face, they would have kept going. "P-pardon?"

"It is a personal invitation," Teela added.

"I'm guesting at the Palace at the moment, on account of having no home."

"Yes. You could stay with me in the High Halls instead; I find the Halls very dull and otherwise too peaceful. Regardless, you will require suitable clothing for your journey to the West March. I assume that very little of yours survived."

"I'm wearing most of it." Kaylin sat. "You're not going to tell me what happened, are you?"

"You can read the report when it's written. You can read any of a dozen reports; Marcus probably won't."

"Teela—"

Teela lifted a hand. "Two of the mages died. We lost four Hawks; three of them were Barrani, one was Aerian. Clint was injured, but not badly; Tain has a broken arm and the disposition one would expect from that."

"Marcus?"

"His fur was singed, as you may have noticed. He's alive. He's alive," Teela added, "because he can move his bulk at need, and he moved."

"I don't suppose the Dragons—"

"The Dragons are, of course, fine."

"The Arcanum—"

"The Arcanum was damaged during the fighting; it is, however, still structurally sound."

"Evarrim?"

"He was not involved in the fighting." The way she said it made clear that no more questions about Evarrim were going to be answered; it also made clear that she would have been happier if he had been.

"What were you looking for anyway?"

"The Arcanists involved with the Human Caste Court and their missing funds."

"Did you find them?"

"All but one."

"Are they in custody?"

Teela stared at her until she felt embarrassed for even asking. "Do remember," she said, "that the Emperor can hold his own laws in abeyance should the need arise, hmm? The Arcanists were expecting trouble; they just weren't expecting the quality of the trouble they did get." She said this with a particularly vicious smile. "I'll meet you here after work."

"But I can't stay in the High Halls."

"Why not?"

"Bellusdeo will kill me."

Teela frowned. "You haven't learned anything from yesterday, have you?"

"What do you mean?"

"Hanging around with that particular Dragon is not good for your health. I'm not sure she's in the clear yet, and if she's not, you won't be."

"I'm in the Palace," Kaylin pointed out.

"Not at the moment, you're not. Your point is, however, taken. I'd prefer to avoid the Palace, if at all possible."

"Why?"

"Because the Emperor isn't terribly happy with the Barrani, its Lords, or its mages, and I'm not assuming that he's going to be entirely happy with its Hawks, either."

"Why?"

"Kitling—think instead of talking, hmm?" She gave Kaylin five seconds to do that thinking, which seemed a tad unfair. "The bomb wasn't thrown by mortals; it certainly wasn't planted by Dragons. Whoever tried to kill Bellusdeo was almost certainly Barrani; it is not inconceivable that they were working in concert with humans."

"If I ask why again, are you going to hurt me?"

"I'll seriously consider it," Teela replied, but her eyes stayed on the safe side of blue. "Bellusdeo is both female and Dragon. The Dragon population has been static for a long time now; the Barrani population hasn't. If we're not at war—and we're not—the war still informs us. Someone doesn't want there to be any more clutches, and killing Bellusdeo pretty much guarantees that."

Kaylin's regular beat was still embroiled in the investigations and magical cleanup demanded by the Emperor and the Imperial Order of Mages. They were drawing to a close, which meant the growing line of concerned citizens—Margot chief among them—were likely to be less of a feature in the various offices the Swords occupied. Which was a pity. Margot's inability to make money by swindling the gullible was a genuinely bright spot in what was otherwise magical chaos and displacement.

The panicked reports of citizens at the edges of the Elani district had dropped to a manageable level in the two weeks it'd been more or less locked down, which meant the Hawks confined to desks in the public office were released to their regular duties. In the case of Private Neya and Corporal Handred, this meant a stroll to the fief of Tiamaris; as Elani was still in lockdown, and it was their beat, they had time in the schedule for low-level investigations of a more incidental nature. As the Hawklord called them.

As the two Hawks headed toward the bridge-crossing that led to Tiamaris, Kaylin filled Severn in on the admittedly scant details of the report Marcus had offloaded, hoping that Severn would drop in on Missing Persons—Mallory's domain—

tomorrow. Mallory didn't have the apparent contempt for Severn that he had for Kaylin. To be fair, Severn didn't have the apparent contempt for Mallory that Kaylin had, either. Severn was much more likely to be granted full records access for a search of those reported missing the past two weeks.

The small dragon chewed on the stick in Kaylin's hair without dislodging it or, worse, snapping it, as they made their way across the bridge and, from there, to the less crowded fief streets. They hadn't bothered to ditch the Hawks' tabard, so the occupants of those streets kept their distance—but they didn't duck into the nearest building, doorway, or alley just to move out of the way. Things improved, if slowly.

To Kaylin's surprise, Tara wasn't in her garden when they approached the Tower itself. Kaylin slowed, ducked around the side of the building, and found it empty, as well. Severn nodded when she glanced at him; he found it unusual, as well.

The Tower doors were shut. Since they had no ward—a kindness offered by Tara, who understood just how thoroughly uncomfortable wards made Kaylin—the two Hawks knocked and then took a step back to wait. The doors took five minutes to roll open.

Standing between them as they opened was Morse. She was alone, which was also unusual; she was on edge, which was worse. "Tiamaris wants to speak with you," she said without preamble.

"Where's Tara?"

"In the mirror room. If she wants to be disturbed, she'll let us know. She's been there for the past three days," she added as she turned and began to lead them into the cavernous, wide halls of the Tower.

"Morse?"

Morse shrugged. "Yeah," she said, answering the question

Kaylin had asked by tone alone. "It's been bad." She paused, squinted, and then said, "Where'd you get the glass dragon?"

Tiamaris was waiting in what looked like a war room. The wall opposite the doors was a vast display of mirrors, none of which were in their reflective state. The whole of the fief, in much cleaner lines than the streets ever saw, was laid out to the left. Across those streets were lines in different colors; one was a bright, sharp red. It demanded attention.

Not even mindful of the distinctly orange color of his lidded eyes, Kaylin came to stand beside the fieflord.

"Word arrived that you encountered some difficulty yesterday," he said, sparing her a passing glance. The glance, however, became a full-on stare when it hit the curled body of the small glass dragon. "What," he asked in a sharper tone of voice, "is that?"

"The reason the difficulty wasn't fatal."

"Pardon?"

"The small dragon—"

"It is not a dragon."

"Sorry. The small winged lizard—" The glass dragon lifted his head and glared balefully at the side of her face. "You're smaller than he is," she told it.

"It appears to understand what we are saying."

"Yes. He doesn't speak, though. He was hatched during the explosion of the Arcane bomb that destroyed a quarter of the building. Given what's left of my apartment, we should have gone down with it. We didn't. Bellusdeo thinks it's because the— He protected us."

Kaylin turned to Severn, who was examining the map with a frown. "The Arkon is doing research as we speak. None of which is relevant at the moment. The red is the last known location?"

The fieflord shook his head. "I will never understand mortals. Yes."

She counted. There were a lot more than one missing boy. "What did the Sergeant tell you?"

"He handed me a report," she replied. "Miccha Jannoson crossed the bridge from the City and didn't return. Are any of these lines relevant to that report?"

Tiamaris lifted a hand, and Kaylin followed its movement. One thread. It started three yards from the bridge, on the fief side of the Ablayne. It was notable for its length: it was short, much shorter than the streets.

"I don't understand."

"Tara spent much time constructing these overlays," he replied, as if that would explain things.

It didn't. "Miccha wasn't a citizen of the fief."

"No."

"The Tower, any Tower, is in theory capable of tracking its citizens."

"That," he replied, "is a statement only partially based in truth. What she can track, should she so choose, is the approximate activity of people within my domain, if she has enough information to work with. Her records of the Barren years are notably scant, but the information she's processed since I accepted the mantle of fieflord are of necessity more complete."

"She couldn't find Bellusdeo," Kaylin pointed out, her gaze moving to the other tracks of red, some much longer.

"She couldn't, no," he agreed. "But there are probable reasons for that, chief among them being she had only a corpse with which to work."

"She has even less in the case of Miccha."

Tiamaris turned to regard her. "She is watching the bridge closely," he finally said.

"What are the purple points?"

"The purple points—and they are not markedly purple to my eye—are unknowns."

"Unknowns?" She glanced at the Dragon Lord. Miccha was an unknown, but Tara had clearly tagged him. "What exactly do you mean by 'unknown'?"

"The fieflord, through the auspices of his or her Tower's defenses, can see anything that occurs within the fief should they be paying attention. It is not, however, a trivial affair on our part. It is less difficult when the Tower is sentient, awake, and watchful, but even Tara has her limits. In the case of Miccha, she noted him precisely because he crossed the bridge and appeared to have very little reason to do so."

"He did it on a dare."

Tiamaris raised a brow. "It was an expensive dare," he finally said.

"You think he's dead."

"I think he will not return to his family." He hesitated and then added, "He is not the only person within my fief's borders to disappear abruptly; he is the only citizen of the Empire to do so and therefore the only person who is directly relevant to your duties."

"A lot of missing-persons reports are filed, Tiamaris. You know that."

"Yes."

"What distinguishes this one from those?"

"There is no obvious commonality among those who are missing. They are variously youthful, elderly, male, female."

"They were reported missing?"

"Two were, directly to Tara. Those are the burnt-orange lines. Relatives of the missing women came to Tara for help a day after their parents disappeared. The orange lines are their known paths and destinations for the day prior to the reported disappearance. She was not, then, at full alert."

"Now?"

He indicated four red lines. "These occurred after the first requests for aid. Those," he added, pointing at lines that were a paler orange, "are possible similar disappearances. Morse has her people out in the streets in an attempt to discern whether or not the disappearances are real."

Morse wouldn't get that information directly, but she had Tara as backup. She asked the questions no one in their right mind—for a fief value—would answer; Tara eavesdropped on the conversations that occurred after Morse left the vicinity of possible witnesses. The citizens of the fief, if they thought about it for a few minutes, could figure out what was going on, but years of survival-based behaviors didn't disappear in a month or two, and Morse caused terror in anyone sane, regardless. Tara didn't.

The fact that the disappearances had been reported at all was an almost shocking display of trust. "That's a dozen in total."

"Including your citizen, yes."

"What do you suspect?" It was clear he suspected something out of the ordinary, and fief crimes encompassed a lot of ordinary on any given day.

"There are ways of remaining hidden; not all of them are one-hundred-percent effective if someone is watching with care. If those reported as missing were dead within this fief, we would know by this point. We have discovered no bodies. Given twelve possible disappearances in total, with no word and very little in the way of clues…"

Kaylin grimaced. "Magic," she said with the curt disgust only found in the Halls of Law.

"Magic," he agreed in about the same tone.

"I think I need to talk to Tara."

Tara was, as Morse had indicated, in the mirror room. If Tiamaris chose to scan fief records using traditional mirrors,

Tara did not; she had a shallow, wide pool, sunk in stone, whose still surface served that function. She stood by the curve of the pool farthest from the door; her eyes were closed. She nonetheless greeted Kaylin and Severn as they entered. She had folded wings, and Kaylin marked the absence of her familiar gardening clothes.

The pool by her feet had become the ancient version of a modern mirror, although the images in the water were not the ones Kaylin had expected. Where Tiamaris had maps of the fief in every possible view, Tara's was focused on a set of buildings, as seen from the street. Kaylin frowned. She didn't know Tiamaris's fief as well as she once had—the catastrophic encroachment of Shadows had destroyed several buildings, and Tiamaris's crews were working on replacing them—but these buildings weren't fief buildings, to her eye. They were too finely kept, too obviously well repaired, and in the fiefs of her youth, that indicated danger.

"They are not, as you suspect, within Tiamaris." Tara turned to Kaylin, opening her eyes. They were the color of dull obsidian. "Hello," she said softly. It took Kaylin a few seconds to realize she was speaking to the small dragon. The dragon lifted his head, stretching his delicate neck. "You are clearly here with Kaylin."

He squawked.

"Can you understand him?" Kaylin asked.

"Yes. He is not, however, very talkative." The Avatar frowned. "Can you not understand him?"

"No. To me, it sounds like he's squawking." The dragon batted the side of her cheek with the top of his head. "Sorry," she told him. "It does."

"You are certain you are with Kaylin?" Tara asked him.

He snorted, a dragon in miniature, and flopped down around the back of Kaylin's neck. Kaylin reached up to rearrange his claws, frowning at the mirror's surface. "Do you know what he is?" She asked Tara.

"No, not entirely. Creatures such as this one were considered auspicious at one time."

"You've seen familiars before?"

"I? No. Not directly. There are some fragmentary histories within my records, but they are not firsthand accounts." She hesitated, which was unusual for Tara. "Perhaps this is not the time to discuss it. I do not judge you to be in danger at present; there are people within the fief, however, who are." Her eyes once again darkened and hardened, literally.

"You're attempting to look outside of the fief's boundaries?" Kaylin hesitated and then said, "Tiamaris can probably get Halls of Law's records access as a member of the Dragon Court. I think you'll find the buildings faster."

Severn, however, had come to stand in silence beside Kaylin. "Why are these residences of relevance in this investigation?" He slid into effortless High Barrani. Kaylin marked it; she wasn't certain Tara did at this point. Spoken language wasn't an impediment to understanding thoughts—why, Kaylin didn't know. Tara had tried to explain it before, but Kaylin was pretty certain she thought in words.

"Yes," Tara told Severn. "They are significant for that reason."

If the concept of mind reading didn't horrify Kaylin the way it once had, she still hated to be left out of the conversation. She turned to Severn. "Why do you know them?"

"It was relevant to my former duties," he replied after a long pause.

Kaylin tensed. It took effort to keep her hands by her side. "You're not a Wolf now."

"No. But it is just possible that it is also relevant to the Hawks' current investigation."

"The one that caused the Imperial raid?"

Severn nodded.

"Arcanists," was Kaylin's flat reply.

"Yes. The property is interesting because it's owned by Barrani; the deed is registered to a Barrani Lord."

"Please don't tell me it's registered to Evarrim."

Severn's silence was not a comfort.

"Severn?"

"You asked him not to tell you." Tara's last word tailed up as if it were a question.

"That's not what that phrase means." To Kaylin's surprise, Tara didn't ask her for the precise meaning, or rather, didn't ask her to explain why the difference existed.

Severn's gaze had fallen to the mirror. "You didn't see this yourself," he finally said to the Avatar.

"No," she replied. "One of the men who crosses the bridge did. He is not a citizen of Tiamaris, but he is responsible for the disposition of building materials."

"A merchant?" Kaylin asked.

"That is what my Lord hopes to ascertain."

"Are you reading the minds of every person who crosses the bridge?"

"Yes. All. It is interesting and challenging, but tedious. It is also very difficult, and the readings may not be fully reliable. Listening to conversations is a much simpler affair. My Lord feels that the disappearances in the fief are not related to the fief itself; he is looking outward."

"You know about the raid on the Arcanum." It wasn't a question.

"Yes. My Lord was informed by the Emperor. It is not," she added with a frown, "information that is to be shared. I'm sorry."

"I'm not. I'll probably regret saying that, later."

"Oh. Why?"

"Because with our luck, it'll be relevant. Who, exactly, did you take those images from?"

Tara gestured and the mirror's image shifted. A man in nondescript clothing appeared in the pool's center. He was an older man; his hairline had seen better decades, but he seemed fit. She thought him in his mid-fifties, although he might have been younger. His eyes were dark, and his brows gathered across the bridge of a prominent nose, but there was a brightness to them, a focus, that implied lively intelligence.

"You are absolutely certain that this is the man?" Severn asked softly. It was the wrong kind of soft.

"Not absolutely," Tara replied. "As I mentioned, it is difficult to read at this distance." Before Severn could speak again, she added, "But he is the only man—or woman—present who is quite so difficult to read."

"And the rest take more effort but produce more certain results?"

She frowned. After a long pause, she said, "There is one person I cannot read or follow."

"You've deployed Morse and her crew?"

Tara nodded. "Morse doesn't like it," she added. "She appears to think I need protection. I am unclear as to why."

"Morse isn't concerned about your physical safety; she's not stupid. Can't you just read her mind?"

"I have. I do not understand much of what she thinks. She is concerned that the people in the fief will somehow take advantage of me."

"I can't imagine why. Can you mirror that image to the Halls?"

"Which?"

"Both."

Tara nodded.

"Be very careful," Severn told her. "Lock it down to a specific person—the Hawklord would be best."

"Why?" Kaylin asked sharply.

"The man in the mirror is influential; he is not considered a friend of the Imperial Halls. He is cautious but political."

"Meaning he might be able to access some of our records?"

"Meaning exactly that."

"Is he Human Caste Court important?"

Severn didn't answer.

"Is he too important to otherwise be crossing the bridge with carpenters?"

"Demonstrably not." Severn forced his hands to unclench. "Yes, Kaylin, his presence here is highly suspicious. There is no reason for his presence in Tiamaris, save at the invitation of the Dragon Lord, and clearly, no such invitation has been extended."

"It has not," Tara said, confirming what was obvious.

"Is he in Tiamaris now?" Severn asked.

Tara frowned. "No," she said without pause. "He did not cross the bridge today."

The two Hawks exchanged a glance. It was the day after the raid on the Arcanum.

"We're going to head back to the Halls of Law," Kaylin finally said. They turned toward the doors.

"Wait."

Kaylin turned back to see that Tara's wings had suddenly unfolded; they were resting at a height that meant severe danger in the Aerians they mimicked.

"Yvander is speaking to someone on Capstone," the Avatar said. Capstone was a hard sprint's distance. "Yvander is one of my citizens."

"Who is he speaking to?"

"I do not know. I cannot see the person clearly."

Kaylin stiffened. "You're certain?"

Tara nodded. In the distance, loud, heavy footsteps thundered down the hall. "I can clearly sense Yvander. I can hear what he's thinking."

"What is he thinking?"

"'I don't have to work for another hour and a half. It should be safe.'"

"What should be safe?"

"A meal and a conversation," Tara replied. "Someone has clearly offered him both."

"Someone you can't see."

"Yes."

"Someone he shouldn't be able to see, either."

"Yes, that is my concern."

The doors flew open; Tiamaris, eyes verging on red, stood in its frame. His voice as he spoke was a Dragon's full voice, caught in the chest of a man. Judging by expression alone, the man part wasn't going to last long. "Tara, the aperture."

She nodded, and Tiamaris turned and stepped back into the hall.

"Kaylin, Severn, follow him. Quickly; we may be too late."

They ran into the hall in time to see Tiamaris finish a transformation that justified both the unusual width of the halls and the height of the ceiling. His eyes were larger and redder as he swiveled his head.

"Yes." Tara spoke out loud for Kaylin's benefit.

"Don't just stand there gaping." Tiamaris's voice shook the ground as he glared at the two Hawks dwarfed by his Dragon form. "Get on."

CHAPTER 5

The aperture, as Tiamaris had called it, was actually a wall, and from the interior side, it looked like solid stone. Given Tiamaris was running at it headfirst, Kaylin wasn't too concerned; if it failed to open, it was unlikely to hurt him. Tara, however, flew ahead. At this height, most Aerians would have run—but her flight was like a loosed arrow; she moved. The wings seemed decorative.

Parts of the rapidly approaching wall, unlike the roof of the Hawklord's Tower, did not separate and retract. Instead, they faded, turning in an eye's blink into a very large, very open space with a bit of ceiling over it. Beyond it, instead of the vegetable gardens that pretty much served as the lofty Tower's grounds, was the length of a street that Kaylin took a few seconds to recognize: it was Capstone.

Capstone at this time of the day wasn't empty—but it emptied quickly, pedestrians moving to either side of the street in a panicked rush at the unexpected appearance of a large copper-red Dragon. Tiamaris's color seemed to shift according to either mood or light; Kaylin, having seen so few transformations in any other Dragons, wasn't certain why. It wasn't the time to ask.

"Tara, we're near the border of Nightshade?"

Tara nodded, scanning the people who were now standing in doorways, against walls, or, if they were lucky, in the mouth of an alley.

Tiamaris drew breath, and before Kaylin could stop him—or before she could try—he roared.

Tara lifted her chin. "There," she said, pointing. "At the edge of the border. Kaylin?"

Kaylin leapt clear of Tiamaris's back and landed in the street. She took off down Capstone at a run. She hadn't asked Tara what Yvander looked like, but at this point, it wasn't necessary: he was near the border, and all but the most hysterical of people who lived on this side of the Ablayne knew damn well to avoid it; there was likely to be only one person near its edge.

Severn caught up with her as she ran, pulling ahead because he had the greater stride. The man in question—dark-haired, slender of build—froze in place as he heard their running footsteps. Given that he'd just heard a Dragon's roar, this was surprising. He hesitated for one long moment and then turned to look over his shoulder. His eyes widened as Severn barreled into him, knocking him off his feet.

Thank gods, Kaylin thought, that they weren't in the streets of their city. The two men rolled to a stop as Kaylin approached them.

She blinked. "Pull him back," she told Severn. "We're too far in."

Severn dragged himself—and the young man—to his feet. "Sorry. The Lady wants to speak with you."

The man blinked. His dark eyes were wide. "The—the Lady?" He didn't seem likely to bolt, and Severn relaxed his grip on a rumpled brown tunic. "Why?" He blinked again and looked around, his eyes widening farther, which Kaylin would have bet was impossible. He turned quickly to his right. "Get Michael," he said. "Michael!"

He was clearly looking for someone. "There's no one else here," Kaylin told him as Severn began to pull him back toward the safe side of the street.

"He was right beside me," the man insisted. "We were—" He frowned. "We were heading to Luvarr's."

"You were heading in the wrong direction. There was no one else with you." Kaylin's hands slid to the tops of her daggers as she gazed down at the street. At the height of day, the boundary that existed between Tiamaris and Nightshade seemed almost invisible. But Kaylin looked toward the fief of her childhood, the street that continued into it, and the buildings that stood at its edge, drained of all color. What was left was gray, black, and white. The border had a width that normal maps didn't give it.

"Kaylin?"

She shook her head. Something about the shapes of the buildings looked wrong at this distance. "Take him back to Tara."

"Not without you."

Yvander was bewildered. "I don't understand," he said in a tone of voice that made him sound much younger than he looked. "Why am I here? Where's Michael?"

"That's a good question. Go back to the Lady," Kaylin said gently. "I'll look for Michael."

"Kaylin—"

"That will not be necessary." The fieflord stood yards away, the Tower's Avatar—and his figurative crown—to his left. "Yvander."

The young man dropped to his knees with no grace at all; Kaylin suspected fear had caused his legs to collapse. "Lord."

There was no official title for the fieflord, because if you were very, very lucky, you never had to meet him. Tiamaris, however, accepted this in stride. He turned to Tara. "Lady, this is Yvander?"

She nodded, her eyes obsidian, her wings high. "You were not with Michael," she said.

"I—I was, Lady— He was just—he was right here...." Severn caught his arm and helped him to his feet, for a value of help that saw the Hawk doing most of the heavy lifting. He then guided him toward Tara, who hadn't moved an inch. As Yvander approached, she lowered her wings.

"Private Neya."

"Lord Tiamaris."

"Tara does not believe it is wise to remain where you are standing."

Kaylin turned to look back at the street. "Tara, can you come here?"

"I? No."

"You're certain?"

"I am the Tower, Kaylin; in exchange for power within the boundaries ascribed me by my creators, I am left with very little beyond them."

"This is now beyond your boundaries?"

"Yes."

"And in theory, that means I'm standing in Nightshade."

Tara was silent for a long moment. "You are aware that that is not the case."

Kaylin nodded slowly. "But I don't understand why."

"Come back to Tiamaris, Kaylin."

Kaylin, however, frowned as she caught movement out of the corner of her eye. Someone was standing at the window of one of the gray, washed-out buildings. He wasn't gray in the way the buildings were; he wore loose robes that might have been at home in the High Halls. She recognized the long, black drape of Barrani hair.

His eyes widened as he realized she was looking directly at him.

"Tara, there's someone here!"

Severn sprinted across the ill-defined border to her side as the hair on the back of her neck began to stand on end. She had enough time—barely—to throw herself to the side before the street where she'd been standing—gray and colorless though it was—erupted in a livid purple fire. She rolled to her feet and leapt again as the fire bloomed a yard away.

The small dragon squawked in her ear; he'd been so still and so quiet she'd almost forgotten he was attached. "Go somewhere safer," she told him sharply.

Her skin ached as her clothing brushed against it, but she didn't need the pain to know that magic was being used. Severn stopped in front of the building as he unleashed his weapon's chain. "Get behind me!"

Kaylin managed to avoid a third volley of ugly purple fire, and the leap carried her more or less to Severn's side, where she narrowly avoided his spinning chain. The fourth gout of flame broke against the barrier created by the chain's arc.

"Kaylin!" Tara said, raising her voice. It wasn't shouting, not in the strict sense of the word. Her voice sounded normal, if worried, but much, much louder.

She heard a curt, sharp curse—in a normal voice, if Dragon voices could be said to be normal. A shadow crossed the ground as Lord Tiamaris of the Dragon Court left his demesne. He landed to the left of where Severn now wielded his weapon, his wings folding as he lifted his neck toward the building that contained the unknown Barrani.

The ground didn't shake at the force of his landing; it gave, as if it were soft sand and not cracked stone. Or as if it were flesh. It reminded Kaylin strongly of the gray stretch of nothingness that existed between worlds, although it in theory had shape, form, texture.

The unmistakable sound of a Dragon inhaling was surprisingly loud when it happened right beside your ear. Purple fire broke against Severn's chain and sizzled where it touched Tiamaris; Kaylin could no longer be certain that the blasts were aimed at her, they were so broad. Tiamaris was angry enough that he didn't appear to notice them.

The Dragon fieflord exhaled fire. Had the building been a regular fief hovel, it would have been glowing. This one, although it had the shape leeched of color, wavered in the wake of the flame, undulating as it slowly lost coherence. If the Barrani Lord was caught in the Dragon's fire, he made no sign, but in the distance, Kaylin could hear weeping. It was soft, attenuated, and clear somehow over the roar of flame.

She reached out and rapped Tiamaris; he didn't appear to notice.

The building continued to waver, melting at last into a gray smoke or fog. She would have panicked, but the crying didn't get any louder; it was almost as if it were entirely unrelated to the demise of the building itself. Only when that building was gone did Tiamaris acknowledge Kaylin.

"You should not be here," he told her in his deep, bass rumble.

"You're here," she pointed out, perhaps unwisely given the color of his eyes. "Severn, can you hear that?"

Tiamaris hadn't looked away, but the question caught Severn's attention. "Hear what?"

"I'll take that as a no. I can hear someone…crying."

"No."

"Tiamaris?"

The Dragon snorted smoke. "No," he said after a pause.

"I hear nothing. I do not wish to remain here," he added. "Which direction is the crying coming from?"

"I'm not sure," she replied. "I think—I think it's coming from Nightshade's side of the border."

"Then you may visit Nightshade," he replied. "But do it the regular way."

"Meaning?"

"Cross the bridge, Private. Both of them. Come. We will speak with Yvander now."

Yvander was already speaking when they returned to the color and solidity of the fief of Tiamaris. He was gesturing, hands moving as if he thought they were wings; Tara's head was tilted in a familiar way, and she was once again wearing her gardening clothes. Her wings, however, remained.

His hands froze as Tiamaris approached. It was almost impossible to maintain unreasoning fear when confronted with the Tower's avatar; it was almost impossible not to be terrified when confronted with Tiamaris.

Tara, however, turned nonchalantly to the great Dragon who crowded the street simply by standing still. "Yvander thought he was with his friend Michael."

Tiamaris nodded.

"The intruder?"

"Gone."

Tara turned to Kaylin. "He was Barrani?"

"He looked Barrani to me—but if Yvander saw him as Michael, there's no guarantee that he was." She hesitated and then added, "He was using magical fire."

"It was not fire," Tiamaris said.

"It looked like fire. But purple."

"Fire is not generally purple," Tara told her. "Yvander, where did you meet Michael?"

"I met him on the way to the Town Hall. I'm due to start work in—" He glanced at the sky, and in particular at the sun's position, and blanched.

Tara, however, touched his shoulder gently. "You will not be removed from your position. Please. Where did you meet Michael?"

"On the way to the site," he replied, his panic receding in the face of her reassurance.

"Please, show us."

An escort of the Lord and Lady of the fief was perhaps not what Yvander would have wished for at the start of the day, but by the time he stopped on a street whose name escaped Kaylin, he was relatively calm. "Here."

Kaylin looked at the building to the left of the street. "He lives here?"

Yvander frowned. "No. He was visiting a friend, he said."

"Good enough." The building was, as far as the fiefs went, in poor repair; the door that in theory kept people out was listing on its hinges. Severn glanced at Tiamaris, who nodded in silence. Kaylin followed as Severn went to investigate. A fief building—especially in Tiamaris, given the damage done by the weakening of the borders—would have to be literally falling down before it remained empty, and this building was no exception; there were two families, at best guess, living on the first floor. The second floor, however, appeared to be empty.

They took the stairs cautiously; Severn gave Kaylin the lead because frankly, these stairs didn't look as though they would support a lot of weight. When she reached the second story, she froze. "Severn? Come up the stairs slowly."

The stairs creaked as he climbed them. The halls were narrow, the ceiling, which looked dangerously warped, low. Neither of these were remarkable, or at least they wouldn't have been in Nightshade, the fief with which they were both most familiar.

"What is it? What did you see?" was the soft question asked when Severn joined her.

"A mage was here," was her flat reply.

"Is he here now?"

"If he is, he's not casting. My arms don't ache. But—there was magic here. I guess whatever it took to disguise himself as Michael involved a decent amount of power."

"Which would make some sense, but a spell of that nature would generally be cast on either Yvander or the impersonator, not a hall in the middle of a run-down building."

"It's not the hall," she replied. She didn't argue with anything else, because all of it was true. "It's the door." Lifting her arm, she pointed toward the room at the hall's end. There, against its closed door, was a sigil, an echo of the identity of the mage who had cast the spell. She frowned as she drew closer. There was an obvious sigil, but around it, or beneath it, lay a far less distinct mark.

She recognized them both. She'd seen them before, in her apartment, just after her home had been destroyed by an Arcane bomb.

The door looked ordinary, for the fiefs; it was old and slightly warped. The hinges were, of course, on the other side, but Kaylin didn't expect them to be in perfect repair, either. She approached the door with care, noting how utterly silent the rooms to either side were. It was possible they were entirely empty—it was the right time of the day for that—but she felt her heart sink a yard, regardless.

Severn nodded as if she'd spoken, and opened a door to their right. Kaylin paused and watched him enter. The door wasn't locked, but frequently, doors in buildings of this nature weren't. A lock guaranteed violence if someone actually wanted to enter; it didn't keep them out. People in the fiefs understood squatters' rights: the stronger person had them. Kaylin and Severn had moved several times, with very little warning, in their early years in Nightshade, but they'd moved unharmed. They'd put up no fight, because the result of a fight was a given; in return, the people who'd kicked them out simply waited for them to walk through the door.

Maybe that had happened here.

Severn returned. "It's empty."

"No sign of who's occupying it now?"

"None." He walked straight across the hall and opened the opposite door, entering more quickly. He left more quickly, as well. "Empty."

He then backtracked down the hall. Kaylin turned to look at the door at the end of the hall, and at the familiar sigils that sat in its center. When Severn returned, she said, "They're all empty." It wasn't a question.

"Yes. The downstairs wasn't. Whatever happened upstairs didn't make a lot of noise."

Kaylin nodded. "Or it happened more than a week ago."

"Strong magic?"

She shook her head. "Weak now. Whatever it was meant to do, it did—but the mages left signatures."

"Michael wasn't working alone, then?"

She frowned. "One of the sigils is almost illegible, it's buried so far beneath the other." The frown deepened. "I've seen a lot of sigils. The stronger one looks normal, to me. The weaker one…" She shook her head.

"You recognize them."

"I'm not likely to forget them; they're what the Arcane bomb splashed across what was left of my home."

His jaw tensed; he didn't. "Don't touch the door."

"Wouldn't dream of it. Tiamaris is an Imperial Order–trained mage. He might see something here I don't."

The good thing about an enspelled door was it forced Tiamaris to let go of his Dragon form; he couldn't fit through the entrance to the building otherwise, unless he planned to make a much larger hole in the supporting wall. His eyes had shaded to orange, but it was an orange that was very close to red. Tara, in gardening clothes, still sported obsidian eyes. They entered the building with Kaylin; Severn chose to scout the ground floor while Tara listened in. She could do that and move.

The stairs creaked ominously under Tiamaris's weight; expecting it, Kaylin waited until he'd cleared them before stepping onto them herself. A fall like this wasn't likely to cause a Dragon trouble, but it wouldn't do much good for her.

Tiamaris strode straight down the hall and paused a yard from the closed door. "You didn't open it?" he asked without looking back.

"No."

"Is magic now active?"

As Kaylin had magic detectors built into her skin by default, she shook her head. Her skin didn't hurt. When Tiamaris repeated the question, she said, "Not that I can sense."

He did something that was definitely magical in response.

"That's you?"

"It is." He reached out and opened the door.

Kaylin cried out in shock and pain, half expecting the door to explode outward at the sudden force of magic she felt. It didn't. It was still in one piece, still attached to its hinges. It didn't appear to have harmed Tiamaris at all.

But it hadn't opened into a normal room, either, even by

fief standards. It opened into fog and gray, dark shadows. Or smoke without the obvious fire to cause it.

Tara said something sharp and harsh in a language Kaylin didn't understand. The door flew shut before Tiamaris could take a step into the room itself.

"Lady?" he said, turning toward her, as Kaylin said, "Tara?" They spoke with the same inflection.

Her eyes were obsidian; wings had once again sprouted from between her shoulder blades. "Do not open the door," she told her Lord softly. "It does not lead to any residence within the fief of Tiamaris."

"Where does it lead, Lady?"

"To the outlands," was her soft reply.

"To the Shadows?" Kaylin asked. "Outlands" was not a word she'd heard Tara use before. "To the heart of the fiefs?"

"No. No, Kaylin. If there was such a place in my domain, I would know."

"But—"

"This is not the same," she continued. "Not for the purpose for which I was created. It is, however, as much a danger to my Lord's people." She didn't mean the Dragons.

Tiamaris's eyes had shaded to a cooler orange; Kaylin was willing to bet that was as calm as they'd get today.

"Do you know what she means by 'outlands'?" Kaylin asked.

"No."

"Tara, do you think it's likely that the missing people walked through that door?"

"I think it very likely," Tara replied.

"Where did it take them?"

"I do not know."

"Is there some way to determine that?"

"Yes," she replied. "Enter the room. It is clear the spell is still active." To Tiamaris, she added, "I do not think they will return that way, but while the entrance exists, there is some possibility. Would you have me destroy it, Lord?"

Yes warred with hope, and hope won, although it was close. "Can you place a guard upon this door, and this building, to ensure that it is not used again without your knowledge?"

"Now that I am aware of it, yes. I cannot guarantee that there are not other points of exit—or entrance—within the fief."

"Why?" Kaylin asked.

"Because such doorways did exist when I was first created; they were not, in and of themselves, a danger; they were a path between specific locations. Once, before the fall of *Ravellon,* such doors existed between the great cities."

"Great cities?"

Tara shook her head; her wings settled into a comfortable fold. "They are gone now. Ruins remain, if that. They were not mortal cities, and against their height, Elantra counts as little. But I did not think to see such a thing again," she added.

"I am not averse to the study of the ancient," Tiamaris finally said. "I spent much of my youth in that endeavor, and it was not always considered either safe or wise. It is possible that Sanabalis may cede some of his mages to the study of this door, should I request it."

"Would you?"

"I would not have you stand guard in this…building…indefinitely; if the Imperial Order assigns its mages here—"

"Do you trust them?" Kaylin cut in.

"They are not Arcanists," he replied. "They are beholden to the Emperor."

"They are, but the fief doesn't operate under Imperial Law."

"True. But I believe it can be argued that the mages chosen will be…ambassadors for the Empire. Diplomats." He smiled.

It was not a pleasant smile. "It will prevent me from destroying them if they are overweening in their arrogance, but it will likewise diminish their self-importance."

"I don't frankly see how."

"Many of the mages are interested in the ancient and the unknown; the choice of those who are allowed to study here, of course, will be mine. If they anger, annoy, or bore me, I will send them home; if they attempt to remain, I will send them home in pieces."

"Why let them come here at all, then?"

"Because there is some small chance they will discover what the purpose of this room is—and was—and while they are here, they will defend it as if it were their personal belonging. Should the Barrani—any Barrani—attempt to access this room and this door from this side, we will know, and the mages will be better prepared than my own humble citizens." He turned to Tara and said in a quieter voice, "It would be wisest, I think, to relocate those citizens who remain in the building."

"There is a real Michael," Tara told them as they left the building and headed toward the Tower, which took longer because there was no portal and no angry Dragon to sit on. "He is a citizen of the fief. He did not, however, approach Yvander in any way today."

"Do you think the would-be kidnapper was someone who knew both Michael and Yvander?"

Tara frowned and shook her head. "I think Yvander supplied both the image and the words he thought he heard. What I do not understand," she said, "is why Yvander was being led across the border, rather than to the building itself. If the room there serves as portal, why was it not used instead?"

"I'm going to guess that the disappearances in Tiamaris

aren't unique. It's possible they've also occurred outside the fief."

Tara hesitated, and Kaylin marked it. The Avatar's eyes once again lost the semblance of normal eyes, becoming black stone instead. "My Lord gives me permission to discuss this. He gives you permission to discuss it as well, but asks that any official discussion—with your Sergeant or with the Lord of Hawks—be referred to him.

"I believe the building I was studying in the hall of perception might somehow be involved, but if the Arcanists attempted to create a portal that is similar to the one you discovered, they would find it much, much more difficult beyond the bounds of the fiefs."

"Why?"

"There is a reason that the Towers were built and a reason they were built here. Beyond the borders of the fiefs, the type of power required would be much, much more significant. If they were very lucky, planned well, and made use of the magical storms that engulfed a large part of the City itself, yes, there is every possibility such a gateway exists in the City proper. The magical storms, however, were not predictable, and I consider their use in this case unlikely. It is not just a matter of power—although power is necessary—but also a matter of precision."

"But they could build gateways like this in the other fiefs?"

Tara nodded. "They are most likely to be found near the border zones; a singularly powerful but unwise mage might attempt their construction within the zone itself."

"What is it about the fiefs that make it easier or simpler here?"

Tara shrugged, a gesture that looked, in all details, as if it could have come from Morse. It probably had. "The same thing that allows Ferals to hunt in the streets. The Ferals don't cross the bridge."

"You don't think they can."

"No."

"If 'Michael' were leading Yvander across the border to Nightshade, it's likely that a portal exists in Nightshade."

Tara nodded. "We have been far more vigilant than Barren was capable of being. Given the recent difficulty with the borders, the ongoing threat posed by Shadows that managed to enter the fief during the period of instability, and the necessity of reconstruction, it is more difficult to conduct large-scale and illegal magics without the possibility of detection."

"You didn't detect this door."

"Not immediately."

They reached the Tower. "Our apologies to the Halls of Law," Tara said softly. "I do not think the missing boy will be found."

The doors rolled open; Kaylin remained on the outside. "If people are disappearing, there has to be some reason. The people Tiamaris listed as missing are all human, but they span age and gender. I've seen many ways humans can be bought and sold, but their value is entirely dependent on age, gender, and appearance. None of those require something as complicated as the portal. None of them require any level of magic. But magic clearly was used.

"The victims aren't, as far as you know, in the city anymore. They had to be sent somewhere."

"They were sent to the outlands," Tara replied.

"Tara, where are the outlands? Are they even in the Empire?"

"Not in the sense Elantra is, no. But if you mean to ask me why those victims came from the fief, I believe it to be because such a portal could be opened here."

"Could it be opened in *Ravellon?*"

"Perhaps—but there is little chance, in my opinion, that the ones who opened the portal would survive the opening."

"So it had to be here. What purpose would random victims serve?"

"There was once a theory," Tara replied, "that mortals were malleable because they had no True Names and therefore no confinement. They are not fixed in shape."

"They are," Kaylin replied sharply. "If you attempt to break their shape, you generally damage—or kill—them." But as she spoke, she thought of the Leontines and their story of origin and fell silent.

"The Ancients did not perceive life the way you do," Tara finally said. "I have not heard the voices of the Ancients for so long, Kaylin. Nor do I hear them now, in this; it is too small, too precise, and too secretive. My Lord will speak with the Imperial Order, but I think it unlikely that the Imperial Order will offer enlightenment. It is possible that the Arkon may have information that is relevant."

"Yvander was being led to Nightshade," Kaylin said. The words were sharp and heavy. "In Nightshade, no one's likely to care."

Tara frowned. "If something is preying on his people, he will. If he does not have sympathy for the individuals who have gone missing," she added, "he is nonetheless Lord in his domain, and he cannot afford to overlook such predations."

"He didn't give a damn about the Ferals," was the sharp reply. "And there were certainly brothels like Barren's, where predators from the City were welcomed."

"He did not turn a blind eye to the latter," was Tara's cool reply. "He profited from it, in a fashion of his choosing."

Kaylin's hands bunched into instant fists. She'd learned, on the other hand, to keep still when she was in the grip of a sudden, unexpected anger. She met Tara's steady gaze and saw that the Avatar's eyes were no longer obsidian.

"I have angered you," she said.

"Yes."

"Why?"

"Because," Kaylin replied, exhaling and loosening her hands, "I hate what you're saying."

"Is it inaccurate?"

"No. If it were inaccurate, I wouldn't be angry. You're not wrong, and I hate that you're not wrong."

"My Lord would be sympathetic," Tara replied. Her wings folded into her back and disappeared as she straightened out her apron.

"We'll take word to the Halls," Kaylin said after a long pause. "If I don't come to visit in the next two months, it's not because I'm angry."

Tara frowned. "You are leaving?"

"Yes. I'm going to the West March." The West March suddenly seemed like a terrible waste of time. People were being kidnapped in the fiefs, and Kaylin and Severn were two Hawks who could navigate its streets. She didn't say this.

On the other hand, standing on the front steps of the Tower, she didn't need to; Tara heard it anyway.

"Kaylin."

Kaylin, shoulders hunched, was looking for something to kick. "I don't want to go to the West March. I want to be here."

"The fiefs aren't our jurisdiction."

Kaylin said nothing for two blocks.

"And that's not why you're angry."

Severn knew her. Sometimes, she forgot how well. "No."

"Nightshade?"

"Yes." She wanted to spit. She couldn't bring herself to say the name. "I'll bet you any money—and I mean any—that there's a portal to wherever across the border. Whoever was taking Yvander to 'lunch' was leading him there."

"I wouldn't touch that bet."

No one still breathing would. "But it makes no sense. The kidnappings. I hate magic."

The small dragon hissed in her ear.

"I'm sorry, but I do."

He nipped her earlobe. Had he been larger, she would have grabbed him and tossed him off her shoulders. As it was, she managed to ignore him. "I think this has something to do with the embezzling. The biggest difficulty we've had in solving this case has been the lack of distribution of the stolen funds. It's not in banks. It's not in drugs. It's not in gems or other concessions. It's not in the hands of merchants."

"You think it's in the hands of fieflords."

She did. "Tara's half-right. They couldn't just grab people off the street. Dozens? The fieflords would have to notice that. But what if they just buy people? Pay off fieflords? It's not much different from killing them in brothels we'd shut down in two seconds on this side of the river. They don't have that option with Tiamaris. He'd eat them for lunch.

"And if it's Barrani, they'd know that. They've been at war with Dragons on and off for centuries. If Tiamaris claims this as his, he's not selling any of it—not for something as mundane as stolen treasury funds."

"What, exactly, would the Exchequer or the Human Caste Court derive from that? Stealing funds to give to Barrani to buy chattel doesn't seem like motivation to risk life and limb—literally. It doesn't make sense."

"No." She slowed. "It doesn't. But I think it doesn't make sense because we don't know where the people went. We're missing part of the big picture. What we're not missing is the fact that 'Michael,' whoever the hells he was, walked Yvander across the Nightshade border." With a great deal of bitterness, she added, "There's no way he doesn't know. He fingered the Arcanum. He knew who to blame. How?"

"You're going to Nightshade."

"I am."

CHAPTER 6

The sky was so gray, it was almost the color of silence. The rage bled away as Kaylin walked; it left a familiar despair in its wake.

It had never occurred to Kaylin, growing up in the streets of Nightshade, that a fief could be almost safe. But in Tiamaris, Ferals were hunted, and the ranks of those who formed Tiamaris's unofficial guard force were growing; people wanted to hunt Ferals here; the young wanted to be heroes. Only the dangerously insane had ever done so in Nightshade, and in Kaylin's admittedly small experience, they were just as likely to kill as the Ferals and for reasons that were just as clear.

In Tiamaris, people came to the fieflord—or Tara, at least—to report their missing parents.

Tiamaris had owned the fief for almost two months, if that, and these were the changes he had made. Dragons were a force of nature, as all Immortals were, but this Dragon, she understood and, in her own way, admired.

Nightshade had owned his fief for far longer than she had been alive. He could have made the fief an entirely different place, just as Tiamaris was attempting to do. He hadn't. He had never particularly cared about the people who eked out a miserable existence in the streets surrounding his castle. They were mortal and no more important than any other insignificant and transitory possession.

The Ablayne came into view. She had seen it so often from the wrong side of its banks that it was almost a comfort. The bridge that crossed Tiamaris wasn't empty, and the men—and women—who walked it weren't attempting to be furtive. They walked it the way the citizens of Elantra walked to any job or to any market. They did blink a little when they saw Kaylin and Severn, but only because they wore the tabard of the Hawks.

With the streets of the city firmly beneath her feet, she relaxed—but not enough. "Will you go back to the office?" she asked.

"If you'd prefer," he replied with only a small gap between question and answer to indicate hesitance.

She nodded, and he accompanied her down the riverside street until they reached a more familiar bridge. This one contained no foot traffic, no obvious guards, no carpenters or linguists; it was a bridge in name only and served as it had always served: as a wall, a way of keeping people in their respective homes.

"I'll be fine," she told Severn. "It's not my death he wants."

"You don't know what he wants."

It was true. She didn't. "I don't always know what *I* want."

"No." His smile was slight. "Mostly, people don't."

"Or they want the wrong things."

"Wrong?"

"Things they can't ever have. Safety. Security. Things to remain the same. Some things," she added quickly. She turned to him at the foot of the bridge. "I want to stay where we are."

He didn't misinterpret, although he could have. Instead, to her surprise, he hugged her. She stiffened and then relaxed, slowly, into the warmth of it. "Don't live in the past," he told her.

"I'm not. It's just—it's part of me. I feel like I barely managed to step out of the shadows, all of them. Ferals, loss, myself. I was kept as an assassin. I'm now paid to protect people from what I once was—and I want that. You—" She swallowed. "What I did for the Wolves wasn't what you did for Barren."

"Excepting the obvious, how was it different?"

"It was legal."

"Technically, what I was doing was legal, as well. Barren was the Law."

"Kaylin—"

"I know." She pulled away, lifting a hand and forcing herself to smile. "We're not doing it anymore. We're Hawks now. I'm not Barren's. You're not—"

He lifted a finger to her mouth and the words ended abruptly. "Go ask what you need to ask. I'll go to Missing Persons and file a report with Mallory and Brigit."

It was hard to imagine that she'd once lived in Nightshade. She knew she had, but the visceral truth of life in its streets as an orphan had eased its constant grip; when she looked at the worn roads and old buildings, she could see them as they were, as they might have been in a different context. She could meet the furtive gazes of strangers, walk down the streets, and evince no surprise or dismay at the way the children and their minders fell silent, shrinking toward the cover of familiar doors or alleys to allow her to pass.

She'd been one of those children, although she'd played on the streets far less often. Some of the older minders—grandparents or great-aunts and -uncles—had been kind enough, but that kindness extended only as far as empty streets and a lack of Nightshade's thugs. If necessary to preserve their own, they would have handed her over in a minute; it was a fact they all accepted.

Your kin wouldn't, for the most part, although that was no guarantee of safety.

Now, Nightshade's mark adorning her cheek, no one would touch her. Most of the people who sidled away had no idea what the mark meant, which was fair; Kaylin wasn't clear on the concept, either. But Nightshade's mortal thugs, and worse, his Barrani thugs, did. It gave her a freedom in the fief that she had never had and never thought to have anywhere on this side of the Ablayne.

That freedom extended all the way to Castle Nightshade.

The streets that surrounded the Castle itself were empty of all but the fortunate few who made small deliveries to the fieflord, and they didn't stop to chat for a variety of reasons. They weren't dressed as foreigners; they were dressed as fieflings. Any delivery made to Castle Nightshade implied wealth, and any wealth was a target. If you couldn't be parted from your wealth while alive, death wasn't much of an impediment.

She approached the guards who waited beyond the portcullis through which the open courtyard was visible. The portcullis served as the entrance to the Castle, but not in the traditional way. It was a portal that moved you from the street side of the metal bars to the inside of the Castle's grand foyer, with a lot of nausea and magical discomfort in between.

Andellen was one of the two men who stood guard. He bowed. "Lord Kaylin." The words immediately caused a similar bow in the other guard. Kaylin disliked the gesture, but understood that Andellen wasn't offering it for the sake of her pride or her position. It was tradition, and given how little tradition existed in his life in the fiefs, she tried hard not to begrudge it.

"Lord Andellen."

"Lord Nightshade is waiting."

She grimaced. "Of course he is."

Passage through the portal was always disorienting, in part because Castle Nightshade's architecture wasn't fixed. Like the Tower of Tiamaris, it shifted in place, responding to the desire or command of its Lord. The foyer was the only part of the Castle that Kaylin was certain remained the same between visits: it was too loud, too ostentatious, and far too bright. Large didn't matter.

She kept this to herself as she rose unsteadily to her feet, wondering, as she often did, if Nightshade deliberately made the portal passage as nauseating as possible to give himself the edge in any negotiations or conversations.

"I hardly think it required," was his amused—but chilly—reply. He was, of course, standing beneath the chandeliers. But his eyes were a shade of blue at odds with the situation, and the color immediately put Kaylin on guard.

"You are cautious," he replied, "as is your wont." He offered her an arm. If she maintained physical contact with Nightshade, the Castle didn't throw up new doors or halls and didn't distort the ones she'd seen before. She reached for the bend of his elbow and stopped as the small dragon reared up on its unimpressive legs, extending his head, his small jaws snapping at air. It was, sadly, the air directly between Kaylin and the Lord of the Castle.

"What is this?" he asked softly, his brows folding in almost open surprise—for a Barrani.

"My newest roommate," she replied tersely. She pulled her

hand back, and the small dragon settled—slowly—around the back of her neck, looping his tail around the front.

"It lives with you?"

She had not come to the Castle to talk about the small dragon. "Yes."

"I…see." He withdrew the offered arm. "Are you aware of what it is?"

"A small, winged lizard," she replied. The small dragon hissed, but did so very quietly. She knew Nightshade would have some interest in the small creature, and at the moment, she didn't care. A cold certainty had settled into the center of her chest, constricting breath.

His expression chilled. "You are, in the parlance of mortal Elantra, in a mood."

"I'm angry, yes."

"Have I done something to merit your anger?" As he spoke, he walked; if she wished to continue the conversation, she had no choice but to follow. "Have you made preparations for our journey to the West March?"

It wasn't the question she'd expected. "I've been given a leave of absence from the Halls of Law, yes. I will be traveling with Teela." The halls of the Castle looked almost familiar, and they led to the room in which Nightshade habitually received guests. Or at least guests who wore the tabard of the Hawk on the other side of the bridge.

"That is not entirely what I meant." He led her to the long couch in front of the flat, perfect table that graced the room's center. There, silvered trays held very tastefully arranged bread, nuts, and flowers.

"You know that the High Court is traveling there."

"Indeed."

"How exactly are you going to survive?"

"Is my survival of concern to you?" He smiled.

She ignored the question and the smile; the latter was harder. "You're Outcaste, and even if the Barrani don't view Outcastes the way the Dragons do, they won't be able to ignore your existence if you're constantly in their presence."

"No," he agreed. "Be that as it may, I have reasons to believe in this case they will hold enmity and decree in abeyance."

"Reasons you'd like to share?"

"At this point, Private Neya, you would not understand them; I believe they will become clear with time. My status, however, given the debt owed you by the High Lord, should not materially affect your own."

She lifted a hand to her cheek, which deepened his smile and lightened the color of his eyes. "Yes." The smile faded. "It is not, however, concern for my welfare that brought you to my Castle."

"No. You already know what I want to ask."

His eyes, when they met hers, were dark, his expression smooth and cool as winter stone. "Ask," he said softly. When her silence extended for minutes beyond awkward, he smiled. It was thin. "I would not have all effort in this conversation be mine. You made a decision, Kaylin. You have come to my fief, my Castle, to ask a simple question. Ask. I will not lie."

She exhaled. "There's been a series of disappearances in Tiamaris."

His expression didn't shift. At all. "Continue."

"One of the people who disappeared in the fief wasn't a native. He crossed the bridge on a dare."

At that, Nightshade frowned. "That is unfortunate."

"Is it more unfortunate than the other disappearances?"

"Of course. That mortal was a citizen of the Empire over which a Dragon claims ownership."

"And the others were citizens of a fief over which a different Dragon claims ownership."

"A Dragon who is in the unheard-of position of also owing loyalty to the Eternal Emperor. I do not envy him the loss of an Imperial citizen within the boundaries of his fief; he will almost certainly be called upon to explain it."

"An explanation has presented itself."

She felt him stiffen, although nothing about his expression or posture changed at all.

"And that?"

"A Barrani Lord of some power appears to have been involved."

"Ah. You call him a Lord?"

"The Barrani who have power aren't generally content to let it remain unrecognized."

His smile was slender, sharp, and laced with an odd approval. "True. Why do you believe a Barrani Lord to be involved?"

"Because you do," she replied, the words as tight and sharp as his smile.

"Perhaps that is merely the arrogance of my kind." He rose. "If events are of significance, of consequence, we assume our own to have a hand in them."

"So do we. Your own." She could find no warmth with which to smile. "I saw him."

Once again he stilled. "You…saw him? The Barrani you accuse?"

"I saw him," she repeated, "in the border zone."

After a significant pause, Nightshade spoke. "You are so certain, Kaylin, that the individual you saw in the border zone was Barrani?"

In response, she folded her arms. "I am."

"The border areas are often…amorphous. What is seen—"

"I don't want to play this game."

"Ah." A brief smile. "Which game, then, would you indulge in, in its stead?"

"You're aware that I'm currently resident in the Imperial Palace?"

The smile vanished. "I was not."

"You are aware that the only home I've ever had I could truly call my own was destroyed yesterday?"

Silence. It was not an awkward silence—but it was. Nightshade resumed his seat, the table dividing them. "I was not." He glanced at the small dragon. "How was it destroyed?"

"An Arcane bomb." Her throat was inexplicably tight; it was hard to force words out. The small dragon rubbed the underside of her jaw with the top of his head.

He asked nothing, watching her.

"The magical signature left in the wake of the bomb is not currently in the records of the Imperial Order."

He nodded, as if the information were irrelevant.

"But that same magical signature can be found in the fief of Tiamaris, near the border, where I saw the Barrani we believe to be involved in the disappearances."

"And your question?"

"People have been disappearing from the fief of Tiamaris for the past week—that we're aware of. How long have people gone missing from your streets?"

"If I say they have not?"

"I'll redefine the word 'missing.'" She pushed herself to her feet, feeling too confined by the stillness enforced by sitting. "Was the unnamed Barrani Lord buying people from your fief?"

"It is not, in the fief of Nightshade, an illegal activity. Imperial Laws have no jurisdiction here. Nor do they in any other fief; Lord Tiamaris may style himself after Imperial rule, but it is choice, not dictate."

"Is Imperial gold currently in what passes for your coffers?"

"We use the resources we have, Kaylin, and we sacrifice the things of lesser import to us."

She swallowed.

"You have done the same in your short past. Perhaps you comfort yourself by telling yourself you had no choice. If it will comfort you in a like fashion, pretend that I, likewise, felt I had no choice."

"How?"

"Pardon?"

"How am I supposed to pretend that? You're the fieflord here. If someone came to threaten you—in any way—the Castle would probably eat them. They wouldn't make it out alive unless it also suited your purpose. You won't—you probably can't—starve. You won't freeze. All-out magical assault probably couldn't destroy these walls.

"Given all that, how am I supposed to pretend you had no choice?"

He raised a brow. "I am almost surprised that you've considered making that effort. Very well. Some two or three dozen of the people who live in the fief have been extracted from its streets, with my permission. I received compensation for their loss."

"Where were they sent?"

"Why do you suppose they were sent anywhere?"

"Because there's a door in Tiamaris that opens into the outlands."

Nightshade's eyes were indigo. "Do not go near that door," he said, all pretense of civility lost. "Do not touch it."

"It's not in your fief, and yes, Tiamaris is well aware of its existence. He protects his citizens."

"As the shepherd protects his sheep."

Stung, she said, "No. As a decent ruler protects his people."

"Is there no difficulty within this city that will not, eventually, entangle you? I ask it, Kaylin, if I cannot command it. You do not understand the danger."

"I understand it better than any of the people who were lost to it!"

"Kaylin." He rose, and the way he stood made her conscious of the difference in their height, their weight, and their reach. She stiffened, bending at the knees as if she would, at any minute, have to throw herself bodily out of harm's reach. The small dragon reared once again, spreading his wings just behind her head, like a slender, glass fan.

Nightshade ignored him this time.

The small dragon had ways of making himself heard, at least when he wanted Kaylin's attention; Nightshade, however, was not the kind of man one bit on the ear or chin. Instead of maintaining his rigid posture on her left shoulder, the familiar launched himself into the closing space between the fieflord and the Hawk, buoying himself up with the silent motion of delicate, translucent wings.

He looked, to Kaylin's eye, tiny and fragile in his defiance, and she almost reached out to grab him and pull him back, but she didn't want to injure those wings.

What Nightshade saw must have been different; he froze in place, lifting a hand as if to indicate harmlessness. Kaylin didn't buy it. The small dragon wasn't buying it, either. He lifted his neck and looked down at the fieflord before opening his jaws to exhale. The motion was that of a dragon in miniature, but what he exhaled, along with his high-pitched, barely audible roar, was not a gout of flame; it was smoke.

Opalescent, swirling gray spread like a dense cloud before Nightshade; it was amorphous enough—barely—that Kaylin could see the rise of the fieflord's brows, the widening of his eyes. He moved—he leapt—to the left, rolling across the floor and coming to his feet as if he were an acrobat.

The dense smoke didn't follow him, but it didn't really dissipate, either; it hung in the air like a small cloud. A small, glittering cloud. They both stared at the small dragon, who pirouetted in the air, which was the only time he took his eyes off the fieflord.

Nightshade spoke three sharp words; the hair on the back of Kaylin's neck instantly stood on end, and the skin across her forearms and legs went numb. The small dragon yawned and returned to his customary perch, which would be her rigid shoulders. He rubbed her cheek with the side of his face.

Three lines appeared beneath the cloud, pulsing as if they were exposed golden veins. Nightshade spread his hands; his fingers were taut but steady. His eyes were a blue that was so close to black Kaylin couldn't tell the difference. All her anger—her visceral, instinctive rage—guttered. The whole of his attention was focused on the cloud, and as he moved his hands, the lines that enclosed it shifted in place, until they touched its outer edge. When they did, their color began to change. It was a slow shift from gold to something that resembled the heart of a hearth fire.

Nightshade spoke softly in Barrani; the words were so low Kaylin couldn't catch them. The magical lines engraved in air brightened, losing their red-orange tint.

"What is it?" she asked, her voice almost as low as his. Barrani had better hearing.

"Step away from the containment," he told her. "If you do not know what it is, I have some suspicion. It is not safe, not even in the Castle." Although he spoke to her, he didn't take his eyes off the cloud. Not even when the small dragon squawked. "You are mortal," he continued. "Mortals walk the edge of hope; it is a sharp edge.

"The question you came to ask has only one answer—an answer you knew before you arrived. Would it truly have offered any comfort were I to lie? Or would your hope blind you so badly you might choose to believe?"

She was silent.

As if he were Sanabalis, he said, "What purpose would such a lie serve?"

"I don't know. Reputation. Community standing. Tact—the desire not to hurt someone else's feelings."

He frowned.

"Yes, they're mortal terms, but I've noted that absent big words, there are certain similarities."

"If I chose to lie to you now, how would you categorize that decision? I am not afraid of you, Kaylin. There may come a time," he added, his glance flicking off the small dragon on her shoulders, "when fear would be the appropriate response, but I cannot see it. Your judgment of me, should you choose one, is irrelevant. Your feelings—ah, that is a more complicated issue, but I will not lower myself to live in such a way as to assuage your fear or your guilt.

"Let me make this much clear: you are valuable to me. You. It is not because you are mortal; your mortality does not, by extension, make the residents of this fief valuable in the same way. Nor will it. I am not beholden to Imperial Law, and I do not choose to indulge in its outward appearance at this time; it serves no useful purpose."

"And if it did?"

"I would acquiesce, as the High Court does. But it would not change in any material way what I feel, either for you or for the mortals you mistakenly assume are your kind. Such feelings, such…interactions…are a matter of necessity; if the weak congregate, they have some hope of survival."

Kaylin was silent for a long moment. When she once again met his gaze, she held it. "Tell me why," she said, her voice heavy but steady. "Why did they buy your people?"

"I am not at liberty to discuss that," he replied. "And as there is no answer I can give you that will excuse the action in your eyes, I am not of a mind to do so, regardless."

Kaylin's walk back to the Ablayne was swift and silent.

CHAPTER 7

Marcus, seated behind a stack of paperwork that made him look smaller, looked up the minute she crossed the threshold that divided Hawks from Halls. His eyes were a pale orange, and given the past week, that was good. His ears flattened as she hesitated.

"Do not tell me that you're handing me more work," he said, wedging a growl between every other syllable.

"Not exactly. I went to Tiamaris."

"The Missing Persons report?"

She nodded. "According to Tiamaris, Miccha Jannoson, reported missing today, crossed the Ablayne by bridge. He disappeared a few blocks from that bridge."

"Disappeared?"

Kaylin hesitated, casting a meaningful glance at stacks of paperwork that weren't in any danger of getting smaller in the near future.

Marcus growled. This caught the attention of the Barrani Hawks; as Sergeant sounds went, growling was generally quiet. The wrong kind of quiet. "What happened? According to the

Hawklord, a request for Records access has arrived from the Imperial Palace."

"The Palace doesn't need permission."

"In this case, it does; the request has been tendered by a member of the Dragon Court, but involves access outside Imperial boundaries."

"We believe—and we have very little in the way of solid proof, Sergeant—that a Barrani Lord is responsible for the disappearance."

Someone whistled. It wasn't Marcus; it was Teela. She approached the sergeant's desk with care. "What very little proof do you have?" She wasn't particularly offended. Two decades of service with the Hawks made Kaylin's claim reasonable on the surface; the Barrani were often peripherally involved in crimes investigated by the Hawks.

Very few of them were Lords. Kaylin turned to Teela. "I saw him."

"You saw him grab the child?"

"Miccha wasn't a child, strictly speaking."

Teela generally considered most mortals children when she was in a mood. "Answer the question."

"No. Not that one."

This caused Marcus's growl to deepen, and Kaylin surrendered. "Tiamaris has been monitoring his fief carefully this past week; Miccha isn't the only person who's disappeared—without an obvious trace—in the boundaries of his fief. The reason he noticed Miccha at all is because of the increased surveillance.

"While we were examining the fief's internal Records, Tara caught something unusual; one of the citizens of Tiamaris appeared to be having a casual conversation with thin air as he approached the border between Tiamaris and Nightshade. The people who've disappeared have done so without struggle or obvious panic, and if someone's going to voluntarily sneak across a fief border, it's always going to be the one that's between the fief and the rest of Elantra."

Marcus's brows rose. They lowered again without comment.

"The Barrani Lord," Kaylin said, still watching Marcus, "appeared only when the citizen in question had crossed into the border zone. I didn't recognize him," she added. "But I would bet money he's an Arcanist."

That caused a different kind of quiet. "What," Teela finally said, "did he do to cause that assumption?"

"The usual."

"And that?"

"Tried to kill me."

Teela's eyes shifted to an instant midnight-blue. Kaylin found it both stressful and oddly comforting. "I didn't recognize the spell, but—Arcanist."

"How did it manifest?"

"Purple fire."

Teela said nothing. When Marcus growled, the Barrani Hawk shrugged. "I concur."

"Pardon?"

"He's an Arcanist. There's more, kitling."

"No doubt the Hawks will hear about it from Sanabalis and the Imperial Order at some point: the Lord was involved in either the creation of, or the protection of, something that functions as a portal to—somewhere else."

"Where?"

"I'm not sure it has a name. Tara referred to it as the outlands. Tiamaris has quarantined the building we found it in, and he's calling in Imperial mages to 'study' it. We think the Barrani Arcanist used the portal to access the fief of Tiamaris." She hesitated, given Teela's eye color, and then said, "The door bore two sigils."

"You recognized them," was Teela's flat reply.

She nodded. "They were the same as the sigils on the Arcane bomb."

"You've been informed that the Imperial mages could only find one?"

"Yes. The second—at least on the door—was subtle; it was pervasive, but strangely amorphous. I'm to speak to Sanabalis about it, but he's so busy that I might be able to put it off for six weeks."

"Private."

"Sergeant?"

"When the alleged Arcanist tried to kill you a second time, was it because he recognized you?"

"No, sir. In my opinion it was because we'd seen him, and we'd interfered with whatever it was he intended. We no longer ditch our tabards when we enter Tiamaris at the request of Lord Tiamaris; it's likely that the Barrani saw only the Hawk." She exhaled. "If there's any way to investigate the financial activities of the fieflords, I think you'll find that a large portion of the embezzled treasury funds are now in the fiefs."

"The...fiefs."

"It's possible that the money was funneled to the Arcanists—or an Arcanist—who then used it to pay fieflords for a few dozen of their citizens. There would be no reports filed and no objections to the disappearances."

"The fiefs are not our jurisdiction," Marcus growled.

"The disposition of the Imperial funds is, though."

"You think the Exchequer was indirectly involved in slave trafficking?"

"No." Pause. "Technically, yes."

"If this is your idea of not adding to our workload, you fail."

"Can I keep the job anyway?"

"Out. I believe you have an appointment at the High Halls.

But first visit Records. The Arkon has sent word about needing another full scan of your marks."

"Given the events of the afternoon, I was really hoping to give that a pass."

"Given the importance of your pilgrimage, and your ignorance of same, that is not considered an option. Don't give me that look—if you have a problem with the decision, take it up with the Hawklord and Lord Sanabalis. Corporal."

Teela nodded.

"I've been extremely appreciative of your duty detail for the past three weeks." That detail had involved hours that would have driven the mortals in the department literally insane; the Barrani worked around the clock with breaks for meals. They didn't need something as petty as sleep, and lack of sleep didn't slow them down at all.

"Not so appreciative that you're offering a raise."

"No. I'm following what I'm told is a time-honored tradition."

"Which would that be?"

"If you want something done, give it to the person who's always busy."

Teela chuckled drily. "You want me to make certain Kaylin survives."

"More or less."

"Yes, sir."

Teela was not in good enough humor that she insisted on driving the carriage after their detour to Records, which was a mixed blessing; driving placed her on the outside of the cabin.

"You are certain about what you saw in the border zone?"

"Given that Yvander was convinced he was walking with a friend in an entirely different part of the fief? Possibly not. But that kind of illusion usually makes my skin break out in hives."

Teela nodded in the absent way that implied she wasn't listening to the answer. Long experience had taught Kaylin that this didn't actually mean she didn't hear it. "Refrain from mentioning this in the High Halls," she finally said. "The Barrani Court expects a certain amount of political fallout from the failed assassination attempt. The Emperor was not pleased." Gaze firmly fixed on the exterior landscape, she added, "What else happened? Before you attempt to tell me that there was nothing, remember what I've said about lying."

"I don't really want to talk about it."

Teela, however, did. "You visited Nightshade. Oh, don't give me that look." Given that Teela's gaze hadn't shifted, this said something. "Kitling, I don't know what hopes you have for Lord Nightshade, but hope, among our kin, is not a double-edged blade. It is single edged, and the edge always wounds. Always. He is not mortal. He does not value what you value."

"Does he value what you do?"

"You don't understand what I value. You assume because I'm a Hawk, I share yours. This is not a safe assumption," she added in case it was necessary.

"Why did you come to the Hawks?"

"For reasons of my own. They are not particularly relevant. They were reasons," she added drily, "you would possibly approve of; your own…were not."

"But the reason I stayed—"

"Oh, hush, kitling. Not all of our heartless plans work as we intend; nor do all of our good intentions. We are where we are, and we can rarely predict where we will go, no matter how firm our beliefs."

After a longer pause, Kaylin said, "I can't tell whether or not you're warning me off Nightshade or telling me not to judge him."

"Can I not do both?" Teela turned to her then. "It has never been safe to know him or to keep his company. That much is true. But this is less about Nightshade, to me."

"How so?"

"He is what he is, Kaylin. Accept that; you will find the Barrani less daunting. He is not mortal, and his concerns are not mortal concerns."

"He sold mortals to the Arcanist," was her flat reply.

Teela's eyes darkened. "That is unfortunate," she finally replied. "You are certain?"

"Yes."

"The same Arcanist—"

"Who was responsible for a portal that led to what Tara called the outlands, yes. And who destroyed my home."

"What is he doing?" Teela said, but she didn't ask it of Kaylin; she spoke to herself. Realizing that she had a rapt audience anyway, she shook herself. "We are almost at the High Halls. I should warn you that the High Halls are in slight disarray at the moment."

"...What do you mean by 'slight'?"

"I did mention that our raid was not entirely conclusive. The Eternal Emperor paid a visit to the High Halls—in person—this afternoon."

"He went Dragon?"

"Ah, no, you misunderstand me." Teela hesitated and then added, "Or perhaps not. He did not, however, arrive at the High Halls in Dragon form. He did arrive at the head of the Palace guard, companioned by the worthy Lord Diarmat."

"And he was let into the Halls?"

"Let us say that a detachment was sent—in haste—to greet him. He was not, by all reports, in an entirely pleasant mood, nor was he willing to embark upon the more delicate dance of diplomacy usually employed between the Barrani High Court and the Dragon Court."

"What happened?"

"Swords were brought, armor was brought—I'm afraid you've probably missed them; they are artifacts, preserved in the Halls, from the wars between our kind."

"The Emperor wasn't impressed."

"I wouldn't say that. They didn't enrage him, however; he was already too close to that state to be concerned about simple armor or weapons."

Kaylin grimaced. "You're enjoying this, aren't you?"

"I assure you, a Dragon in the High Halls—"

"I meant tormenting me."

"Oh, that. Yes, I admit your very mortal patience is a delight to try on occasion. I have to get it out of my system before we reach the High Halls and I'm forced to call you Lord Kaylin in a serious way."

"As opposed to the way you use the title in the office?"

"As opposed to that, yes." She smiled. She had a beautiful smile.

"So the Emperor was hunting for the missing Arcanist in the High Halls?"

"Yes."

"I don't understand."

"I believe there is some confusion. He wasn't hunting for the Arcanist because of the Arcanum's interference with the Human Caste Court; the investigation into the matter of the Exchequer, while a growing annoyance and a severe inconvenience, is unlikely to bring the two Courts to the brink of open conflict." She paused. "It is likely, however, given your current suspicions, to cause far, far more concern to both Immortal Courts. At the moment it is in the hands of the Tha'alani and the Imperial Order of Mages."

"Ugh. Let me guess: the Human Caste Court is claiming that they were enspelled."

"Very good, kitling."

"Is there any possibility that's true?"

"If greed is a spell, yes, in my opinion. The Tha'alani will sort some of it out. At the moment, it's uncertain how many of the Caste Court were involved in covering up for the Exchequer because they were expressing racial solidarity and how many were being heavily bribed. We have our actuarial experts working on that, as well. It is just possible that the Caste Court was collectively the victim of severe extortion; Nightshade indicated two Arcanists, one of whom perished and one of whom is missing."

"It's not likely he'll flee to the High Halls."

"No. As Lord Evarrim will, however, be present at the High Halls, it would be best if you tucked your pet under your tunic until we reach my rooms, if at all possible. I don't think I need to tell you to—"

"Avoid him like the plague?"

"Indeed. I realize you are not fond of him. He is my cousin, and I am not fond of him, either."

"Do you have any idea who the Barrani was?"

"I believe so."

"What are the Emperor's chances of catching him?"

"Not, at the moment, high. It would also be an interesting fight, although I think I would place odds on the Emperor."

"Speaking of the Emperor—"

"He would have been content to leave the investigation—and the usual negotiations that occur when the Law and the High Halls collide—in the hands of the Halls and the Hawklord."

"But?"

"Patience. You will recall one other event of significance that occurred yesterday?"

"My apartment was destroyed."

"Very good. Yes. Your apartment was destroyed, and by some stroke of luck, folly, or very peculiar destiny, neither of its two occupants joined it."

"He's pissed about Bellusdeo."

"He is, indeed, angry about Bellusdeo."

"Did the Barrani even know about Bellusdeo?"

"Demonstrably."

"...How many others are likely to try to kill her?"

"After the Emperor's visit? Only the suicidal. We're immortal, not invulnerable."

Kaylin frowned. "How do you feel about her?"

Teela's eyes narrowed. "That is an unwise question."

"Which means you won't answer."

"Which means I will answer."

Kaylin lifted a hand. "I don't want to hear it."

"Then, next time, don't ask. It wouldn't trouble me—at all—if she died. It would not have troubled me at all had the attempt on her life been made in any other location. Or rather, had it been made while she wasn't dogging your footsteps like a foolish, bored child. The Dragon Court already shadows the High Halls, as it shadows all of our kind; what need have we of more of them?"

"Teela—"

"We serve the Emperor."

"I don't think he'd consider your opinion appropriate service."

"No, he wouldn't. Bellusdeo has two points in her favor. She apparently likes—and respects—you, something that most of the Immortals of any power or significance fail to do, and she has, purportedly, argued at length with both the Captain of the Imperial Guard and the Eternal Emperor himself in an attempt to elevate your stature."

"How do you know that?"

"I am part of the High Court, of course."

"Which is never allowed anywhere near the Imperial Court. You've got a lot of spies in the Palace?"

"Kitling, please."

Kaylin allowed—barely—that it had probably been a naive question. "But I don't think the High Court cares whether or not she likes or respects me."

"Ah, I wasn't clear. She has two points in her favor where my opinion is concerned. Neither of those points will hold much sway where the rest of the High Court is concerned, but I'm sure you're aware how much I care."

"You wear the Hawk."

"Exactly." Teela grimaced. "No one was happy when word of her arrival reached the High Court. It's been somewhat tricky for the Barrani Hawks, but as one of the few who is also a Lord of the Court, it's been trickier for me. The others simply remained outside of the reach of the High Court."

"They can do that?"

"They know the mortal city quite well. Yes, they can. It's not considered politically wise in most circumstances, but given the probability that they would be required to spy on Bellusdeo in the best possible case, it was prudent."

"You went to Court."

"I did. I am not particularly afraid to deny a request that has no merit. Bellusdeo is a Dragon, and it is probable that if she survives, there will be young Dragons again, but I cannot see that as a material threat in the near future. The heart of the fiefs is a greater danger, and the Emperor is, in my opinion, critical if we wish to keep the Shadows in check. Evarrim does not agree; he feels all that we require are the Towers, now active." Her frown was cool and slow to develop. "The Dragons and the Barrani are not at war, at the moment. But war has oft been our state in the past, and it is clear that it is a possibility in the future, as well. Fewer Dragons, in that case, would work to our advantage."

Kaylin said nothing very loudly.

"You asked, kitling."

It was true. She had. And she pretty much hated the answer, even if it didn't surprise her. But she didn't—and couldn't—hate Teela for it. And why? Because Bellusdeo was a power. She was immortal. She had once been Queen. Hating Bellusdeo wasn't in any way the same as selling gods alone knew how many helpless and powerless people to an Arcanist.

The small dragon nudged her cheek with its head; she ignored him until he bit her earlobe. "Can you just promise me one thing?" she said when she had stopped her very Leontine cursing and had covered one ear with her hand.

Teela lifted a brow.

"Can you hold off on the whole war thing until after I'm dead?"

CHAPTER 8

Fittings for Barrani clothing were definitely not the same thing as fittings for uniforms. For one, there was no Quartermaster. There were Barrani, but they appeared to have been vetted by Teela, because they treated Kaylin with abject—and genuine—deference. Kaylin found that, more than anything else in the Halls, truly unsettling, because Teela didn't even seem to notice. Kaylin did. She usually noticed the exchanges between those who had all the power and those who had none; she'd been on the zero end of the scale for a majority of her life, and in her case, old habits died hard.

These Barrani—two men and two women—also failed to notice the small dragon that was nesting, at the moment, in Kaylin's hair. The dragon, on the other hand, didn't seem to find this troubling.

"What, exactly, is disturbing you, kitling? Has someone poked you with a needle?" Teela's tone was cool and regal, although her eyes were green. She spoke Barrani, not Elantran.

"Just—nothing. Nothing."

"If someone is clumsy enough to injure you, even in so minor a fashion, I will deal with it."

Kaylin wondered if Teela had said this on purpose, because Teela was perfectly capable of being deliberately cruel. "I can deal with it myself," Kaylin said stiffly, this time in Barrani.

"Ah. So you merely desire permission?"

"Teela—"

The Hawk lifted a hand. "Endure for a moment or two longer," she said. "I will not have you presented to the rest of the Lords who have chosen the pilgrimage in inappropriate attire; as befits your station, you are expected—by title—to know better. If you fail to do so, it is not upon you that their derision will fall."

That stopped her cold. "Upon you?"

"Very perceptive. If they insult you while I am present, I am bound by custom since I have claimed you as my *kyuthe* to defend you. It is therefore unlikely to occur, and if it does, it will be because an enemy of my kin wishes to engage me." She smiled. Her smile was slender and very sharp. "I have no reluctance whatsoever to rid the Court of my enemies or the enemies of my line, but I wish to do it on my own terms. I would rather not reward them with a challenge over something as trivial as your attire; if they seek to provoke me, let them at least be creative."

Kaylin exhaled the rest of the breath she would have used for more angry words. "I'm never going to understand the Barrani."

"You needn't sound so morose, Lord Kaylin. They are unlikely to understand you, either."

"Yes, but I'm unlikely to try to kill them for fun."

At the end of two hours, the attendants offered graceful bows to Teela, who accepted them as her due. When they left, she glanced at the door and then spoke three sharp words. Or at least three sharp syllables; Kaylin didn't recognize the language.

"Many of my kin in particular dislike being ruled by a Dragon. Given the history of our two races, that is unlikely to surprise you. If it does," she added darkly, "refrain from sharing."

"Very funny." Kaylin found a nearby cushion that was about three sizes larger than anything she'd ever owned. She sat on it and then, surprised by how soft it was, sprawled flat on her back instead. The dragon leapt off her head before she landed, and set up a loud squawking that lasted a good thirty seconds, while Teela chuckled. "Now that one of the Barrani Arcanists has attempted to assassinate Bellusdeo, the Emperor is watching. And he's pissed off."

"The Emperor is always watching. But yes, he is angry. It is possible that there exist, among the High Court, Lords who would do much to inflame his fury."

"Because they're suicidal?"

"Because it would rekindle war, Kaylin. They think, at this point, we would have the advantage in a war—and with the appearance of your Bellusdeo, that advantage is likely to dwindle with time."

"What do you think?"

"War bores me," she replied in a tone that perfectly suited the words. "And treason, only a little less. They are both so frequent and hold so few surprises; if you read up on the history of the Barrani—in the High Court texts, not the sanitized dribbles in the Halls—you will find that treason, like war, is an age-old practice for the very conservative among my kin. I feel it has been long enough that those same conservatives might consider it attractive again.

"If you will therefore condescend to be moved, I will feed you and escort you off the grounds."

The food was good. The escort, however, went less smoothly. Teela was there, all right, but as they left whatever set of rooms Teela occupied, the Halls got a little more crowded. It was the wrong kind of crowd; the Barrani didn't do milling with any competence. Also, two of them were in armor.

Teela didn't appear to be concerned, if you failed to notice the color of her eyes. Kaylin tensed. This was a fight in which she might be helpful to Teela if circumstances were perfect. Sadly, perfect would involve the sudden disappearance of all but two of the Barrani who loitered here, obviously waiting.

The glass dragon was sitting across her shoulders; she felt him shift position and lifted a hand to press his slender body firmly back down. "Not here," she told him quietly. "I don't think it's a good idea for us to separate."

He stopped struggling the minute the last of the words left her mouth, and pressed himself into her shoulder, looping his tail around her neck so tightly it reminded Kaylin why she didn't care for necklaces.

"Lord An'Teela."

"Lord Darrowelm." Teela offered a polite—shallow—bow; it was, however, graceful. If the man to whom she addressed the bow was offended, it didn't show; his eyes had been blue from the start. "Has the Emperor returned?"

At this, Lord Darrowelm's eyes narrowed. "He has not. The High Lord has convened an emergency session of the High Court. Given the constraints of time and the matter of the Emperor, he felt it possible that you had not been informed."

"The High Lord is, of course, correct." Her eyes could not be any bluer.

"Lord Kaylin, you are also commanded to attend."

★★★

The six Barrani did not magically dissolve as they headed down the halls, Teela and Kaylin at their center. They made no move to draw weapons; something as trivial as speech didn't apparently occur to them. Kaylin had been the Hawk on duty in marches to the gallows that were joyful in comparison. The small dragon on her shoulders had relaxed enough that Kaylin could easily breathe; he did insist on random hissing, which the Barrani ignored.

The door that opened into the forest through which one had to pass to approach the High Lord's throne was taller and wider than Kaylin remembered; it looked completely unfamiliar. On the other hand, the architecture of the High Halls seemed to be about as predictable as the layout of Castle Nightshade; the lack of stability didn't faze the Barrani. They'd probably had centuries to get used to all the ways in which it could change shape.

The forest, on the other hand, did look familiar. They stepped through the door into the middle of trees, and the footpath that wound around their roots resolved itself, in the distance, into a more carefully laid path of interlocking stone. The small dragon hissed in her ear; when she failed to look at him, she felt his teeth on her left lobe. She didn't even curse under her breath; Barrani hearing was too good. She hoped that she wasn't going to be escorted to the High Lord with blood trailing down her neck.

When they got out of here—if they did, in one piece—they were going to have a long chat.

The path opened up into a much larger circle, girded by slightly curved benches, most of which were occupied. The center of the circle itself was also occupied, and as Kaylin passed between two of the outermost benches, Barrani heads swiveled in her direction. She weathered the inspection, missing her uniform.

Lord Darrowelm and his escort did not stop moving until they'd passed through most of the crowd; when they did, the two thrones of the High Court came into view. They were both occupied.

The Barrani escort immediately sank to one knee; only Darrowelm and Teela were left standing. They bowed. Kaylin hesitated for a heartbeat before she bowed as well, remembering that she was a Lord of the High Court, mortal or no.

The High Lord bid them rise.

"Lord An'Teela. Lord Kaylin."

"High Lord." Kaylin glanced to his left. The Consort sat beside him, the platinum of her hair trailing down her shoulders, where some of it spilled into her lap. She wore a simple pale gown, and her feet were bare. Her eyes, however, were a cold blue, and when Kaylin met them, she offered no obvious acknowledgment.

Clearly, she was still angry.

"Have you come to the High Halls at the behest of the Halls of Law?" the High Lord asked.

"No, High Lord."

He waited. Fumbling with High Barrani, she said, "I am here by the grace of my *kyuthe*." Teela gave her no hints, in part because Kaylin didn't dare to look away from the High Lord to receive them. "We are to journey to the West March together, four days hence."

"So I have been told. Why do you seek the West March at this time, Lord Kaylin?"

"I wish to witness the recitation of the regalia." Had she had any idea she would have to stand in front of the High Lord like this, she would have practiced the making of what now felt like totally feeble excuses.

"Ah. Why?"

Because Lord Nightshade wants me to hear them. The words didn't leave her lips and not for lack of trying. Her jaw locked in place; for one long moment it was all she could do to breathe. She felt Nightshade's presence like a literal weight against her chest.

The High Lord noticed, of course; he said nothing, but his eyes, which weren't very green to begin with, shaded into blue.

"I've—I've heard the story the Dragons tell the Leontines," she offered instead—when she could speak. "I've seen it; I've touched it. It didn't change or affect me, because I'm not Leontine. I've been told the regalia is a—a story told to Barrani, but it's supposed to be similar in some fashion. And the Lords of the High Court listen to that story at least once."

His eyes remained blue. "Very well. I will not command otherwise; you are correct in your assumption. I admit I am curious to see what effect, if any, such recitation will have; you are, in theory, mortal."

She bowed, mostly to hide her expression; he bid her rise, probably because he knew.

"We have not yet finished our discussion, Lord Kaylin. Come, approach me."

She glanced at Teela; Teela didn't meet her eyes. She didn't move her head at all.

Kaylin approached the throne. The Consort turned toward her, her eyes still the same frigid blue.

"We have heard that you suffered the loss of your home in the City."

Sarcasm, her early and best defense mechanism, rolled over and exposed its throat under the Consort's gaze. She swallowed and nodded. "It's true."

"Is it also true that you offered the hospitality of that home to a Dragon?"

Gods damn it. "Yes."

"Why?"

"Because," she said, trying to force exasperation out of her tone, "she's a Dragon. She wanted to stay in my home. I am a Lord of the High Court, but I am not Barrani. I had no safe way of refusing her."

"Nor any safe way of accepting her presence, either."

She failed to point out that the Arcane bomb had been designed—and probably thrown—by a Barrani Lord of the High Court in which she was now being interrogated, and that took effort.

"Where is the Dragon now residing?"

"In the Imperial Palace."

"And you?"

"In the Imperial Palace."

"I see. Would you not consider making the High Halls your home? You are a Lord of the Court."

"I don't intend for the Imperial Palace to be my permanent home," she replied, evading the question.

After a long pause, he nodded. His eyes were a darker shade of blue. "Very well."

She started to retreat, and the Consort rose from her throne. "Lord Kaylin," she said in a Winter voice.

"Lady."

"What are you wearing across your shoulders?"

"A small, winged lizard."

The Consort approached, and the little dragon lifted its translucent neck, raising its head so that it rested against Kaylin's left cheek. She glanced at it and saw that it was, opalescent eyes wide, watching the Consort—and only the Consort. "I have never seen a like creature." Her eyes were indigo. The dragon hissed; Kaylin felt its wings lift part of her hair as they rose. She said nothing, but when the Consort lifted a hand, she took an involuntary step back.

The Consort then lowered her hand. "Where did you come by such an exotic pet?"

The hells, Kaylin thought, could not be worse than this. Any answer she considered sounded flippant or evasive, but she was certain silence would be worse. She did not want this woman to be any angrier at her than she already was. Swallowing and hating the anger and the argument that had led to it, she said, "From an egg born to mortal parents during the worst of the chaos that occurred before the Norannir arrived in our world."

The Consort's eyes narrowed. "It was born during the magical upheaval in the City."

Kaylin nodded.

"And it hatched when the portal opened?"

The Consort knew. She knew what Teela suspected. She knew what the old stories said. And why wouldn't she? She was a Barrani High Lord, the mother of her race—a race that gathered power as if it were air or food. "No."

"No?"

"No. It remained unhatched until my home was destroyed."

"Do you understand what it is that you have?"

Kaylin swallowed. "I understand what some people think it is."

"And did you then make your choice to accept the threat of that portal and the Devourer because you wished to obtain it?" Oh, her voice was cold. There was no magic in her words; if there had been, Kaylin was certain she'd be dead—and in so many small pieces they wouldn't be able to bury her. "Is that why you refused my request?"

Kaylin, however, was beginning to find the anger that

lurked beneath her fear of offending the Lady any further. "I refused your request," she said, "because thousands of people would have died if the portal hadn't opened."

She heard Teela's sharp breath; it was a warning.

"And I was right. The Devourer did not destroy the world, and thousands of people who would have starved, or worse, are now alive in the fief of Tiamaris." She might as well have been speaking to stone. "I had no idea what would hatch from the egg—if the egg even hatched at all—and even if I had, it wouldn't have occurred to me to risk an entire City—"

"An entire world."

"An entire world, then. I had nothing to gain."

One pale brow rose. "I believe there are some dozen members of the Court in which you now stand who would disagree with that."

"Yes. And they're all Arcanists. I'm not. If this is, indeed, a familiar, how does it help me?" The contrary creature began to rub the side of her face with the side of his.

Teela cleared her throat. Kaylin turned to look at her; her eyes were not a comforting color. "Lady," she said.

The Consort lifted one pale, perfect hand. "I will hear your words at a later time, Lord An'Teela," she said coolly. "At the moment, I am interested in Lord Kaylin's rather colloquial explanation. You claim that the egg itself did not hatch until the assassination attempt?"

"Yes."

"And at that time?"

"An Arcane bomb destroyed my apartment. The egg hatched when the bomb went off. The small dragon may have afforded us some protection."

The Consort's lips thinned. She turned to the High Lord and tendered him a very low bow. "My Lord," she said quietly, "I would speak with Lord Kaylin in a more private place."

The shape of his eyes shifted ever so slightly; it meant he was as surprised as Kaylin by the request. It certainly didn't appear to be made with any affection or warmth. After a pause, he nodded. Kaylin wasn't certain how she felt about it herself, but as usual when surrounded by Immortals, her certainty—or lack thereof—didn't matter.

The Consort turned and walked toward the back of her throne. She didn't turn to see whether or not Kaylin followed; Kaylin did. She knew where the Consort was leading her.

There were no obvious guards around the perimeter of the fountain. It was, aside from one Hawk and one Barrani Lord, deserted. Kaylin met the Consort's blue, blue gaze as they stood in a tense and awkward silence.

It was the Consort who broke it. "You have not returned to Court since the portal opened—and closed."

It wasn't what Kaylin had expected. "No."

"Why?"

Kaylin hated these types of questions. She hated the test inherent in their nature. But they were alone here. The Consort, entirely for reasons of her own, had conceded that much. "I thought you'd still be angry."

"I am." She waited. When Kaylin failed to find more words, she turned again. "I am not the High Lord," she said.

Since this was more or less obvious, Kaylin nodded.

"Among my kin, it is always wisest to keep those disinclined toward you within your view. Especially when they are people of power. Yet you come only now, and I am certain without the intervention of Lord Darrowelm, you would not be in Court at all. I ask again, why? Is my anger considered so slight, and the threat it poses so insignificant, that you feel the exercise of due caution beneath you?"

If Kaylin's jaw had not been attached, it would have fallen

off. It did drop open and hang there unnoticed for a minute, anyway. She took a step forward and stopped; the Consort's eyes were still the wrong shade of blue. "No—no that's not why—" She drew a breath, lifting her hands to disentangle the Dragon's wings from hair that would never be as obliging as the Consort's.

"Among my kin," she said, "we avoid angry people. Anger is—anger. Most times it's not even our fault. But when someone with too much power is angry, everyone suffers. I learned that in the fiefs. I was so far beneath the fieflord I could have been a cockroach. Didn't matter. If the fieflord was angry and I was in reach, I suffered."

"And I am now to be compared to an Outcaste or a mortal?"

Ignoring that because it wasn't what she'd intended, although it was what she'd achieved, Kaylin rushed on. "This time, it was my fault. It was," she continued, "but I don't—and can't—regret it. I took a risk that you would never have taken. Maybe if I had—" She shook her head again. "I couldn't come here without some sort of apology. And I can't apologize."

"Oh? Why not?"

"Because I was right."

"And I, wrong?"

Careful, Kaylin. "You were right about the risk. You were right about the possible consequences. But so was I—and in the end, what counts for me is that the world is still here and the People are alive. Not more, not less." As she spoke, her shoulders fell and her chin rose. "You're the only Barrani at Court, outside of Lord Teela—with the exception of the Lord of the West March—that I was happy to see. You were also the only one who was happy to see me. I knew I'd broken that. I didn't want to—"

"Accept it?"

"Maybe. Or maybe I wanted it to be entirely your fault."

The Consort smiled; it was not a warm expression. "Very well, Private Neya. I am angry. And I am of my kin; the fact that you were proved materially correct does not ease the anger—it deepens it. But the majority of our argument has happened beyond the prying ears and eyes of the High Court; if you intended my humiliation, you did not plan with care."

"I never wanted that. I don't want it now."

"What do you want, then?"

"I want you to stop being angry. At me. I don't care if you're angry at the rest of the Court for the next several centuries."

"You are so guileless," the Consort replied. But her eyes were a paler shade of blue. It wasn't a blue that would become green anytime soon. "I will not ask you of your Bellusdeo."

"I'm not aware I mentioned her name."

"You did not. But it was, of course, known to us. She is not what the Dragons have become, over the centuries."

"No."

"Are you fond of her?"

The question surprised Kaylin. "Does it matter? She's a Dragon. I'm a private."

At this, the Consort chuckled. Kaylin missed the sound of her laughter. "No, I don't suppose it does."

"I want to strangle her half of every day, if that helps."

"Oddly enough, it does; I can't imagine why. Did you truly not understand the nature of the creature you now possess?"

"I didn't. I don't now. I kept the egg because it was—it was a baby, even if it was a total anomaly. I wasn't certain it would ever hatch. He's taken to living on my shoulder. He hisses a lot. Sometimes he bites my ear. I'd never even heard the term 'familiar' until Bellusdeo mentioned it." She hesitated and then added, "But...I like him."

"He is yours. Yours or not, he is a danger to you, if I am not mistaken."

"He can stand in line." The dragon nibbled on her ear with impeccable timing.

"Will you take him with you when you journey to the West March?"

Kaylin nodded.

"Very well. I believe I will join the pilgrims who venture to the West March this year."

CHAPTER 9

Kaylin's jaw dropped. It closed more quickly this second time. "Y-you're going to the West March?"

"Yes. Although it is not mandatory for me, I have not traveled to the West March since the Leofswuld. It will be the first time that I have set foot in those ancient forests as the Keeper of the Lake, and such a journey, given the change in my station, is almost mandatory."

"Is the High Lord—"

"The High Lord is not of the opinion that such travel on my part is wise at the moment. He has not, however, forbidden it; I will be under the protection of my brother, after all."

"Only when you get there."

"The recent occurrences have made the enterprise more fraught, I will admit. The Emperor was…ill pleased…with the turn of events."

"Is the Arcanist the Emperor is looking for even here?"

"He is not, as you surmise, within the High Halls. Whatever else you may think of us, we are not so unwise as to attempt the assassination of any Dragon in such a fashion. I will not lie; it is considered an evil and a necessity to bow to the rule of a Dragon, no matter how theoretical that rule might be. Should the Emperor attempt to retaliate, we are not without power here; the High Halls would withstand the fury of the Dragon Court for far, far longer than the Imperial Palace."

"Do you know where he is?"

"He?"

"The suspect."

"I do not know if you will believe me, Lord Kaylin, but no, we do not. If we did, he would be—possibly regrettably—dead. An act of that political scope and magnitude is never wisely undertaken without the direct permission or at least tacit consent of the High Lord. No such consent was given, not even obliquely. There will be no peace between the two Immortal Courts while the assassin is at large." She glanced once again at the fountain. "The one opportunity that arose from the threat of the Devourer—the meeting of the Lords of the two Courts—might yet be saved." She turned. "You will, no doubt, hear of this, given your oath of allegiance."

"I don't think you understand what the rank Private entails."

"Perhaps not. The High Lord has made clear to the Emperor that the matter of the renegade is not a matter for the Caste Court, in his opinion; as the action was taken with no reference to, and no respect for, the Lord of that Caste Court, he is willing—barely—to wash his hands of the affair." She turned back, her smile slender. Kaylin, a private, understood exactly what this meant: the Barrani Caste Court would allow the Imperial Courts to prosecute the would-be assassin as if he were a common, mortal criminal. It was an almost historical decision, and Kaylin had no doubt at all that it would be an extremely unpopular one for the High Lord.

"Do you agree with his decision?"

One pale brow rose. "He is my Lord," was the cool reply. "I find you difficult. I at first thought to treat you with the open affection one reserves for a very intelligent, very loyal pet. They are qualities I prize, and loyalty is in short supply among my kin; it is not absent, but it is always qualified. You are not, it is clear, obedient, and I do not hold the leash to your loyalty.

"But I find it difficult to ostracize you. I am uncertain why. Perhaps there is a deeper reason that some of my people choose to serve your Hawks. I am angry still. But to my surprise, I can see a time in which that anger might at last be laid to rest in a way that does not involve your unpleasant and untimely demise." She smiled. It was a cutting, edged smile very like the ones that occupied Teela's face when she was angry. "At the very least, if I have not—yet—chosen to end your life, I refuse to allow any of my kin to forever deprive me of my prerogative to do so.

"It is not an act of forgiveness on my part; nor is it an act of mercy." Eyes still the wrong shade of blue, she approached Kaylin from the left. The small dragon raised its head to meet her steady gaze. This time, when she lifted her hand—gingerly, palm open to indicate its emptiness—he stretched his neck and very gently touched the center of her palm. "It is a striking creature," she finally said.

"Around the office," Kaylin replied, sliding into Elantran, "we call that 'cute.'"

"And you will take him with you when you travel to the West March." She exhaled once and turned to face Kaylin. "You frustrate me, you anger me, and you surprise me. You have not yet bored me. I warn you not to start." Before Kaylin could think of a reply, the Consort continued. "Perhaps our use of the word 'caution' and your use is separated by circumstance of both birth and experience. Regardless, I will tell you to be careful."

"Of him?"

The dragon lifted its translucent head.

"No; I would not waste breath on a warning that I knew in advance would serve no purpose. Barrani Caste laws are not Dragon laws; there are those who seek to both shelter and support the Arcanist. Were there no Dragons involved, he would now be Outcaste. The High Lord's rule is too new for such an action to be taken without extreme caution, but his preference has been made clear. You have some experience with the Outcaste," she added, eyes narrowing. "I will not ask for details; you bear Nightshade's mark. I would ask you to consider the company of Lord Andellen on your journey." She turned.

Kaylin, however, froze on the spot in the way people did when they'd processed enough information and boiled it down to bad news. "Wait, Lady."

"Yes?"

"Are you telling me you think our missing Arcanist is going to the West March?"

"If he is wise, no. But wisdom has not been demonstrated in either of the two investigations involving the Imperial Law. There is considerable danger."

"I'll have Teela."

"It is not the direct threat that should be your concern."

"What should?"

"I am not inclined to be more helpful at the moment. I am certain you will have an answer to that question if you are both patient and clever."

"What is his name?" she asked the Consort's retreating back.

The Consort didn't reply. But the fact that she'd mentioned him, nameless or no, made Kaylin a little bit happier. This

Consort, with her dark, hard eyes, wasn't the Lady Kaylin had first met—but maybe, in time, she would be.

The emergency meeting of the High Council took the better part of four hours, and if Kaylin was nervous—and she was—her stomach didn't care. It would have been embarrassing under normal circumstances; it was terrifying here.

As the High Lord and his Lady had no more direct words for Kaylin, she remained utterly silent. Teela spoke four times, once to ask a question; she wasn't the only one. Evarrim spoke; he was angry. He didn't reference the small dragon, though. Darrowelm was as quiet as Kaylin. As Kaylin didn't recognize most of the other Lords by name, it was harder to track them; she couldn't just ask Teela who they were. But she listened. The Consort had made clear that the would-be Outcaste Lord—whose name was frustratingly never mentioned, possibly because of his pending status—had sympathizers among the Barrani.

Teela was not in a good mood by the time they were dismissed. The Barrani, as a whole, were in the same mood as Teela. It made the Consort look friendly. Kaylin thought about dragging Teela to a pub, but that wasn't going to happen in the immediate future, either; the dismissal apparently required each Lord to approach the throne, in a long line, as if they were paying their final respects.

This took another hour and a half, and involved another bow five feet from the seated High Lord. Kaylin wondered briefly if etiquette lessons in this Court would be as onerous as they were in the Dragon Court.

She watched carefully as the Lords that preceded her approached the throne; she noted the style of each one's bow and counted the seconds they held them. It was never longer than ten; it was never less than three. Given she was only an honorary member of the Court—one whose oath of fealty was to the Imperial Law, if not the Emperor himself—she elected to hold her bow for ten seconds.

When she rose, the High Lord said, "Safe journey, Lord Kaylin. Do not forget my brother's ring; it is a sign of his favor, and in the West March, it is akin to Law."

"Why did the Lady ask to speak with you in private?" They were the first words Teela spoke, and she spoke them only when the carriage was halfway from the High Halls to the Halls of Law.

"Mostly? To let me know she was angry in a place where my temper wouldn't embarrass her."

"I thought it courageous of you to speak at all."

"I didn't have much choice. To be fair, she wasn't the only one who was angry."

"You refer to her question about the familiar?"

"Yes."

"It was not an unreasonable question, kitling."

"No, of course not. Who wouldn't put an entire world on the line for the off chance of getting their hands on a creature that doesn't sleep and won't leave them alone?" The small dragon bit her ear, but not hard enough to draw blood.

Teela eased into a chuckle. "You are not Barrani, clearly."

"If she was asking the Barrani, I wouldn't have cared. They would have said no, regardless."

"But in their case, it would have been a lie?"

"You wouldn't do it."

"I? No. A smaller city, on the other hand—"

Kaylin glared, which made Teela laugh. "Try to be less predictable, kitling."

"As long as we don't have to go back to the High Halls anytime soon."

"We won't." She tapped on the roof of the carriage and it began to slow. It was not, however, anywhere close to the Halls of Law.

"Where are we going?" Kaylin asked as a familiar building with a large hole in its walls loomed into view.

"To find a ring."

"Ironjaw said he'd fire anyone who let me get close to the crime scene."

Clearly other people's jobs were not Teela's concern.

Some of the Hawks were still on duty; they could be seen at the height of the scaffolding. Kaylin knew that over half the building had been evacuated, pending repairs. There was some argument in progress about the financial jurisdiction of those repairs. Kaylin had a strong interest in the resolution, but no ability to influence it.

The Hawks let her in, which is to say, up, after a brief exchange of words with Teela. Kaylin climbed the scaffold's ladders with ease.

Luckily—for a value of luck that had two sides—Joey was on duty. Unluckily, so were two Imperial mages. Teela fielded their questions, which were curt and full of the irritability mages displayed when the work they didn't particularly enjoy was extended by an unhelpful interruption. On the other hand, that interruption included a small, translucent dragon.

Here, Kaylin's ignorance proved useful; she had nothing to hide, because she had no solid information to give them. She carefully failed to mention the word *familiar;* on the other hand, she chose to answer their questions before she offloaded questions of her own. Yes, they had found evidence of her few belongings in the wreckage. No, those belongings had not miraculously survived the detonation of the bomb. As proof, they had buckets—literal buckets, as those were most easily raised and lowered—of cloth scraps, wood splinters, glass shards. She recognized some of those shards as mirror shards. The mirror was the most expensive item she owned, or had been. She also found the handle of her wardrobe.

"Business face," Teela whispered as Kaylin turned it over in her hands.

Kaylin nodded. It wasn't the first time an Arcane bomb had exploded in the city. It wasn't even the first time she'd had to survey both the wreckage and its detritus. It was just the first time it was so personal. She tried to set it in the proper context and surprised herself by mostly succeeding.

"What, exactly, are you looking for?" the older of the two mages asked. He was not a young man, as he'd pointed out at least three times. He'd also introduced himself as Feluann Harcastle, of the Order of Imperial Mages.

"A ring," she replied.

Feluann nodded. "Barrani work?"

"Yes."

"You will have to claim it from the Halls of Law. It seemed valuable, and it was unharmed by the explosion itself; the Hawk on duty at the time didn't want to leave it lying around in the buckets used as receptacles."

Kaylin thanked him, meaning every word. It was one of the rare occasions in which she felt grateful for the existence of the Imperial Order of Mages, and was proof that, on occasion, the small dragon—and her ability to be polite about his existence—was actually a positive.

Getting the ring back was trickier than getting the information from Feluann had been, possibly because the Hawks on duty in Articles and Evidence weren't all that impressed by the cute, small dragon. Kaylin had to go to Marcus, bare her throat, and wait fifteen minutes in front of the chaos of his desk before she had his attention; she had to spend another ten minutes explaining why she needed the ring back. In theory, it was part of the evidence left after the explosion; in practice, Marcus was just sharing his mood.

"I'm going to the West March," she reminded him. "I'd like to start my stay there without giving offense before I even open my mouth."

Marcus glared.

"It's a ring he gave to me as a sign of my status as chosen kin. I can't show up without it if it's still in one piece."

Leontine sense of fashion warred with Marcus's hard-won knowledge of the Barrani. Given the fact that his primary contact with the Barrani were his Hawks, he struggled a bit before growling across the office to a waiting Caitlin. "Mallory's not going to like it."

"Mallory's in Missing Persons."

"Yes. But Articles and Evidence overlap our offices; believe that he'll hear about it."

Kaylin tried to look suitably penitent; the Leontine growled. "Go. Don't cause any trouble before you leave, or you might not make it."

"That won't break my heart."

"Not your heart, no." He growled to make his point; his fur rose an inch. "And if you're thinking Mallory will have time to forget in the two months you'll be on vacation, think again."

"No, sir," she replied. "It's Mallory. Two months will just give him time to agitate for my expulsion. Again."

Severn met her before she left the office. He was quiet. It was the wrong type of quiet.

"Are you all right?" she asked for the third time. He'd failed to hear it the previous two.

He nodded. His silence took them to the front doors and

down the stairs into the streets, where they joined the flow of traffic. He didn't add any words to what wasn't a conversation; he hadn't asked about the High Halls, either. They made three more blocks before Kaylin stopped walking.

It took him a third of a block to realize he'd left her behind; he turned back, where she stood watching, arms folded.

The line of his mouth shifted and thinned; he took one long breath. When he released it, he almost looked normal, for Severn. "Is it that obvious?" he asked.

"A little."

His smile was slight, but there. "And if I tell you I can't talk about it?"

"Is that what you're going to tell me if I ask?"

He nodded.

"Fine. I'll try my hardest not to ask. Have you eaten?"

He shook his head.

"Why don't we head—" She stopped.

"—to the Palace?"

She nodded. "The one good thing about living with Dragons is I probably won't have to scrounge for food, and I won't have to borrow your money."

His brows rose. "I don't believe I've ever lent you money."

"At least twice a month, every month, since we've been partnered."

"You've been keeping track?"

She started to walk.

"That money wasn't a loan, Kaylin."

"I intend to pay it back—that makes it a loan."

"First, with the way you handle money, you won't be able to pay it back. Second," he added, his voice rising on the second syllable as she opened her mouth, "it wasn't meant as a loan."

"Doesn't matter."

"It does. If you look at every attempt to help you as a burden or an obligation…"

"You'll stop?"

He shook his head. "I'll try, if that helps."

"Not really." She clenched her jaw to stop more words from following. Severn was already stressed. They did not need to have this argument today, especially since it wasn't likely to end before they were in earshot of the Imperial Palace guards. "Do you care if Bellusdeo's hanging around?"

"Does it matter?"

"Probably not. If she's in the Palace, she's not likely to be bored. Really, really aggravated, but not bored." She hesitated. "I'm sorry."

He raised a brow and then shifted his gaze off her face. "Don't be."

The small dragon lifted his head, bumped the underside of Kaylin's jaw, and then spread wings. Before she could stop him, he launched himself at Severn's head. He did not, however, snap, claw, or bite; instead, he slid down the back of Severn's neck, where he more or less fastened himself onto Severn's shoulders.

Severn didn't miss a step.

Kaylin stumbled. "He's never done that before," she finally said.

"Jealous?" His lips curved in a genuine smile; she was happy to see it, even if it was at her expense.

"Just surprised." The little dragon swiveled his neck and regarded her with wide opal eyes. She wasn't certain if he was annoyed, happy, or smug. "Maybe he can stay that way for a couple of months."

Severn hesitated. "It probably won't help you," he finally said.

"Why?"

His smile deepened. "I don't have permission to speak about it yet." Because he was smiling, she took the opportunity to wheedle.

Dinner came half an hour after Kaylin had reached her rooms. Before dinner arrived, a message from the Arkon was delivered; Sanabalis was kind enough to deliver his own message before the dishes had been delivered to the dining table. Sadly, his message arrived in person, where it couldn't be safely ignored.

"Corporal," he said, nodding to Severn. "Private. May I enter?"

"I don't mind," Kaylin replied. "Bellusdeo might, but she's apparently not here."

"She is with Lord Emmerian at the moment. She spent the afternoon with Lord Diarmat."

Kaylin winced in sympathy. "Are they both still standing?"

"They are. I will concede that Lord Diarmat does not, however, consider Bellusdeo charming."

"Lord Diarmat doesn't consider anyone charming."

Sanabalis chuckled as he took a seat at the table. The chairs in the Palace, or at least in these rooms, were solid enough to take a Dragon's weight. Given that Dragons ran the place, this made sense, although it probably made furnishing these rooms incredibly expensive.

"Lord Diarmat knows I'm being sent to the West March, right?"

"Have you informed him?" Sanabalis's eyes were a lovely, lambent shade of gold, the bastard.

"No. Since the Halls of Law are sending me to the West March, I assumed the Imperial Court would be informed. Given especially the long reports of all my movements Lord Diarmat asked me to read."

"Ah. I believe Lord Diarmat made clear the consequences of missed lessons?"

"He canceled the last one without notice."

"The obligation is not, of course, mutual." The corners of his eyes were etched in lines Kaylin was certain were getting deeper by the second. "They are not my lessons, Private. You are not, at the moment, my aide. Given Lord Diarmat's current disposition—"

"His constant disposition?"

"As you say. Given that, my intervention—with no pretext of the necessity of your presence in matters that concern the Imperial Court—is likely to cause you rather more difficulty than it alleviates."

"I'd appreciate it anyway. I won't have to see his face for two months, and I'm sure lessons with Bellusdeo will drive the minor irritation of me out of the picture in that time."

"Immortal memory," Sanabalis replied. "I believe he intends to reschedule the lesson before your departure."

She was torn. She didn't want to go to the West March. On the other hand, the silver lining to that coming cloud was the utter absence of Diarmat and his lessons. Bellusdeo had made the lessons bearable. She felt free to speak her mind and did so without hesitation. She could say things that Kaylin couldn't even dream of saying. Kaylin, for her part, was wise enough to appreciate the Dragon's words without adding any fuel to the fire that was Diarmat's temper.

But regardless, Kaylin was still trapped for hours in a room that contained Lord Diarmat. "They're going to send me."

"Indeed. I believe Lord Diarmat wished to make his opinion clear—and permanent. Some concern about your absence has been raised in other quarters. The Emperor has considered the future costs of bargaining in bad faith with the particular informant involved. He will not, therefore, order you to remain."

"Teela's going."

"So we have been informed." Reaching up, he lifted a familiar heavy chain over his head; dangling at its end was a round golden pendant. "Wear this while you are in the West March."

She hesitated. "I'm not leaving for three days. Four. One of those."

His eyes finally shifted color, heading to a bronze that still seemed cheerful considering the past two days.

"Don't you need it?"

One brow rose. "Kaylin."

She took it and glanced at the table; he cleared his throat. Only Marcus would have been louder. Giving in, she set it around her neck. "It's a thick, heavy chain," she told him, tucking the pendant into her shirt, where it was hidden from casual inspection. "If it gets caught on anything, I'll be asphyxiated. Or break my neck."

"Don't get it caught on anything, then. I will not take offense at your desire to hide my pendant while you are in the Palace—or in the City limits. You will, however, wear it while in the Court of the West March."

"Yes, Sanabalis."

"If you are humoring me with the intent to ignore my order at a safe distance, the ability to light a single candle after months of effort has clearly gone to your head."

She was silent.

"Private Neya, bearing that pendant while you are within the heart of the Barrani old forests was my condition for allowing you to leave this city. It serves as a warning to the Barrani should they desire to be less than civil. I do not expect you to avail yourself of its particular properties; even at that remove, it would be considered a diplomatic disaster."

"More of a disaster than breathing fire at most of the High Court this afternoon?"

"Yes. You are not the Emperor. You will wear it, or you will find yourself without employ upon your return to the City." He vacated his chair and turned to Severn. "Corporal."

Severn rose and bowed.

"Well, I guess that settles that," she said when the door closed. She took a chair near food that was cooling.

"He did say it was an order," Severn replied, joining her.

"He's also said he's not directly in the chain of command."

Severn chuckled. "He's larger, meaner, and vastly more knowledgeable. You've been in the Halls too long if you think that counts for nothing."

"I'm wearing it, aren't I?"

"Not happily. I'm not certain why you're objecting."

"It's an open declaration of ownership."

"That's harsh."

"Dragon ownership. I can't think of much that's more likely to annoy Barrani Lords who don't spend all their time in the shadow of the Imperial Palace. I have the *kyuthe* ring. I don't think I need the implied—and distant—threat literally hanging around my neck."

"The man who can take away your pay does."

"Fair enough. I wish you were coming," she added as she began to eat.

"Oh? Why?"

"Cowardice. I hate being the only mortal in a gathering full of Immortals who think killing each other cleverly is the height of good manners."

He laughed. The small dragon startled at the sound of the laughter and left his shoulders to hover in the air above the table between them. When he decided it was safe—if he truly felt threatened—he once again perched across Kaylin's shoulders.

"It's not just that," she continued when he'd settled down enough that she could readjust the fall of her hair. "It's this." Lifting her hand, she brushed her fingers across Nightshade's mark. "The Barrani here are all used to it by now. I don't know how the Barrani we meet in the West March are going to react. Here, Nightshade is a fieflord before he's Outcaste. There, I'm not sure it'll matter as much."

"The Lord of the West March declared you *kyuthe* with full knowledge of that mark."

She nodded, pensive, and Severn exhaled. "I'm going."

"You can't. Nightshade said—"

"He will understand the change in circumstances."

"We're not speaking about the same Lord Nightshade, obviously."

"I won't be present as a Hawk."

CHAPTER 10

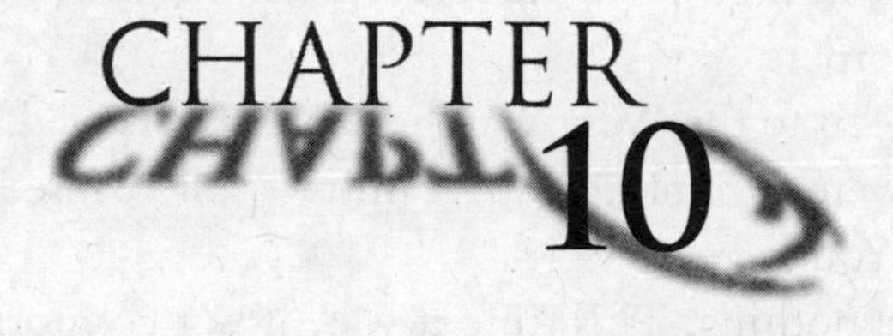

The silence was sudden and loud. Severn didn't break it, but he met her gaze and held it—not the way cats do and not as a challenge; it was less comfortable, and more vulnerable, than either.

"This is about the missing Arcanist," she finally said. Her throat felt dry.

He nodded.

"The Emperor was angry."

"Demonstrably."

She gave up on food and pushed herself away from the table, toward the edge of the large embroidered rug that lay beneath it. "Why you?" she demanded, although she kept her eyes on her feet.

He said more nothing. This time, the edges of the carpet held her attention; he finally said, "You did say you'd like me to—"

"As a Hawk, Severn. As a Corporal of the Hawks."

"I am a Corporal of the Hawks."

"Marcus didn't order you to go to the West March."

Silence. Then: "No. I've taken a leave of absence."

No doubt with pay. She tried to cling to the petty resentment; it was too thin to support her.

"Kaylin."

She turned, palms out, as if she were begging. "Why you?" She knew what it meant. He was going as a Wolf. He was going as a hunter. He'd received orders to kill—someone. Imperial orders.

"I've been to the West March before. I survived."

"You weren't hunting an Arcanist—" She paused. Looked at him. "You were."

He said nothing. This time it was, if not comfortable, expected. "I survived."

"And that scar?" The scar that hadn't existed in their lives in the fief of Nightshade was white.

"I survived." He walked toward where she stood, and placed his hands over hers; his were very warm. Or hers were cold. "I don't intend to die there. This time, if things get dangerous, you'll have my back."

She slid her fingers through his and tightened her hands. "Only if you let me know when you need me. I'm not a Wolf."

The door opened before he could reply. Bellusdeo strode into the room, her stiff skirts making as much noise as her feet did. She stopped, noticed their clasped hands, and snorted. Loudly. "Corporal."

The word was a curt dismissal. Kaylin, annoyed, opened her mouth; Severn tightened his grip on her hands. "You'll know."

She shook her head mutely, unwilling to let go of his hands. Severn was a Hawk. He wasn't a Wolf anymore. But the Wolf Lord intended to send him to the West March on a long—and dangerous—ground hunt.

"Kaylin," he said, smiling, "I can't feel my fingers."

She looked down; her knuckles—her hands—were almost

white. "Promise," she said while Bellusdeo fumed in the background.

"I promise. Let me leave before Bellusdeo becomes angry."

"Too late," Bellusdeo snapped.

Kaylin knew that these were technically joint quarters, but the Dragon's attitude annoyed her. Kaylin had put up with weeks of Bellusdeo's intrusive presence and had even lost her home to it; she felt she was owed a little leeway. But she also knew the Imperial Palace favored ill-tempered Dragons over justifiably annoyed humans. She let go of Severn's hands.

The small dragon wuffled in her ear. He then began to eat her hair, and she lifted her hands to disentangle his jaw. She also let her hair down—he squawked—and put it up again more carefully. He snapped at the stick instead. "Don't eat this," she told him, glaring. "This is the only one I have."

"I'm sure you can get a dozen more," Bellusdeo told her as she shoved a chair away from the table and sat. "Just ask the Seneschal. They owe you something."

"Technically, they don't. The Emperor is not held responsible for the illegal actions of his subjects; the damages done by said subjects are therefore not his responsibility."

"You're quoting legal scripture at me?"

"The laws of the Norannir may have been different." Kaylin turned to Severn, who was waiting, his hands behind his back. "I'll see you tomorrow?"

He nodded. He looked tired, to Kaylin—and Severn almost never looked tired.

"What," she asked Bellusdeo, after Severn had left them, "is annoying you?"

"Imperial Court etiquette."

Kaylin grimaced. Fair enough. She glanced in the direction

of the door. "If you're not sick to death of talking to Dragons, I have one more stop before I'm done for the night."

"And that?"

"The Arkon. He sent a message before dinner arrived, 'requesting' my presence in the Library at 'my earliest convenience.'"

Bellusdeo looked at her hands, which were now in her lap. In a much more subdued tone of voice, she said, "I'm sorry."

Kaylin tried for humor. "The Arkon isn't your fault."

One golden brow rose in an arch. Bellusdeo wasn't biting. "You don't deserve this. This Palace, these Dragons, the loss of your home. If I were—" She shook her head and seemed to lose about three inches of height as she sank farther into the chair. "I have no lands here, no currency, and very little power of my own. There is nothing I can do to—"

"There's nothing you need to do. You're not to be held responsible for criminal activities, either, unless they're yours." Kaylin tried to find a smile and was surprised at how easily it came to her face. "Let me go talk to the Arkon. If you hear him shouting, you can come and rescue me, and we'll call it even."

"Or I can go with you to prevent it."

Kaylin winced. "You really haven't spent enough time with the Arkon," she said as she headed toward the door. "I'll be back as soon as I can."

The Arkon was in one of the almost featureless rooms in which none of his precious collection was housed. This room contained a table, four chairs, and walls that rose like the upper half of a sphere; there was no obvious aperture in the ceiling, but it otherwise reminded Kaylin of the height of the Hawklord's Tower. There was a mirror on the wall; it had a very workmanlike frame, and wood could be seen in small patches where gold leaf had worn thin.

"Private Neya," the Arkon said. His eyes were bronze.

"Arkon," she replied, tendering what she hoped was a perfect bow. It was certainly a better bow than she would have given a month ago; if she'd learned nothing else from Diarmat, she could now bow in a way that wouldn't embarrass Imperial Guards. If, on the other hand, the Arkon even noticed this improvement, he hid it well.

"I see you've brought the glass dragon."

She nodded.

"Good. I expected to see you somewhat earlier, as did Bellusdeo."

"I was in the High Halls. There was an emergency meeting of the High Court," she added, "because the Emperor apparently breathed fire on some of its Lords."

"I imagine they survived it."

"They did. They were happy about the survival, but less than impressed with the fire."

The Arkon nodded. "I have been informed that you intend to leave the City. With the small dragon."

Kaylin nodded. Sanabalis had strongly implied a meeting of the Dragon Court had taken place over that very issue.

"I see you are wearing Sanabalis's seal."

It was hidden. Clearly, it was designed to be recognized by other Dragons—without actually being seen. "He won't let me leave without it."

"Good. Why, exactly, are you going to the West March?"

"Wasn't that discussed?"

"Some nonsense about a debt owed an informant was mentioned; I am not interested in hearsay. Why are you going?"

"It's not hearsay. In return for information about the Imperial Exchequer and the Human Caste Court, I'm to go to the

West March. In theory, I'm to accompany Lord Nightshade; in practice, given Teela and the Consort are also going, I'm not sure what's going to happen." When the answer seemed to darken the color of his eyes, she said, "Given the events of today, I'm not even sure it's smart for me to leave the City. People have been disappearing from the fief of Tiamaris. We're pretty sure we've figured out how."

"I assume this is not the normal kidnapping the Halls of Law were meant to deal with?"

"No."

"And it differs how?"

Kaylin exhaled. "The Barrani Arcanist suspected of being responsible for Bellusdeo's attempted assassination appears to be involved."

"Why," he asked in the severe tone of voice reserved for a busy man who's forcing himself to tolerate interruptions, "is his affiliation with the Arcanum relevant?"

She bit back the extremely sarcastic retort that came to mind. "I recognized the signature of his spells."

"I see. Continue."

"He either created or made use of a portal extant in Tiamaris."

"A...portal."

"Yes. Tara said it led to the outlands. It seemed very much like Shadow magic to me."

The irritation fell away from the Arkon's expression. "The outlands? You are certain that is the word she used?"

"Yes."

"Did this portal occur in the border zone?"

Kaylin was surprised. "No. The portal—behind a warded door—exists in the fief of Tiamaris, very close to the border between Tiamaris and Nightshade. Tiamaris has said he'll petition the Imperial Order for volunteers to study it."

The Arkon rolled his eyes. "You are certain that the Arcanist—"

"The signatures that marked the door were the same as the sigils left in the wake of the Arcane bomb."

"I will send someone, with Tiamaris's permission, myself."

"Why?"

"It cannot have escaped your notice that the Imperial Order has discerned one signature at the sight of the detonation, not the two you claim to have seen. I wish to send someone who I consider competent to examine the door to ascertain that there are two sigils."

Kaylin frowned. "You don't think there are."

"I do not think he will find two, no. I would, however, prefer to be proved wrong in this case." He rose. "The Barrani fugitive in question was not—in theory—to be found within City limits."

"The fiefs—"

"Are not within those limits, yes. But we did not use simple hearsay to determine this. If he chose to remain in the border zone, this would explain much. You will be traveling to the West March."

"I'm going to listen to a True Story that the Barrani—not the Dragons—tell. That's all I know."

The Arkon rose. "You will carry the small dragon with you. If Lord An'Teela is correct, it is, by circumstance of birth and emergence, a familiar. I have spent the day attempting to extract information of a less dubious nature from my personal archives. I have also taken the liberty of consulting with records not accessible to the Imperial mirrors. It would be preferable if you honored the informant's request next year—I believe the event is annual.

"I am aware, however, that this reasonable advice is not to be followed, and I do not even have the satisfaction of placing blame at your feet. It is vexing." He raised a brow. If Dragons weren't famous for their lack of humor, Kaylin would've guessed he was joking, or at least trying. "I have therefore summoned you here to give some small warning. There is a danger to you. If, as suspected, the creature is a familiar, he is not, yet, yours."

She glanced at the small dragon's face, which was easy because he was attempting to head-butt her nose. "He seems to be."

"He is attached to you, yes. But there is something complicated about the owning of a familiar that is not clear to me. There appears to be some challenge, not only in the summoning of a familiar—and there are four tales that hint at resultant disaster—but also in retaining the familiar. In one of the older tales, a Sorcerer of possible Barrani extraction by look summoned a familiar at great personal cost."

"Possible Barrani extraction?"

"The racial term was not used; no race was mentioned. There are two images accompanying text that is only barely decipherable, and the proportions of face, hands, and height are in keeping with the Barrani. I am willing to admit that this could be a function of artistic interpretation; some of the symbols on his robes and in his hands—yes, in, not on—are not clear enough to assign." The Arkon cleared his throat. "The relevant passage implies heavily that the summoned creature did not consider the summoner worthy. Records: first and second images."

Kaylin frowned. In the first image—or what she assumed was the first image—stood a man in long robes; they were a blend of white and gold, and words had been written across the hem and the trailing edge of extremely impractical sleeves. "His hair's the wrong color for Barrani." It was the color of burnished copper.

"Indeed. I did not say the assumption was definitive. He is not, however, Dragon, and I do not think him human."

"It's a painting," she pointed out.

"It's probably a children's story. Attempting to glean useful fact from it is almost madness, but unfortunately at the moment, it's all we have. I did not ask you to examine the images in order to critique my findings. I draw your attention to the second image."

She frowned. The man in his white, runed robes, with long hair and eyes that seemed glittering blue—not, in Barrani, a good sign—was also depicted in the second image; he was no longer, however, alone. "What's that?" Kaylin asked.

"A very good question. I believe the artist is attempting to render the familiar in its incomplete state."

"He looks nothing like mine."

"No."

"In fact he—or it—looks like a large tear in the painting."

"Yes."

"Why?"

"Well, according to the legend—according to what I could decipher—the Sorcerer failed the familiar's test."

"My familiar has a shape."

"At the moment, yes. It is not clear from the context of the story whether or not the familiar had a prior shape before this scene occurred in the narrative."

"What happened after this scene?"

"The familiar left."

"Oh."

"The Sorcerer, however, did not survive it."

"...Oh." She glanced at the small dragon, who was staring at the images as if they were fascinating. "How did he die?"

"It is not recorded. Ah, no, it is recorded, but the words used, besides *death,* are not clear to me."

Kaylin nodded. "There's something else, isn't there?"

"There is. I am not entirely certain they are not related, although at the moment, I can point at no concrete reason why they should be. You said the creature ate one of the marks on your arms."

"Yes. Just after he hatched."

"Has he repeated this since?"

"No."

"Has he, that you are aware of, eaten anything else?"

"...No. He chews at things on my plate when he's bored. Or at least when I think he's bored. The chewing changes the shape of the food, but not much of it seems to be missing."

"So, at the moment, in the past two days, the only sustenance the creature has had is one mark from your arm."

She nodded.

"Has it shown any further sign of hunger?"

"No."

"Does that strike you as natural?"

"I don't know—snakes don't eat three meals a day."

The Arkon chose to ignore this. "You are going to the West March to hear, to witness and experience, what you call a True Tale."

She nodded.

"Do you not feel even the slightest concern about his reaction to the words of that tale?"

Kaylin blinked. The small dragon flicked her ear with its tail. "No," she finally admitted. "Not until now."

He rose after a long, weary sigh. "I suggest you consider it. If you cannot command the creature—and it seems clear to me, from brief observation, that this is the case—you may find the recitation of the regalia more challenging than even the High Court could predict."

She hesitated.

"Private?"

"Did anything happen to Bellusdeo today?"

One pale brow rose. "Define 'happen.'"

"She's not happy."

"I can't imagine why. She has lost her home, her people, and the stewardship of a large country; she has arrived in the place of her birth centuries after she left it. The Imperial Court is uncertain of her disposition—and frankly, that takes a great deal of effort—and she is uncertain of her future in the Court. Anyone she knew in her childhood, save only myself, is now either dead or sleeping. She has asked permission to attempt to awaken two; it has been refused.

"The formality the Court has adopted displeases her; she feels it is in keeping with Barrani traditions, and she has far less love of the Barrani than even Lord Diarmat." He stopped in the doorway and lifted a hand to grip its frame. "She will adjust, Private, but it is not easy. The two people to whom she feels closest at the moment are absent; one is in the fief of Tiamaris, and one is about to leave the Palace for at least six weeks. She petitioned the Emperor for permission to accompany you and was informed that she would have to petition the High Court.

"This was, of course, before the…incident. Even were the High Lord to grant that dispensation—and it is highly doubtful—she would not be permitted to leave without… some anger. She cannot fly in this City unless she is within the aerial boundaries of Tiamaris, which is not large for the span of her wings."

Kaylin raised a hand as he drew breath. "I'm sorry. I get it."

"You are willing to accept the loss of freedom, because in your earlier life, absent Imperial Law and Imperial dictate, you felt you had none. It is not as simple for Bellusdeo. She was caged when she existed in the Shadowlands; she is caged here in a different way. I have spoken with the Court," he added, his voice softening. "And I have made clear that she is not a cage bird. But she is of value, Kaylin. If we are immortal, if we have forever, she exists as hope and possibility only so long as she lives.

"You may think the Arcane bomb was not significant enough to kill her."

Privately, Kaylin did.

"Bellusdeo is also of that opinion. Lord Sanabalis, however, is not."

"Why?"

"It is his suspicion that without the magical interference of the hatchling, the bomb would have destroyed the city block in which it was detonated. The magical signature, while recognizable, is strangely muted. The Imperial Order of Mages is less certain, but at least one mage concurs with Sanabalis; he feels the power was leeched from the area of effect at precisely the moment it began to expand. I am not certain a more definitive answer can be achieved."

"You told Bellusdeo this."

"I believe Lord Emmerian was tasked with informing her. She accepted the information, but has since demanded to know why the Arcanum is still standing."

It was a question that would have been very familiar in the Halls. "I'll talk to her," she said.

"I would consider it a…personal…favor. If she were not the only female, I fear she would have chosen to take the long sleep of our kind."

"And that's not an option now?"

"It is an option. We cannot prevent it should she so decide, not easily and not cleanly. But if she struggles and argues, she is aware of her responsibility. I do not think she will force that option until Maggaron, at least, is dead."

Kaylin headed toward the door, paused, and then said, "You like her, don't you?"

"That is almost impertinent, Private Neya. But as I have asked you a favor, I will overlook it. Yes. It is possible that I have become sentimental in my dotage."

"Immortals don't have a dotage."

"It is a figure of speech. We do not, as you imply, grow weak or forgetful with age, no. But even in our lives, we know innocence and ignorance. Bellusdeo was born in my youth. She—and her sisters—were the definition of *difficult;* their lack of respect was accepted, barely, because they were both female and young. In my youth, I may have found some of the rules that governed the Aerie more restrictive than I would now. Bellusdeo frequently circumvented those rules and tweaked the noses of those who attempted to forcefully apply them.

"She is not so very different now, but now she knows loss. She cannot easily become the girl she was, but those are the only memories she has of this land. I appreciated her, yes. I do not wish to see her suffer."

Bellusdeo was waiting in the first of the large rooms near the entrance to their quarters. A rectangular rug lay above the dark wood planking, navy blue broken by colorful interlocking patterns, beneath the heavy chairs strategically scattered about the room. There were windows, in a curved bow, to the left of where the Dragon sat, back toward their half-curtained view. A fire was burning in a fireplace that ran half the length of the wall; it was surrounded by a mantel above which a wide, long painting sat. It was of a seascape, absent people.

Bellusdeo didn't look up when Kaylin entered the room;

she didn't look up when Kaylin took the nearest chair and sat in it. She looked up only when the small dragon, grumbling, pulled himself off Kaylin's shoulder and flew more or less directly at her face. Kaylin, horrified, shot out of her seat and tried to grab him; he was remarkably fast and easily evaded her hands.

He didn't evade the words that followed, but she wasn't sure he understood many of them. On the other hand, with her luck, he'd learn to speak and those would be the first words out of his mouth. While she was in company.

Bellusdeo, however, laughed, and the sound was arresting; she was, momentarily, delighted at the small, darting creature and Kaylin's total inability to exert any control over his flight. When she managed to stop laughing, she looked up at Kaylin; her eyes were an odd shade of copper. She wasn't angry; she simply wasn't happy. Kaylin wasn't certain if Dragon eyes had a color that meant sadness; she couldn't imagine any other Dragon of her acquaintance feeling it.

"Why don't we go out?" she said, before her thoughts caught up with her mouth.

"If you feel like walking the City under an escort of the Imperial Palace guard, Lord Emmerian, and a random mage, I'd be delighted."

"That sounds…grim."

"It does, doesn't it?" Bellusdeo rose. "I'm sorry. I owe you at least fifty apologies. I'm going to be terrible company, and I drove your Corporal out of the rooms the minute I entered them."

"He's used to worse."

One golden brow formed a distinct arch.

"What about if we had a small escort of Imperial Hawks instead?"

The other brow joined it. They both fell as the Dragon's eyes narrowed. "I fail to see how this is going to be helpful."

"Some of them will be Barrani?"

Her silence was expected and chilly. Her eyes, however, didn't shift color. "I am not fond of Barrani."

"No. Most Dragons aren't."

"And they're considered so harmless by mortals that 'going out' with them is natural?"

"No. But they're Hawks first, Barrani second. Some of them are even my friends."

"You refer to Teela and Tain?"

"I do."

Her head tilted, she thought about this for two minutes. "I will ask Lord Sanabalis."

"Ask the Arkon instead."

Teela and Tain appeared at the palace in under half an hour. Kaylin knew this because the Seneschal's face was a distinctly ashen shade when his presence was announced by the door ward. The Hawks hadn't been escorted to the door, either; they'd been left in the main hall, where the density of Palace guards had no doubt severely and suddenly increased.

Bellusdeo was no longer wearing the expensive silks and dyes of clothing suitable for a Lord of the Court; she was, instead, wearing clothing suitable for a trip to the market. Getting that clothing had been a challenge; Kaylin wasn't certain how she'd managed it. Then again, she was capable of some magic; maybe it was illusory.

Kaylin's clothing wasn't. "You're sure about this?" she asked as they followed the agitated Seneschal down the long hall.

Bellusdeo smiled. Cats could only dream of having a smile like that. It lasted until Teela and Tain came into view, whereupon it stiffened without actually falling off her face. "You are certain you trust them?"

"With my life. Not, sadly, with my dignity."

"Very wise," Teela said from down the hall. "We've been instructed by the Hawklord to curb the most egregious examples of self-indulgence." Kaylin could almost hear the Hawklord's voice.

"You're off duty."

"And if we don't wish to remain that way permanently, we're going to compromise a little." She smiled her best smile, which sadly was all edges. Her eyes, however, were emerald-green. "Lady Bellusdeo. You are not enjoying your sojourn in the Imperial Palace?"

"No more than you enjoy your visits to the High Halls," the Dragon replied in a chillier tone.

Teela laughed. "A fair reply. I can honestly say I've never met a Dragon Lord like you."

Bellusdeo's smile lost some of its chill. "I hope I haven't been too large a disappointment."

"Disappointment? No. I owe you a debt," she added. "I haven't been bored for weeks now."

As compliments went, it was third-class. Or at least that's how Kaylin felt about it. One look at Bellusdeo's expression made clear that Kaylin was not a Dragon; she seemed genuinely pleased.

Kaylin stared at the two of them, then glanced at Tain, who was smiling his lazy, broad smile. "What you don't understand, and won't no matter how often we explain it, is the role boredom has in our lives. We live forever, if we can defend ourselves. We've seen everything. Life loses urgency. Loss dims, humor dims. If we say someone's not boring, it is an accolade." This was more than Tain usually said in a night out, probably because it was hard to get a word in edgewise when Teela was speaking.

Bellusdeo nodded. "It is not meant as an insult, nor is it meant as a backhanded compliment." Her smile brightened. "Come, let's go out into your city and alleviate boredom."

Kaylin, slowly trailing behind, wondered why this had seemed like such a good idea at the time.

When she entered the office the next morning, she was appalled at how noisy it was. She was also dimly aware that the noise level hadn't changed. Severn, idling at his desk, glanced up from a very neat pile of paperwork. When he caught sight of her face, his brows rose.

"You went out drinking with Teela and Tain."

"Yes."

"Why? It had to be your idea—they wouldn't let Barrani, even Hawks, anywhere inside the Palace."

"Bellusdeo was in a bad mood."

"...So you took her drinking with Teela."

"For the first pub, yes. By the end of it, I was trying to get her to go back home. By that point, she wasn't listening."

"Was she drinking?"

"Yes. But I don't think it had much effect on her."

"Was there—"

"They didn't start an all-out brawl, no. There were two fights. They were short. Bellusdeo finished one of them."

"I don't want to know."

"Good."

"I want plausible deniability."

"Very funny." She sat at her desk. "I want water."

The truth, once the headache had subsided a bit, was that she didn't regret the evening. Teela was in a better mood than she'd been in since Margot had all but destroyed the investigation into the Exchequer, and Bellusdeo had returned to their apartment with eyes of radiant gold. Sadly, she'd entered the Palace humming a ditty with extremely questionable lyrics, and she smelled like pipe smoke. It was Kaylin who'd received the dirty looks, of course.

CHAPTER 11

Three days later, the journey to the West March did not start at a reasonable hour. In theory, the caravan was to leave at dawn. In practice, it did. But as usual, wedged between theory and practice was the fact that the pilgrims were expected to meet at the High Halls, prepared for the voyage, before that dawn arrived. Kaylin, whose body considered morning to be somewhere around the vicinity of noon when it had a choice, managed to make it on time, in part because Severn dropped by the Palace. He didn't have keys, of course, but apparently didn't need them to make it as far as the door.

The door ward announced Severn's presence in a voice that could wake the dead. It certainly caused Kaylin to roll out of bed and reach for the knives she no longer wore in her sleep. Bellusdeo had a bed but hadn't bothered to use it. She had helped Kaylin pack, although *help* was a very subjective word.

"I've ordered a carriage," she told Kaylin as she handed her the pack. "It will take you as far as the High Halls. I do not believe it will be allowed onto the grounds."

"If we're lucky, it'll be allowed onto the block."

Bellusdeo winced. "That is possibly correct." She led them to the doors and stopped there, looking pensive and almost entirely unlike a Queen. "I wish I could go with you," she said. It was wistful, not whiny; she knew why it was impossible.

Kaylin hugged her tightly.

"Thank you for your suggestion the other night," Bellusdeo said. "Even in my own kingdom, there was very little activity that was that...casual. Your Barrani friends are interesting, Kaylin. Inasmuch as Barrani are capable of caring, I think they care for you. Teela is going with you."

"Yes."

"Try to observe what she does. Try to mimic the parts that are unlikely to cause friction."

"I'll assume you don't mean get drunk and start fights."

Bellusdeo smiled. "She is unlikely to do either among her kin. I do not believe she relishes the opportunity to travel to the West March, either."

"We can go out somewhere when I get back. Just promise to remind me to drink less next time."

The smile deepened. Bellusdeo hugged her tightly and then pushed her gently but inexorably out the door.

The caravan, as Teela had called it, was in the main unlike any caravan Kaylin, as a Hawk, had inspected. The Barrani, clearly, did nothing common. There were wagons, yes, but the wagons were enclosed in colorful cloth—white, green, and gold with hints of various shades of brown that suggested tree bark without ever descending to its solidity. The wheels were slender and high; the driver's seat, in colors that matched the cloth, wide and—to her admittedly inexperienced eye—comfortable.

There were also carriages. Kaylin had seen Barrani carriages before; these were similar, although their colors were different. They matched the gaudy, bright colors of the wagon coverings. The crest that was usually engraved, or painted, or both, on the doors was different, as well.

"It's the insignia of the Lord of the West March," Teela said.

Kaylin jumped and spun.

"You chose that dress, did you?"

To Kaylin, the dresses were pretty much of a kind. They were soft, light, and possessed long skirts that nonetheless allowed almost full freedom of movement. This one was a cream color. Most of the others were much, much brighter than Kaylin's normal wear; none of them were black. "Yes, why? It was one of the ones you sent to me; I thought they'd all be acceptable."

"It's the most…drab."

Bellusdeo had said something similar, which Kaylin recalled. "Look, Teela, I don't want to draw a lot of attention."

"Well, you could be dressed irreproachably and you would still draw attention. First: you are not Barrani, and we are going to the West March. Second, and of vastly more import, you have not managed to leave your small companion behind."

Kaylin ignored the last comment. "I don't notice you criticizing Severn's clothing."

"Because Severn's clothing, while conservative, is not inappropriate."

"Damn it, neither is mine!"

"And he doesn't respond to teasing at all. He's both attractive and very boring at the same time."

Teela was dressed as a Lord of the High Court. Gone was the comforting and familiar tabard of the Hawks; gone was the practical leather. She carried no sticks, either; instead, a scabbard hung from her left hip. It was as fine as the jewelry that dripped off her fingers, wrist, and neck.

"Please don't tell me I was expected to wear jewelry."

"The only important piece for you is the ring." Teela lifted a languid arm. "You don't like my jewelry?"

"No one—not even the nobles that crossed the bridge for their entertainment—wore jewelry like that in the fiefs. It's practically a demand."

"To be robbed?"

"And killed, yes."

"And it's been eight years since you called Nightshade your home."

Kaylin nodded. Hesitated.

"Kitling."

Surrendered. "You know he's going to be in the West March, right?" she whispered in a voice so low Severn wouldn't catch it, and he was standing beside her.

Teela's smile was almost feral. "I have not been informed of that fact." Her voice was sweet and soft. "And as a Lord of the High Court, I am certain I would have been if such an… unusual…exception were to be made. Come. You and your Corporal will ride with me."

Kaylin, however, froze.

Teela sighed pointedly. "Kaylin?"

"Please tell me that's not Evarrim."

"If you insist."

"Please tell me truthfully that Evarrim isn't coming to the West March."

"Oh, truth." She shrugged delicately. "Since he is demonstrably here, I cannot fathom why you are even asking."

"Kill me now."

"Nonsense. Dead, you will provide no relief from the interminable boredom."

Everybody needed a purpose in life. Kaylin, however, wished fervently for a better one at this moment.

★★★

The best thing about the carriage ride was that Teela did not insist on driving. The most surprising thing about the carriage—other than the fact that it was actually almost comfortable—was the fourth passenger.

"Andellen!"

"Lord Kaylin."

"…You're coming to the West March."

"While you live, by the grace of the High Lord, I am granted the rights and privileges of a Lord of the High Court. Yes, I intend to travel to the West March." He glanced at Severn. "I was not informed that you would be joining us."

"I am a little-known Lord of the High Court," Severn replied. "But as you are sworn to the service of Lord Nightshade, I will tell you this. I am not here at the request of Imperial Hawks; nor am I here to serve or protect Lord Kaylin."

"Yet you have received an invitation to the gathering."

"In an informal fashion, yes."

Andellen nodded, as if he could easily read between the lines of Severn's reply. "Lord Kaylin."

"Yes?"

"What are you wearing?"

It took her five seconds to realize that he wasn't asking about the dress, which was too bad, because that one, she was less worried about answering. "It's a small dragon."

"I highly doubt that."

"Why?"

"I have seen, as you call them, small dragons, if by *small,* you meant to imply *young.* They would not be so easily draped across your shoulders, even as hatchlings."

The small dragon lifted its head, pressed its cheek against Kaylin's; she assumed he was staring at Andellen, but didn't turn to look. He'd become much more aware, in the past few days, of when people were talking about him. It didn't seem to bother him. It did make him curious, though. She glanced at Teela. Teela didn't seem to mind Andellen, although Andellen had chosen to forsake the High Court in service to an Outcaste Lord.

Kaylin exhaled and explained.

Andellen's eyes narrowed as he listened. He was staring at the small dragon. The small dragon must have been staring back. She would have told Andellen he was wasting his time, but the only person she'd ever seen win a staring contest with a cat was Teela, a Barrani.

"The newest talk is the presence of the Lady in our gathering," Teela added casually.

"Is it bad that she's here?"

"For you? I cannot fully say; you find minor things needlessly upsetting. But to us, it is significant."

"Why?"

"Lord Andellen, please answer the question. I will no doubt be tasked with answering many, many more during the long weeks of travel and would like to preserve some of my energy."

"She is the Lady of the Lake." Andellen did not seem overly concerned or resentful at Kaylin's lack of knowledge. "You fail, consistently, to understand her significance to our people as a whole. If she is not the woman we would have chosen—"

"She's perfect for it."

"It is not a statement of preference, Lord Kaylin; it is merely observation. She is oft considered too sentimental to hold such a position, but not one of the Lords of the High Court has any say. She is not appointed; she just is. There is an undercurrent of fear because she is seen as weak. If we do not breed as quickly as mortal races, children are still our future, and without the Lady, there are none."

"So…she's Bellusdeo."

"Bellusdeo is the female Dragon currently in residence in the Imperial Palace?"

"Yes."

"She is, and is not, the same. If, among all the females born to clutches, only one would ever be fertile, she would be."

"But there are no other female Dragons. Not in this world."

Andellen nodded. "True. Bellusdeo is a weakness to the Dragons and their flights in the same way as the Lady is to the Barrani. The Lady does not travel."

"But she lived in the West March—"

"Before the death of the previous Consort, yes. She did. But now? If she dies, we are plunged into a chaos of seeking. Those who would attempt to take her position—and there are not a few—must take the test. Most are doomed to failure. And while they fail, there will be no children. There will be none until a successor is found. The previous Consort did not leave the High Halls."

"At all?"

"At all. The Court gossips as a way of passing the time. Your…pet would be worthy of far more note were it not for the presence of the Lady."

"What does the gossip say?"

"I am not, except on sufferance, heavily entwined with the Court as it is currently composed."

She exhaled. "Teela?"

"There are two possibilities. One: she travels because the Lord of the West March is in danger. If she were not who she is, this would not be credible. It is, however, a possibility. The second? That there is an event of import at the gathering itself and that your presence, Lord Kaylin, is a danger she seeks to offset."

"If it was a danger, I wouldn't have been given permission to attend."

Teela raised a brow. "You do not understand the High Court. If the High Lord sought to deny permission, Evarrim would have countered him."

"Evarrim's not the High Lord."

"No, he is not. But the High Lord is Barrani, Kaylin, not Dragon. He is Lord while he maintains his position against those who seek to unseat him."

"And why Evarrim?"

"Because he wishes to separate you from the City and your defenders there. Certainly the Dragon whose pendant you currently wear. Evarrim has some standing in the Court. As you were granted the title of Lord, and as you have not made the voyage to the West March, it is well within your rights, by law."

"I'd sooner die than be in his debt."

"I imagine, in the short term, that is the idea," was the agreeable reply. "The Lady is angry with you at the moment. But angry or no, she chose to speak to you in private and not in the heart of the Court over which she presides. This can be looked at in one of two ways." She stopped speaking and waited.

"Teela—"

"It won't harm you to try to think like a Barrani for the next two months. It may well prove to be of practical benefit."

She had a point. "I don't hate this just for the sake of hating it; I hate it because I have to pretend I'm Evarrim."

Teela chuckled. "You could, instead, pretend that you're me."

"Fine. You win." Kaylin fell silent for a few minutes, during which the wheels began to turn. They didn't even creak. "The most obvious would be that while the Lady is angry, she's not willing to consign me to pariah status."

"Yes, that is the most obvious, and if she were mortal, that might well be the case. She is Barrani, and in most cases it would be inconceivable. It will, however, be considered possible precisely because the Lady is known for her weaknesses in that regard."

The silence was longer and more thoughtful. "It's possible the Lady thought that a public argument would not go in her favor. If that was the case…"

"Yes?"

"She would conduct the argument in private. The assumption being that she would consider me no threat, or less of a threat than the loss of face the argument would cause in the High Court."

"Very good."

"There is a third possibility."

"Oh?"

"That the Lady considers me an equal."

Teela did not, to Kaylin's surprise, laugh. "Very good," she said softly. "Andellen?"

"The third possibility will never be spoken of in public. You are mortal, Kaylin. You are tolerated because you are Chosen. If the Lady, the Mother of the Race, condescends to consider you her equal…"

"It's bad."

"It would be bad. It would be bad because no one in the High Court who has not served in the position she now holds understands the whole of the power—and the ability—that comes with it. Nor do they fully understand you. It makes you much, much more of a threat."

"So they'll ignore it."

"They will not speak of it."

"Which isn't the same."

"Which is not, as you surmise, the same."

* * *

The caravan did two things that Kaylin had not expected. First, it continued to travel well past sunset. In and of itself this wasn't shocking. The Hawks had, in emergencies, been sent into the streets on patrol at later hours of night. But she had been under the impression that caravans, like most of the working world, tended to plan their routes around the sun's light.

"Perhaps mortals do. There are inns within a day's easy travel along the Imperial roads, it is true. It is also, however, irrelevant. When we are three days out of the capital, our road will diverge from that most commonly used."

"But we—"

"The Barrani High Court and its Lords do not often make use of mortal inns."

"Why not?"

"For one, they require money. In and of itself, given the nature of mortal inns, this is not surprising, although it is considered distasteful by many of my kin. Second, and of more import, they frequently ask that we sign their ledgers as…proof of our stay." As she spoke, she glanced pointedly at Severn.

"This is a problem? You're not doing anything illegal."

"We are not. But legality is oft in the eyes of the Emperor."

"Given the number of your party, you could probably refuse to sign."

"We could, but the interaction would be unpleasant for all involved. We do not travel to the inns."

Kaylin had, she hoped, prepared herself for camping out.

By the time night had truly overtaken the whole of the sky, the air was cool. The carriage, on the other hand, was on the stuffy side, even with open windows and a dwindling lack of the hot air speech produced. Teela and Andellen had dispensed with speech; Teela looked bored, which would have been worrisome if there had been anything she could do in a carriage—short of driving it—that could be dangerous. Andellen looked thoughtful. Severn was silent and watchful; Kaylin had gone from restive to sleepy. The small dragon squawked once when the tilt of her head threatened to crush him, and he'd nipped her ear to make his point, before rearranging himself in a pile in her lap.

Barrani didn't sleep. Clearly Severn didn't sleep when facing two Barrani, either.

Kaylin, however, began to nod off, jerking herself awake when the carriage wheels hit something on a road that was, in the best case, purely dirt.

Severn glanced at her; she couldn't tell if he was smiling or not. He didn't speak. Instead, he lifted an arm, and after a brief hesitation, Kaylin leaned against him.

Is this unfair?

He stiffened for an instant, and she started to sit up, but he folded his arm carefully over her shoulder.

No, Severn, I mean it. Is this unfair? I don't know if— I'm not—

Idiot.

The small dragon gave a small wuffling snort, as if he agreed.

"Easy for you to say," Kaylin mumbled. *I don't want to—I don't want to hurt you. I don't want to be hurtful. You don't deserve that.*

Kaylin, two things.

Two?

First: you think too much. Second: I'm a big boy. Let me decide what causes me pain. You get to decide what causes you pain. Don't make choices for me.

But—

Although it would no doubt amuse Teela, we're in a carriage with two Barrani companions. I don't expect anything, and even if I did, here would not be the place I'd choose. Sleep, Kaylin. Sleep. I'll keep watch.

She drew one deep breath, exhaled, and leaned into his side, remembering as she did the faraway streets of Nightshade on Winter nights before anyone she knew had died. His arm tightened, but not uncomfortably, and she drifted off to sleep.

True to Teela's word, the wagons didn't stop at an inn; they didn't stop on the road, either. Kaylin had assumed that there would be campgrounds tucked to one side of the road. Campgrounds, fire pits, tents—these were the things she'd been instructed, by Hawks who had done some travel on the cheap, to expect.

Joey had never traveled with Barrani.

CHAPTER 12

She was still sleeping when the carriage rolled to a stop; the sound of doors opening woke her, although they didn't wake her quickly. She could sleep standing up, as long as she could lean against a wall and fold her arms; she could certainly sleep while seated. But she rarely fell into a sleep as deep—and dreamless—as this one had been. She felt the urge to pull covers over her head and ignore sunlight, although she had no covers and it was demonstrably not morning.

Severn was content to wait until she'd managed to shake off sleep; Teela and Andellen were not. The cabin was empty and silent for a few long minutes; Kaylin stretched as far as the cramped ceiling would allow. "Where are we?"

"I'm not certain. The last time I traveled outside of the City, I wasn't traveling with Barrani Lords."

She looked out the window and froze.

She'd been told, by Joey, to expect campgrounds, which he described as dirt with a fire pit somewhere in its center. A place where you put up tents and hoped the ground wasn't too lumpy. Campgrounds were characterized by proximity to water.

The water part was true; Kaylin could hear it. Everything else was wrong.

There was light here. It was a rich, ambient gold, not quite sunlight, but a cut above the flickering shadows of fire or torch. It yellowed the trunks of the standing trees and rose to gild their branches. She couldn't easily see a source for that light.

"Look up," Severn said softly as he climbed out of the carriage. He offered her a hand; she took it without thinking; he was warm.

There was a clearing here, although it was now so crowded with carriages it looked like the drive of a large, pompous manse on the night of an important event. "Are there more carriages than we started out with?"

He nodded. He looked relaxed, but she was holding his hand; he was tense. If Severn was at ease with the Barrani Hawks, he clearly had two categories for Barrani. Which made sense, given Evarrim was also here. The reminder pushed the last of sleep off the figurative cliff of her mind.

"Where did everyone go?"

The light caught the play of his smile as he looked down. "Inside. We've been granted passage."

"Passage? To where?" She looked around at the empty carriages; even the horses that had drawn them were nowhere to be seen.

"Follow me," he told her, although she would have had to follow anyway, as she was still attached by the hand. The dragon had taken up his usual position as smooth, scaled scarf, but his eyes were bright and his head flicked from side to side as they walked toward the trees.

City streets weren't as well lit as this. They weren't as lovely, either. There was something about the shape and sheer height of the surrounding trees that suggested majesty in a way that was entirely unlike grand architectural edifices. She heard crickets in the distance, but the sounds of the City were entirely absent. Even the sounds of their footsteps as they walked were hushed and muted; there was no stone beneath their boots.

Severn led her to a tree.

It was four times her width—or larger—around the base of the trunk, and its roots lay in living knot-work above the ground. They parted almost naturally in only one place, and Severn followed the gap. "Umm, Severn?"

He glanced down.

"This is a tree."

And smiled. "It is. It's also where we're headed."

"They walked into a tree?"

"That's exactly what they did. There was a distinct pecking order to entry."

"That's why you didn't wake me."

His smile deepened. "Teela's spoiling for a brawl; I recognized the expression. At this point, I don't think she cares what the excuse is. If we enter last because you fell asleep and couldn't be bothered waking, no insult is offered."

"Are you kidding? They're Barrani. They can take insult at anything."

"They were mostly insulting each other. It was subtle. The Consort, of course, entered first." He walked right up to the bark of the tree and let go of her hand. "Can you see it?"

She couldn't. "I see a lot of bark."

Severn drew a small knife from his belt.

"Please tell me we don't have to bleed on the tree."

He cut the mound of his left palm in answer. It was a clean, shallow cut.

"I do not believe the Barrani. And they're worried about signing a guest book?"

He placed his palm against the bark of the tree and Kaylin watched as the trunk began to fade from view. In its place she could see a long hall that stretched from where they were standing into a distance that ended with one forbidding door. Before she could say more, Severn turned to her and handed her the knife. He took a step forward.

She didn't even try to follow him. The instant his feet were on the other side, in the hall, the hall vanished; the tree returned like a particularly unwelcome morning. She lifted her hand, gritted her teeth, and opened her left palm.

The small dragon leapt off her neck and shoulders and attacked Severn's knife. Kaylin nearly dropped them both, because he'd landed on her right hand. When she attempted to pull the knife away from his little, snapping jaws, he breathed on it.

She watched as the knife's blade melted.

Two things occurred to her. The first: this knife hadn't been cheap. The blade was hard enough to keep a decent edge—Kaylin hated the grinding sound of blade against stone—but worked in some way she didn't understand that prevented rust, and Severn was quietly attached to it. He was not going to be happy. He wouldn't say a damn word, either.

Second: the blade wasn't molten; it wasn't even hot. The steel dripped and elongated, flowing toward the ground as it separated entirely from the knife's handle. She cried out and tried to catch it, dropping the now bladeless handle in the attempt. Only as the liquid metal pooled in her palm did a second thought catch up with her, and by then it was too late.

But the metal wasn't hot. It wasn't even warm. It was cool, shiny in the golden glow of tree light.

"Gods damn it," she said to the angry, small dragon. "Why did you do that?"

The small dragon hissed, his wings folded flat against his back. He still clung to her right arm, though. He made a squawking noise that managed to sound entirely pathetic, and she surrendered. "Look, I'm sorry. Don't make those eyes at me. This was important to Severn, and he doesn't have many important things."

The small dragon then launched itself off her forearm, where he alighted on the fallen handle. Catching it in his claws, he flew back up, but this time, he landed on her left wrist, just above the cool, metallic puddle in her cupped palm. He let the hilt go; it landed on top of the liquid and sunk a bit. Kaylin wasn't even surprised when he then nosed around that hilt to reach the small, silver pool, although the squelching noise it made was a bit revolting.

But the small dragon did something—snort, breathe, it was hard to tell—and she felt the metal squirm. She held her breath as it began to shift in place, sliding over her palm and the stretch of her fingers. It lengthened farther, hardening as she watched, until it was once again the shape and weight of a blade. It was also attached to the hilt.

It didn't look like the same knife, mind. But at least it was a knife. She gripped the hilt tightly in her right hand. "Shall we try this again?"

The small dragon hissed, and Kaylin decided his answer was no. "Look, I don't want to spend the night sleeping under the wheels of a carriage, and I'm sure as hells not going to sleep in those seats."

Hiss. Wings extended for good measure.

"You have a better idea?" She reached out and splayed her hand against the tree's bark. Nothing happened. "I can't just stand here pounding on the trunk. Severn's probably getting worried, and if he isn't—"

"I am."

"—Teela is." Kaylin turned around to face Teela.

"What, exactly, are you doing, kitling? I understand it was a long day for a mortal, but you're more than accustomed to long days, and you don't normally spend time talking to yourself. At least not out loud."

"I'm talking to the dragon."

"And he's answering?" Her tone was so flat, Kaylin couldn't tell whether or not the question was sincere.

"Not precisely. He doesn't seem to want me to cut my hand."

Teela looked down at the dragon, who dug claws into Kaylin's exposed skin. Given she was wearing the bracer, he had to stretch a bit to find it.

"I don't suppose he told you why?"

"No such luck. To be fair, I don't much like the idea myself. I don't sign a ledger in my own blood."

"You don't stay in inns." It was true. "And it's blood, not name."

"You wouldn't be signing your True Names in a ledger, Teela."

"Even the casual names can be manipulated for information if enough people know or use them."

"But not blood?"

"Kitling, the Consort is waiting. You can probably be excused if you stand out here all night; Barrani expect a certain amount of ignorance from mortals. I, however, cannot. Give me your hand."

The dragon squawked. It was a louder, more forceful sound than the usual one. It almost had timbre.

Teela lifted one dark brow. "I see. If you have an alternative?" She glanced at Kaylin and added, "I cannot believe that I am speaking to the creature. You are a terrible influence, Private Neya."

"Sorry. On the other hand, I'd kind of like an answer to the same question."

The dragon lifted its neck and bared fine, slender teeth.

"A better answer. One that makes sense." To Teela, she added, "Why do your wards need blood, anyway? The wards in the High Halls don't."

"This is a very different magic," Teela replied. "But it is a magic that guarantees a certain privacy and safety. The Shadows surrender no blood that the great ones recognize as living."

"It must be different. It doesn't make my arms itch."

Teela chuckled. "Kitling?"

Kaylin raised the knife slowly, and the small dragon snorted. He pushed himself up, off her arm, and toward the trunk of the tree, as if he would attack it. It would have been almost comical, had Teela not drawn such a sharp, silent breath. "Do not let him breathe on it, Kaylin."

And she was supposed to stop him how? But Teela's tone was deadly serious. Kaylin took a step forward; the dragon was hovering very close to the bark. Before she could grab him, he reached out and bit it.

Teela relaxed, for a value of relaxation that wouldn't pass muster in the corps. Kaylin stiffened. She'd seen what had happened when he'd bitten Severn's knife. But after a few very tense seconds, the tree had not melted or turned to a liquid version of itself; its light had not shifted or dimmed in color. When Kaylin reached out to touch bark, it was solid and rough beneath her palm.

She started to speak and forgot what she'd been about to say; the tree began to fade.

Teela was utterly still as she watched the very unusual door open. Only when it remained that way did she draw breath again. "Fail to mention this," she told Kaylin.

Kaylin nodded as the dragon flew back to her shoulders. He seemed smug, although she wasn't certain why she thought so; his expression hadn't really changed all that much, although his eyes were slightly more lidded.

"And don't just stand there staring. I told you, the Consort is waiting."

The halls were even taller than they had appeared when Severn had stepped into them. She could only see the ceilings at the farthest point, where a closed door waited. To see them above her head, she had to look so far up she had problems maintaining her balance. Frowning, she looked at the floor instead. It was pale; she'd thought it was gray, but the light in the halls was markedly different from the light on the other side; it was almost white.

Bending, she touched it. "It *is* stone."

Teela nodded. "If you could save your inspection for a less inconvenient time, it would be greatly appreciated."

Reddening, Kaylin rose and straightened out the skirts of the dress she wore. "Are the walls stone, as well?"

"No."

"The ceiling? I'm walking, Teela."

"No."

"Does this door want blood, as well?"

"No. It is not a traditionally warded door." The Barrani Lord frowned. "Or rather, it is not a ward in the sense that you know it. Anyone who has entered the hall should be able to pass through the doors, but anyone unfamiliar with these halls who has entered them tonight offered the great tree some of their living blood. I am not entirely certain how the door will regard you."

"I was willing, Teela. He wasn't." She glanced at Severn's knife. In the brighter light of the hall—a light, it had to be said, that didn't seem to have a source—the knife was markedly different in shape: longer and narrower. It wouldn't fit the sheath it had come from.

The door, however, did roll open as Teela approached it. It opened into a round, low hall. Archways much smaller than the door and lower than the ceilings surrounded the wall's perimeter, leading into cloisters in the distance. The floor itself, however, was occupied by one large table; it was a rounded oval, around which elegant, tall-backed chairs had been placed. Food was spread from one end of the table to the other, and several silver pitchers stood between the plates. None of the food had been disturbed—or touched, by the look of it.

At the head of the table, the Consort sat, her hair a white spill down her shoulders. Her eyes, even at this distance, were a remarkable shade of blue when she turned to look at the new, late arrivals. If the floor had opened and swallowed Kaylin, she would have been grateful.

"Lord An'Teela. Lord Kaylin."

Teela nodded.

Kaylin, on the other hand, resorted to the use of knees. She fell to one and bowed her head so low her chin touched the space between her collarbones. "Lady."

"I trust you had little difficulty finding the entrance? Lord An'Teela was concerned, although Lord Severn seemed to manage, and he seldom leaves your side." Kaylin, on one knee, was acutely aware that half the room had stopped talking. She assumed they were now watching her; she didn't check. She also didn't lift her head; she waited.

This was the Barrani version of standing in front of Diarmat's desk at attention, the difference being she didn't hate the Consort. She hoped, some day in the near future, the reverse might once again be true.

After fifteen minutes, talking resumed in the hall; voices rose and fell. Clearly, Kaylin abasing herself in front of the Lady of the High Court only had brief amusement value. Barrani at their most political often spoke in the most pleasant, soft voices. Their laughter—and they did laugh—was cool and almost musical to the ear. On the very rare occasions Teela's voice had become so pleasant, she was at her most dangerous; one step away from killing. Not a killing rage—the Leontines had cornered the market on that. The Barrani just seemed to get more and more chilly. If it wasn't for the color of their eyes, they might even seem to be growing more friendly, not less.

Teela left Kaylin on the floor, presumably to take a seat at the table.

The Consort began to speak, but not to Kaylin. *I've survived this before,* she told herself. The small dragon seemed content with his perch of more supine-than-natural shoulders; he didn't hiss, didn't squawk, and didn't unfurl his wings.

Dinner continued; she could hear the enticing sound of cutlery, of glasses moving and sometimes clinking. She was hungry, and having spent most of the day in cramped quarters, she wanted to move. But she stared at the floor and her foot instead. She'd done this before.

The Consort continued to speak to the Lords of the Barrani Court. If she glanced in Kaylin's direction at all, she didn't spare the time to say the single word that would allow Kaylin to rise. Kaylin did not rise. Her leg cramped; her hips stiffened. She waited. Music began to play somewhere to her right. A stringed instrument, joined, in time, by a flute.

This helped. It didn't make a difference to her empty stomach, but it did lessen the impact of the noise it made.

I take it back. This is worse than Diarmat. It was more subtle than Diarmat, but as the time stretched on, it was infinitely less pleasant.

When the Barrani began to leave the table and the hall, she lowered her face a few inches, inhaling and exhaling deeply, as if this were an entirely physical endurance exercise. It was. She knew, at that point, that dinner was out of the question. If she wanted food, she would have to rise. If she rose without a word from the Consort, the last hour, or longer, had been a total waste of time and effort.

The hall emptied. The music ceased. Kaylin's head was still bowed, but it felt about four times heavier than it had when she'd first knelt. She closed her eyes and began to recite legal metrics, the earliest and most important of her lessons with the Hawks.

She felt a hand on her shoulder; she didn't move.

"She's gone," Severn said. "They've all left the hall for the evening."

She considered, briefly, remaining in this posture until they returned in the morning.

"There's still food left."

And abandoned the idea. Her legs wobbled as she rose; Severn offered her a hand, and she took it.

"The Consort did notice," he told her as he led her to the table. The food left here made it clear that the Barrani didn't consider food an important commodity. Then again, she'd never met a starving Barrani.

"Did her eyes get any greener?"

"Not appreciably, no. Why did you take so long?" he added.

She froze. She had forgotten Severn's knife. The small

dragon attempted to move most of his body so it was out of Severn's line of sight.

Severn raised a brow; he'd noticed, of course.

Exhaling, she handed him the knife. "This is yours. I'm sorry."

He glanced at it. "That's not my knife."

"It's what's left of your knife. Mr. Small and Squawky wasn't keen on my cutting my hand and bleeding on the tree. I had your knife—I'm really, really sorry—and he bit the blade."

He lifted the knife and examined it carefully as she continued to speak.

"The blade melted after he bit it."

"Melted?"

"Yes, but not because it got hot. It just...melted. It turned into silver liquid. I know you really liked that knife. I wasn't happy. He knew I wasn't happy. So he—he tried to change it back. This was the result."

Severn was now examining the edge of the blade—by shaving some of his arm hair. "It's sharp."

"It's too long for the sheath. I'll buy you a new one the minute we get back to the city."

He gave her the "with what money?" look.

"I'm not paying rent this month."

He turned his attention back to the knife. "If you don't mind, I'd like to keep this."

"It's yours anyway." She looked, with longing, at the food on the table, but didn't touch any of it. "You're not angry?"

"You're not the one who destroyed it. The small dragon appears to be trying to hide, on the other hand. Did he let you cut your hand with this knife?"

"No."

"How did you get in?"

"He bit the tree. I'm thinking of letting him attack a few door wards when we get back."

Severn smiled. "Not advisable," he told her, picking up a plate and putting it firmly in her hands.

"Oh, probably not." There was fruit on the table. Some cheese. Different hues of wine, which she decided not to touch. There was bread in very odd shapes, some meat that she assumed was venison, because there weren't a lot of cows or sheep here. "Teela wasn't happy."

"No. I don't imagine she would be. She told you to keep this to yourself?"

"More or less."

"It's good advice."

"I know. You don't count," she added as she began to eat.

There was no Seneschal, no innkeeper, and no native guide to lead them to their rooms after Kaylin had finished eating. There was, in fact, no one in sight except Severn. "Is it always like this?"

Severn nodded.

"What happens to the dishes?" There didn't appear to be much in the way of an obvious kitchen, either. Kaylin assumed it was beyond one of the many evenly spaced archways.

"You're a Lord of the High Court. Dishes are not your concern."

"Right. Do you know where we're supposed to be staying?"

"Not yet. Watch this carefully." He left the table, left the circular floor, and headed toward the first of the open arches. She followed, finding the utter absence of noise disturbing. It wasn't that she liked hearing catfights, dogfights, and drunks singing off-key, to name a few, but they were a constant intrusion that reminded her that she lived in the City. There was no city here.

The small dragon rubbed her left cheek with his nose; his eyes were wide opals. He, like the room, made no sound. Severn's feet did. So did hers. She tried to lighten her step. He passed the first arch and headed toward the second, following the subtle perimeter the exits made.

When he approached the fourth, the floor beneath his boots began to glow. It was a light very similar to the gold shed by the trees that served as sentinels and doors. "This way," he told her, following that light. It expanded a yard beyond his feet, no farther, but it continued to hold that position as he walked.

"You're sure I'm allowed to go this way?"

"Look at your feet."

She did. The floor beneath her boots was the same gentle gold as the floor beneath Severn's. "If I weren't supposed to go this way, there'd be no light?"

He nodded.

"Have you ever tried just walking through a random arch?"

"Yes."

"What happened?"

"I survived. If a Wolf is hunting here, and he has permission to enter, this is not the place to attempt to make the kill. Ever."

She fell silent, grateful for the moment that the path they were following was the same, and uncomfortable with his example. She ignored it, because it wouldn't lead either of them anywhere she wanted to go tonight. "Does it work differently for Barrani?"

"I can't say for certain; it's my suspicion that it does."

Something about his tone was slightly off. Kaylin frowned and stopped walking. After a moment, so did Severn, and the light across the floor lengthened between them.

"Is he here?"

"He?"

"The Arcanist you were sent after."

He didn't answer.

★★★

The small dragon flew off her shoulder, which startled them both, and landed on the glowing portion of the ground between them. Kaylin took care not to step on him as she closed the gap. For good measure, she slid a hand under his belly, scooped him up, and drew level with Severn while he waited.

"Sorry. I know you're not supposed to talk about it. When I start asking questions, I forget to check them at the mouth."

He chuckled.

"I'll try harder to remember."

His smile was slight and resigned as he began to walk again. "Don't."

"Why?"

"Because it'll just make you self-conscious. I don't care if you ask, as long as you don't mind if I don't—or can't—answer. You're capable of being careful, but frankly, I don't want to be treated as if I were Lord Diarmat. I don't need you to be afraid of me."

"Good. It's not likely to happen anytime soon."

The lights beneath their feet continued to guide them, but unlike small dragons, they weren't impatient. The hall seemed to move at a gentle curve toward the right, and as the lights finally ceased their slow progress just ahead of their feet, they stopped at a door. It was, unlike the door that had fronted the great hall, narrow and made of a pale, pale wood. The hinge was invisible on the exterior of the door—if it even had a hinge.

"Is this my room or yours?" Kaylin asked, looking at the floor.

Severn's smile froze, but it didn't entirely desert his face. His scars did whiten, though, especially the one along his jaw. "This might be a problem. Try opening the door."

"Not if I have to bleed on it." She examined the door with

care; she couldn't see a ward on its surface. Or a lock. Or, if it came to that, a bloody handle or doorknob.

"You don't. That's only the price of entry."

"For every single stop?"

He nodded. "Unless you've been there before, yes."

She stalled for time. "So you hadn't been here."

"No. Not in this particular way station. Farther on, yes."

"Why farther on?"

"I don't have a dislike of inns, and I'm perfectly willing to sign a ledger under an assumed identity. The Barrani Lords have issues with that. But the Barrani roads to the West March don't follow mortal trade routes."

"Can I ask how you even found those way stations?"

"You can ask. At the moment, I can't answer." He lifted an arm and placed a palm against the door's surface, as if it were warded. The door swung open, its movement completely silent. Kaylin still couldn't see any evidence of hinges. If it had just faded from view it wouldn't have been any less natural.

"I guess this is your room," Kaylin said as Severn stepped across the threshold. She lingered by the door as he entered the room. The light that had pooled between their feet didn't follow him.

She turned to look down the hall; it was dark. But it was a dark that reminded her of a moonlit night. She could make out the shapes of the walls and could even see another doorless arch in the distance. What she couldn't see was any movement of the golden light beneath her own feet.

She took a step away from the door; the light remained where it was. She took two steps; it didn't move. "Severn?"

He was watching.

"Do you think this is my room?"

"The door opened for me."

"Yes, but..." She pointed at the light. "Maybe the built-in guide won't work for me because I didn't bleed on the tree."

"It was working earlier."

"Yes, but—" She glanced into the chamber beyond the now-open door. What she'd assumed would be a single inn-like room was not. Or if it was, people were expected to sleep on the floor or the low, long chairs. There was no desk, but there was a flat table; in all, it reminded her of the room in which Nightshade entertained visitors. The walls were a pale blue; the floors, a dark-grained wood. In the center of the room, a small tree stood; it looked like a sapling, but Kaylin didn't know enough about trees to name a species. "If I'm not supposed to be here, will something bad happen if I step across the threshold?"

"Not immediately."

"What happens eventually?"

"You'll find the room either too hot or too cold; you'll find everything slightly off. If you remain in the room, you'll begin to notice unpleasant, small details."

"Such as?"

"An excess of insects. Spiders, small beetles."

"Cockroaches?"

"In your case, probably."

"None of those are likely to kill me."

He laughed. "No. Me, either. But the air gets stuffy, and if you can't or won't take a hint, it becomes absent. It's not unlike being buried alive, but without the dirt." He walked farther into the room, and as he did, Kaylin noticed a recessed arch along the right wall—a wall that, in theory, led back into the hall they'd emerged from.

She hesitated. The small dragon flew up to her shoulder and gently bit her chin. She took this as a hint and stepped into the room, waiting for the room to react. While she waited, she genially cursed the Barrani. She couldn't imagine any other race coming up with something so subtly unfriendly.

But it wasn't too hot or too cold, and the air in the room was light and pleasant. "Do all the rooms have trees growing out of the floor?"

"I don't know. I haven't seen all the rooms." Severn reappeared. "There's a bath here. The bedroom's on the other side of the bath."

"You realize that the bath should be in the middle of the hall, right?"

"In a normal inn, yes."

"And the bedroom would be across the hall?"

He nodded. "It's not that different from Castle Nightshade."

She grimaced. "Thanks." After another awkward pause, she said, "Do you think they normally put two people in the same room?"

"I don't know. It's the first time it's happened to me, but there's no complaint department here. I believe you can leave and spend the night in the carriage if you want."

"What do you mean, 'believe'?"

"I've never tried."

"This whole setup didn't bother you the first time you had to stay in a way station?"

"I slept with a knife under my pillow, if that helps. And I didn't sleep much."

Fair enough. She entered the room that Severn had said contained a bath. It was very much like the baths in the High Halls—not as large but just as ostentatious. On the other hand, there were towels, rather than attendants.

"Kaylin—"

She shook her head. "It's not as if you don't randomly show up in my apartment from time to time. I don't need to have a room of my own. Not," she added quickly, thinking of Bellusdeo, "while I'm on the road." She knelt by the side of the large, shallow pool and plunged a hand into the water. It was warm. It was, in fact, on the edge of almost too hot. Barrani baths weren't actually about being clean, though. And the hot water reminded her that her legs hurt, in large part because she'd been left in what she hoped was a perfect kneel for far too damn long.

"Bath first," Severn told her quietly.

The small dragon sat on her shoulder while she lounged in the water, letting her hair float around her like dark kelp. He appeared to be cleaning his tail, and reminded Kaylin very much of a hairless, translucent cat.

"Why are you here, anyway?" she asked when he brought his nose to her cheek and started rubbing. She lifted a hand and began to scratch his nose, wondering idly if magical creatures were capable of feeling itchy. This one certainly didn't appear to need food, which meant the rest of the caretaking duties usually associated with pets weren't an issue, either. He did seem to enjoy being scratched and rubbed, though. And he didn't answer the question, although he lifted his head and craned his neck toward what she assumed was the bedroom.

"Does it have two beds?" she asked.

The small dragon tilted its head in her direction.

"I'll take it that's a no."

CHAPTER 13

There were bathrobes in the bathing room. Kaylin wasn't surprised when one of them fit her perfectly, although she did find it creepy.

Then again, she found Barrani homes creepy. It never looked as though anyone actually lived in them. Caitlin's home was much neater and tidier than Kaylin's, but there were things in it. Small paintings, several scarves—all gifts—an assortment of small boxes. Just…things. She reminded herself that this was the equivalent of a roadside inn, which wasn't meant to be a home. But the room would have fit right in at Castle Nightshade. The Barrani didn't form sentimental attachments to things. They barely, as far as Kaylin could tell, formed sentimental attachments to other people.

Severn, seeing that she hadn't fallen asleep and drowned, left the room to take a bath.

Kaylin did what she often did when she was in a strange room on her own: she paced. She observed. The room was large. The walls, rather than being flat, curved on a gentle slope to form the ceiling. The floors were of bare, pale wood.

There was an armoire that seemed to conform to the curve of the walls, but when she opened it, it was both empty and far too deep; there was a table, not a desk, that held one low bowl of water in which three flowers floated. Severn had stowed his pack to one side of the bed and his clothing on top of it; his bedroll and blankets were set to one side, again on the floor. Clearly he didn't trust the armoire.

Or maybe he liked a little bit of mess, as well. Her clothing was heaped in a pile in the room that contained the bath.

She checked the marks on her arms—they were a nascent coal-gray—and checked her bracer. The gems were flat and lifeless. The small dragon chewed strands of her hair, content to perch and make small animal noises while she walked.

She turned her attention to the bed. As beds went, it was round. Round was not the normal shape for a bed in any room Kaylin had ever seen. Kneeling by its side, she lifted the sheets and looked beneath it; there were more than the usual number of legs, some of them in the center of what she assumed was a frame that supported slats.

When she rose, she sat heavily on the left side of the bed. "Ten years ago, this wouldn't have been a problem," she told the dragon.

"It isn't a problem now," Severn said.

She froze and then swiveled slowly to look at him; he was wearing a bathrobe. His hair was wet in the messy, toweled-dry way; in the room's light, his eyes looked darker. "I am not Barren."

She flinched.

"I'm not Nightshade," he continued. "I'm not a bored, self-indulgent noble. And I'm not a young Hawk whose jaw you could easily break." He walked over to the right side of the bed and sat. He looked a lot more comfortable than she felt. "Nothing will happen tonight—nothing that you don't start."

She swallowed and turned to face him. "There's too much light in here."

Severn glanced toward the ceiling and whispered a single Barrani word. The lights began to dim. But they dimmed slowly, as if there was an invisible window that now opened onto sinking sun. He lay back on top of the covers, while she crawled under them and pulled them up to her chin. They were large and heavy, and they hid her toes. She hated having her toes stick out.

"There are no monsters under the bed," he said, grinning.

"I know. I'm not a child."

"You checked." It wasn't a question.

Since it was true, she rearranged her pillows. "Do you think the Consort is ever going to speak to me again?"

Severn accepted the change of subject. "Yes."

"Without blue eyes?"

"Yes."

"Soon?"

"No. I think she was reluctantly impressed tonight, if that helps."

It shouldn't have, but it did. She fell silent for a long moment. "I'm not good at starting things."

"I know. And I'm not good at waiting."

"You waited for seven years."

"Yes. I don't really want to wait out another seven, but I can. It's not the waiting that's hard."

"No?"

"It's the not doing. It's knowing that you're here and I can't safely touch you if I ever want to touch you again. It's knowing that Barren's dead, and I can't kill him."

"Morse needed to kill him."

"And you didn't?"

She closed her eyes. "Not as badly as Morse did. I saw him die. That was almost enough."

"But he's there, between us."

"Yes." She swallowed. "It's not just Barren."

"No. If I can ask one thing of you tonight, please don't mention their names."

She nodded and then said, "Yes. I mean, you can ask, and I won't."

Night continued to fall in the room, the shadows shifting from gray to indigo. Kaylin listened to Severn's breathing and forced hers to match his, until they sounded like one person. One person and small dragon, who curled up against the top of her head.

"Don't you ever get tired of it? The waiting?"

"Not yet."

"Will you?"

"What do you think?" He shifted position in the bed; she felt the tug of covers as he slid beneath them. "Is that what you want?"

"...No."

"Then don't ask again. I didn't waver when you tried to kill me the first time, in the Hawklord's Tower. I didn't give up when you tried to kill me in the Foundling Hall. But enough time has passed, Kaylin." He shifted again and whispered a different name. "Elianne."

"You almost never call me by my name."

"I call you by the name you chose. What you're called doesn't change what you mean to me. I don't know if we'll ever get past what I did. I want to try. If you know it's impossible, tell me. I'll deal with it."

She wanted to say something, but all the words were messed-up, wrong words.

"But don't give me your version of pity, either. I don't want it, and I don't need it. I made a life that has space for you in it, but it's still my life."

She slid onto her side, facing Severn's profile; it was now night-dark in the room. She wanted a breeze, an open window—her own window, warped shutters and all. She could see his profile clearly; the line of his nose, his lips, his chin; she could hear his deep and even breathing.

"Are you sleeping?" she asked softly.

"…No."

"Can I?"

He turned to face her. "Yes. If you want, I'll keep watch."

"I don't think anything's going to attack us here."

"Is that a no?"

It wasn't. In the Winter, they had often slept in shifts in the fiefs, because in the Winter, finding some warmth could be a matter of life and death, and people who thought they could afford to be merciful were often corpses by morning. She didn't know if Severn had slept well in Nightshade, but she had. Severn kept watch; he was there; he would wake her. There was something strangely comforting about her discomfort. She could feel his breath in the space between them—and there was space between them. And she thought she wouldn't mind if there was less of it, because it was dark and she couldn't see his expression. She could hear his voice, and she thought there was nothing in his voice, ever, that could remind her of Barren and her own self-loathing.

But she couldn't quite bring herself to bridge the gap, and she knew if she didn't, it wouldn't be bridged. She even thought she understood why. If something happened, it had to be because she was certain; something as feeble as "not minding"—tonight—wouldn't cut it. "I'm afraid of change," she whispered.

He didn't answer. He lifted a hand and then, in silence, lowered it. She thought it trembled.

Kaylin was woken by her most familiar adversary: sunlight. She pulled covers over her head and reached for the shutters, because she could do that in her sleep, she'd done it so often. Unfortunately, there were no warped shutters, because, among other things, there was no window.

"Given the Consort's reaction to your late arrival last night, are you certain you want a repeat?"

A cold bucket of water would have been less effective. Kaylin leapt out of bed in a panic that would have done Marcus proud. The small dragon made a sound between a squawk and a shriek, and she apologized—loudly—because she'd probably half flattened him in her rush.

She headed immediately toward the bath chamber, but didn't manage to reach it because someone had moved the armoire. It was no longer nestled harmlessly against the far wall; it was practically jutting out of the arch through which the bath could still be seen.

"I officially don't like Barrani way stations," she said, coming to a halt. "Is it too much to hope that you moved the closet?"

"Stranger things have happened, but no, I didn't. Nor did I ask that the armoire be moved."

The closet's door swung open. It creaked, which must have been deliberate, because it certainly hadn't creaked that way when she'd opened it last night. Kaylin strongly disliked the idea of a sentient, moving closet. "Is this dangerous?" she asked as she approached the widening door.

"I think it unlikely, depending on your definition of danger."

"Has this ever happened to you?"

"No."

She noticed that he had his hands on his dagger hilts, but that he hadn't gone as far as unwinding his weapon's chain. She entered the closet, small dragon firmly attached to her shoulders. The door did not swing shut at her back. As she'd half expected by this point, the closet wasn't empty. It contained one dress. The dress was an emerald-green, similar in color to the ones Teela often wore when at Court, with sleeves that appeared, on casual inspection, to be mostly holes.

"All right," she told the room. "I'll wear it."

The dress came with a cape. The cape was mostly fabric, on the other hand. The neckline would hide Sanabalis's chain; the holes were diamond in shape and started at the shoulders, ending at the wrists in a chain of exposed skin. This was on the outside of her arms; the bottoms were long, trailing swathes of green. The skirt was loose enough for a full, fast stride.

Kaylin disliked skirts for a number of reasons. On the other hand, any weapon she could carry here was purely for show and a modicum of comfort.

"Kaylin?"

She glanced up at Severn.

"There are boots, as well."

There were. They were the same color as the dress. She bent at the knees, lifted one, and whistled. They were very supple—even soft. Carrying them into the room's brighter light, she examined them carefully. They were flat, the heels a stiff leather. They looked, on first inspection, like boots that would be far, far more comfortable than the ones she'd been wearing, but they would stand out like a sore thumb if she happened to be in any other clothing.

They fit her feet. She hadn't, at this point, expected they wouldn't. And they were so comfortable it almost felt as though she wasn't wearing boots at all. "These," she said, "are keepers. I hope." Eyes rounding, she turned to Severn. "None of this stuff disappears when I leave the way station, does it?"

"I don't know. I've never had a room be this critical of my clothing before."

The small dragon didn't seem to mind the clothing, which was good, given his reaction to the things he did mind.

"Breakfast?" she asked when she'd finished with the boots' laces.

He nodded and offered her an arm.

Kaylin regretted her decision to accept the guidance of a mute closet the minute she entered the great hall. The floor helpfully lit the way beneath their feet, so reaching the great hall itself took only a handful of minutes, but as they passed beneath the last arch, the general din of Barrani conversation took a distinct dive. Silence spread in a widening circle, as if Kaylin were the rock dropped into a still pond.

Her hand tensed where it lay across Severn's lifted arm. "This was not a good idea," she whispered.

He didn't reply. He did slow his pace to accommodate Kaylin's hesitation, but he continued to walk, and as she was holding his arm, she followed. The small dragon lifted his neck until his head was level with her gaze. But he didn't look at her or demand her attention; instead, he seemed to be surveying the gathered High Court.

The Consort, in her radiant white robes, sat once again at the table's head. To her left and right, Barrani Lords were seated; Kaylin didn't recognize them immediately. But they turned to look at her as the encroaching silence at last caught their attention. With it came the Consort's.

Even at this distance, Kaylin could see that her eyes were blue. She looked for Teela and Andellen, the only two Lords in this room she could be fairly certain were friendly. She found Teela first.

Teela's eyes were also an unfortunate shade of blue.

Severn continued to walk. Kaylin's legs moved automatically to follow; there were empty seats nearer the foot of the table than its head, and that's where Severn seemed to be leading them. He nodded, politely, in the direction of the Lords of the High Court. Kaylin, after a pause, did the same. It seemed to be working, but before they could reach the empty chairs—and the food that had suddenly lost its appeal—the Consort rose.

"Where did you obtain that dress, Lord Kaylin?"

"In a closet, Lady."

The silence broke in several ways. Small, hurried conversations and asides sprang up around the table as the Barrani High Lords began to speak at once and over each other. Even in shock, the jostle for position was evident. One or two of these Lords attempted to catch Kaylin's attention and failed. Kaylin's gaze was all but riveted to the Consort's, and the Consort didn't blink.

"From a closet in this way station?" she finally asked.

Kaylin hated the color of her eyes. She'd spent seven years—more, really—telling anyone who would listen that she didn't care what other people thought of her. She'd all but shouted it from the rooftops in the first few months; she'd certainly made it clear to any poor sod who'd listen for more than five minutes.

She almost never said it now, because the truth was she did care. She didn't care about the opinion of random strangers she didn't know and would likely never see again. That part was true. But she did care what Marcus thought. Or Teela, or Tain. Or Caitlin.

And she did, clearly, care about the Consort's opinion. She didn't want this woman to dislike her. But she didn't regret the decision that had caused the Consort's anger, either. It was not high on the list of things she'd travel into the past to change; it was nowhere close.

"Lord Kaylin?"

"Yes. From a closet—I call it a closet because to me, that's what it looked like—in this way station. This morning." She hesitated, because the Consort was angry and she didn't want to make it worse. Kaylin now examined the dress with minute attention to detail. But it was a dress. It had none of the beading and none of the lace—certainly none of the boning—that human Court dresses generally boasted. Its hem skirted the edge of the boots that matched its color, but there was no obvious train, nothing to trip over if she were to be forced to run at an all-out sprint. The sleeves dripped toward the skirt's hem, and they would cause problems in a fight, but they didn't restrict the movement of her arms, either.

There wasn't much in the way of gold thread, or silver; it was, excepting only the adjoined, diamond-shaped holes, a fairly simple dress. Teela's current dress was more complicated; the Consort's was certainly more regal, and in any case, both women naturally looked stunning, a state Kaylin felt no need to achieve because it was impossible.

The Consort smiled. It wasn't friendly, but it wasn't smug, either. She nodded and added, "Join us, Lord Kaylin," in a tone of voice that caused the man to her right to move. He moved, on the other hand, exactly one seat over, which left no room for Severn. Severn, whose eyes did not shift color when he was angry.

But she recognized a command when she heard it, and she headed toward the seat that had been vacated for her use. She drew eyes as she walked the length of the curving oval table to reach it, too.

"Why did you choose to wear the dress?" the Consort asked as Kaylin sat.

She stopped herself from shrugging. "The way station seems to have a mind of its own. I thought it meant me to wear the dress because the dresses I did have weren't appropriate. Somehow." The fact that the way station had probably been built by Barrani should have been a clue. "Can I ask why—or how—the dress was a mistake?"

One pale brow rose. "It is unlikely to be a mistake on the part of the way station," was the Consort's eventual reply. "But none of our kin would have worn that dress assuming it was insignificant."

"Most of the Lords are male."

"Ah, yes. But what would be offered to a male would be different in form; the cloth would be the same."

"I'll leave it here."

"I rather think that a poor idea, Lord Kaylin; you are, of course, free to make the attempt."

She wanted desperately to talk to Teela, who was down the other side of the table and whose eyes were about as blue as the Consort's. Since talking to Teela wasn't in the cards, she ate. She wasn't certain what she was eating—some of it had the texture of mushrooms. It wasn't her favorite texture, but there was very little food she wouldn't eat if it was placed in front of her. There was a golden liquid that seemed too pale and too delicate to be ale or apple juice; she stuck with water, instead. But she tried, as she ate, to use the multiple utensils on either side of her plate in exactly the way Tara had taught her.

Eating beside the Consort wasn't as grueling as eating in front of Diarmat would have been. She told herself this several times. The Consort did not speak to her again, although she wasn't obvious about her silence. She spoke very little to the man on her left, either, concentrating on her food, although that concentration didn't actually involve eating any of it.

When the bells started to chime—and they sounded like wind chimes, to Kaylin's ears—the Consort rose in silence. She left the table—no one else did—and headed toward the wide, flat set of stairs that led to the arches surrounding the lower hall.

One of the arches moved forward, as if to greet her. As it did, it grew taller and wider, its peak flattening as its frame expanded. The slightly shadowed interior of the arch also shifted, tearing as Kaylin watched. Beyond it lay the very different shadows of forest in daylight. The Consort didn't step into the forest, though; instead, she placed both hands on the left and right sides of the frame, which required her to extend her slender arms to their full length.

Light spread from the palms of her hands and traveled up toward the peak of the arch, where it shone like a diamond, cold and hard. She spoke three long words, and they were words, although they each contained enough syllables for a paragraph. Kaylin didn't understand them, but at the same time, she knew they meant gratitude. Complicated, complex Barrani gratitude.

The light was like starlight brought close and made personal. No one seated in the hall spoke a word; it was so silent, Kaylin wondered if they'd forgotten to breathe as well or if breathing was somehow a breach of etiquette. They remained seated, which confounded the rules of rising-as-respect that had been demanded by Diarmat—even though, in theory, much of the torturous etiquette arose from the Barrani.

While the light at the height of the arch burned at its brightest, the Consort lowered her arms, drew her hands to her side, and left the building. Only when she'd completely passed beneath the standing stone did the rest of the Court rise to join her, relaxing as they followed.

Severn was the first to join Kaylin as she rose. She wasn't above palming some of the food, although she didn't shove it into the long, deep pockets—the practical pockets—of the dress.

"Remind me," she said as she fell into step at his side, "to ignore advice from silent closets in the future."

When he failed to reply, she turned her head to catch a glimpse of his expression; it was grim.

"Kitling," a familiar and distinctly female voice said. "I honestly cannot take you anywhere." Teela slid a hand onto Kaylin's shoulder; the small dragon hissed.

"Is everyone just leaving?" Kaylin asked, because it seemed as though everyone was doing exactly that. "Some of my stuff is still in my room."

"It won't be," Teela replied. "The way stations open—and close—in a very particular way, and on the rare, rare occasions mortals have chanced upon them, they often wake beneath the trees from a very unusual…dream."

"Are they all like this?"

"No. Some of them are actually interesting."

Kaylin turned to stare at Teela, but it was impossible to tell whether she meant this as a joke. "I can't leave in this dress."

"You will find that materially inaccurate," Teela replied. "I do think the boots are a nice touch."

They were at the tail end of a loosely formed line, which dwindled as the Lords of the Barrani Court passed beneath the arch. "If you could stop mocking me—for just a few minutes—and tell me what's special about this dress, I'd really appreciate it."

"It's the fabric. We call it the blood of the green." She let go of Kaylin's shoulder and approached the standing arch. "I will go ahead. Corporal Handred, I suggest you do likewise."

"Why, exactly?"

"You will understand shortly. Don't worry, kitling," she added in Elantran. "It's highly unlikely that you will be detained, and if you are, the Consort will no doubt bespeak the way station to negotiate your release."

"I wouldn't bet on it."

CHAPTER 14

Severn didn't want to exit the way station before Kaylin did. Teela all but insisted, and while that usually worked in the office, Kaylin could practically see Severn digging his heels in.

"Teela, does it matter?"

"It is a precaution, nothing more." Teela's eyes were blue.

"For his sake or mine?"

"For his."

Which pretty much settled that, except for the glaring and a few more chilly words on Teela's part. She departed first, her stride a little on the long side.

Which left Kaylin and Severn alone in the hall. "Was he here?" she asked quietly.

Severn glanced at her. After a long moment, he shook his head.

"Neither was Nightshade."

"You looked?"

"I don't have to. He wasn't in the way station last night."

Severn nodded. "It's unlikely that the Arcanist would stop here. We're still within the boundaries of the Empire. If he is wary—and he must be—he will not leave much of a trail until we are closer to the West March itself."

"Nightshade—"

"Nightshade is different. The Arcanist is wanted by the Emperor, for crimes against the Empire. He is not, yet, Outcaste. Nightshade was made Outcaste by the current High Lord's father. It is a judgment that crosses boundaries."

"He lives in the fiefs, which are at the heart of the same city as the High Halls."

"Yes. But the concept of treachery to the race isn't entrenched in the Barrani Caste Court in the same way it is in the Dragon Court. A Barrani can be made Outcaste by subtle political maneuvering. It's not unlike assassination. A Dragon? No."

"You think he'll come out into the open in the West March?"

Severn frowned. "I don't know. The Consort is waiting," he added, changing the subject.

"I'd like to be able to leave the way I arrived," Kaylin told him, staring up at the light. "Is that what you did?"

"I didn't travel with the Consort, the High Lord, or the Lord of the West March," he replied. It was evasive, and he knew it.

"So you didn't have this whole leave-taking ceremony."

"No. But I didn't stay at this way station, and given the rest of the Court, it's probably wisest to follow."

"I'm not sure I like the light."

Severn nodded. "I know." Smiling, he offered her his arm; she slid a hand over the top of his wrist and they both took a step forward. The small dragon's head was higher than hers; if Kaylin didn't trust the light, he seemed fascinated by it. She raised her free hand and clamped it firmly over his body. He hissed.

"Sorry," she told him. "I can't afford to have you eat that." She suddenly felt certain this was both a possibility and a danger, and she walked more quickly toward ostensible freedom.

When her foot touched forest floor on one side, the light suddenly fell, as if it had weight and substance. It struck her head that way as well, and she let loose a couple of indiscreet Leontine words; both of her hands were occupied.

Before she could let go of either Severn or the small dragon, Severn caught her around the waist and pulled her the rest of the way through.

After the initial pain of the impact, she felt a sudden rush of heat; she hoped it wasn't blood and lifted her hand to the crown of her skull. The pain was gone. What remained was warmth, and the warmth flowed into her hand and down her arm, traveling as if it were corporeal. It almost was; she could see silver light surround her arm as it traveled.

The dress absorbed it as if it was liquid; Kaylin's skin absorbed it, as well. She felt the marks on her arms begin to react; they became warmer. They were only partially hidden by the fall of green cloth, and she could see they now shone a pale, pale gold.

Teela was waiting, her eyes a sapphire-blue. The rest of the Court was waiting, as well.

"So," the Lady said.

The green dress had not disappeared with the way station. Kaylin's pack and bedroll were on the ground beneath the bowers of the nearest tree, beside Severn's. She shook herself and headed toward them.

Andellen was about as happy as Teela, which made the first hour of the carriage ride pretty chilly. Not that it wasn't a little chilly to begin with; it was only barely dawn, and the color of the sky—absent the City skyline—was one Kaylin generally experienced on the long, hard shifts of the emergency midwives' calls. She drew the cape that had accompanied the dress more tightly around her shoulders, surprised at just how much fabric there was. It wasn't wool, it wasn't oiled, and it wasn't particularly heavy, but it was warm nonetheless.

"Teela, your face is going to crack if you don't say something soon."

"My apologies, Lord Kaylin."

Ugh. Barrani moods could be unpleasant and unpredictable, but Kaylin knew this one. She turned to Andellen instead. "Lord Andellen." Trammeled by High Barrani, she clenched her jaws briefly before she continued. "Does the dress have significance for you, as well?"

"It does. I am a Lord of the High Court, and my name is my own."

"You've seen it before."

"I have seen the blood of the green once before."

"When you went on your pilgrimage to the West March?"

"On one of them, yes."

"Why is it significant? Does it have something to do with the regalia?"

He turned to stare out the carriage windows. "You will have to discuss this with my Lord," he finally said, failing to look at her as he spoke.

No one liked to think of themselves as the person so uncomfortable with silence they babbled just to stop their nerves, especially not Kaylin, whose ability to make small talk was notable by its absence. But the tenor of this particular silence was better suited to rival gangs sizing each other up before the daggers came out than a carriage. It was better suited to a corpse than a carriage.

"I don't care if you speak nothing but Leontine for the next three hours, Teela," Kaylin said. "Tell me what you think I've done wrong. Taking Nightshade's offer of information to Marcus doesn't count. The Hawks needed that. You know we did."

"It's my considered opinion that the presence of Bellusdeo would have put an end to the worst of the difficulties," was her clipped—and eventual—reply.

"That's hindsight. We didn't know the would-be assassin was also involved with the embezzlement."

"It is." Teela lifted a delicate hand to her brow and massaged her forehead. "You will etch permanent wrinkles in my face in spite of my immortality," she said. "Let me give you some advice. In the future, if you see unfamiliar clothing in a strange—and possibly dangerous—environment, do not put it on."

"I won't. But can we talk about the present instead of the future?"

"At this point, I'd rather hear your endless litany of complaint about Margot or Mallory, a situation I would have sworn impossible." Her tone was sharp, but her eyes had lost the worst of the blue. They weren't green, but in the right light, Kaylin could now pretend they were. "There are decades in which those robes, or in this case that dress, are not seen."

Kaylin frowned. "Have you ever worn this dress?"

Andellen glanced at Teela.

Teela said, "No."

"You're lying."

"I frequently do. Why do you assume I am doing so now?"

Since the reason was Andellen, a man reinstated to the High Court only for the length of Kaylin's remaining life, Kaylin said nothing. Andellen's expression stiffened, and he once again turned his gaze toward the landscape passing by the carriage window. It was a controlled, stiff movement.

"Doesn't matter. What happened when you wore this dress?"

Teela turned to Severn. "Corporal, I suggest you distract her."

"Fine. I'll change the subject." Kaylin surrendered. "Who made the way stations?"

Andellen's lips twisted in what Kaylin assumed was a grimace. It wasn't. He was trying not to laugh. "My apologies, Lord Kaylin," he said when she glared. "As an attempt to change the subject, it would be considered poor."

"I am reminding myself," Teela added, "that I was sent here to preserve your life. It is remarkably difficult at this specific moment."

The small dragon hissed and spread his wings.

"Oh, please," Teela snapped. "You are only slightly more terrifying than a difficult cat."

Kaylin reached up and loosely clamped her palm over the small dragon's jaws. "Does wearing this dress mean I'm supposed to do something when we reach the West March?"

Teela exhaled heavily.

"Wait—were the Lords present hoping that one of them would be wearing it instead?"

"Very good. The blood of the green by no means appears every time the regalia is recited. It's considered a significant event when it does." As Kaylin opened her mouth, Teela lifted one hand. "If you ask whether or not you can pass the dress on, I swear I will hit you. But yes, kitling, the Lords who have chosen to undertake this journey now have another reason to resent the fact that you're breathing.

"Honestly, if I'd realized how much of a pain this was going to be, I would have let Marcus rip out your throat and be done with it."

"We needed the information Nightshade gave us."

"Yes. And if Nightshade weren't a fieflord, I would seriously consider killing him myself."

Andellen, who rarely spoke Elantran, nonetheless stiffened.

"It's mostly Nightshade I'm angry at," Teela continued. "This is just his kind of game. If I didn't know better—and sadly, I do—I would say that he somehow arranged for you to have this dress." Her eyes narrowed. "Have you spoken with him at all since we left the City?"

"No."

"Good. I can't forbid it, but if I could, I would. The recitation is largely ritual, but Kaylin, as an unusual hanger-on, you'd be tolerated. You're Chosen; you bear the marks. But this? This is almost too much." Teela fell silent. Kaylin tried to find the value in awkward silence, and the carriage continued to roll.

By the time the carriage came to a halt, Andellen knew quite a bit more about the Hawks' office politics—and office gossip—than any Barrani who hadn't taken the Oath of Service. He knew more about the pragmatic approach to the application of the laws as well, although given he was Barrani, that would probably come naturally to him, regardless. He also learned about the midwives, Marrin of the Foundling Hall, and Evanton.

Evanton interested him, but any substantive question he asked was interrupted by Teela. If this bothered Andellen, it didn't show. He was remarkably calm and accepting for a Barrani of any stripe; had he been Tain, the two would probably have come to blows by this point, although daggers would be another few hours away.

The sun set; the moons rose. There was enough light to see by, an indication that the skies were relatively clear. There had been two stops, both brief and both meant, as far as Kaylin could tell, to give relief to the horses that drew the carriages. Those horses were, compared to the normal horses that drew cabs in the City's streets, what the Barrani were to the mortals who also walked the same streets. She found them intimidating.

Then again, she found the horses that pulled the mail wagons intimidating. It was their size. Treating something that big as if it were a well-trained dog was outside Kaylin's skill set. She thought the horses beautiful, in a sweaty, muscular way, but only at a distance. Severn didn't have that problem.

On the second of the breaks, Lord Evarrim approached Kaylin. Teela, annoyed, was nonetheless there to run immediate interference.

Evarrim, however, smiled affectionately at his cousin, tendered Kaylin a very deep bow, and rose. "Lord Kaylin." His smile was pleasant; it appeared to be friendly. There'd been an absence of friendly smiles for the entirety of the day, which made his seem even more attractive—but in truth, not by much.

"Lord Evarrim." She returned his bow and, when she rose, saw his brows had risen slightly.

"Your Court form, Lord Kaylin, has greatly improved and in such a short time." A friendly smile did not prevent the usual condescension.

The small dragon had sunk claws into every part of Kaylin's body where his paws were attached. He was rigid, and his little wings were high. Evarrim noticed, of course. His eyes frequently slid off Kaylin's face to rest a few inches to the side.

"I mean no harm to your master," Evarrim told the small dragon. "I merely came to offer her both my respect and my congratulations."

"Thank you. They are appreciated entirely in the spirit with which they are offered."

He raised a brow again and his smile deepened. "An'Teela, it is a pity your *kyuthe* is mortal. In a century or two, she might truly find her way in the Court otherwise." He nodded; the nod contained less grace and more regard than the much more formal bow. "It is auspicious, Lord Kaylin. Very seldom have the stars begun their alignment so far from the West March."

She glanced at Teela.

"Or perhaps you are not aware of all of the customs." The smile that now adorned his lips was the usual, edged affair.

"I could never claim to be cognizant of all of the customs of the High Court," was Kaylin's pleasant reply. Curiosity warred with dislike; they were pretty evenly matched. Dislike won, but it was close.

"No, indeed. Very few of our kin could make that claim, and many of our kin have no pretensions; they are not now, and will never be, Lords of this Court. But you, my dear, are."

"Never is a long time, given Barrani live forever."

"You are aware of the risks one takes when one wishes to assume position within the High Court."

She was. It was, in all but one case, an all-or-nothing proposition, where all was eternity and nothing was the usual death and hells. She nodded.

"It was a test that you were not, ultimately, forced to take."

"I did."

"You live, Lord Kaylin, regardless of your name; you are mortal, and yet a Lord of the High Court. It was not unexpected to those who know the marks you bear. And perhaps it should not have been unexpected that you would be chosen as the harmoniste, given those selfsame marks. Perhaps," he added softly, "it was even known. You are here now. You wear the blood of the green, and you have already been granted one of the illuminations." As he spoke, his eyes once again fastened themselves to the left of her cheek, where the small dragon sat rigid and glaring. "And, of course, you carry a creature that the entire Arcanum finds fascinating. We shall have to hope that you bear up under the weight of the several responsibilities you now carry."

The small dragon hissed; she raised her right hand and clamped it over his jaws. Seeing this, Evarrim's eyes shaded to a darker blue. Teela was almost standing between them, and if that wasn't enough of a hint, Severn came to stand by her side, his left hand hooked prominently into the links of his weapon chain.

Andellen, however, chose to observe in silence.

"It is far too late to treat her as a child, An'Teela," Evarrim said, his voice dropping several degrees.

Teela said nothing, but she didn't move until Evarrim bowed again, turned, and walked away.

"What," Kaylin asked in a voice as quiet as she could, "is a harmoniste? I can guess what the illuminations are, in the context of this morning."

"It's a word," Teela replied curtly. "In other contexts, it's a pretentious word," she continued after a pause in which she chose to slide into Elantran.

"Which contexts?"

"In music, it is a word with softer verbal edges than *composer.*"

"The only thing I know about music is what I like."

"The same could be said of your knowledge of food," Teela replied, pursing her lips. "I have mentioned that if Nightshade does magically appear, I am likely to attempt to kill him myself?"

"A time or two."

"Good. I should not like to take you by surprise."

"Harmoniste?" Kaylin prodded.

"There is another use for the word."

"Clearly."

One black brow arched at the tone of Kaylin's voice. "It involves the harmonization of parallel tracks of text or narratives."

"Words."

"Words, yes."

"Teela—"

"The role of the harmoniste is not always required, nor do we know before we leave the City itself and begin our trek to the West March. We have no say in the choice of harmoniste and no way of assigning the responsibility. We have no way of revoking it, either."

"Teela—"

"Your job is easily explained, but not easily done. When the recitation begins, you will hear words. Given it's you," she added with a very unladylike snort, "you'll probably see them. I have no idea whether visualization will make that job any easier." She lifted a hand as Kaylin opened her mouth again. "While I realize you have the characteristic impatience of the mortal, I am not, in fact, taking ten years to get to the point. The call to gather the horses has just gone out."

Kaylin had not heard a sound.

"And we will therefore be milling here for some tens of minutes yet. Learn patience."

Kaylin swallowed. The small dragon slowly settled back onto her shoulders.

"If you were to do your job with written words, you might have the time to note, consider, and think about it."

"Teela, what is my job?"

"It is simply to listen to the disparate threads of the recitation and draw them together into as cohesive a narrative whole as you can."

Kaylin thought she was about to lose her brows to the skyline, her eyes widened so quickly. "I won't even understand what the words mean!"

"No."

"I'm supposed to be able to tell how separate parts of a story I don't understand can be somehow worked into one story?"

"Crudely put, but yes, Kaylin." Her eyes had dimmed to a color that could pass for green in the low light. "Before you begin to panic—"

"Too late."

"Before you begin to panic more, consider this carefully. You've heard Lord Sanabalis tell the tale of the Leontines. You didn't understand the words he spoke—but, kitling, you did. You couldn't translate them as he spoke them, but when he had finished, you knew the story of the Leontines, both their creation and their corruption. I am not worried about your abilities in this regard."

"But?"

"I am very concerned about the illumination."

Kaylin fell silent, although she had no intention of letting the silence last. "You wore the blood of the green when you went to the West March the first time."

"No, Kaylin, I did not."

"But you said—"

"If I recall correctly, I said that I've never worn that dress. You did not choose to believe me."

"Because you were lying."

"But regardless, I did not wear that dress when I first arrived in the West March; when I first arrived in the West March, I was not a Lord of the High Court. I did not control my family's lands, and I was not considered the heir, in the unlikely event of the death of my father." Gazing deliberately toward the carriages that were beginning to line up, she continued. "I was young then."

Kaylin frowned. "Teela…"

"Yes?"

"How old are you?"

Teela glanced at Andellen. "I was under the impression that question was considered rude."

"Only if I'm asking it of a mortal, which you're not."

"I am older than Lord Andellen," she replied.

"Older than Tain?"

"Yes."

"Did you— Were you brought here as a child to listen to the regalia?" Kaylin's voice had dropped and her words had slowed as she'd asked. She remembered hearing that there was a reason that the recitation of the regalia to children was no longer permitted. And she remembered that the Barrani had tried to use the regalia as a method of empowering the race by altering children they had been willing to use as experimental subjects.

"Kaylin," Severn said before Teela could answer. "The carriages are ready." He caught her elbow and tugged it, and she followed, stumbling as she turned to look over her shoulder at Teela's back.

Teela didn't join them in the carriage for the last leg of the journey. The ride was silent, but the silence wasn't awkward in the same way, and it was a silence that Kaylin therefore felt no need to fill. It descended as she considered Teela as a child—itself an almost impossible task, given Kaylin had never seen a Barrani child and couldn't imagine one—in a carriage like this one, heading toward the West March to listen to a story that might literally remake her. Nightshade hadn't given Kaylin any details, but his tone and his expression had made clear that the cost—to those children—had been high.

But…Teela was Teela. She was a Lord of the High Court.

She had her followers, her guards, and a position in the Court that implied she was respected, even if she had chosen to go slumming with the Hawks. No one expected her stay in the Halls of Law to last, or at least, no Barrani did. Maybe not all of the children had been harmed or transformed?

Kaylin wondered if Teela was contemplating memories of a time when she had been helpless, when her life had been under someone else's control and her fate had been a matter of whim.

It was unsettling.

No, Kaylin thought, fidgeting, it was worse. Teela was not a person to whom anyone could offer comfort. Not if they wanted to live.

"Lord Kaylin."

She looked up at Andellen.

"Lord An'Teela will be, in mortal terms, all right. This is not the first time that she's traveled to the West March; it is unlikely to be the last. If past experiences trouble her, they do not stop her. When she came to the West March as a Lord of the Court, she wore the blood of the green, as you wear it now. She arrived in a position of strength, and she fulfilled the duties demanded of her."

"Was there any other option?"

"Yes. She could have failed."

Kaylin fell silent.

Severn took up the slack. "What would the consequences of failure have been, in that case?"

Andellen now fixed his glance out the window, which seemed to be a very common Barrani pose while riding in a carriage, at least given the trip so far. "Understand," he began, which couldn't be considered promising, "that the punishment is not meted out by the High Court. It is not a consequence of failure to obey a Lord's command. If there is a mechanism by which the harmoniste is chosen, it is one beyond the comprehension of the majority of the High Court. Given the prestige and the perceived power granted to those who assume this role, believe that attempts at discovery have been made throughout our history."

"That's not an answer," Severn replied. If human eye color changed, his would be analogous to Barrani-blue at the moment.

"No. I was never chosen. My experience is therefore based on very limited observation and hearsay."

"Understood."

"The task set the harmoniste varies in difficulty and complexity."

Kaylin lifted a hand; Severn glanced at her. Andellen, however, continued to stare at what passed for road in the moonlight. "How can it vary? The regalia is supposed to be a true story, in the sense that it involves True Words. It is, or can be, transformative."

Andellen nodded. "That much is correct. The regalia, however, is not a single story. I believe, if you ask, my Lord will tell you that the recitation involves stories, a plurality of stories."

Kaylin nodded.

"Those stories are not one thing, Lord Kaylin. They are not a single narrative."

"That's what I'm supposed to do, isn't it?"

He raised a brow as he finally turned to meet her gaze. "No. Not in that sense. When the recitation begins, the gathered Lords listen until it is done."

Probably without fidgeting, which Kaylin was doing right now, even though she was deeply interested in the subject matter. "Who tells the story?"

"Generally? The Lord of the West March."

"So he chooses which of the stories are told to the gathered Lords?"

"No."

She blinked. "He's telling the story, somehow, and he doesn't choose?"

"That is correct. You will understand when you yourself are audience to the tale."

"I'll probably be a bit distracted."

Andellen did not smile. "Not even you could be so distracted that you fail to see what occurs. If the Lord of the West March did, indeed, choose, there are tales for which he would not have survived the telling. He does not choose."

"Why the Lord of the West March?"

"Because he is the Lord of the West March; it is for that reason, and no other, that the Barrani hold the West March tightly. It has never fallen to an outside force, be that force as great as the three Flights of the Dragons. It is not simply a title, Kaylin."

"So he doesn't choose. Given that I'm now the harmoniste, I guess that makes sense. Which means no one knows what story they'll hear when they arrive."

"Indeed."

"If the story is the wrong story—"

"'Wrong' is a very subjective word. But some stories are longer in the telling—in all ways—than others, and they press a weight upon the Teller, and a burden upon the harmoniste. It is not often that the harmoniste fails," he added softly. "But when they fail, it is because the burden of disparate stories is too great; they cannot contain, or perhaps find, the meaning that informs each. They have no way of forcing the stories to overlap, and instead of a complex, complicated, and cohesive narrative, they are left with chaos and disorder."

"It drives them insane?"

Andellen was silent for a long moment. "No," he finally said. "I think in your case, that is all we have to fear, but I am not entirely certain. Understand, Chosen, that I, Lord Teela, and every other Barrani here, are alive solely because of the existence of True Words. The harmoniste, in their role, must understand what is being said on a level that is more visceral than mere linguistics. They must somehow hold the thread not of a single word that grants life but of the equivalent of pages. Those pages will come to them all at once, and if they falter, their name is swept away when the words leave."

CHAPTER 15

The way station of the evening was not part of a tree. It was, instead, part of a cliff—the bottom part. She saw this because she was almost hanging out the window at the time.

In the night, with moonlight silvering the forested land, the cliff was a solid sheet of black. Light appeared only when the carriages at the head of the long caravan came to a stop and their passengers sought breeze and open sky.

"Do you recognize this one?" Kaylin asked when she was allowed the same freedom.

Severn nodded.

"Is it a lot like the tree?"

"Very like, although the interior is architecturally different."

"Does this mean we're no longer in the Empire?"

Andellen coughed.

Severn raised a brow. "No. I have a map if you want to look at it. We won't be outside the Empire for at least a week."

"A week of days this long?"

"Yes. The Barrani carriages are superior in all ways to

the carriages or caravans we would otherwise use, but heavy rains still slow them down."

Kaylin hung back when it came time to enter the way station; she'd seen what the dragon on her shoulder had done once, and she wanted to make sure that no one else did. The Barrani approached the cliff face, touched the rock as if it were a warded door, and then stepped forward into nothing. They did this in a line that started with—that waited for—the Consort and continued until only a handful of the Lords of the Court were left. There had been some subtle jockeying for position, but in truth not much.

When most of the line had dispersed, Kaylin began a slow walk toward the cliff's face. Teela was there, waiting. Andellen was not. Neither, to Kaylin's relief, was Evarrim. Teela, on the other hand, looked less grim; she even smiled when Kaylin approached.

"Sorry about the morning," she said in Elantran. "I'm feeling a bit cooped up, so I wanted a change of pace."

"Walking?"

The Barrani Hawk lifted both brows. "Walking? Me? Hells, no. I was driving. And I was in a foul enough mood that I decided against driving the carriage you were in—you complain too much."

"Teela—"

"Have you ever heard a Barrani complain about my driving?"

"…No."

"Well, then." She glanced at the stone face of the cliff. "Are you going to enter, or are you going to stand here all night?"

"Given this morning, I'm thinking of camping in the tent."

"Oh, I'm certain the wildlife would love that." Teela folded her arms and leaned against the stone's surface. She also raised an eyebrow. Severn stepped into the gap that followed; he placed his palm against the cliff face. He didn't bother to cut it first.

"I'll see you on the other side," he told her.

"Coward."

That got a smile, but it didn't keep him on the Kaylin side of the door. He walked through the stone, which rippled only slightly in his wake. This left Kaylin standing beside a lounging Teela. Teela no longer looked angry, which was good; she looked bored, which was bad.

"Why don't you go on ahead?" Kaylin asked without much hope.

"Given the previous way station, I'll wait."

Kaylin lifted her left hand—she always touched door wards with her left, because it was her off hand—and pressed it firmly into the stone. The stone was cool to the touch, smooth and hard. Her arms did not start tingling the way they usually did when magic was involved; her hand didn't go numb. But the rock didn't part, either. She glanced at Teela. In the dim light that surrounded the door, her eyes were a mix of green and blue.

Surrendering, Kaylin nudged the small dragon's head with the tip of her chin. "Go on," she told him softly. "Unless you're going to be reasonable about me spilling my own blood."

The dragon peeled himself off her shoulders and rose in a lazy swirl of wings. Hovering in front of the stone, he opened his delicate jaws. He bit the rock.

Since Kaylin was now expecting it, she observed him carefully. The rock was more or less flat, and it was certainly hard enough that biting it should have caused the dragon serious difficulty. But his nose seemed to dip beneath the surface that Kaylin's hand couldn't penetrate, and as he closed his teeth, it seemed to grow amorphous, almost cloudlike. It was too much to hope that Teela hadn't noticed, but ever the optimist, Kaylin glanced at her fellow Hawk. Teela was watching the dragon, and only the dragon.

He came back to Kaylin's shoulders and wrapped his tail loosely around her neck. Taking a deep breath, Kaylin entered the way station.

Stepping through the way station's door was not unlike stepping between the giant statues that served as both pillars and warnings outside the High Halls in the City of Elantra. The ceilings were, in her opinion, of a height with the ceilings of the High Halls, but these halls looked far grander because they were wider, the floors laid out in a smoky-green marble that caught light and returned random flecks of color. A small army would be dwarfed by these halls.

She took a step forward and was surprised that it didn't echo.

Teela's, however, did. "The door, you'll be pleased to note, has not been broken by the interference of your pet."

"Pardon?"

"I could not enter without touching the door myself."

"But not bleeding on it."

"Not this time, no. I have been here before. So, apparently, has Corporal Handred." Her eyes, in the much brighter light of the way station, were a deep emerald.

Teela slung an arm around Kaylin's shoulder, which caused the dragon to hiss in outrage, because he happened to be on most of it. She moved her arm a bit, but didn't let go. "Kitling, you honestly need to find less territorial friends."

"You could lead by example."

Teela snorted. "I'm Barrani. Don't ask for miracles."

They began to walk down the hall. If the first one had seemed long, this one seemed endless. Kaylin could jog here and keep in top shape without ever hitting a door. "You're not angry?"

"No. I'm impressed." With Barrani there was often no practical difference. "I would never have surrendered my blood to the station if it were not absolutely necessary to enter it."

"You're not worried?"

"I am, of course, worried, but I reminded myself on the drive here that you've been nothing but a constant worry since you were a child."

"I wasn't a child when we met, Teela."

"Oh, hush."

Because no argument had delayed her—and Kaylin wondered if the delay was the reason Teela had stayed behind—they reached the dining hall very shortly after everyone else had. The tree station, as Kaylin now thought of it, had contained rounded rooms, rounded arches, rounded ceilings; even the table had been a large oval.

The cliff station was not given to such indistinct lines; everything was hard, solid, and squared. The table itself was—to Kaylin's eye—one giant slab of coal-gray stone. It gleamed beneath lights that were bright and well-defined; they were much harsher than the lights of the tree station. The chairs were actually benches—of stone, of course. But the table was wide, and cloths of different colors had been laid across its center. So had food.

Kaylin wondered how the food had gotten there, who had prepared it, and how they were paid, because that was the kind of thing she wondered about the Barrani. If it was all done by magic, it was a magic she wanted to own, especially if the magic also involved the cleanup. But at the moment, none of the impressive-looking food had been touched. None of the Barrani High Court had taken their seats; indeed none of them seemed interested in the food. Kaylin was, but the sight of a room full of Barrani—even a room this size, because it was huge—most of whose backs were turned toward her, implied that hunger was trivial.

"Teela?" she whispered, because Teela was still attached to her shoulders.

Teela had become as still as the rest of the Barrani.

"What's happened?"

She glanced at the Barrani Hawk and saw that her eyes had darkened to a shade of blue that suited midnight. In the absence of an answer, Kaylin started to try to wind her way through the crowd, but Teela's arm—and hand—tightened.

And then she heard a familiar voice and froze herself.

"Welcome, Lord Kaylin."

It was Nightshade's.

At the mention of her name, the Barrani Lords nearest to the back of the room swiveled to face her. Their eyes were a uniform blue that was not quite as dark as Teela's.

"Lord Severn, I see you have chosen to accompany Lord Kaylin." She still couldn't see him, but his voice had hardened, the way water did when frozen. Kaylin glanced briefly at the High Court; no one seemed to have drawn a sword, and the Consort had not yet ordered Nightshade's immediate death. He was Outcaste. Kaylin's understanding of the Barrani High Court would never be considered complete, but she would have bet her own money that an Outcaste Barrani was subject to the death penalty if he was foolish enough to set foot anywhere near the ruling class of his race.

Nightshade wasn't just near it; he was at its heart. She heard his steps. As he seemed to be the only person walking, it wasn't hard.

But she heard the way Teela drew breath when he at last

walked into view. She felt Teela's grip tighten, and at this point, it was likely to leave a couple of bruises. Since bruising and Teela's company weren't strangers—or at least Kaylin being bruised—she barely noticed.

Nightshade was dressed in flowing ivory robes, but those robes were edged in a blue that defied Kaylin's description. It wasn't dark, but it wasn't pale, like sky; it wasn't green, but it didn't shade into the purple. Instead, it seemed to encompass all these things. As he drew closer, she realized that the ivory was, like the blue, not entirely fixed; it was white, it was cream, it was a range of shades simultaneously.

He wore a tiara. She couldn't recall seeing it before and, regardless, didn't like it—it reminded her too much of Evarrim's, although the stone that hunkered in its peaked center was not a ruby. It was…an emerald. It was an emerald that Barrani eyes seldom approached, the green was so deep and so pure, and even Kaylin, who owned very little in the way of jewelry, knew it was worth a small fortune—where *small* in this case probably covered the whole of the block she'd lived on until an Arcanist had decided to play.

Nightshade was smiling broadly; he was, as far as Kaylin could see, the only Barrani present who was. Even Andellen, whose face she caught in the crowd, had turned a shade of white that was pale, for Barrani skin. His hands were in fists. The mark on Kaylin's cheek was warm; she automatically lifted a hand to cover it.

Nightshade approached and gently caught that hand and lowered it.

Teela said nothing, but the temperature dropped anyway, and she didn't let go of Kaylin's shoulders. But Nightshade's moment of elegant smugness was ruined when the small dragon on Kaylin's shoulder lifted his head—and his wings—and faced the fieflord squarely. The small dragon hissed and his wings rose, but his claws dug in, as well. It was clear his opinion of Nightshade hadn't improved.

Given the color of Nightshade's eyes, neither had his opinion of the small dragon.

Clearing her throat, Kaylin said, "Why are you here?"

"I was summoned," he replied gracefully, choosing to look away from the small dragon as if he were inconsequential.

"Impossible." To Kaylin's surprise, the voice was Evarrim's.

"Demonstrably not, Lord Evarrim," Nightshade said, turning.

"You are Outcaste."

"The green does not choose to recognize the politics of the High Court." Nightshade tendered Lord Evarrim a deep, respectful bow. "Nor, apparently, do its many hearts."

Hearts?

These ancient fortresses, Kaylin. They are the hearts of the green; did you not know?

She shrugged her hand free of his, too aware of the feel of his skin. The Lords that surrounded them in a loose, tense circle moved slightly to allow the Consort to pass between them; she came to stand a yard away from Lord Nightshade, her expression unreadable.

"Ah," Nightshade said, "Lady." He did not bow, although he did incline his chin. A small ripple passed through the crowd, but no words—at least none that reached Kaylin's ears.

"Lord Nightshade." She paused and then added, "Calarnenne."

He smiled then, and he offered her a bow that was the essence of obeisance.

The Consort did not speak until he rose again, except to give him leave to rise. Kaylin tried not to feel a pang of resentment; clearly an Outcaste fieflord was granted a measure of respect that a Lord of the Court who was late for dinner was not. "You were summoned," she said, no question at all in the words.

"I was, Lady. I apologize if it causes you any inconvenience."

"It will, of course, cause a great deal of inconvenience, as you so put it. Does my brother know?"

"Given my status in the High Court, I felt it unwise to burden him with that information. He does not."

She glanced at Lord Andellen. "And your liege?"

"It did not concern him. I am Lord."

Around the two, Barrani Lords began to relax; no one, however, moved.

"And did Lord Kaylin know?"

"No, Lady."

"How strange, given your relationship. Lord Kaylin?"

"It never occurred to me that Lord Nightshade would appear here. Or anywhere else the Barrani High Court congregated. No, Lady. I had no idea."

"Do you understand why he is here?"

Gods damn it. "...No, Lady. Forgive my ignorance."

The Consort lifted one platinum brow. "Perhaps I shall," was her eventual response. To Lord Nightshade, however, she said, "You must be weary from your travel, Calarnenne. Join me." It was not a request.

Nightshade was not a Lord of the Court, but he nodded and bowed again. "With gratitude, Lady."

Kaylin, mouth slightly open, watched as Nightshade offered the Consort his arm. He led her through the crowd; given the height of the Barrani, she lost sight of them both fairly quickly.

"Teela, my arm is numb."

Severn, however, whispered her name, and she turned. "Nightshade's mark," he said softly. "It's glowing."

Great. "Does it at least match the dress?"

★★★

The Court now dispersed, but the anger and confusion that had stopped them in their tracks still conspired to rob them of many words. Kaylin understood why: the Consort had spoken; she had invited Nightshade to join her, and she had used the acceptable public form of his name. While she did not deny him, they could not, unless they wished to publicly place her in the wrong.

But they moved stiffly and without their characteristic elegant grace. Teela, on the other hand, didn't move at all.

"Teela," Kaylin repeated. "My arm. Numb."

Teela glanced, with blue eyes, at Kaylin's face; the blue darkened into a shade that was almost indigo.

"Tell me. Why is he here, and why is no one trying to kill him?"

"The robes he wears," Teela replied, "are as significant to the West March as the dress you also wear."

"And the tiara?"

"It is also, as you surmise, significant. It is possibly more significant than the robes themselves. Or the dress."

"What does it mean?"

"Lord Andellen informed you that the Lord of the West March serves as the vessel for the regalia and its recitation."

Kaylin nodded.

"There have been exceptions."

"This is an exception?"

"Clearly." Teela slowly relaxed her grip. The small dragon had already lowered his wings, but his neck was now high, his head at a level with her cheek. He surveyed the moving crowd as if it could, at any instant, become an immediate threat. He was obviously smarter than he looked.

"Nightshade will recite the regalia?"

"No. The Lord of the West March will do that."

"I don't understand."

"No, you don't."

"Teela, would it kill you to explain something to me for once?"

Teela glanced at the table, where the seated Lords were now watching Kaylin with barely veiled curiosity—and hostility. "In this case, or at least in this context, I do not think it would work in your favor, no."

Kaylin exhaled and nodded. "Are we going to eat?"

"Yes. At the foot of the table." Teela began to walk, and Kaylin followed her like a badly drawn shadow. Severn joined them.

Teela did not relax at all during the meal. She also ate very little and drank nothing that didn't look like water. Her movements were minimal and deliberate, and her attention—her obvious attention—was given to any part of the room that didn't have Nightshade in it. Since the room was huge, and since Nightshade occupied one seat—albeit the one to the right of the Consort—this shouldn't have been hard. Apparently, it was.

Nightshade, however, spared no glance for Teela; he spoke with the Consort. She spoke with him. He might have been a favorite of the Court and its High Lord, given her expression and the texture of her laughter, which spanned the length of the stone table and filled the echoing heights of the dining room's ceiling. There was nothing fake in it; there was nothing glittering and constructed, either. The Consort appeared to be both relaxed and delighted. Kaylin recognized this; she'd seen both, in her time. Her time, however, had apparently passed, and eating very fine food between an utterly rigid Teela and a totally silent Severn emphasized the loss.

* * *

Dinner was awkward for Kaylin, but the rest of the High Court, excepting only Teela and Evarrim, took their cue from the Consort and slowly resumed their pleasant discussions. Which is to say, their discussions: Barrani could speak enchantingly and musically about the most torturous of murders. Wine, food, and water disappeared in large quantities as Kaylin watched. She did eat—she was hungry—but the food pretty much tasted like proverbial ash in her mouth. After the eating, no one excused themselves from the table; it wasn't the Foundling Hall, after all. Barrani Lords remained, some seated, some rising to drift between seats to enjoy the company of others of their kind.

Only when the Consort rose did that stop. People fell silent, again taking the whole of their social cue from her. Lord Nightshade rose with her and remained by her side. Kaylin paid attention because this hall had no obvious exits in a raised circle in the distance, unlike the previous hall. Or at least that's what she told herself. She rose when the Consort rose, as well. At one time, she might not have noticed.

The Consort bowed her head; white hair pooled down her shoulders and across her dress as she closed her eyes and lowered her chin. She lifted her hands until they were almost at the level of her chin; it looked as if she was praying, something the Barrani did not do. She spoke in a language Kaylin didn't understand, although it sounded very close to High Barrani. It was frustrating; Kaylin initially assumed she couldn't understand because she couldn't hear, and she listened intently, closing her own eyes in order to concentrate fully.

But what she did hear didn't resolve itself into any known words; the familiarity of the syllables failed to cohere in equally familiar ways. She knew that the Consort offered thanks. She could assume that those thanks were offered to the way station or to its guardian, whoever or whatever that was—but no name, no rank, no title returned on the tide of those syllables by the time they'd drawn to a close.

When the Consort again fell silent, she lifted her head, opened her eyes, and waited.

Kaylin's unasked question about the nature of exits from this particular hall was answered a few seconds later: the walls began to move. They didn't become ethereal or transparent—that would have been too quiet and far less dramatic. No, they moved as if they were part of some giant stone clockwork. It was not silent; the ground beneath Kaylin's feet trembled in a way that implied an earthquake without actually producing one.

But as sections of wall began to recede, pulled away in all directions by that loud, grinding mechanism, halls—or the outlines of halls—were revealed. The dining hall was bounded on all sides by floors that did not match what had moments ago been the interior; they were stone, but they were a pale stone, not quite alabaster but not any marble that Kaylin had ever seen. At the corners of the far end of the room, doors now appeared.

"What happens when you're not traveling with the Consort?" Kaylin asked Severn. She asked it quietly, waiting until most of the Barrani Lords had departed for those doors. They seemed to know which doors to take; Kaylin saw no trail of light on the floor to guide their feet.

"The hall never becomes enclosed."

"Why does it make a difference?"

"Perhaps," Teela said, "my ancestors had the same general patience with etiquette that you once had, and this was simply a method of enforcing correct behavior."

Something about the way this was said made Kaylin turn instantly. The Barrani Hawk was quiet for a long moment.

Then she shook herself. "I will adjourn to my room. I cannot believe it contains any surprise more unpleasant than the dining hall did—and if it does, I will be able to vent some of my growing frustration." She smiled as she said the last bit; it was a cold, hard smile.

"The Consort outranks everyone seated in this room," Severn said when Teela was gone.

Kaylin nodded.

"But absent the Consort, the ranks will settle out in a similar fashion. The Barrani do not travel in groups of equals; there are subtleties of lineage and birth order that govern all interactions."

"The Hawks—"

"The Hawks, and the Barrani who wear it, are outside of the Court paradigm. When the Consort is not present, Kaylin, the Barrani with the highest rank will take the head of the table. It is his—or her—duty to offer the plea to invoke the station's activities."

"Plea?"

"Yes. The Consort is graceful and even happy to perform this duty."

"Most Barrani would sooner cut off their own tongues."

Severn smiled. "Indeed. But they open and close the hall in a similar fashion, unless they wish to avoid the way station. At most times of the year, they do. The stations are not seen and are not invoked often; the loss of comfort is less galling than the brief loss of dignity."

"It's ritual," Kaylin pointed out as Severn began to walk toward the door farthest to the left. "How much dignity do they stand to lose?"

Severn shrugged. "They're Barrani, remember." Halfway down the hall, he continued. "No one can escape this hall without the permission of the ranking Lord—or Lady. If they wish to leave and the Lord does not agree, they have the option of attempting to kill the Lord and change, by his death, the balance of power. It is a very pretty jail."

And it was a jail, Kaylin thought, that had once housed a young Teela.

"There are very good reasons why that attempt is seldom made," he added. "The station enforces peace, even if that peace is Barrani by definition. Poison loses efficacy, if applied to drink or food." He spoke as if he was certain. She didn't doubt that he was.

"How do you know this stuff?"

"I was taught it."

"Yes, but by who?"

Severn's smile deepened. "You wouldn't know the man."

"Was he?"

"Was he what?"

"A man? Because I can't imagine anyone who's not a Barrani Lord would know any of this stuff. Except maybe Evanton. And Evanton doesn't travel."

"He was a Barrani Lord." After a pause, Severn added, "He was also a Wolf."

There were no lights in this hall, no subtle path to guide the two Hawks as they reached the door. The door opened into a hall that was easily wide enough to accommodate dragons in their flight form. It was also tall enough. It was, however, very fine. Although the walls were of stone and the floor of cold marble, there were veins of gold in the pillars that rose to the heights, and the odd glitter of something that might be a gem if it were removed and cut. Kaylin, trying to fit this hall into what she'd seen of the layout, gave up. Like the tree station, the cliff station apparently wasn't bound by the laws that governed competent architects. Nor did it appear to be affected by the consequences that governed incompetent ones.

But the squares of marble beneath their feet began to glow as they walked.

This time, however, Severn's path stopped outside one door, and Kaylin's just kept moving. Given the new occupant in this particular station, she hesitated. Severn was equally happy. But he accepted it with the same quiet grace he accepted anything he couldn't change.

"I'm not willing to take the risk," he told her as she opened her mouth. "Not with you—and you would be the one to be at risk if you attempted to stay in this room. Nightshade cannot control the station."

"You're worried that's where I'll end up."

"Yes, but so are you."

"I— He always makes me nervous."

"I know. I'm only worried because you wear the blood of the green, and he wears its crown."

"Is that what it is?"

"Yes. His robes are also ceremonial—I've seen paintings, but this is the first time I've seen them in life. They're not as significant as the crown." He touched the door and it swung open into a large, well-lit room. "Go," he told her quietly and left her standing in the hall.

But she knew why. If he didn't leave now, he wouldn't leave—and as the station had decided he was to occupy this room, failing to do so could be fatal. He was willing to take that risk with his own life. Kaylin, conversely, wasn't.

As his door swung shut—and at a far greater speed than it had opened—she began to walk.

Kaylin followed the light. She followed it with reluctance, because she was afraid she would end up in front of Nightshade's door. But the small dragon on her shoulder was so relaxed he seemed to be sleeping; his eyes were shut, his wings were flat against his back.

The halls widened and branched, but they were always very tall, and the walls remained unadorned cut stone. The only thing that interrupted the smooth, flat stone were door frames, also of stone, and their recessed doors.

She was aware of Severn as she walked. Aware that he wasn't sleeping, bathing, or even sitting still—which he so often did; he was pacing. He was pacing, his weapons in either hand. She couldn't see him, although she knew by now it would be possible if she concentrated. She didn't; she could feel the daggers in his hands as if their hands were momentarily one.

The light continued to guide her until she stopped in front of a door that looked, to her eye, like any other door in the station so far. The small dragon woke then, stretching everything except the tail that loosely encircled her throat. There was no obvious door ward across the door's center; there was no obvious knob or handle, either. She lifted her palm and touched the door, and it rolled open.

She was buoyed for a moment by the hope that the room was otherwise unoccupied, because the room revealed by the opening door appeared to be empty. That lasted maybe ten seconds. Rooms in the station were complicated and large; there was never just one of them.

Teela entered the main sitting room from an arch to the left. She wore a bathrobe and not the finer dress in which she'd sat, blue-eyed and almost silent, through most of dinner. Her eyes rounded.

"Kitling? What are you doing here?"

"Apparently," Kaylin replied as she entered the room, "staying for the night."

CHAPTER 16

Teela's eyes were a shade of blue that could be mistaken for green, and to Kaylin's surprise, the green deepened as the Barrani Hawk approached. "The station led you here?"

Kaylin nodded. "I'd complain to the management, if I were you. I'd do it myself," she added as she entered the room and the door shut—without help—behind her, "but I can't find it. Is there a closet here?"

"There is. It's empty." She paused and then added, "It was empty." She turned, bathrobe catching the ambient, strange light, and led Kaylin from the sitting room to the bedroom. There was, as there'd been at the previous station, one bed. But as Kaylin had, in her youth, managed to sleep in a much, much smaller and lumpier bed beside Teela, it wasn't really a problem. The closet, as Teela had called it, was on the right-hand wall as she entered. Unlike the previous station's armoire, this closet was built-in, or at least the door implied that.

Kaylin found her packs very close to the door, on the floor. "Yes," she said to Teela, who hadn't bothered to follow. "This is where I'm supposed to stay."

"Take a bath first."

"Will you help me with my hair?"

"Of course," Teela replied as one dark brow rose to near invisibility beneath the line of equally dark hair. "It's always been my life ambition to be servant to a troublesome mortal."

"The one thing I like about these stations," Kaylin said, submerged in water that was on the edge of pleasantly warm, "is the lack of servants. No one's rushing about, or hovering with towels, or watching me."

"I'm no one?"

"You're not rushing all over the place."

"I have some dignity." It wasn't, on the other hand, a strictly human variety. Teela had shed the bathrobe and slid into the bath beside Kaylin. Since it was a Barrani bath—which, by any normal definition, meant a pool full of warm to hot water—there was a lot of room. She spread her arms across the stone lip and kept her hair above the water.

"So…do any of the other guests have to share rooms?"

"I doubt it. The stations enforce peaceful coexistence."

"So I can assume the station wouldn't dump me in a room that also contained Evarrim?"

Teela laughed. Her eyes were still green; if it weren't for the surroundings, they might have been in the office on a day that didn't involve the investigation into the Exchequer. "That would be a safe assumption, yes. It would not be entirely correct."

"Great."

The Barrani Hawk laughed again. "He is powerful, Kaylin, but he is not in and of himself as dangerous as some of the other Lords."

When Kaylin turned a skeptical look on Teela, Teela said, "He is almost alarmingly direct for a Lord of the High Court.

If he doesn't like you, you will know; if he wants something that you possess—and he's aware that your death is the only way to transfer that item into his own possession—you'll also know. He does play games," she conceded as Kaylin continued to stare, "but not with any great artistry."

"Is there a way to get the station to give me a room of my own?"

"I honestly don't know."

"When you use the word 'honestly,' it usually means something different from when I say it."

Teela nodded genially and upended a pitcher of water over Kaylin's head.

Fifteen minutes later, Barrani hair clips notwithstanding, they were both soaked, and the marble floors had become a disaster waiting to happen. The small dragon absented itself after the first pitcher, squawking in outrage.

Kaylin's hair, on the other hand, felt a bit cleaner. "Who made the stations?" she asked, treading water in the pool's center.

"The Ancients," Teela replied with a snort.

"Why?"

"They were probably tired of babysitting their creations. Us," she added. "Either that, or they were bored and decided to be constructive. Think about it. You've had experience with the needs of children—a roof over their head, food, clothing, and a need to separate them before they blacken each others' eyes."

Since this was a charitable description of the Foundling Halls on a bad day, Kaylin grimaced and nodded.

"It takes a certain amount of concentration and effort on your part. It probably took a similar amount on the part of the Ancients. They had a better way of eliminating it, that's all."

"Then why the harmoniste? Why the Teller?"

Teela fell silent in a way that implied the silence would hold.

"You were chosen," Kaylin continued. "What did it mean for you?"

"Not what it will mean for you," Teela replied. "My circumstance was…different." Her eyes were still green, but they were a darker shade of green. She looked at Teela's wet face, framed by equally wet hair that reached into the water and flowed freely around her shoulders. Kaylin hesitated and then decided against pressing her. Everyone had reasons for silence and the secrets silence contained. No one knew that better than Kaylin.

But…breaking that silence in Kaylin's case had been like breaking shackles and chains. It was true: it had. But it was a choice she'd made, and the choice itself was part of the freedom.

"Kitling," Teela said, flicking water at Kaylin's face, "you even think loudly. Your lips are moving."

"I'm worried," Kaylin replied. "And waterlogged."

"That is the usual outcome of a bath."

"I don't usually have a pool when I bathe; I have a small basin with barely warm water."

"If you weren't too lazy to boil enough—"

Kaylin threw up her hands, which caused a cascade of water. "Fine. I'm lazy." She pulled herself out of the pool by its edge and navigated dangerously slippery floors as she headed toward towels that she hoped had survived the deluge. "I'm worried," she said, words muffled as she applied dry towel to wet everything else.

"About yourself?" Teela asked.

"Of course about myself. I have no idea what a harmoniste is—"

"I told you."

"Yes. And I'm always good at applying theory to real life."

Teela chuckled. "You aren't terrible at it, kitling. In a decade, I think you'll be very good. But it's not just that."

Kaylin exhaled, knowing full well how annoying Teela found it when someone worried about her. She was fairly nonracist about the annoyance; she didn't like it when Tain did it; she didn't like it when the rest of the Barrani Hawks did it, and she certainly didn't appreciate it from the merely mortal. She did make an exception for Caitlin, but everyone did that, even Marcus.

"Kitling, if you tell me you're worried about me, I'll give you something to worry about." Case in point.

"You've been on edge since we left the City," Kaylin said as she avoided meeting Teela's eyes. "If I'd known that the West March—if I'd known what it meant—"

"You would have forbidden me from traveling there?" Her voice was distinctly chillier.

"No, it's not that...." Mostly because Kaylin stood no chance at all of forbidding Teela anything. "...It is that."

Teela sighed heavily as she pulled herself from the bath. She caught Kaylin's shoulders in her hands and turned her around so that they were facing each other. Kaylin was wrapped in a towel; Teela showed the usual Barrani reticence about nudity. Her eyes weren't green, but they weren't quite blue, either. "Kaylin, I am not you."

"I know." Kaylin shook her shoulders free, picked up Teela's discarded bathrobe, and handed it to her. Teela took it, slid it over her shoulders, and watched as Kaylin did the same. The small dragon decided at this point it was safe to land, and did so. He didn't, on the other hand, seem to care for wet hair in his face, so it was probably convenient that he didn't actually breathe fire.

"Why are you worried?"

"I don't know." Kaylin headed into the bedroom.

"What are you worried about?"

"Teela—" Kaylin turned. "First, I don't really want you to be so pissed off again that you don't speak to me for an entire day. Second, I don't want you to be so pissed off that you blacken my eye."

"I promise I will not blacken your eye."

"What about the first one?"

Teela raised a black brow. "Sometimes, kitling, you take your chances. I don't know what the hells you're worried about, so I don't know whether or not it's offensive. I'm not promising anything I can't deliver. Not," she added, "to you."

"Why were you so angry about the dress?"

"I don't recall saying I'd answer questions." Teela walked over to the bed and sprawled across its width. Since the bed was large, none of her body parts draped over the end, the way they did when she did this in Kaylin's apartment.

In Kaylin's previous apartment.

"I wasn't angry at you," Teela said. She reached out and grabbed two pillows.

Kaylin raised a brow in a fair attempt at mimicry. "It just looked that way, right?"

"It just looked that way, yes. I was against this from the beginning," she added. "I was against it, but I accepted it—we did need the information. But if I'd known that you'd end up wearing that dress, I would have cut off the Hawklord's wings first."

This shocked Kaylin into momentary silence. The silence caught Teela's attention; she lifted her face off the pillow. Her eyes were still the same odd shade of not-green, not-blue. "What is your worst childhood memory?"

Kaylin blinked. Sometimes Teela could change the subject so quickly, it gave her whiplash. "My what?"

"You heard me."

Finding room for herself on the bed—toward the headboard, rather than the foot—Kaylin grabbed the last pillow and curled her arms around it. The small dragon hissed in her ear and readjusted himself. "Finding my mother. She was dead," Kaylin added quickly. "I was five, I think."

"Five mortal years of age."

Kaylin nodded. "Do you even remember being five?"

"Of course. The Barrani do not forget."

"The Barrani don't get sick. My mother did."

"We don't get sick the way mortals do. The belief that we are immune to disease is not entirely accurate, but we are immune to diseases that afflict mortals."

"And you don't grow old."

"Not once we reach maturity, no."

"Does it take a long time to reach maturity? Don't make that face; this wasn't covered in class."

"In terms of your years, yes, we take much longer than mortal children of any race. We have a long coming-of-age, a long childhood, in comparison. I am not considered young by my people." She reached out and ran her fingers through Kaylin's wet hair. "You should stop cutting your hair. And maybe leave it down a little more."

"My hair gets in the way of everything. It even gets caught in doors."

Teela snickered. "I remember that. I remember the first time you cut it—Caitlin shrieked. You've got to do a lot to make Caitlin shriek."

"Not apparently." Kaylin rolled over. "Why did you ask?"

"Ask what?"

"What my worst childhood memory was."

"I was curious."

"You were thinking of yours."

Teela nodded, her hand stilling, strands of dark brown,

some with split ends, twined and drying around her alabaster fingers. "You've heard a bit about the regalia." When Kaylin nodded, Teela continued. "And you know that the recitation can grant power—stature—to the Lords of the Court."

She nodded again. "Does it work for everyone?"

"No, kitling. It is not entirely random, although it is not entirely predictable, either."

"Especially for the young. The children are too young and too—" Kaylin grimaced, desperately wanting Barrani memory "—unanchored in their names. I think. I didn't learn what that meant. But...I was told it is now forbidden for children to hear the regalia at all."

"It is considered one of the worst of our crimes, an act of treason against our race. It is one of the few crimes the Barrani take seriously."

"But, Teela, you—"

Teela nodded. The lights in the room had dimmed; Kaylin wasn't certain when. Color faded to shades of gray in slow stages. "Yes, kitling. I was brought to the West March when I was a child. I was one of the children who were destined for greatness." The words were bitter, but they were softly spoken.

After a long pause, Kaylin asked, "Did you know your parents?"

"Pardon?"

"Barrani never mention their mothers or their fathers. Sometimes they mention cousins, but to be honest I find that confusing. As far as I can tell, every Barrani is every other Barrani's cousin."

"Mortals seldom mention their parents, either."

"Are you kidding? I can tell you sixty-five things about Joey's mother on a slow day. I can tell you Reena's mother's pissed about her marriage, and Kathy's mother is pissed about her lack of children. Clint's mother, well, that's more complicated. I'm not sure I want to meet his father, though."

Teela laughed. "Stop. I surrender. Very well. Barrani don't speak about their parents much. But compared to mortals, they don't speak about anything much. Mortals always feel that the minutiae of their lives are interesting. I am not particularly interested in the ephemera of their daily existence. They will speak about the bargain they found in the market in the morning, about the lineup at the well, about the run in their socks—anything. All the time. It's one of the best things about your Corporal—he doesn't chatter."

Self-consciously, Kaylin said, "I do."

"Yes, well. I've learned to find your babble interesting. Or at least tolerable. I will admit it didn't even take that much effort; you had so much energy when you were thirteen you were like a puppy or a kitten. Even people who don't care for pets seem to like the puppies and kittens, have you noticed?"

Kaylin failed to answer, which made Teela laugh. Being the butt of Barrani laughter was never fun, but at least Teela was laughing. "Teela? Your parents?"

"My mother, like yours, is dead. And at least we have this in common, kitling; of my childhood memories, it is the one that haunts me. But we differ in one regard: I didn't discover her corpse; I watched her die."

Kaylin's arms inexplicably began to tingle and itch. It was the marks. "Teela, are you using magic?"

"No." Teela pushed herself up into a sitting position. "Why?" The word was sharper and smoother in the darkness.

"My arms. The marks are tingling."

"They aren't glowing."

"...No. But—" Kaylin shook her head. What else did she expect in a place like this? "Sorry. I don't know what's bothering them. They're not getting any worse."

Teela reclined again, but she was now on guard. Perhaps because she was, she could continue. "My mother died in the West March."

Silence. Even the small dragon was utterly still, as if he could understand the import, the gravity, of every word.

"Teela—your father—"

"You have a Hawk's ears," was the fond answer. "Yes, kitling. My father killed her."

She thought of Severn, in the darkness. She had promised that she wouldn't mention Steffi or Jade, and she'd kept that promise, but Teela's words brought them back, like cold, accusing ghosts. Severn had not killed her mother. But Severn had killed Steffi and Jade.

"Did he survive it?" Kaylin finally asked, voice thick.

"For a few centuries, yes."

"He's dead now?"

"Yes."

"Teela—"

"Yes, kitling. I killed him."

"Did you—before that, before he killed your mother—did you love him?"

"You are such a mortal. Of all the questions you could ask—most pertinent how I managed to kill him, given his superior rank, his superior status, and his relative power—you ask that one. Not a single one of my kin, not a single member of this High Court, not even the Lady, would think to ask that question." The words were laced with affection and fondness; in the dark it didn't matter what color Teela's eyes were.

"When I was a child," the Barrani Hawk continued, relaxing into her familiar, full-body lounge, "I did. But I loved as a child loves, in ignorance and with a desperate desire to have that love returned. I believe it is the only time I lied to myself in my earnest fervor. My father was not a young man when I was born; I was the youngest of his children at that time and the only daughter. My brothers are half brothers; my mother was a new wife. She came from the West March," Teela added. "She was not accustomed to life in the High Court; the Courts of the West March are different."

The tone of her voice was not the same in the darkness. Kaylin reached out and wrapped an arm around Teela's shoulder.

"I know mortals think all Barrani look alike—it's really quite confounding. To me my mother was beautiful, far more beautiful than the Lady."

"Than you?"

Teela laughed. "Far, far more beautiful than I. She had a voice that could stop songbirds in their tracks; they would sit on her arms and shoulders for hours, listening. They could starve to death, that way, and never notice. I loved her voice," Teela added. "Many did. My father, among them.

"You are aware that we do not have many children. We have brothers and sisters, sometimes—I was never graced with a sister."

"Until me?"

She laughed again, and this time, she draped an arm across Kaylin's neck. The dragon hissed; they both ignored him. "Until you, kitling, although I think I daydreamed of having an older and wiser sister. We seem like we breed, but we breed slowly, if at all. There are whole families whose proud lines faded from existence because no children were born to them over the centuries. But my father was blessed in his choice of wives, and my mother bore him a child: me.

"My mother was an only child. Her parents were not significant, and more: they were not Lords of the Court."

"Did the Court exist then?"

"Oh, yes. And the High Halls existed as well, although the territory was bitterly contested by the Dragon Flights. We were a people—my father's people—bred for war. But I do my mother's kin a disservice, Kaylin; she was not some gentle rustic, living in peace and harmony with nature in the outer reaches of our lands. Regardless, her parents had not chosen to undergo the test of name. They had no rank and little obvious wealth; their wealth, such as it was, was in their only child.

"They were fools," she added roughly. "Fools, all. They spoiled her, they adored her, they indulged her; they dried her tears—and she cried them. No one of my kin would have cried so openly as she; we wouldn't have dared. But she did. She apparently cried at my birth."

Kaylin, who had seen many, many births in her tenure as emergency volunteer at the Guild of Midwives, said, "That's a normal reaction."

"Only for mortals. Not for Barrani. It is considered a poor start to a child's life."

Kaylin said nothing. She could hardly remember her own mother's face, she'd been so young when her mother died. But…she remembered the feel of her mother's arms, her lap, the soft sound of her voice. She remembered braiding her mother's hair. She remembered feeling loved.

"My mother followed her parents' path. She was overjoyed at my birth, at my existence. But she was raised in the West March, and she raised me in the High Halls. I remember her," Teela said, her voice softening and slowing. "I remember her beneath the endless heights of the ceilings in the halls. Sometimes she would sneak us both into the forest that surrounds the High Lord's seat. There were forests in Elantra at the time, although they were dwindling; they were not considered safe. But the forests of the High Lord were.

"She taught me the names of trees, flowers, weeds. She knew them all."

"I envy you," Kaylin whispered.

"Why? Aside from the usual."

Kaylin hit her with a pillow. "I can't remember what my mother looked like, not clearly. I remember images, but—they're so far away now. Barrani remember everything."

"They remember what they notice, yes. But, kitling, let me ask a different question. Do you remember, clearly, what your mother's corpse looked like?"

Kaylin flinched. But in the darkness, she realized she couldn't. She could remember what she felt. She could still feel it, if she concentrated. She could remember the feel of her mother's cold, stiff hands and the utter absence of her breath. But she remembered them because what she'd felt wouldn't leave her; they were twined and anchored in her emotions. "...No."

"I remember. I remember what she said before she died. I remember where she was wounded and how often. I remember how her blood flowed, and, kitling, I remember the color of her eyes. I remember her expression and if I reach out, like this, I can almost touch it." Her hand now rested against Kaylin's forehead.

It was the first time that Kaylin clearly understood how double-edged the gift of near-perfect recall could be. She couldn't, even if she tried, see the two bloody corpses of her girls—and they were clearer, and the emotional scar newer.

"No gift comes for free," Teela whispered. "Your kind consider mine gifted, blessed. Consider the cost and the price paid for those gifts. I would be you," she continued, which was almost shocking. "Even given your life to date, given your losses, I would be you. You live in the moment, Kaylin; your past does not walk so clearly and heavily beside your present, and your future? It is always shadowed, a thing made of hope, dream, and fear. You barely have time to learn who you are before the burden of that knowledge must be laid down."

"But we're—"

"Yes. You are weak. My kind can enslave you without much effort. You are killed by the slightest of storms, the smallest of fires. You are feeble in your age, and you lose so much so quickly. I imagine that if I was granted my idle wish, I would loathe it in the end. But that is the nature of wishes. Do not forget it."

"You turn everything into a lesson, don't you?"

"Oh? What have you learned from brawling?"

"Don't get caught by the on-duty Swords, don't give your real name, and, most important, avoid drinking with Barrani when at all possible."

Teela laughed and hit her with a pillow; she hit hard, even at play. She always had. "My mother died attempting to spirit me away from the West March. When she understood fully what my father intended for me—for me, kitling, but not for his sons—she was horrified, terrified."

"She didn't know?"

"She was foolish, I told you. He knew what her reaction would be; I am certain he knew what he would be forced to do should she discover the truth. I do not know how he intended to hide it. Perhaps he truly believed that I would emerge as a significant power at the end of the recitation, and I would be his: his daughter, of his line. Perhaps he thought that she would forgive him when she realized that he had favored me—*favored* me—with the chance at such a gift.

"But she was raised in the West March, and she was afraid. She pleaded with him, she begged him. My mother, on her knees. It is an image that burns me still. When he agreed to abide by her wishes, she knew. She hugged him, she hugged me, she took me home. But she knew.

"The worst of it is this: I wanted that power. I wanted to be the golden child. I wanted to be my father's pride." She fell silent.

"I never knew my father."

"I spent centuries wishing I had never known mine. Sometimes ignorance is a blessing." Teela exhaled. "And sometimes, it's not. My mother knew he'd lied. She tried to save me; she didn't come alone. I told you she grew up in the West March. The Lord of the West March would clearly not be moved; the recitation could not be conducted without his consent. Even were that consent reluctantly given, he would be bound by it; he could not afford the loss of face rescinding that permission would cause.

"She could not, therefore, approach the Lord of the West March. I believe, had the Consort of the time been present, she might have had luck pleading her case there. But the Consort very rarely travels to the far reaches of the West March. You are blessed."

Kaylin wondered why half the blessings she experienced felt a lot like curses.

"She went to her parents instead. She called upon her kin. Her parents understood both her fear and her frenzy, and they bespoke others; they avoided the Lords of the Court, and they sought no aid from the Lord of the West March. Before you ask, the Lord who held the West March of that time is not the man who has claimed you as *kyuthe*. Your Lord of the West March is in no way the same. He is soft and more sentimental, and it is my suspicion that had he been Lord of the West March at the time of the recitation, it would never have taken place.

"But my father was an influential, powerful Lord. He could be refused a request, but not a request that the High Lord had already granted. In the end, my mother and her kin appeared before the recitation had begun, and they demanded my release.

"My father, of course, refused and ordered them to leave. They did not leave."

"They fought," Kaylin whispered.

"Yes. And they fell. In and of itself, that was a crime—but my father's men did not draw swords first and they acted, arguably, in defense. I should tell you now, in case it becomes relevant, that shedding blood within the circle of the green is considered a severe crime."

"As large a crime as attempting to alter Barrani children?"

"No. But at the time, no such crime existed. The Barrani of the West March fell to the superior blades of the High Court. I tried to stop them," she added, her voice an uncharacteristic whisper in the darkness.

Kaylin didn't have to close her eyes; it was dark. But she wanted to, for just a minute. She could imagine that she might've done the same, and she knew the way it would have ended.

"My mother knew they would fail when her people began to die. She didn't fight. Instead she prayed to the heart of the green."

"Wait, she prayed?"

"A figure of speech." Teela's silence had the quality of thought. "Perhaps that is the wrong word in your tongue. Beseech?"

"'Beseech' makes more sense if we're talking about Barrani."

"Beseeched the heart of the green, then, to little effect. My father killed her. He did not attempt to spare her life; he was angry. She was his wife and known as his wife, and she had traveled with the High Court and the children. She had betrayed him, and she had done so in full view of the High Court; she could not be spared." Teela's voice sounded so dry, so matter-of-fact.

"Did he even try?"

"No, kitling. I told you—he couldn't."

"But—but if you accept that, if you can accept that..."

"Yes?"

"I don't understand why you killed him. Why you felt you had to kill him."

"I loved my mother," she replied.

Barrani sometimes made no sense. Kaylin could understand the need to kill the man who had murdered her mother; she had no problem with that. But Kaylin was certain that no explanation, no circumstance, that caused her father to murder her mother would ever be acceptable to her. If she could understand fully and completely the reasons for the killing, how could she hate him enough to enact revenge?

Kaylin had spent almost seven years of her life planning ways to kill Severn should she ever meet him again. But once she had learned the why, the machinery of revenge had rusted out beneath her.

"Your lips are moving again, kitling."

"They are not." Kaylin would have hit her with a pillow, but Teela apparently had all of them at the moment.

"We're not the same. Don't spend too much time trying to make that comparison. I understand why he killed her. But in the end, she died because of me."

"That's not true. You didn't kill her."

"Had I not been in the West March, had I not been a candidate for the recitation, she would never have moved against my father. No more would I; in our fashion, we both loved him, and the things we wanted from him were not dissimilar. She would have raised no hand—or voice—to spare the other children; they were not hers."

"Teela, why was she so concerned?"

"She never explained it to me. But after the recitation, it became very clear."

Kaylin frowned. "There's something I don't understand."

"There's a lot you don't understand. Which particular element is causing confusion now?"

"You were there. Your mother failed to save you. You were one of the children who was forced to listen to the regalia. Which is now a great crime. Yet you're still Teela. If what happened to the children was so horrifying, why didn't it happen to you?"

Teela rolled over, switching from stomach to back; she stretched her arms high above her head, exposing her armpits. Kaylin knew, from unfortunate experience, that Teela wasn't ticklish, and in any case, it seemed like the wrong moment to make a second attempt. Wrong or no, she did consider it.

"I don't know," she finally said. "It was a question asked of me often in my childhood. Even as I matured, I was watched, tested, and cautioned."

"Were you the only one spared?"

"Yes."

"And it was obvious that the others were—"

"Yes, kitling. It was obvious within the day. It was obvious that something had gone wrong within the hour, although not all the children so affected manifested the change immediately. It was," she added softly, "a long, long recitation. The harmoniste collapsed immediately upon its conclusion, as did the Lord of the West March. Only the Teller was spared that fate—in a fashion.

"We were taken to the station in the West March. It is

not so often used for visitors; there are halls within the West March that are usually left open. But the deaths in the circle of the green closed many doors that day.

"Had we not been in the station, I do not know what would have happened. There are theories," she added softly. "There are theories that were argued for hundreds of heated hours in the High Halls upon our return. Some of the Lords—those who had not accompanied our group—were adamant that we try again. They pointed to the very unusual circumstances that preceded the recitation: the blood in the circle, the deaths, the almost unheard-of length of the regalia that had been offered to the triad.

"But the Lord of the West March, upon recovery, forbade any further attempt. The High Lord himself traveled, in haste and at personal risk, to the West March, and when he returned, he ended all discussions. He would not countenance such a risk again, for we had lost some dozen of our children in that attempt—and given the numbers of our young, it was significant."

"Do you know what he saw?" Kaylin asked when Teela's voice once again ebbed into silence.

"Yes. He saw the way station. He saw what it contained. The children, the young, were not the only losses—and in my opinion, the Lords of the Court who died within twenty-four hours of the recitation's end were considered the bigger loss."

"Did the children kill them?"

"Yes. And were it not for the anger of the citizens of the West March, the death count would have been much, much higher; we would have been welcomed in the homes and the halls where they dwelled. The station was a prison; it contained the transformed."

"But…you were in the station."

"I was."

"And you survived."

"Yes. I was one of only a handful to do so. My father was another, but he lost three lieges in his flight."

"He saved you."

Teela said nothing.

"Teela—"

"Enough, kitling. I have not spoken of this for centuries. If you are now afraid for me, don't be: I returned to the West March as an adult. On that journey, watched by every member of the Court, I was chosen as harmoniste. It stilled their fears."

"And yours?"

"What did I have to fear?" she asked. But her voice—her voice wasn't Teela's voice; it was too raw and too bitter. Kaylin was silent for a moment; she sat up in the darkness. "Kitling, I am not you." There was a note of warning in her words. "I traveled to the West March in the dress you now wear—well, a longer variant—and I stood as harmoniste, and I did not transform, I did not become monstrous, I did not kill the Lords of the High Court, present and watching like wary vultures. I became fully, and finally, adult."

"Was it hard?"

"It was…difficult."

"And I'm making you go back."

"No, kitling, you are not. You couldn't make me do something I did not want to do. I am here because I suggested it to Marcus." She rolled onto her side, facing Kaylin. "I am a Lord of the High Court. I am a Lord of note in that Court. But I'm also a Hawk. As a Hawk, I play by ridiculous, labyrinthine Imperial rules. I support equally ridiculous Laws—how many books does it take to contain them all, anyway?—and I wear a tabard, as if I were the lowest of my own guardsmen. I walk—walk, mind, not ride and not drive—the packed and dirty streets of Elantra, in the service of a Dragon—"

"In the service of his Laws."

Teela snorted.

"It's not the same thing, Teela."

"—and I spend as much of my time living outside of the High Halls as I possibly can. I'm not overly fond of mortals," she added. "But before that gives offense, I am even less fond of most of my kin. The Hawks," she added, her voice shifting, "became important to me. I do not know when it happened. I don't even understand why, but I offered to accompany you to the West March because the Halls of Law needed the information Nightshade dangled in front of the Hawklord.

"I did it as an adult; I did it knowing what the West March means to me. If you attempt to feel guilty about my presence here, I will be insulted. And what have I told you about deliberately insulting the Barrani?"

"It's a very bad idea."

"Is that all I said?"

"No. It was longer and had more concrete lists of consequences. But that was the gist of it. I'm not allowed to worry?"

"Worry if you like. But guilt? No. Your guilt is an attempt to deprive me of the ability to make an adult choice—and accept the resultant consequences—and given what I endured to become an adult, I can't allow it."

Teela settled her head back into the pillows, since she still had all of them. "At this very moment—and I'm certain I'll regret saying this—I'm actually glad I came. It was a shock seeing you in that dress. I am worried, and I was upset. But it's been a long, long time since I last spoke about my mother to someone who would truly understand the loss."

"You were talking about her death."

"I know. But talking about her death, I remember her life—or at least the parts of it that overlapped with mine. She did everything she could to save me."

"I think she did save you, in the end."

"Oh?"

"You said she begged the heart of the green for something. I think we can both guess what it was. You were the only one to survive, so maybe the heart of the green was listening." Kaylin relaxed and sank back into the bed again. "Hey, are you going to hog all the pillows? Give me one. Give me one and tell me more about your mother. Or the West March. The good bits," she added.

CHAPTER 17

In the morning—and the light was ambient morning light, although here, too, the rooms lacked anything that resembled windows—Kaylin felt calmer. Teela was already awake, because Barrani didn't need to sleep; they kind of dabbled in it, as if they understood it was supposed to be a good thing but couldn't quite get the hang of it.

But Teela's eyes were the same color, when Kaylin saw them, as Kaylin's dress. The good thing about dresses that were entirely magical was they appeared to be self-cleaning. And self-ironing, too. Kaylin slid into it, vastly more comfortable with its color, its length, and that fact that, for this journey, it was hers than she had been before she'd been dumped in Teela's room. The small dragon perched on her shoulders, mumbling to himself.

"You know," Teela said, "if he is a familiar—and I am almost certain he is—the stories about their grandeur and power seem to have missed the mark."

"They probably weren't aiming for truth."

"No, probably not. They're stories, after all."

"Are you ready? I'm starving." She headed toward the closet, and Teela cleared her throat loudly. "Right. I forgot. The bags will get tossed out when we leave. Hey, Teela, what did the light mean?"

"The light?"

"The one that hit me on the head just before we left the last station."

"We talk about the alignment of the stars when we talk about the recitation. The stars referred to aren't literal. They are also referred to as illuminations. The light offered as you left was a single illumination, but it was offered so early in the journey it implies that there will be more. There is some correlation between the illuminations and the complexity of the tale. A harmoniste isn't always chosen; a Teller of Tales is even rarer."

"When you were a child—"

"Yes. We had all three. The harmoniste barely survived, and he was much changed."

The breakfast table was the same one at which dinner had been served the previous evening; it was peopled by the same Lords, although most of their clothing had changed. The Consort sat at the head of the table, and to her right sat Lord Nightshade. Kaylin felt her cheek grow warmer and she started to lift a hand to touch his mark; Teela caught the hand instead and kept hold of it.

"It would be best if you failed to acknowledge the mark."

"Is it glowing?"

"Slightly, yes. I don't think the color works with your dress." Her grip tightened, but not painfully. "You could wear a large sack over your face, and everyone would still be aware of the mark; there's no way to hide it from Barrani. There's no need to let it make you feel self-conscious, either. On most days you don't even remember it's there anymore. Make this one of those days."

Kaylin glanced at her; she was smiling. "Look, there's your Corporal; he's saved us seats."

Teela's version of "saved" was entirely inaccurate; Severn was mortal. There were seats near his end of the table because no one with any desire to climb to the upper echelons of the Barrani High Court could see any advantage in conversing with him. Teela steered them both toward Severn's end of the table.

"You ended up at Teela's?"

"More or less. But Teela doesn't need much sleep."

Teela, being Barrani, took her place on the intricate stone bench without making a sound. "Did you sleep well?" she asked Severn.

He nodded. The morning meal was mostly a variety of bread and fruit cut into not entirely appealing shapes. There was cheese, as well as…fish. The fish was raw. Teela laughed out loud at the expression on her face.

"It won't kill you," she said.

"No, it won't." Because she had no intention of eating it.

"Well, don't eat too much," the Barrani Hawk said, entirely disregarding her own advice.

"Why not?" was the immediately suspicious question. "Did you eat all the cheese, Severn?"

"I've decided I'd like to drive the carriage today."

"No way."

"You can't exactly forbid it, kitling."

"Probably not, but I can try. Severn, help me out here."

Severn laughed. He was—he looked—entirely relaxed. For the next fifteen minutes they might have been sitting on the admittedly battered benches in the mess hall, on a day with no Exchequer hanging over their collective heads. The presence of the Barrani Lords did nothing to quell that impression; they were like a backdrop, and at least they weren't sitting across a desk in the public office, complaining about armies of giants. Or evil chickens.

But it couldn't last. Not here. Barrani, having finished eating and probably aware that they'd be stuck in carriages—or on foot—for the long and grueling day of travel ahead, now began to rise.

One of those Lords was Nightshade.

It was interesting to watch him move. Even the Lords who failed to speak a word to him—and they comprised two-thirds of the Court present in the hall—couldn't quite ignore his passage; not the pointed way they could ignore Kaylin's. He drifted down the side of the table, pausing only to speak with Andellen, who, no surprise, answered.

But when Nightshade laughed, everyone fell silent, even Teela. Court laughter was generally unkind; it was a variant of Court gossip and had the same edge, albeit absent the actual words. The only exception to that in Kaylin's admittedly small experience was, or had been, the Consort. She was not, however, laughing now. Nightshade was.

His voice was full and open; he seemed to be genuinely amused—almost delighted—by whatever it was Andellen had said. One look at Andellen's face made clear that he was also highly amused; they were sharing a joke of a kind that had no place in this Court.

Nightshade drifted down the table and at last reached Teela. He offered her a full bow.

She lifted a black brow in response; her eyes were now blue, but it wasn't the indigo that they'd fallen into when she'd first laid eyes on him the previous evening. "Lord Nightshade," she said, which caused a small whisper to rise from the portions of the table near enough to hear her. Given they were Barrani, it was a large portion.

"Lord An'Teela," he replied, rising. "It is always a pleasure to see you."

That was pushing it.

"Forgive my boldness. It has been long indeed since I have traveled with the High Court; it reminds me of younger days."

Teela nodded; it was cool and much stiffer than her normal nod. "When did you become aware that you would be the Teller? I did not see you in the Hallionne on our first night."

"No. I did not, as you might expect, travel with the High Court at the time."

Kaylin noted that he hadn't answered the question, and he glanced at her, reminding her that any mental notes taken were like large sandwich boards in his view.

"Indeed," he said, although she hadn't spoken. Teela and Severn both turned to look at her as she reddened. "To answer your question, Lord An'Teela, I knew before I set out."

Teela froze. She wasn't one to fidget much to begin with, but even the movement of breath seemed to stop.

Nightshade's smile grew an edge. "It is interesting, is it not? I woke to find the crown within my castle. I did not, however, have any knowledge of who the harmoniste would be."

"But you knew there would be one?" Kaylin asked.

"I did. There is never a Teller without one. There are recitations at which there are neither. Consider the recitations an event of varying difficulty. At times, if the difficulty is considered great, the green grants the Lord of the West March a harmoniste. But if the recitation is to be very difficult, a Teller is also chosen."

"How does the green, whatever it is, decide?"

"No one knows for certain. As the position conveys both honor and stature, were it understood, it would be contested."

"I bet. I'd also bet that every High Lord here, with the possible exception of the Consort, is trying to figure out how you managed it."

His smile was deeper and less cold. "Yes, they are. But if I were you, I would not be so quick to dismiss the Consort's curiosity."

Kaylin hesitated again.

"Yes," he replied, although she still hadn't figured out how to ask the question. "The Consort and I are well acquainted. She was not happy when I was forced to depart the High Court; she is not displeased that I am—even in a very limited fashion—at Court once again."

"Lord Kaylin," the Consort said from the table's head. "Lord Nightshade."

Nightshade turned toward her and bowed instantly.

"We will depart." The Consort's voice was cool.

"Lady," Nightshade said.

The Consort turned from them both, and then she turned back, her eyes on Kaylin's face. Or on, Kaylin thought, the mark that adorned her cheek. She said nothing, offered nothing, before she once again turned away.

The same standing arch opened in the dining hall, some yards away from the head of the table over which the Consort presided. This time, however, the Consort did not leave first; she indicated that the Lords of the Court were to precede her. They were graceful in their acquiescence; they stepped through the arch and vanished instantly.

As Kaylin, Severn, and Teela were at the foot of the table, they joined the progression at its tail and approached the Consort only after the room was all but empty.

The Consort turned to Lord Nightshade. "Lord Nightshade, the rules that govern the taking of an *Erenne* are clear, and the High Lord has chosen to uphold them. You will not attempt to enforce your hold upon Lord Kaylin while you are in this Court."

"I am already Outcaste, Lady," was his neutral reply. "There is little incentive for me to obey such strictures now." He bowed again and, without another word, walked through the standing arch.

Kaylin approached the arch; Severn and Teela waited by mutual—and silent—consent. When her toes were on the edge of what she classified as inside, she raised both her hands in mimicry of the Consort, cupping her palms. "Come on," she told the shining light. "I'd really rather you didn't give me a concussion."

Teela snorted in a very un-Barrani-like way as the light began its descent.

"What?" Kaylin demanded, not taking her eyes from the soft, round glow.

"You make even the mystic mundane."

"Easy for you to say—it wasn't your head it smacked the first time."

The third day of travel wasn't any kinder than the first two, and at the midday break, Kaylin was sore. The idea that she could be this sore when she'd done no walking, running, or drill work had come as an extremely unwelcome surprise. Severn smiled when he saw her expression. "It gets easier."

"I don't believe it. At this point, I'd feel better if I ran after the damn carriages."

Food on the road wasn't the complicated and intimidating fare that it was during the dinners and breakfasts that book-ended the day; it was almost normal. "Are we the only ones eating?" she asked Severn as she plunked down on a patch of ground beneath one of the larger trees in the clearing.

"Probably."

"Why?"

"In case it's escaped your attention, the Barrani don't 'grab a bite.'"

Teela sauntered over and almost sat in Kaylin's lap, her way of indicating that Kaylin should move over. She also held out a hand, and Kaylin, sighing, broke off half her sandwich and placed it in the Barrani Hawk's open palm.

"Most Barrani," Severn amended.

"I haven't noticed them holding back in the mess hall."

"There's less food in the mess hall."

"And most of it's terrible," Teela added. Her eyes were a shade of green that looked normal; Kaylin, even surrounded by Barrani Lords, felt herself relaxing. "You've started a storm of discussion."

"You mean gossip."

"I feel 'gossip' is an unkind word."

"Says the Barrani Queen of the cutting, sarcastic rejoinder."

Teela laughed, which did attract attention. It was a different kind of attention than it usually attracted.

"What have I done this time?"

"The second illumination. I don't think we've ever had a harmoniste take two this early in the voyage."

Kaylin's hunger dwindled, and not because she'd eaten enough. "How could they even tell? Does it show?"

"Demonstrably." Teela was enjoying herself. It was annoying, but it was better than rage. Kaylin, eating her diminished lunch, forcefully reminded herself of this.

"Severn?"

He shrugged a fief shrug. "It's not visible to me."

Great.

"Don't make that face," Teela told her, rising. "And finish up. We're about to start moving again."

"We only just stopped!"

One black brow rose. "We have a long way to go, kitling." The smile smoothed itself off her face. "And we're nowhere near the West March yet. There are four small stations in the next few days. They won't cause you problems, because they don't confer illumination; they merely offer safety. They are not as complex." She examined her skirts for crumbs. "Corporal."

Severn lifted his chin and met a gaze that was darkening.

"No matter what you see, now is not the time."

He nodded as she turned and made her way toward the carriage, where the horses were—damn it all—being strapped back in.

So it went. For the next four days, the stations were, as Teela had implied, smaller and less overtly impressive. The rooms, for one, didn't magically appear and disappear; the dining hall didn't change shape or lose doors. The flooring in the halls did light up, and rooms were still not a matter of personal choice, but they always led to either Teela or Severn, and Kaylin was comfortable now with both.

Nightshade was cool and remote; the mark on her cheek didn't even warm in his presence. The only time he physically approached Kaylin during the four days—and the fifth—was when Evarrim was also on the way. Even then, he left after he'd headed off Evarrim.

The Consort was unfriendly, but Kaylin expected that.

Familiarity with the small dragon didn't diminish Barrani interest in his existence, but given Nightshade and the Consort's chilliness, the Lords—with the single exception of

Evarrim—were content for the moment to maintain a strict look-but-don't-touch approach.

On the fifth night from the cliff station, the Barrani caravan paused by the side of a river. It was, in Kaylin's opinion, wide enough to be called a lake, but Teela insisted this was not the case. The Barrani Hawk was quiet in a way that suggested reflection as she stared at the slowly moving water. Kaylin was staring, too—at the total lack of anything that looked like a bridge. Or a barge.

The Lords began to congregate on one large, flat rock on this side of the river as Kaylin watched. "How are we supposed to cross that?"

"You'll see," Teela replied. "Come. The Consort is moving into position now."

The small dragon actually perked up at the words, lifting his head and blinking as if he'd emerged from a long, long sleep and couldn't quite get it out of his eyes. Kaylin was reminded of just how sharp his tiny claws were when he dug them through layers of priceless green cloth as he began to bob up and down. "I think he's excited."

Teela chuckled. "He looks it. He really is disarming. Watching the two of you together makes it very hard to take him seriously."

The small dragon squawked in outrage. Given the pitch and the volume of his complaint, it wasn't conducive to being taken more seriously. Even Severn raised a brow and shook his head, smiling.

Teela led them to the outer edge of the rounded rock that was serving as an impromptu viewing platform. The horses and carriages had been held back. "There's not a lot here to graze on," Kaylin observed.

Teela raised a brow. "Graze?"

"Well, the horses have to eat something."

"You think there's been enough to graze on in the past week?" The Barrani Hawk shook her head. "You don't know much about horses, do you?"

"Not Barrani horses," Kaylin said.

"Not about any horses," Teela replied. "Regardless, no, they're not being left here tonight."

"What are we doing with them?"

It wasn't Teela who answered.

"The horses are a concern. This isn't a safe patch of forest."

Kaylin stared at Severn. While she didn't know much about forests, and travel so far had involved hours on end in a fancy box stuck on wheels, nothing had struck her as dangerous. "Not safe?"

Teela and Severn exchanged a glance.

"These lands were heavily contested during the last Draco-Barrani war," Severn finally replied. "A lot of magic was used, in both offense and defense. In at least three areas, the magic ran out of control."

Kaylin glanced at her arms. The marks were flat, coal-gray; they didn't itch, and they weren't glowing. "There's no magic here right now."

"What you're wearing could be considered magic," Teela replied, "but it's not giving you hives."

True.

"If you wander off what passes for road here, you'll see large patches of land in which nothing natural grows. Unfortunately, at random intervals, unnatural things grow instead."

"Why were these lands so contested?"

"The Hallionne," Teela replied. "Watch."

The Consort was speaking. Her words didn't carry; her voice did. It was sweet and low, but something about it made all Kaylin's hair stand on end. In case she missed the significance of this, her arms and her legs began to itch. "I didn't even know she could use magic," she muttered.

"She's the Mother of the Race," Teela said, both brows lifting.

"Well, yes, but—"

"But?"

Put that way, it did sound stupid.

The Consort continued her low, urgent speech. There seemed to be no physical component to her spell at all. But when she stopped speaking, the waters of the river suddenly came to an abrupt halt. It wasn't as if someone had inserted a long, invisible wall between the two banks; the currents just…stopped.

The Barrani High Court took a few steps back when the water began to move. It didn't move in a way that suggested the currents were once again flowing—it roiled; water sloshed up the rock and across the Consort's feet. She stayed her ground. So, Kaylin noted, did Nightshade. He stood to the right, and a large step back, from where the Consort had begun her compelling speech.

The small dragon leapt from Kaylin's shoulders as she watched. He didn't go far; he flew in tight circles above her head. She was grateful he wasn't a pigeon or a seagull. The waters, Kaylin noted, were rising. She wouldn't have been surprised had they lifted themselves right out of their bed.

Having thought that, however, she was.

CHAPTER 18

Kaylin had, once or twice, watched glassblowers at work. Although the water didn't have the color or obviously molten texture of semisolid glass, that came closest to what she now watched. The water rose in an orb that caught sunlight. But it also caught moonlight, night sky, and gray dusk, none of which were actually present.

She watched as layers grew up around this floating orb, taking a different shape, a less circular one. "Those are—those are wings," she whispered. They were: they were like a watery sculpture of a moving, gliding Dragon. The jaws and the tail were last to form, because the wings seemed to stretch out forever. When it was done, the riverbed was bone-dry beneath the very strange shadow this sculpture cast.

Its eyes opened.

"Severn—"

"Yes," he said softly. "It's meant to be a Dragon." Something about his tone of voice made her tear her gaze away from what the water had formed. His eyes were wide with something akin to wonder, his lips half-parted, his head lifted. Strands of his hair had fallen into those eyes, but he didn't notice. What he noticed was the Dragon.

Kaylin thought she wouldn't be surprised if it spoke.

But she jumped two feet back when it roared. She'd heard a lot of spoken Dragon in the past few weeks—most of it the discussions between Bellusdeo and Diarmat—and this? It was a Dragon's voice. It shook the stone beneath their collective feet.

"This always happens?" she whispered to Teela when the Dragon paused for breath.

"Yes." Teela's expression was grim.

The small dragon rose higher, and higher again, until he was at the level of the water Dragon. He was also almost invisible; the light of the day passed through him, and he didn't have the warped and wavering colors of the rest of daylight's spectrum to lend him visibility. But even at this distance, she heard what passed for a tiny dragon's roar: a squawk. It was the sound chicks daydreaming of being Dragons would make.

But comical or no, it caught the Dragon's attention.

Teela's breath was sharp enough to cut. "This," she said in a grim tone that matched her expression, "on the other hand, is different. Call him back."

Kaylin stared. The Barrani Hawk pivoted to face her. "Kaylin, this is not a joke. Call him back now."

She didn't even have a name for the small, inconvenient creature. "It's not like I tell him what to do," she said between clenched teeth. "Hey! Come back here!"

Teela's eyes, which were blue, almost fell out of her head.

The water Dragon roared, its voice deeper, louder. It was the sound of a tidal wave crashing into ships and buildings. Kaylin's mouth went dry. But the small dragon squawked and squawked in reply—if it was a reply; she had the impression that he hadn't shut up once, deafening Dragon notwithstanding. He seemed remarkably unimpressed, and given the way the entire Barrani Court—Consort and Nightshade included—now turned to stare at her, she wanted a little of his self-confidence.

Or a lot.

Severn stepped nearer, wonder draining from his expression. What was left was familiar: he had her back. Teela, by her side, didn't budge—although she still looked outraged and annoyed. "I do not believe this," she said in evenly spaced Aerian. She could have spoken in Leontine, but an appropriate Leontine phrase sounded too much like "I'm going to rip out your vital organs and eat them while you are still alive—and watching."

The water Dragon opened its jaws and sucked in air. Something made of water shouldn't have been able to inhale so loudly that everyone on the ground beneath it could hear the sound.

"Hey!" Kaylin shouted at the small dragon, hands to either side of her mouth. "Get back down here!"

The water Dragon exhaled. A plume of what looked like smoke left its wide, almost transparent jaws. Folds of roiling mist enveloped the small dragon, who seemed intent on having a staring contest with its opponent, while hovering in place and making pathetic noises.

Kaylin held her own breath as the larger Dragon's slowly dissipated. She started to breathe again when she saw her own small dragon still hovering in the air; whatever the water Dragon had chosen to throw at him hadn't killed him. It had, however, annoyed him; she saw the small creature suddenly dart toward the water Dragon.

"I have a really bad feeling about this," she said to Severn and Teela, both of whom were watching the skies. Turning, she sprinted toward the Consort. "I don't know what you're doing," she said, voice low, syllables crunched together, "but call the water Dragon back. Call it down if you can."

The Consort turned to look at Kaylin. "Call it back?" she said, voice cool.

"I know he's small but he—"

Nightshade said, "Lady. If it is at all possible to accede to Lord Kaylin's request, I feel it wise."

"I am not responsible for the shape the water takes, as you well know."

"Is it important it stay in the same shape?" Kaylin asked, hoping the small dragon was stupid enough to just bite the bigger one. She was afraid he would breathe instead, and she remembered the hanging, opalescent cloud in Castle Nightshade. It had been a small cloud; she was certain that a large cloud was beyond the small dragon. But…she wasn't certain what the small dragon's breath could do. If it were in any way related to the Shadowstorms that were darker but similar in texture, it didn't have to be large.

"Can you not call your familiar back?" the Consort demanded, her gaze once again on the skies.

"…No."

"Are you certain it's a danger?"

Given the relative size of the two flying dragons, it was a fair question. "Yes."

The Consort raised both her arms; they were trembling. "Lord Nightshade," she said, voice soft.

"Lady." He glanced at Kaylin. "Watch the skies, Lord Kaylin. If there is a moment at which you might intervene, you will know it." He raised his arms, and he caught the Consort's right hand in his left; their fingers intertwined as the Consort began to sing.

The Consort's song wasn't gentle. What she sang wasn't meant to soothe or to calm. She didn't start banging shield with sword, but that was probably because she didn't have them at hand.

What shocked Kaylin into stillness—she'd already fallen silent—was Nightshade's voice when it joined the Consort's. She had never heard Nightshade sing before; she'd never really considered it a possibility. Most of the singing she'd heard in her life was in taverns and in the dim recesses of her early childhood memories of her mother. Neither were like this. Nightshade's voice was strong. It was strong, deep—she would have predicted that, had anyone asked. But it blended with the Consort's, giving her the melody and folding itself around it, supporting and strengthening the tone and texture of her notes. He took nothing from her in her strident challenge; he gave instead.

Kaylin felt tears start and didn't know why; she couldn't understand a word they sang. The song wasn't any form of Barrani she recognized.

The small dragon darted around the large one. It had the advantage of size; it could pivot neatly and easily. The large Dragon, however, could almost match it, which was dizzying given the difference in their proportions. The Dragon roared as the song continued, and Kaylin watched as both dragons—water Dragon, glass dragon—slowed their roaring, their turning, and their snapping as the song continued.

They watched the Consort and Lord Nightshade; they listened.

What happens now? Kaylin thought, watching, eyes watering, mouth dry.

In answer, the water Dragon began to glow. In his chest, as if he had swallowed sunlight, a bright, pale gold shone. His wings unfurled, extending far beyond their previous reach; they thinned as they spread. She could see the shape of pinions, the hint of something that would be leather if leather were liquid. No dragon wings she'd seen, not even the small ones, resembled these.

The Dragon's neck shrank, dwindling until it no longer looked Draconic. Its jaws receded as well, collapsing into the form and shape of a face that resembled the Barrani. It was not a Barrani face; the flying water creature was too large for that. But its cheekbones, its slender taper, its chin—no, she thought, *his* chin—were similar. What the neck and jaws had done, the Dragon's tail now mimicked; it dwindled.

All that was left of the form were wings that were no longer Dragon wings; his claws had already completed the transformation into long, slender limbs. He looked like a living, moving work of art, even to someone whose whole interaction with art was "I know what I like." But the light in the center of his chest—which now shone where his heart would be—continued to glow, and as it did, Kaylin understood why: it was a word. It was a living word, a True Word, an immutable rune.

Even at this distance, the shape of its many lines and scores were distinct and recognizable. But they were also complex, dense; the word began to rotate, turning on an invisible vertical axis as she watched, as if to display the whole of its three-dimensional, complex self. It reminded her, in complexity, of the single glimpse she'd had of the Outcaste Dragon's True Name. She knew it wasn't a word she could speak, and if this water were somehow alive—as the name at its heart implied—trying wasn't an option. She'd be dead before she could get her mind around the first of its syllables, if she could even figure out where to start.

She had no doubt at all that this was what Nightshade had told her to watch for, but his confidence in her abilities to interfere were hideously unfounded.

This water being looked down at the gathered Barrani,

expression impassive, as the Consort's song faded on a single attenuated note. She lowered her arms, and as she did, Nightshade's came with them. Kaylin was shocked to see that the Lady was literally sweating.

The small dragon alighted daintily on the water Dragon's—no, the water being's—exposed shoulder. Whatever animosity he might bear a small dragon, it seemed contained to, confined in, the Draconic form; he didn't appear to notice the small creature's presence.

"Daughter," this being said as he alighted in the dry riverbed, yards away from the rock on which almost all the Barrani now congregated. "Why have you wakened me?"

The Consort lifted her chin. "Your dreams had grown wild and dangerous, Hallionne Kariastos."

He turned slowly, gazing across the landscape that surrounded the riverbed. "Was I dreaming?" he asked softly. His voice, Kaylin thought, could break hearts, just by being heard. She hated to cry in public but could feel tears sliding down her cheeks, regardless.

"You were, Hallionne."

"A dream of Dragons," he said after a long pause. Lifting a hand, he removed the small dragon from his shoulders, cupping him in a palm. "Small dragons indeed, and strange, to wake me so completely."

The small dragon squawked.

"Oh?" He turned then to look directly at Kaylin. "Are you certain that I have woken at all?" Still carrying the small dragon, he walked across the riverbed, leaping up to stand on the large, round rock. He held the dragon out to Kaylin, whose arms—and mouth—felt momentarily frozen.

"He is yours," the winged man said. "And you are mortal."

She managed to nod.

"Mortal, and yet, you wear the blood of my brother, and

you stand at the entrance to the lands under my protection. Do you come seeking my protection?"

She had no idea what the right answer was. Nor did any of the Barrani, even the ones she knew, rush in to supply it.

He smiled. The small dragon hopped off his hand and onto Kaylin's shoulders, where it draped itself like a soggy scarf.

"If you do not seek protection," the man said after a long pause spent studying Kaylin's tears, "accept instead the offer of my hospitality." He turned toward the riverbed and gestured.

From out of the dirt and the stones over which the water had run, a large arch now assembled itself. It was not as subtle as the trees or the cliffs had been. Kaylin had, until the moment all the water had deserted the river, expected to somehow walk through it holding her breath to find the way station.

What surprised her, however, wasn't the arch—given where the arch had come from, expecting magic made sense. It was the Barrani reaction. The Lords of the High Court were silent, and to a man, their eyes were blue. Glancing at Teela, Kaylin amended that: to a person, their eyes were blue.

"I really hope that creature is useful in some way," Teela said in very quiet Elantran. "Answer his question before he decides you're being rude."

Kaylin looked back at the man. "I would greatly appreciate the hospitality."

His smile, like his voice, could melt hearts. "Enter, and be welcome."

Kaylin was the first person through the arch. She was therefore the first person to enter the way station for a good fifteen minutes, during which time she looked around the hall. It was not, like the cliff station, sharply angular in construction, and although there was stone, much of it seemed to be crystalline.

The floors were solid, but they were vaguely translucent, and to Kaylin's eye, something large was moving beneath them.

The front hall was rounded in the corners, like a worn die; its walls curved up toward the large room's center. There were mirrors at even intervals around the wall, although when Kaylin approached them, she realized they weren't reflective.

"Records," she said. Nothing happened, which is what she'd expected. She tried calling for Records in each of the languages she knew and got the same blank gray for her trouble. She even lifted a hand to touch one, but the small dragon hissed in her ear until she lowered her palm.

"Where is everyone?" she finally asked.

The walls and the inactive mirrors failed to answer. There were no doors that Kaylin could see, either, so further exploration would have to wait—for something. She would have headed back out to see what was happening if the arch had been a two-way convenience. It wasn't.

"Next time," she told the small dragon, "remind me not to enter first."

He squawked agreeably.

"I don't suppose you have any ideas?"

Squawk.

"Fine." Kaylin approached one of the mirrors again. They were large, long ovals, taller than the mirror in the Hawklord's Tower. Frowning, she tried a few different High Barrani phrases; after all, this was a Barrani way station. When she hit the long, polite phrase that indicated hunger—a simple declarative "I'm hungry" wouldn't do—the flat, lifeless surface of the mirror in front of her began to move. It moved like dense cloud seen at a distance—except she was standing inches away.

The roiling folds of mist began to harden. As they did, they took on familiar forms and shapes; she could see a long table, with benches to either side. There were candles on the table, and large, shallow bowls—or plates with funny lips; it was hard to tell. There were goblets and glasses, as well.

Everything in the mirror was gray, but when the scene had finished asserting its solidity, color appeared in a rush, like the spread of fire over dry brush.

"Well, then," Kaylin said to her sole companion. "Shall we?"

Kaylin stepped through what was obviously a portal. She didn't experience the horrendous sense of dislocation entering Nightshade's castle always caused, and again wondered if that dislocation was simple, ancient malice. The floors in the dining hall were solid hardwood, in planks with a very light stain; it added a warmth to the room. In all, she liked the interior of this station better than the other two.

There were no doors leading to, or from, the hall—but there were mirrors, very similar to the one she'd entered, spaced evenly along the walls. Interspersed with mirrors, some of which weren't dull gray, were odd adornments: what looked like small banners. Kaylin approached them and realized two things: the hall was huge, and the banners were therefore not all that small. Neither were the mirrors. She guessed that there were no physical halls in this building, if you could call it a building at all.

She glanced with longing at the table.

The Consort still hadn't arrived; no one had. Until the Consort arrived, neither end of the table could be designated as the head—there were no visual cues. There were chairs, not benches, at either end of the table, but the chairs were identical. Kaylin's preference—when she was allowed to sit and eat—would definitely be the foot of the table, as it would be farthest from anyone with clear Barrani political ambition.

Her stomach complained.

As there wasn't anyone in the room with her and the food was just sitting there, Kaylin finally decided that rules of etiquette didn't count. She grabbed something that looked like sticky bread and carried it to the farthest wall, where the crumbs wouldn't be immediately visible. The small dragon insisted on biting it a few times as well, although as far as she could see he didn't actually eat any of it.

Fortified, Kaylin returned to the table, unable to just choose a chair, but less resentful about it.

The first person to arrive was not, in fact, a person, although she recognized him immediately. It was the water Dragon in his second form. He smiled—the same smile—as Kaylin executed a formal bow and held it long enough to indicate deep respect.

"The hall is not to your liking?" he asked. His eyes were a shade of gray that was almost black, and they had no pupils. They reminded her very much of Tara's eyes.

"It's my favorite hall so far," she said quickly. The last thing she wanted was for the hall to be refashioned beneath her feet.

"The food? Is the food not to your liking?"

She had the grace to hide her fingers, some of which were still a little on the sticky side. "Are you—are you this station?"

"Station?"

"We call—well, I call—these buildings way stations."

"I am a Hallionne," he replied.

"That wasn't your name?"

He smiled. "I am Kariastos. Hallionne Kariastos. These stations of which you speak are called the Hallionne."

"They remind me of other buildings," Kaylin told him. "And you remind me of the Avatar of the Tower of Tiamaris."

"I have not heard of this Tower."

She started to tell him about it and caught the words before they left her mouth.

"This Tower's Lord is a Dragon?"

Her suspicion about Kariastos hardened into certainty at that point. "The Barrani and the Dragons are no longer at war."

"This Avatar of whom you speak—"

"I didn't speak, but yes, she's like the heart—or the soul—of the Tower. Her name is Tara. I don't know if she'd recognize the word *Hallionne*. I'll have to ask the next time I visit her."

He glanced around the room. The ceilings here were much taller than they were in the foyer.

"Will you not sit?"

"I can't."

He raised a brow.

"I mean, I can, but it's frowned on."

"Oh? By who?"

Kaylin blinked. "I'm a Lord of the Barrani High Court," she told him, speaking softly and scrubbing the words of as much inflection as she could.

"You are mortal."

"Yes. A mortal Lord of the Barrani High Court. I'm the newest member of the High Court, and that means I'm the least significant member."

"I fail to see the logic in that statement."

"The Consort—the woman who sang to you—is the most important member of the High Court. Until she's seated, no one sits, unless she gives orders to the contrary. I have no objections to this," she added as quickly as High Barrani allowed.

"Very well," Kariastos replied. "But this is my station, as you call it; I am the host. I have not been fully awake for a very long time. Come, you have accepted my hospitality. Sit. You break no rules." When she didn't immediately move, he added, "You wear the blood of the green, mortal or no. The rules that govern the Hallionne in this case are clear. You are welcome here, and your welcome is not dependent on the High Court."

She was silent, considering her options.

"Perhaps the young ones have forgotten," he continued. "And if it is necessary to remind them, I will wake my brothers from here to the heart of the green, and they will explain our ancient rules more…clearly."

"No! That really won't be necessary." She headed toward a bench.

The Avatar cleared his throat loudly.

Kaylin gritted her teeth and changed course, landing in one of the two formal chairs that bracketed the long table. "Do you even eat?" she asked as the table shifted and plates began to move—on their own, which wasn't appetizing—toward where she now sat.

"I require sustenance, yes. If you mean will I join you, the answer is also yes. I would be a poor host otherwise."

After the first fifteen minutes, in which the hall did not become noticeably more occupied, Kaylin began to relax. Hallionne Kariastos was intimidating in the way Tara was intimidating; he didn't blink, he watched every movement, listened to every syllable, and answered questions she hadn't asked. If it weren't for her long exposure to the Avatar of the Tower of Tiamaris, Kaylin was certain she would have found this creepy—at best.

But like Tara, the Hallionne seemed to expect…nothing. He could read her thoughts with the same ease Tara could and with the same self-consciousness. Being read wasn't an act of exposure, because there was no judgment behind it. She would have liked to see Severn and Teela, but had to admit that the meal, after the first quarter hour, was the most re-boring she'd had since she'd joined the High Court on their journey to the West March.

"Your small creature," he finally said. "Where did you find him?"

"He was given to me."

"He is a very...unusual gift."

"He hadn't hatched at that point, and no one knew what was in the egg."

"I...see. He may be of aid to you, in the future. Treat him well—and, Lord Kaylin, name him if you can."

"Does it matter? He's alive without a name."

"Your companion is not mortal, Lord Kaylin. He is only half-alive. You understand some of the nature of naming and some of the nature of truth but not the whole of either. You go to the lands called the West March by the Barrani; you go to the heart of the green. Words are spoken there that can shift the nature of those who listen if they are not anchored."

She set her fork down. "Is it dangerous?"

"It is. As you suspect."

"Will something happen to him?" She'd considered any number of possible tragedies, and none of her scenarios had involved the small dragon. He squawked.

"I cannot clearly see," was his somber reply. "But he is like a vessel that is only partly filled. Handle him with care, if you wish to make use of him. If you cannot name him—if you cannot hold him—do not take him to the recitation. Your part in it, I fear, will be long, and it will be difficult; the tale is forming."

She frowned. "You know what the tale will be?"

"I? No. But I hear the movement of words, and it is a storm. I would not have said a mortal would survive it, but you bear the marks of the Chosen; you may." The Hallionne rose. "I will return shortly," he said, "with the rest of my guests."

* * *

The rest of his guests were, in Kaylin's estimation, half the High Court. This half included the Consort; to her surprise, it did not include Nightshade. Severn wasn't the first person through the portal; he was close, though. Teela was on his heels.

They both relaxed—marginally—when they saw her.

"I'm fine," she said quickly. "Where is everyone else?"

"They have elected to bypass the hospitality of the station for the evening," Teela said stiffly.

Kaylin frowned. "Why?"

"Because the Hallionne is awake."

Her frown deepened.

Teela rolled her eyes. "You've been closeted with the Hallionne for the better part of an hour, and you don't understand?"

"...They don't want him to read their minds."

"No. It is a singularly unpleasant experience."

"Kariastos is like Tara," Kaylin offered.

"The Avatar of the Tower of Tiamaris?" When Kaylin nodded, she said, "And how often have Barrani guests visited that Tower?"

"Well..."

"Does Castle Nightshade possess such an avatar?"

"Not that I've seen."

"I invite you to consider the reasons for that. We value our privacy highly; it is the reason we are able to take advantage of immortality."

"Oh. But you're here."

"Yes. I am aware that the Hallionne are not my kin. They value peace; they protect their domains. I am willing to take the risk of what the Hallionne sees in my thoughts; were he sleeping, he would touch them in his dreams, regardless. Many, however, are not."

"The Consort is here."

"The Consort is one of the few who has less choice; she woke him." Teela's eyes narrowed as she glared at the small dragon who occupied Kaylin's shoulders. "I would like to know why it was necessary; awake, he did not seem to feel your pet was a threat at all."

The small dragon growled. It was the first time that he'd made that particular noise.

Teela raised a brow, and Kaylin turned to Severn, hoping the shift in position would break what looked to be the beginning of a staring contest. If Teela were intent on it, she could probably outstare a tree, or at least stare at it while it grew, aged, and withered, which counted as a win in Barrani books.

The Consort was indeed present. She glanced at the table and then took the chair that Kaylin hadn't occupied for thirty minutes; Kaylin stayed on her feet while the denuded Court assembled around her. There was the usual jockeying for position, but the entire atmosphere was subdued. Kaylin wasn't certain why she thought that, either. The Barrani were talking, as they always did; they ate, they drank, they seemed as animated as they'd been at any other meal.

"Lord Kaylin," the Consort said, lifting her chin. "Come. Keep me company while I dine." There was one empty place beside the Consort.

"It can't be any more dangerous than eating with the Hallionne," Teela whispered. "Go."

Hallionne Kariastos did not stay for the meal. He welcomed the Barrani into his home and then spread his wings. They put Aerian wings to shame, they were so long and so utterly perfect in shape and form. "Welcome," he said as he rose. "I will see that your horses are properly stabled and cared for. Eat and drink in peace." He then flew up toward the center of the ceiling—and vanished.

"I'm sorry," Kaylin said, as she took the seat that the Consort had indicated. Severn and Teela were relegated to the safe end of the table, which was the one Kaylin had been occupying.

"You do not seem uncomfortable in the presence of the Hallionne. It is unusual."

High Barrani, Kaylin. "Perhaps, Lady. Or perhaps it is because I am mortal."

The Consort raised a white brow. For a moment, she reminded Kaylin of Teela.

"I spend time in the Tower of Tiamaris. I'm accustomed to the Avatar of the Tower, and Kariastos seems a lot like the Tower's avatar. Except more Barrani."

"The Avatar of the Tower reads your thoughts, then?"

Kaylin nodded. "I don't think she tries. But thinking is equivalent to talking really loudly if you're anywhere in the Tower. She can listen to any conversation held in the fief itself, but that does take concentration and effort. Hallionne Kariastos is a little like Tara. He hears the words I'm doing my best not to speak out loud."

"You do not feel this is deliberate on his part?"

Kaylin thought about this for a long moment. "No," she finally said. "I really do think he's barely aware of the difference between what's spoken and what is thought."

"This does not disturb you? Mortals have feared the Tha'alani for as long as both races have been forced to coexist."

Kaylin had been one of them. "I don't fear the Tha'alani now," she replied, keeping heat out of her voice with effort. "Because I understand them better. If every thought we've ever had could be examined and understood by every person we came in contact with, we would have a better idea of what people were really like."

"You, of course, feel this would be beneficial."

"I don't think we'd be so quick to judge others." Kaylin shrugged. "Maybe if we could stop doing that, we wouldn't spend so much time judging ourselves, either."

"And perhaps where mortals are concerned that might be an improvement; you spend far too much time on your regrets and your past fears."

Kaylin managed to keep her initial response to the words to herself. They were probably true, after all.

"Do not look so ill-pleased, Lord Kaylin; the Hallionne is likely to blame me, and it appears you have his favor. The Barrani do not spend the time in…introspection…that mortals do. If we did, eternity would be a curse; it is not. My kin therefore do not suffer the Tha'alani gladly—or at all."

"The Hallionne—"

"With luck," the Consort continued, "and a modicum of self-control, the High Court will not be severely denuded by the absence of the station's intercession. Be that as it may, they will remain on the far side of the river, awaiting us in the morning."

"But you're here."

"I am less concerned with the Hallionne."

Kaylin raised a brow, and the Consort grimaced. It was the most natural expression she'd willingly offered Kaylin since they'd left the City limits. "And, as you refrain from pointing out, I woke him. If all my Court chose to absent themselves from this station for his waking hours, I would nonetheless be required to attend him."

"Would apologies help at all?"

"In this case, perhaps. I believe that the regret you feel at the necessity of the intercession is genuine; if you had the ability to constrain your…friend…you would do so. It is time," she added and rose.

The Court fell into the usual hush that resembled manners. "We will retire," she told them as she stepped away from the table and glanced at the flat surfaces of large nascent mirrors that were placed evenly against every wall. Kaylin expected them to shift and change as they opened portals into the rooms in which the guests would spend the evening.

"That is what would normally occur," Hallionne Kariastos said. Kaylin looked around the room; his voice was present. He wasn't. "I am currently occupied; there is some minor difficulty on the surface."

The Consort stiffened.

"Yes," he replied, although the Consort hadn't chosen to put the thought into words. Kaylin glanced at the rest of the High Court; they were now watching the Consort in a deliberate silence that seemed almost predatory.

"Predatory?"

Damn it.

"Lady," the Hallionne said, "I find her entertaining. The rooms will be active now," he added. The mirrors began to form images.

Kaylin wondered if she'd have a room of her own or if the station, confused by the stigma of mortality, would assign her yet another roommate.

"You will be assigned a room, Lord Kaylin," the Hallionne replied in a distinctly less friendly voice. "It appears at least one of our guests wishes you harm."

They were Barrani. If none of them wished her harm, that would have been shocking.

The Hallionne laughed, and Kaylin froze at the sound of his voice; it was a sudden rush of unadulterated enjoyment, and it made her skin tingle. Sadly, that was literal.

* * *

The Barrani High Court emptied the halls without any of its usual lingering. The Consort did not leave first, as was the normal custom. She remained in the dining hall, indicating with a regal nod that the High Lords should feel free to precede her. Teela and Severn stayed behind, until they were two of the only people in the hall, the others being the Consort and Kaylin herself.

Only then did Hallionne Kariastos choose to join his voice by making an appearance. He wore different clothing, in shades of green and brown. It wasn't the clothing that caught Kaylin's attention first. There was blood on his right hand.

The Consort glanced at Teela; they didn't speak. Kaylin was surprised that the Hallionne remained silent, as well.

"Kitling." Teela's eyes were blue.

"You're staying the night, right?"

"I am. I believe Lord Severn had some concerns or some possible business of his own to attend."

Severn, however, smiled grimly and shook his head. "Not tonight."

"No," the Hallionne replied. "If the Court wishes to reside in the realm of insects, wildlife, and inclement weather, it still resides within reach of my power. If you wish to kill Lord Iberrienne, you must do so on a different evening."

Severn nodded.

Lord Iberrienne. It was the first time she had heard him named. She looked at Severn; he met her gaze without blinking or flinching. Or moving. This was the man he'd been sent to hunt. No, she thought, feeling cold and still. This was the man he'd been sent to kill. And Hallionne Kariastos knew it.

One look at Teela and the Consort made clear that they knew it, as well.

The Hallionne chuckled. "Lord Kaylin, if I killed all the

visitors who planned to execute—or assassinate or, more generally, murder—other guests, I would have no reason for existence." When Kaylin frowned, he added, "They would all be dead. It is the nature of children."

It was absolutely not the nature of children.

"Very well. It does not concern me if Lord Severn intends harm to another guest; it is my responsibility to insure that no attempt is made within my domain. The death of a visitor is a profound failure on the part of the Hallionne. If the Hallionne is, as I am, wakened, it is also considered one of the very few profound insults any sentient being can offer. We are not concerned with the wayward damage caused by rabid—or dangerous—pets, or rather, we take no insult from the damage they do." He glanced pointedly at the small dragon before he gestured.

All of the panel portals instantly dimmed; images of rooms—which, for the mortals, looked inviting—vanished. "My secrets," he said softly, "are my own. I understand why your kin choose to keep theirs from me. Lord An'Teela, or Teela, you alone have walked this road before."

Teela's eyes darkened perceptibly.

"We are not kin, you and I, but the Hallionne understand the concept of kin. It is a far weaker concept than that of hospitality and defense, but it is there, and it rises, at last, to the surface. You seek to protect the Chosen for reasons that are unusual. She is not your keep, not your pet; she is not yet your equal. While she resides within any Hallionne, she will be safe.

"Lady, I understand your rage and your grievance, and I find it fair. Therefore I ask a boon of you. I cannot demand it; it is against the nature of the Hallionne to enforce any request that does not reflect their primary responsibilities."

"If you seek my forgiveness…" she began.

"I do. But not yet. She has committed a crime against you;

it is not in her mind a crime, and as her grave risk amounted to little, she has some justification in this view. But her risk removed the Devourer of worlds from the great stretches of emptiness that exist between worlds; if she risked as much here, she is the unheralded and entirely unknown savior of other worlds not yet discovered. And the Devourer now resides within the Keeper's gardens. He sleeps," he added softly.

"Wait, you can hear him?" Kaylin broke in.

Hallionne Kariastos smiled. "Perhaps; perhaps it is more accurate to say he hears us." His smile was radiant. "But you interrupt me. Lady," he continued, turning once again to the Consort. "If she survives her role as the heart of the tale, she will have done a service that even you could not perform, guardian of all names and all life to your kind."

Kaylin didn't much care for the conditional in the last statement. Judging from her expression, neither did Teela; Severn was remote.

"Lord Severn understood from the moment you donned the dress," the Hallionne told her, which caused Severn to stiffen, "that your life was at grave risk, although perhaps his concern has been for your sanity."

Kaylin shrugged. "According to the office, I don't have much of that to begin with."

The Consort said, "I would not be indebted to Lord Kaylin."

The Hallionne frowned. "She has been chosen; she wears the heart of the green. Perhaps at a different time, you might petition the Hallionne to allow you to carry her burden—but not on this occasion, Lady. To take her role in this tale is to take almost as large a risk with the fate of the Lake of Life as Lord Kaylin did."

The Consort said nothing.

"And even so, you would have to wake the all of the Hallionne, and you are, as your kin, very reluctant to do so." His frown shifted; it was a very Tara-like transformation. "You are angry with her, but you are uncomfortable with the thought of her death. Unusual."

"Perhaps," Kaylin said in High Barrani, "she wants the opportunity to enact vengeance herself, and my death in the West March would deprive her of the—"

"You do not even believe that is a possibility."

"What would you have of me?" the Consort asked. The Hallionne did not answer.

CHAPTER 19

The Consort exhaled. "She is a child. Wayward, yes, and foolish beyond belief, but ignorant, as children oft are. I would see her punished for the choices she made, but I would not see her perish. She is not here because she is a Lord of the High Court, although you are no doubt aware that she is that. She is here because the mortals required information that could only be obtained if she agreed to make the journey."

"And she does not understand, Consort, why you are here."

The Consort's lips compressed; Teela's expression didn't change at all. "Does her ignorance signify that much? She was willing to risk the names, Hallionne."

"Indeed. But without her intervention, what ruled as High Lord would not be the brother you loved. Nor would the Lord of the West March now reign in the green."

The Consort did not respond to his statement, not directly. "She does not understand the significance of the heart of the green, but, Hallionne, no one of us do. I was willing to wake you—"

"Because of her."

"No. Because I am the Mother of the Race and very little in the way of politics in the High Court will harm me. No matter how ambitious they are, the Barrani require children who will wake."

Hallionne Kariastos inclined his head. "You are all children," he said softly. "And were your games not so deadly, I would be content to let you play them. Lord Kaylin," he added, "accompany the Consort. Lord Severn requires sleep, and he does not sleep well in your presence; it is distracting."

Kaylin avoided looking at Severn's expression.

"Lord Severn," he continued, "you will come to no harm in this station, but you must now watch yourself on the road." That left only one unembarrassed person in the room, which clearly wasn't acceptable. Hallionne Kariastos turned to Teela.

Teela's eyes were very blue; she'd affected the stance that generally meant "I'm bored, and I'm thinking of relieving my boredom on you if you don't get out of my way." The Hallionne was clearly an expert in body language.

"An'Teela. This is the third telling. Listen well, and understand the whole of what it means, and you will be free."

The Consort was not pleased to have company. Or at least Kaylin's company; Kaylin had no idea whether she'd had company at any of the previous stations. She wasn't about to ask, either, and cringed at the thought that Hallionne Kariastos would actually answer the question anyway.

He was, however, silent.

The room—once they'd cleared the portal—looked like a giant crystal bubble through which floor had been laid. There were no doors between rooms, although there were rooms, one being a significant bath. Kaylin wasn't certain she wanted to take a bath, though; the water was running from one end of the bubble straight through the other. It was clear; there was no mud bed or small rocks, but it kind of looked as if there should be. With fish.

While she hesitated, the Consort disrobed and entered the water, her white hair spreading like a layer of submersed snow or ice, carried by the currents. "If you intend to sleep at all tonight," she said in her crisp, exact High Barrani, "you will of course do me the courtesy of bathing first. There is exactly one bed."

"You don't need to sleep," Kaylin replied in Elantran. She did remove the dress and dumped it in a pile near the wall at the farthest point away from the stream. This room didn't have the corners she'd usually use instead.

"Ah, I forget. You spend time with An'Teela."

Kaylin splashed as she entered the stream, and almost jumped out again—the water was hot. This caused the Consort to arch a brow. The small dragon—briefly detached at the shoulder while she disrobed—peered out at the consort, flicking air with his tongue as if asking a question.

"I'm sorry about the dragon."

"You are not, that I'm aware of, in control of him. Or were you referring to the Hallionne?"

"Both. I didn't mean to get dumped on you tonight."

"I am aware that the choice was not yours." The Consort exhaled. "Everything my brother has ever said about me is clearly far more accurate than I wished to credit."

"Which part?"

"I am overly sentimental—a grave, grave failing—and naively optimistic." She used Elantran for the last word, as if there was no equivalent in High Barrani. Thinking about it, there probably wasn't. "He also feels I give far too much credence to views that are not my own, regardless of how deeply held and very correct my views are."

"It's not something I've ever been accused of," Kaylin admitted.

"No, but you have so few years to form correct views it's more easily forgiven." The Consort frowned. "That, by the way, is an example of behavior my brother criticizes. I find it difficult to hold you in the contempt you so richly deserve."

Kaylin hadn't really noticed that the Lady was having any difficulty in that regard.

"It's vastly easier when you're not actually standing in front of me. Or kneeling. That was impressive, by the way. I think it made an impression on the rest of the Court."

"Probably not a good one."

"It affirmed that you were aware of your position, and in that sense, no, not good. But it also showed that once you've made a decision, you live with its consequences. The humiliation would have caused most of them to abandon the attempt." She slid farther into the water, until its small currents crested the underside of her flawless chin.

"I knew that Lord Nightshade would come," she continued, surprising Kaylin, "and I did not trust him." She spoke in Elantran again. "I knew you would honor your promise, not because you are mortal, but because you are so much yourself."

"But Teela—"

"And," she said, voice softening, "I know An'Teela's history."

"You knew Nightshade when he was a Lord of the High Court."

"I did. He was also a close friend of my father's, inasmuch as Barrani can be said to have close friends."

"But if he's Outcaste—"

"Yes. It was entirely my father's decision."

"Why was he made Outcaste?"

"I do not know. That is the truth, Lord Kaylin. I was…fond

of Lord Nightshade. I came in part because of him, in part because of you, and in part because of the Imperial Wolves."

Kaylin froze, hot moving water notwithstanding.

"Lord Iberrienne is not yet Outcaste. He is, by Imperial standards, a wanted criminal, but the crime for which the Emperor was so understandably enraged is not—and cannot be—considered a crime against our race. The Emperor's rage, however, was predictable. The assassination attempt should not have occurred without consultation with the High Lord."

The fact that it did implied the High Lord's concerns weren't significant to the assassin and his supporters. "It's insulting?" Kaylin asked.

"Yes. It is a grave insult. It is for that reason that my brother is...angry."

"He's trying to have Iberrienne declared Outcaste."

The Consort nodded.

"You don't think he'll succeed."

"Should he declare Iberrienne Outcaste, Iberrienne will be Outcaste. But there are costs."

"Can I point out that Iberrienne tried to kill Bellusdeo while she was living with me in my apartment?"

The Consort nodded. "That fact caused far more friction in Court than the attempt itself."

Kaylin blinked. "Why would anyone care?"

"You fail to understand your own significance in this Court. You have seen the Lake of Life. It was you—not my mother and not me—who retrieved the whole of the High Lord's name from those waters. It is my belief that you could, should it become necessary, choose names and give life to our young, should I fall or fail."

"Iberrienne couldn't know that."

"Perhaps not. Ignorance, however, is not an excuse. It is clear that you find favor in the High Lord's eyes. More than that is not necessary. It is not because the High Lord values you, you understand."

Kaylin had spent enough time around Teela—barely—to nod. "It's because he's said I'm important. Killing me is a slap in his face; it has nothing to do with me."

"Yes. Iberrienne, however, was unrepentant; he considers you a threat and a—what was the word?—abomination."

"Good to know where I stand. Not surprising, but still."

At that, the Consort smiled. "It is further complicated by Evarrim. Iberrienne is his cousin."

"That's not supposed to mean anything, according to Teela."

"Ah. In terms of either affection or survival, it does not; in terms of public face, it does. If Evarrim has not yet disposed of his cousin—"

"No one else is allowed."

"Yes. And?"

"Evarrim wants the small dragon."

"Indeed. He is not, however, the only one." The Consort watched the small dragon for a few silent breaths. "He really doesn't seem very impressive."

"But he's cute."

"When he is not issuing challenges to the Hallionne, yes. The High Lord will not be happy when he hears of this turn of events."

"He didn't want you to come here, did he?"

"No. He did not forbid it, but he counseled—strongly—against it. I believe at least two of the Lords are here at his behest; he will know before morning of the day's events." She fell silent. "So much upheaval, Lord Kaylin. It is not just you; it is everything. The Devourer who sleeps—and dreams. The Hallionne. Calarnenne's presence as the Teller. You. A female Dragon. It has not even been a mortal year."

"I wasn't responsible for the Exchequer, if that helps." When the Consort failed to respond, Kaylin grew more thoughtful. "I think Iberrienne may well have been."

The Consort stiffened, her expression chilling. The water, however, remained on the edge of too damn hot. "The Exchequer difficulty, such as it is, is venal; it involves mortal wealth. I find it difficult to believe he was involved."

Kaylin ground her teeth. "Every crime I've investigated in which the Barrani were implicated involved money." She managed not to shout.

"How many of those crimes involved a Lord of the Court?"

"At least one."

The Consort's brows rose. "That is a serious accusation, Lord Kaylin."

And one it would help no one to make. Kaylin reined in her fraying temper, reminding herself that Immortals always saw mortals, and by extension mortal things, as inferior. Railing against it changed nothing. Hating it just gave Kaylin ulcers; the Immortals didn't care. "It's also in the past. I shouldn't have brought it up."

The Consort inclined her head. "The current difficulty?"

"People have been disappearing from the fiefs; dozens, maybe more. I'm certain a Barrani Lord is involved in those disappearances, because I saw him."

"You did not make this accusation at Court."

Teela had said it would be unwise. Kaylin bit her lip. "No. I knew I wouldn't be in the City, and I thought the criminal would be. But he's here, and that changes things."

"He is already under Imperial death sentence."

"It's not his death that worries me." Even as the words left her mouth, she knew they weren't true. If he died, he would die because Severn was successful. He probably deserved death. Severn didn't deserve to be his assassin. "He didn't just grab people off the streets; they didn't leave their fiefs by bridge or road. They left through a portal."

The Consort's eyes narrowed.

"The Avatar of the Tower of Tiamaris said the portal leads to the outlands."

The silence was significant; it chilled the water. "If such a thing existed within the fiefs, given the circumstances, do you not think it likely that Lord Iberrienne would have availed himself of its use?"

The Consort, like Teela, seemed to know what "outlands" meant. "Only if it was safe."

"How many of the mortals were taken?"

"I don't have an exact count."

"Tens? Hundreds?"

"At least a dozen from Tiamaris; my guess, given access, is higher from Nightshade. If such portals exist only in Tiamaris and Nightshade, than we've lost maybe fifty. If they exist at the edge of the borders in all of the fiefs, hundreds."

The Consort rose. Water rolled off her as her hair drifted down her body in a wave. Her eyes were blue, but her expression remote; Kaylin didn't feel that this shift was directed at her. "When did this occur?" she asked. Unlike Teela, she apparently had a sense of modesty; she grabbed the bathrobe that was loosely draped on wall hooks as thick as her wrist.

"Within the past couple of weeks, at most. The documented cases—"

"There is Imperial documentation?" When Kaylin failed to answer, she added, "At this time, Lord Kaylin, the Emperor is already…difficult. The High Court does not wish to push him past sensible rage."

"There is one case, and one only, that exists in Imperial Archives. The most recent one," she added. "The rest of the archives that exist—in whatever form—exist within Tiamaris."

"And not," was the dangerously perceptive reply, "within the fief of Nightshade?"

"You'll have to ask Nightshade yourself."

"That is a very Barrani answer. I'm surprised. I will speak with Calarnenne." She waited.

Kaylin pulled herself out of the water. She felt uneasy, and it was getting worse, not better. "Tell me what happened to the children exposed to the regalia," Kaylin said. "I think—I'm afraid—the disappearances are somehow connected."

The Consort's expression froze in place. "They could not be. The Lord of the West March would never countenance it."

"I'm not accusing your brother of a crime. It never occurred to me that he could even be involved. I don't understand what's happening here, but I'm beginning to think I should be grateful for the destruction of my home. If no attempt had been made on Bellusdeo's life—" She drew breath, clamping her jaws shut on the rest of the words. "Let me try that again."

The Consort said nothing.

"Lord Iberrienne is involved in the disappearance of some of my people. He chose people whose absence wouldn't be noted by either the Emperor or the High Lord. I believe he sent them someplace else, and if he's traveling with us, it's possible that he sent them ahead." She watched the Consort's expression; rock was less giving. But her eyes were darker, and they seemed for a minute to reflect nothing.

"I am weary," she said, rising.

"Lady, is it possible that Iberrienne might somehow attempt on nameless mortals what was attempted, previously, on the Barrani children?"

"Can you see any advantage—at all—to Lord Iberrienne in such an action?"

"No." Kaylin turned away. In a low voice, she added, "I was hoping you could."

"Given the results, and given that he is aware of it as a Lord of the High Court, I cannot.

"Lord Kaylin."

Kaylin turned.

"I am concerned. What you have said is disturbing, especially given my distance from the High Lord and his lieges. But it is not disturbing to me in the same way, or for the same reasons, it disturbs you. You are worried for your missing mortals."

Kaylin nodded.

"They are mortals you have, in all likelihood, never seen."

"I know."

"This is like your Norannir all over again."

"No. It doesn't involve the possible end of the world." The silence that followed the words was too bitter, too still. The Consort's eyes were a very dark shade of blue, but they glittered now, as if they had hardened. Or frozen. But her voice, when she spoke, was soft.

"I would like to remain angry with you for the next two centuries. If I were my mother, I would, in fact, be able to sustain this rage for the rest of your existence."

"Two centuries should more than cover it."

"Two centuries? I am struggling with a year. I feel it is my right—and my duty—to censure you. But it takes effort. It is hard to watch and listen to you and remember just how dangerous you were."

"Barrani have perfect memory."

"Yes. And demonstrably imperfect emotional reactions; I consider it a failing, but I am only mother, not designer. I cannot extract a vow for future good behavior, in part because you cannot make a binding vow." She lifted a hand as Kaylin opened her mouth to ask the obvious question. "A binding vow is exactly what you would expect; it is a long, complicated procedure that involves the True Name of those who swear the oath. I am not certain what its effects would be on you—and in any case, it would be a waste of effort; if I wanted to kill you, there are far less complicated and taxing ways.

"I want to see you learn the error of your ways. I want you to suffer the consequences of your decisions. But you muddle in things that are so large, even the wise cannot fully comprehend them. There seems to be only one way in which such lessons could be learned, and for reasons that are not clear—to me—I am not willing to allow you to commit suicide.

"It would be markedly easier if you would at least make these appalling decisions for the usual reasons."

"Those are?"

"Personal gain. Monetary profit." The Consort's eyes were now a shade of blue that would have fit in at the Halls of Law on a day that didn't include assassination attempts or the Exchequer.

"You'd be less conflicted?"

The Consort frowned. "I would be as angry; it would be less difficult to maintain the anger. But that is not what I meant. When people are motivated by a desire for personal gain, they are much, much easier to predict—unless they're incredibly foolish. It is hard to predict what the monumentally foolish or willfully ignorant will consider profitable."

"If it will make it easier, I am doing what I do for personal gain." Kaylin headed slowly toward the bedroom. The bed was round. It was also in the center of the room, like a squat, soft table. To her surprise, the Consort followed. "I want to be able to look at myself in the mirror."

"The sad thing about this discussion," the Consort said,

"is that you believe what you're saying." The Consort, who wasn't Teela, pulled up a rather fine chair.

Kaylin shrugged as she climbed in. "Sometimes. I know that the choices I make—they're luxuries. I have something now. It's not what you want—"

"Oh? And you are now an expert in the desires of the Consort of the High Court?"

Kaylin reddened. "No."

"Good. You are telling me that you are just as self-interested as Evarrim."

"It's not the way I would have put it, but…yes." Kaylin rolled onto her stomach and propped herself up on her elbows, which sank. "At least we're not boring."

The Consort's brow rose, but a smile tugged at the right side of her compressed lips. She rose from the chair in which she'd been sitting and made her way to the bed; Kaylin moved over toward one edge. The Consort, unlike Teela—and the rest of the Barrani Hawks, for that matter—didn't lounge. She didn't strew herself across the mattress, taking up most of the room and all the pillows. She lay down instead, folding her arms beneath her head as she stared, wide-eyed, at the ceiling.

"I am sentimental," she told Kaylin. "As a child—and I had a long and simple childhood by all accounts—I was indulged at Court; I was the daughter of the High Lord. I played," she added with just a trace of self-consciousness. "But as I grew, I came to understand the politics that governed the Court. I can remember my shock and distaste. I can remember," she added with a rueful smile, "the disbelief. I think, sometimes, when I look at you, I see what I can no longer have. I don't want to destroy it, but I envy you."

Kaylin wondered if anyone was ever happy being themselves. The Consort was undeniably beautiful, and she would remain beautiful all her life. Beautiful, healthy, youthful. She could speak at least three languages—probably more; there wasn't a door that would remain closed to her if she chose to truly enter Elantran society. She had money, she had servants, she had…everything. And what did she envy?

"When I learned that my brother would be High Lord, it was difficult."

"But you knew—"

"I knew, but I didn't understand at the time what it meant. The Lords of the Court lined up behind each of my two brothers in an attempt to offer them support—physical, magical, and even monetary—for their attempt to secure the throne."

"But—"

"Yes. It is the way of things for so many of my kin. My mother took me aside and explained in no uncertain terms that such a contest was expected of the Barrani who would be High Lord. It was a way of ascertaining that the ruling Lord was strong." The Consort lifted a pale brow.

"Weren't they both her sons?"

"Yes."

"And she accepted this?" Kaylin's brows, on the other hand, could no longer be seen, they were so high up in her hairline.

"Of course. She was the Consort; my father, the High Lord. She was not…happy. But she accepted it. I did not. I could not. I went to my brothers in anger and fear, and I threatened them." She smiled; it was a painful expression. "I threatened them."

"With what?"

"I told them that if either of them did not survive the death of my father—either one—I would abandon the Lake of Life."

Kaylin rolled onto her side. Her brows were still invisible.

"You may now point out that my anger at you is an act of hypocrisy, if you like."

"I need permission?"

"Yes, as a Lord of the Court over which I preside."

Kaylin laughed, the situation was so ridiculous. As she laughed, the bed shook, and the Consort began to laugh as well—albeit in a startlingly beautiful, musical voice.

"My brother—the one who became High Lord—was so angry. He had never been so angry with me before—or since. The brother who became Lord of the West March—and that's an interesting and complicated story as well—refused to enter what became a raging argument. He offered no opinion; he offered no solution. He said nothing.

"Do mortal men do this?"

"What, say nothing?"

The Consort nodded. "I confess that I was almost angrier at my younger brother for his refusal to speak than I was at my older for his disapproval. I did not make a binding vow," she added, "because neither of my brothers would countenance it. It was…difficult. I did not realize at the time that my older brother intended to vacate his claim; neither he nor I realized that my younger brother would refuse to accept it.

"I do not know what would have happened if you had not stumbled so haphazardly into the High Halls at the side of An'Teela. The Hallionne is right," she said. "And he reminds me." She closed her eyes. "My younger brother would have let the Court fall before he lifted the High Lord's crown. He loved us both. It is a weakness," she added, her voice softer. "And I know it. But I can't hate it. I can't despise it. In myself, yes. But not in him.

"And not, apparently, in you. Sleep," she added. "The Hallionne is singing. Can you hear him?"

Kaylin shook her head. "What is he singing?"

"An ancient song. Even I don't understand the words," the Consort replied. "But his voice conveys the sense of it."

Kaylin strained to catch a single note, but absent the Consort's breath—and her own—the room was silent.

"It promises sleep, dreamless sleep, and safety; it promises a gruesome and terrible death to my enemies." Her smile was wistful. "I have not heard this song in centuries."

"You haven't gone to the West March in centuries?"

"Ah, no, I have. But the Hallionne have not been wakened, and even were they, this is a song sung only to…children. Do mortals not have such songs?"

"Yes. We call them lullabies, but in general, they don't mention gruesome deaths."

"Ah. Mortals are strange. My people believe that our children must be prepared to face the future."

"Mine, too, I think. But our parents have hope that the future for their children will be peaceful." She closed her eyes and listened to the deep and even breathing of the Consort as she drifted off to sleep.

"Hallionne Kariastos?" she whispered, staring at the ceiling, confident that any word she spoke, in any tone, would reach his ears.

"Yes, Lord Kaylin." He didn't accompany the sound of his voice.

"Thank you."

She felt his smile and wondered at that; he was nowhere in the darkened room. "She is dearer than a daughter to me. That is the word?"

"Yes."

The Consort and Kaylin entered the dining room side by side the following morning; they entered late, given the look of the gathering. No one sat until the Consort took her seat, which left Barrani Lords milling in subtle silence. The silence grew more pointed, much of it aimed at Kaylin, as the Consort chose a seat. Kaylin looked with longing at Teela before joining the Consort.

Breakfast was, as dinner had been, constrained and near silent. The Consort rose to signal the end of breakfast, as she always did. The diners rose with her, abandoning their desultory meals; they were as tense as she was, at least as far as eye color went.

"This will be a little different," she told Kaylin as she approached an empty patch of floor behind the chair she'd occupied.

"No arch?"

"No. The Hallionne is awake." She didn't lift her arms; she didn't chant—or sing. Instead, she spoke. "Hallionne Kariastos, we thank you for your hospitality and your protection. We must depart now, for the heart of the green is waiting. Will you allow us to leave?"

Hallionne Kariastos appeared a yard away from where the Consort stood. His arms were folded across his chest, and his wings were high. They settled as he studied the Consort's remote expression. He turned to survey the Court; his eyes were narrowed, but they were still obsidian. "I will," he said. "But I will accompany you, Lady."

He gestured, his arms rising in a steeple reminiscent of the Consort's in the previous stations. A portal appeared to his right. It wasn't an arch, and it had no glowing keystone, but the lack didn't make Kaylin feel any easier.

The Barrani were silent; usually meal conversation drifted away from the table when they did, lingering in small clutches as they stood in line. This morning, no one spoke. Kaylin wondered if the Hallionne had paid nocturnal visits to the courtiers.

"Yes," he replied. "I availed myself of the opportunity to

speak with the Lords of the Court; it is seldom afforded us." Since he looked at her when he answered the question she hadn't asked out loud, several of the Lords turned to look at her, as well; they were clearly less amused.

The Consort left immediately. Teela was, to Kaylin's surprise, third in line; she left without looking back. Severn lingered, and as Kaylin took her customary position at the tail of the line—even given the line was much shorter and much more subdued—the hall emptied. As she approached the portal, she saw the river; water flowed through its bed in the normal way. "Is that the other side?" she asked Severn.

He nodded.

"Chosen," the Hallionne said before she could enter—or exit. She turned to face him. Only Severn remained in the room. "I note that you are not fond of the illuminations."

"It's not the illuminations," she lied.

He raised a brow.

"Okay, it is the illuminations. I have no idea what they're supposed to do or be, but they upset the Lords of the Court. That," she added, "and I don't like being smacked on the head at the best of times."

His brow rose. "I understand." He held out his right hand. She stared at it. "I will not, as you put it, drop light on your head. But your role as harmoniste will be difficult; you are not Barrani, and you are not moored in the name you have taken as your own. What the Hallionne give is an attempt to strengthen you."

"But the illuminations don't always exist when a harmoniste is chosen."

"No. In this case, they would even if the harmoniste were Barrani. You are not; we expect you to have grave difficulty. What we can offer, from the recess of sleep, we have offered. I am awake," he added, smiling. "Come."

She placed her hand in his; he tightened his grip instantly. Because Severn was standing at her back, she didn't try to pull her hand free; it would only draw his attention to the fact that her hand was now trapped, and that would probably upset him.

Her dress began to glow, the same way it had when the light descended from the height of the arches. "You are An'Teela's *kyuthe,*" the Hallionne said.

"I'm not—"

"Officially?" His smile was still as breathtaking as it had been the first time she'd seen it. When it faded, she had the visceral urge to say or do something—anything, really—that would bring it back. "If you succeed—and the Hallionnes are divided on your chances—you might be the only person who can offer the help she has needed for so long."

CHAPTER 20

Offering Teela help was similar to baring one's throat when an insane lunatic was waving a knife around. Wanting to help was fine, as long as it was clear that the desire was your problem—and you never attempted to make it hers.

"Tell me why she needs help. Tell me why she's needed help for so long."

He shook his head. "I am not as you are. You are the harmoniste. Calarnenne is the Teller. Story is primal, Lord Kaylin; if you can make sense of it, you will know the answer to your question."

Which, while disappointing, was about the answer she'd expected. She said, "Can I have my hand back now?"

"Not yet," he replied. "Lord Severn?"

Severn glanced at Kaylin, who nodded. He then walked through the portal.

"What the Barrani High Court seems to forget," the Hallionne said when Severn had emerged cleanly on the other side, "is that while there are stronger protections within the

Hallionne itself, all the outlying lands are under my dominion."

"The Barrani are immortal," she pointed out. When he lifted a brow, she added, "They don't forget."

"Event is neutral," Hallionne Kariastos replied. "It is in the interpretation that it becomes personal. When the Barrani look back on events, they recollect them, but they give weight to differing factors; it is why a single event can be viewed so differently. Time, event—they are not true."

"They aren't lies."

"No; that is not the dichotomy. They are subjective, indeterminate."

She nodded, as if she agreed, to end the explanation. "My hand?"

"I intend to escort you out. Come."

Although the transition, when seen from inside the Hallionne, looked instant, it wasn't. It was very much like the portcullis that led into Castle Nightshade—without the dizziness and the nausea. "You are in control of that, you know," Hallionne Kariastos told her.

"I'm not. No one voluntarily makes themselves sick."

"I believe the word you are looking for is not *voluntarily,* but *intentionally*. You do not like the space between spaces, the emptiness between worlds."

"Castle Nightshade is in this world."

He raised a brow. "So, too, am I. But the laws and the rules that govern the Hallionne are not the laws of the external world. To reach them, you must step past the known. You grip the known too tightly. You cling to it in places where it is—at best—irrelevant, and at worse, inimical. Let go, and you will find the passage much smoother."

"How do I let those laws and rules go?"

"I do not know. I am not mortal."

"Is this why you're holding my hand?"

He smiled. "It is. I will release you if you prefer."

"No thanks." She tightened her grip in case the words hadn't fled her mouth fast enough.

He laughed. "We are not, by nature, cruel," he told her. "But perhaps our definition of *kind* is open to interpretation." He stepped onto the far banks of the river, Kaylin at his side.

The Consort was waiting. Her arms were by her side, but her hands were curved and stiff; her eyes were a very dark blue. Teela was standing at her side and three steps to the left; her hands were behind her back. It was what she did in the office when she was tempted to draw a weapon and end an argument, that being very heavily frowned upon.

To the Consort's left was a Barrani Lord that Kaylin didn't recognize. In front of her, most of the Court was arrayed. Severn stood about two feet from where Kaylin and the Hallionne emerged, well back from the gathered crowd. The Hallionne released Kaylin's hand. For the first time since the tree station, the Lords of the Court were not surreptitiously—or openly—watching her as she stepped outside. They were watching the Consort; the Consort was, for the moment, silent. That level of silence, with that depth of blue eyes, made Kaylin momentarily forget she could speak Barrani.

In case she hadn't, Teela shot her a warning glance. Severn raised an arm to keep Kaylin from the periphery of the loose formation, but the Hallionne glanced at that arm, and Severn lowered it without a word. When Kaylin accompanied the Hallionne, Severn fell in to her right.

Who died?

She felt his surprise.

Three Lords.

She clenched her jaw to prevent it from dropping. *Evarrim?*

No. Neither Evarrim nor Iberrienne were harmed.

Is it bad if I'm disappointed?

His chuckle was felt; it didn't escape into his expression and it certainly didn't leave his lips.

Is it clear why they were killed?

It is not completely clear to me, no; I just arrived.

Guesses?

He didn't offer any. She had by that point reached the Consort's side—at the side of the Hallionne. The Consort failed to look at her at all; she failed, which was more surprising, to look at the Hallionne.

Kaylin was familiar with Tara; she knew what the Tower could do in her own domain. In the Tower, her will and her knowledge were absolute; nothing could penetrate the Tower defenses when the Tower itself was active. But in the streets of the fief of Tiamaris, her power was still significant and her word was law. It was law in part because Tiamaris deferred to her; she, in her turn, deferred to him in all matters of governance that didn't involve the Shadows she'd been created to defend against.

Kaylin suspected the Hallionne was not inclined to that sort of compromise, given he dealt almost solely with Barrani. The first words that left his mouth pretty much confirmed that suspicion.

"How dare you?"

Silence. The Consort lifted her chin but did not speak.

"He is the Teller. Do you understand what you have done?"

It was Teela who spoke. "He is Outcaste. To the Barrani High Court, it is significant; his role as Teller, given his status in the Court, is unprecedented." Her eyes were the same color as the Consort's, but her tone was the dry and objective one she used to deliver verbal reports in the Halls of Law. "A natural consequence of his status and the appearance of the crown of the Teller is disbelief and suspicion."

"Suspicion?" Hallionne Kariastos frowned. "You suspect that your Lord Calarnenne is capable of manipulating the heart of the green?" The word *outraged* did not adequately describe his expression.

Outcaste. Nightshade.

She glanced around the riverbank. She couldn't—didn't—see him.

I am here, he told her. *I am…not uninjured.*

Where is "here"?

I am under the Hallionne's protection.

If you were going to accept that, you could have stayed in the station and saved yourself the trouble.

I am not, as are fully half of the Lords on this journey, comfortable in the Hallionne when the Hallionne has been wakened.

She grimaced. *You live in a Castle that's practically the same.*

I am the Lord of the Castle; the Castle is not Lord over me. If my Castle possesses—or is possessed by—an avatar similar to the Tower of Tiamaris's, I would never see it wakened. I expected some difficulty, he added.

Where's Andellen?

He is likewise retained by the Hallionne. But yes, he was critical to my survival. The Hallionnes are aware, but they are not as instant in their response when the difficulties occur outside the stations, as you call them.

The three dead?

Nightshade didn't answer.

"It is impossible," the Hallionne said in a tone of voice so chilly it was a wonder the river hadn't frozen in its bed. "Do you think that the Hallionne—even sleeping—would not be aware of tampering? Do you think we would allow it?"

Teela shrugged. It was a classic Hawk shrug, which made

Kaylin wonder just how much of Teela was really visible in the office. It was different from Teela at Court, of course, but was it any more genuine?

"It is unwise," the Consort said, speaking for the first time since Kaylin had emerged from the portal at Hallionne Kariastos's side, "to insult the Hallionne; it is vastly more dangerous to insult the heart of the green. While he journeys with us, Lord Calarnenne is granted the protection of the Hallionne and the blessing of the heart of the green."

More silence. If they hadn't been Barrani, they would have looked like foundlings caught filching treats from the kitchen.

"There are three dead," she continued when everyone failed, as a group, to speak. "I would see no more dead before we reach the West March." She turned an icy glance upon a Lord that Kaylin didn't recognize. "Lord Iberrienne."

Oh.

"Lord Evarrim. I wish to speak with you both. Hallionne, if you would care to grant us some privacy?"

Hallionne Kariastos's interpretation of the request was not what Kaylin's would have been. Had he been Kaylin, he would have assumed it was a polite variant on "get lost." Instead, he raised both arms, and the Consort, Evarrim, and Iberrienne disappeared.

"It is," he told Kaylin, "in accordance with the Lady's wish. She can wake the Hallionne; she understands how to speak with us, although she finds it difficult at times."

"Were they involved?"

"She does not wish the matter to be discussed with the Court."

"And the three?"

"What she wishes is no longer relevant; they are dead. They attempted to break the peace of the Hallionne and felt such action might succeed should they remain outside my walls.

It is an act of folly, and such lack of wisdom in men of power often precedes their deaths."

Neither Lord Iberrienne nor Lord Evarrim were dead, which meant they hadn't been involved in the attempt.

"No," Hallionne Kariastos said. "They are canny."

The Consort went missing for an hour. While she was in discussion with the Lords Evarrim and Iberrienne, Teela began to gather the horses and hitch them to the wagons. Severn helped her; Kaylin tried and the second horse stepped on her right foot. The Barrani Hawk looked down her perfect nose. "They know you're afraid of them," she said in a tone that implied only imbeciles would be. "I honestly have no idea how you handle the foundlings with an attitude like that. Do you follow them around begging them to listen to you?"

"They don't outweigh me by this much, for one."

Since neither Teela nor Severn appeared to have feet that attracted hooves, Kaylin let them work. When they were finished, the Consort reappeared, bracketed by two Lords that didn't, to Kaylin's eye, look particularly chastised. The Consort approached Hallionne Kariastos on her own, although the distance between the Consort and the rest of the Court guaranteed them neither privacy of thought nor safety, given the Hallionne's mood.

She bowed to the Hallionne and spoke in a singsong voice. It was similar in texture to the song she had sung to awaken him, but lighter and more sorrowful.

"It is a song of leave-taking," the Hallionne told Kaylin. The Consort nodded. "There are three, but of the triad, this is the most gentle." He frowned. "That is the word?"

It was an Elantran word. "Yes, I think so."

He smiled. "The Hallionne will wake as you approach; they are waking now."

A whisper went around the clearing at this bit of news.

"You are welcome to return, Lord Kaylin, should you require refuge."

"I don't, but I require Lord Nightshade and Lord Andellen."

"I have taken the liberty of sending them both to the next station; they will be there when you arrive."

Kaylin blinked. Teela caught her arm and dragged her toward their carriage before she could ask the Hallionne the question that immediately sprang to mind in the wake of his statement.

The Hallionne laughed. "If you cannot stomach even a small walk between my home and this river, you would never survive the long walk. It is not to be undertaken lightly, nor is it to be undertaken at your behest; the Hallionne decide."

"Honestly, kitling, you might as well shout every stray thought that enters your head."

"He wasn't angry."

"He wasn't, no."

"I don't care if the Lords of the Court were annoyed."

"No—and you should. The Hallionne's replies made you look frivolous and ignorant."

Kaylin shrugged. "I'm not frivolous. I am ignorant, at least when it comes to the customs of the Hallionne. No one thought to inform me, and this is not covered in racial-integration class, so please, don't start."

"Speaking of not starting," Teela replied in Elantran.

"Who attacked Nightshade?"

"It may come as a surprise to you, but I wasn't there."

"But you—"

"I understand all the reasons why someone would attack him. Or why they'd be suspicious; it's bloody suspicious. Nightshade, Outcaste, is granted the crown of the Teller from his fief? In his Castle?" Teela snorted. "It's almost too much to be believed."

"The Hallionne believes it."

"Clearly. And frankly, that's good enough for me, but only barely. I've never liked Nightshade; in his youth, he was feckless and self-indulgent."

Kaylin's brows rose.

"What?"

"I've never met a Barrani, except maybe the Consort, who couldn't be called self-indulgent. I'm wondering if you're even using the word in the right way."

Severn very pointedly looked out the window, which framed the passing landscape, most of it thick tree cover. The sun was out; it was definitively morning. But the shadows in the forest were so dark it was impossible to tell what the sky really looked like. There was only barely a road here; even the Barrani carriages weren't up to the task of making the ride smooth.

"Do you know why Nightshade was made Outcaste?"

"No. None of us know. Have you asked the Consort?" Teela smacked her forehead. "Never mind. It's you; of course you've asked."

"She didn't know, either. Or she said she didn't."

Teela joined Severn in pointedly staring out the window. Except for the small dragon, who seemed to be snoring, it was pretty quiet for the morning hours of the journey.

In the afternoon, the caravan came to a halt in what looked, to Kaylin's admittedly inexperienced eye, like a patch of dense forest. Kaylin thought to stay apart from the others. Sadly, the small dragon apparently had ideas of his own in this regard. He flew off her shoulder while she was trying to scare bugs away from her lunch, and headed straight for the Consort. Kaylin cringed.

The small dragon had a kind of lazy flight pattern that made him appear slow; he wasn't. Kaylin ran through three small groups of Barrani eating lunch before she'd almost caught up with him, and she only managed that because the small dragon had stopped a foot away from the Consort's face. If he breathed small chaos clouds, she was going to strangle him. Or worse. He turned his head and squawked at Kaylin as she ran up and shoved an arm between his body and the Consort.

The Consort said, "I am not concerned, Lord Kaylin. I am surprised, and possibly flattered, by his interest."

"He probably wants to steal your food."

"He is welcome to it. I find I have little appetite at the moment."

Kaylin hesitated briefly and then sat a yard away from the Consort; the Consort had a log, but she could make a dirt heap look vaguely thronelike just by sitting on it. "Lord Evarrim mentioned this morning that Lord Severn once served the Wolves."

"You know I can't talk about that, right?"

"You frequently speak of things that would be considered unwise. You are careful when discussing Lord Severn?"

"And Teela, if that helps."

"And An'Teela, yes." She leaned toward Kaylin, lowering her voice. "I know that Lord Severn values you. He does not value his position at Court, and I have little influence over him."

Thinking about Severn, Kaylin drew her knees to her chest and rested her chin on their tops. "Nobody really does. I mean, he follows orders, but he knows which orders are mandatory and which are discretionary. Outside of that, no one tells him what to do."

"I believe you could."

"Why? What is it you want me to ask him?"

"I want him to abandon his hunt."

Kaylin was silent for a long moment. The small dragon took the opportunity to return to her shoulders. "Why?" she asked, stalling for time.

"The Hallionne will wake," the Consort replied. "Hallionne Kariastos is concerned."

"About Severn?"

The Consort's brow rippled briefly. "You are inexperienced," she finally said, "or feckless. You have not learned to hide your thoughts behind thoughts that are similar; there are no layers to them. Hallionne Kariastos hears what you do not say, but more, understands that it does not discomfit you. He finds your interaction with the Tower of Tiamaris fascinating and puzzling.

"Forgive me; I wander. He cannot as clearly perceive the thoughts of Iberrienne or Evarrim; neither chose to dare the confines of his hospitality. But he recognizes something about Severn. Severn, he says, has mastered the art of silence. He cannot tell what Lord Severn is thinking."

"At all?"

"Hunger, exhaustion, apprehension, yes. But he is certain there is more."

"...Because of me."

The Consort's smile was brief. "Because, as you say, of your own thoughts and the things you most fear. But it is more than that. He recognizes the weapon Lord Severn wields. He does not wish to see it wielded within the confines of the domain of the Hallionne. He offered warning against its use in the green. Although it would cause me no pain were Iberrienne lost here, I ask you again: ask Lord Severn to forgo his hunt."

It was what Kaylin herself wanted.

"I can't." When the Consort didn't reply, she continued. "Severn takes his duties seriously; it's part of who he's always been. I can't ask—not without insulting him—unless the fate of the world is hanging in the balance. Literally. If he asked me not to pursue an investigation, I'd be angry."

To her surprise, the Consort glanced away. When she looked back, her eyes were a paler shade of blue, which made no sense. "Apologies, Lord Kaylin. I felt it my duty to try."

"You didn't expect me to say yes."

"I did not expect you to attempt to influence him in this regard, no. But to say yes? Many, many people do. It is a lie of convenience. Their various excuses for failing to carry out the action to which they'd agreed are also conveniences. I thought there was some chance you would accede—outwardly—and some that you would ask for more time to think about it."

"So this was just a test?"

"No. I would have been disappointed had you agreed, but I did feel I had to ask. I will not, of course, order you to do so. The situation is complicated at the moment. Lord Iberrienne feels that Lord Nightshade was the Imperial informant. There is only one fate for those who betray their people."

Kaylin said nothing. The silence was loud and uncomfortable.

The Consort glanced at the carriages as the Lords began to return to them. "Do you like this Dragon?"

Kaylin blinked. For someone graceful, stately, and never in an obvious hurry, she could turn and shift direction on a penny. "Bellusdeo? I do. I think you'd like her."

"I think there's some small chance of that, which is why I have no desire to meet her. Come," she added, catching Kaylin's arm. "We're about to start moving. Ride with me."

They started to walk toward the carriage when the small dragon suddenly stiffened. His wings rose in an instant; had they been sharp, they would have cut off her nose. His claws dug into the dress as he drew himself up to his full, and not very impressive, height.

"Lady," Kaylin said, tensing as she turned toward the heavily wooded forest—or at least to her right, because *heavily wooded* pretty much described all angles of view in this space.

The Consort's eyes widened; at the same time they veered toward indigo.

Something was growling in the distance, and those growls were accompanied by the breaking of branches and undergrowth.

The Barrani had been taking their rest in small groups of two or three; they rose as the growls increased in volume.

"Lady," Kaylin said, drawing daggers, "are these Ferals?"

The Consort didn't answer, not with words. She did, however, draw a sword. Teela joined them, and Severn—making only slightly more noise—was a few yards behind. "An'Teela," the Consort said.

Teela had also drawn a sword. For some reason, the Consort and Lord Teela made swords look as if they were the appropriate weapons of choice for women in long dresses.

Kaylin felt her daggers were out of place at Court, but they were the weapons she knew best, and from the sounds of the growling—and as it approached, it resolved itself into many voices, not one—she'd need them.

When the first tree fell, she flinched; the daggers felt extraordinarily small and flimsy. Severn's weapon chain was out, and he'd already started to wind it up; the Consort watched him—him, not the forest—with a fascination that verged on polite horror. When the second tree fell—and it sounded as if the tree had been struck by lightning—she once again turned to face forest.

"Kitling—"

"I don't get it," Kaylin said as Elantran fell out of her mouth. "We're not in the City. There shouldn't be Ferals."

"If it makes you feel better," Teela replied in her familiar street drawl, "these aren't Ferals. Ferals don't take trees down because the trees are in their way."

"But they're—"

"Yes. They're Shadows. And we're not far out of range of the next Hallionne; they shouldn't be here. Consort—"

"Hallionne Kariastos said nothing about the Hallionne Bertolle. It must still be standing—"

The third tree that fell caused their small group to break up instantly, leaping to either the right or the left, because the trunk toppled into the encampment. Horses screamed. Barrani voices rose in sharp command, not panic.

The panic occurred some five seconds later, as the creatures who had knocked the tree down now converged on the closest Barrani present: the Consort.

Severn moved. His chains were spinning in their vertical circle two feet from the Consort and her readied sword as the first of the creatures hit.

Teela was right. These weren't Ferals. They were almost as tall as the damn horses, but distinctly less pleasant. They had what appeared to be fur by the way it caught light—but the light was wrong, and the fur rippled in a way that suggested something other than skin. They didn't have hooves; they had claws at the end of padded, multiple-toed feet. Six of them, at best guess. They had tails.

Their damn tails were barbed. They had one set of jaws—at least at the moment—but when the first beast really opened its mouth, it seemed to go on forever, and there were at least two rows of teeth in both the upper and lower jaws. The first of the creatures crashed into the spinning blade-barrier and lost parts of that impressive jaw. It shed a lot of blood.

Unfortunately, momentum carried the rest of its body straight into Severn.

The Consort moved before he crashed into her. Teela was already swinging her sword; she wasn't flailing. Something headless was.

Kaylin counted four remaining creatures. She backed away as quickly as she could; her retreat was made hazardous by the appearance of a new, giant log in a very inconvenient place. She stumbled as her feet hit it, and failed to find her footing; the small dragon leapt off her shoulders as she fell awkwardly to her knees. She looked up in panic and saw that he'd flown, claws extended, into the face of the nearest creature—the one, in fact, who was heading toward her. He was more cautious than the front-runner of his pack had been; clearly their pack mate's loss of half a face meant something to these beasts.

A volley of arrows flew past her head just before she rose. Since they more or less hit the creature who was almost in her face, she tried to ignore the probability of friendly fire. The creature rumbled. It had a voice that was like a dragon's in timbre, but not in volume—thank god.

"Get out of my way," it said to the small dragon. It was speaking bloody Elantran.

The dragon squawked, and as the creature attempted to eat it, she saw the characteristic enlargement of chest that meant dragon breathing, writ small. A small cloud of smoke left his translucent jaws and he darted toward the ground as the jaws snapped air a second time. They closed over the cloud the small dragon had exhaled.

She'd had no idea what the cloud could do; she knew what it looked like: gray, opalescent, Shadowstorm writ small. Now, for the first time, she would know.

The small dragon came flying back to her, but it didn't land on her shoulders; it flew above her head in tight circles, making very strange noises.

The creature, on the other hand, began to stagger. Kaylin was more careful in her retreat this time, using the high side of the rounded log as a guide; she watched as the creature began to writhe, opening and closing his great jaws as if he were trying to disgorge what he'd accidentally swallowed. He snapped at air, clawed at ground, and finally rose on hind legs—the middle and back pair—and attempted to claw out his own throat. Literally. Blood followed from the rents in flesh made by his paws.

Beyond him, another creature emerged to step cautiously into the gap.

Arrows continued to fly as Teela and the Consort appeared from around the fallen tree; Teela was bleeding. The Consort was not, although her pale dress was bloodied. Severn was limping slightly; he carried the bladed ends of the chain in each hand, but he didn't set it spinning again. One of the blades was also dark with something that looked almost like blood—it was wet and slick, but it definitely wasn't his.

There were two other Barrani Lords who had made it this far who joined the Consort, blades drawn; there were four Barrani Lords who were now attacking one of the beasts in concert. That, she thought, was a dance that was so perfectly harmonized the four might have been sharing one mind. Given how Barrani felt about that, she highly doubted it.

The carriages were in disarray; half the horses had panicked, but not all. She saw that some of the Lords had gathered them and were keeping them calm. When she looked back at the four Barrani Lords, she counted three.

"Kaylin!"

She leapt over the log as the creature that had swallowed

the small dragon's breath teetered and fell, still jerking spasmodically. The log collapsed when he hit it, and then the wood began to…melt.

Kaylin called out a warning to the fighting Barrani on all sides; she wasn't certain if the log's change of state was due to the small dragon's breath or inherent in the creature itself. She had an answer a few minutes later, when the three Barrani brought down the creature they'd been fighting. It was inherent in the creatures.

The downed beast didn't hit the log; it fell across the road to much shouting and general panic. Given its jaws and claws and the utter silence of the Barrani who'd faced them, this probably meant they knew a lot more about these creatures than Kaylin did. Evarrim appeared, a Barrani Lord at his side, and they began a complicated verbal dance that Kaylin's skin immediately identified as magic—and at that, significant magic.

They levitated the carcass of the creature between them; when it was above the ground, Kaylin could see that the ground had shifted into familiar patterns of chaos. It was no longer the color of combined dirt and undergrowth; it no longer had their textures, either. Instead, it was the color of black opals, but repellant, and it appeared to be, in places, liquid and chitin.

She'd seen similar patches of ground in the fief of Tiamaris, and she knew it was dangerous. But so, apparently, did Evarrim and his companion; the body burst into flames, and the fire was hot. She watched carefully. As the fires continued to burn, and the creature continued to float above the forested path, she saw two distinct signatures emerge from their combined efforts.

She recognized one of them immediately. It had been attached to the Arcane bomb that had destroyed her home.

CHAPTER 21

The other bodies were disposed of in a similar fashion; the beast felled by the small dragon was approached last. Evarrim began to gesture, and Kaylin now recognized the fluid, defined movements of his magical focus. Sanabalis would have been less than impressed; he didn't approve of foci. He considered them crutches, a way of tricking yourself into attaining the correct state of mind to channel magical power and shape it.

The marks on her arms, legs, and back made clear, however, that Evarrim's magic was not minor, and even Sanabalis accepted gestures and words in spells that took time to bring to fruition. Evarrim's signature was bolder than Iberrienne's. In and of itself, this didn't imply that Evarrim's power was stronger, but the two Barrani Lords had been working in concert for almost two hours, and it was Iberrienne who appeared to be flagging.

Iberrienne's signature adorned the wreckage of her home, but it wasn't the only one. Kaylin hesitated as she watched the two men work. If a criminal were both careful and well connected, Arcane bombs with disparate signatures could be used; the signature itself wasn't enough to wholly implicate the caster as a criminal. Why, she didn't know—what other uses were there for Arcane bombs?

Kaylin. It was Nightshade's disembodied voice. *What has happened?*

We ran into the forest version of Ferals. They're dead. We have two injured. We've lost two horses; the Ferals appear to have broken into two groups and attacked the caravan from either end.

She felt Nightshade's genuine regret at the loss of the horses. The injuries sustained by the Barrani Lords did not trouble him at all. *Are you in the Hallionne? Hallionne Bertolle?*

We are, he replied. *There has been minor difficulty. If the Consort now assumes there's been a breach, tell her that she is correct; it is subtle. I have been able to lend power to the Hallionne, but it is not within my power to waken it.*

Kariastos said—

Yes. Kariastos implied that he would see the Hallionne wakened. I have reason to believe that this was true, but Bertolle is not… completely present.

Kaylin would have asked for more information, but she was interrupted.

"What killed this creature?" Evarrim demanded. Loudly.

Kaylin turned in the direction of his voice. The small dragon was once again perched on her shoulder, staring out at the world. She considered silence as an option.

The Consort, however, said, "I believe he swallowed the familiar's breath."

Evarrim's brows rose toward his tiara. He swiveled in Kaylin's direction. Iberrienne, however, did not. "You had your familiar attack the creature?"

"Not precisely."

"What, precisely, did you do?"

"Nothing." She'd stumbled over a fallen tree, but felt no pressing need to share that with a member of the Arcanum. "He attacked the Feral."

"It is not, by any definition, something as harmless as a Feral."

It was true. Among other things, dead Ferals stayed dead; they didn't dissolve the ground around them, turning it, in the process, to chaos.

Evarrim drew sword for the first time that day. The Consort stepped in front of him. She moved quickly. "Lord Evarrim." Her voice was cool. Kaylin couldn't see the color of her eyes; the tone implied endless blue.

"I wish to see the effects of the familiar's breath on the creature," Evarrim told her evenly.

"And you require a sword for that?" Kaylin muttered under her breath. She was solidly ignored.

"Now is not the time or place. Such a study could take days, and we are already two hours behind schedule."

"It would not take days—"

"It would take days," she repeated, "if done with any consideration for safety."

He wanted to argue. His eyes were perfectly visible to Kaylin. But after a long, long silence, he sheathed his sword. "Lady."

"Lord Evarrim." She turned to Kaylin. "Come. The horses that survived have been gathered; the way will be slower and the carriages may be more crowded, but it is now imperative that we spend as little time on the road as possible."

The Consort said very little until the carriage had been on the move for at least half an hour.

Teela and Severn had joined Kaylin and the Consort; Kaylin privately thought the Consort had chosen them because it was the Hawks or two of the other Lords. The Lords would not, of course, complain about her choices, but they weren't happy with them.

"Nightshade said he needs your help."

The Consort actually grimaced; she was tired. "With what, exactly? The whole of the High Court, excepting only Andellen, is in the caravan; no one is likely to attempt to end his life for hours yet."

"Hallionne Bertolle isn't fully awake. Nightshade suspects there's been a breach in the Hallionne's defense."

Teela stiffened but kept silent; the Consort closed her eyes. When she opened them, she stared out of the window, hands folded—and tensed—in her lap. "That would explain much. It is unusual to be attacked on the road itself."

"I don't understand where they came from. I mean, they're Shadows."

"Yes."

"But they're here, and we're pretty far outside the City."

"They did not come from the heart of the fiefs," she replied. "If you think that all Shadow exists in the heart of the fiefs, you fail to understand the nature of the ancient wars. There are other places, older and wilder; they are not contained the way the heart of the fiefs is now contained, although they are considered far less dangerous. The Hallionne are part of the defense against their encroachment."

Kaylin frowned. "Why were the Shadows here?"

"That is the question that now concerns us. Two of our number are tracking the beasts; they are not particularly careful when they hunt."

Kaylin hesitated.

"Yes?"

"Is it safe to send out just the two?"

"They have had experience tracking creatures such as these."

When Kaylin failed to reply, the Consort sighed. "No, of course it isn't safe. But it is information that the Hallionne may not be able to gather; the Shadows don't roam the lands within which the Hallionne are situated unless something is gravely wrong with the Hallionne. Did Lord Nightshade offer any other word?"

Kaylin shook her head.

"I think," Teela said softly, "they intend to gather at the edge of the Hallionne's domain."

"Yes," the Consort replied.

It was Teela who called a halt to the caravan, although it was the Lady who conveyed the orders. This time, the horses were gathered immediately; bows were strung in silence. Both Iberrienne and Evarrim traveled the two sides of forest that enclosed the road. Accustomed to the subtle bickering that well-mannered men and women of power employed, Kaylin found the swift and silent way they worked together unsettling. Very few words were exchanged; curt orders were given. Magic was deployed along the outer edges of the caravan. It was subtle and, for magic, painless, although she was instantly aware of its presence.

The small dragon's grip tightened as Kaylin stood her ground. Severn had his weapons out; he was silent as Barrani and as watchful.

"Teela."

Teela glanced at Kaylin.

"I think they're coming."

"They are. You can hear them?"

"No." She tilted her head at the small dragon, indicating the source of the suspicion.

Teela regarded the small dragon for a long moment; breeze moved her hair. In the dimmer lights of the encampment, her eyes were almost black.

"Are there more of them than last time?"

The Barrani Hawk nodded. "I should never have agreed to this exchange of information."

"You didn't. The Hawklord did. Worry about yourself."

Teela nodded, but she looked at the small dragon. "Keep her alive, if you can."

The dragon snorted. He was as tense as Teela looked. When he launched himself off her shoulders, Kaylin drew her daggers.

The Barrani reacted first. Arrows flew. Kaylin heard soft thunking sounds as they hit their targets; they were followed by grunts of pain. This time, the creatures hadn't bothered with the heavy growling or the casual destruction of trees. They hadn't charged in; they had padded forward as silently as something the size of a horse could.

That changed when the archers made clear they'd been spotted. Kaylin, standing behind the more heavily armed Barrani, froze when she saw the creatures leap into the front line; in the moonlight, they were coal-gray. She couldn't see their eyes, but she could hear their voices; they once again spoke in Elantran—apparently to issue orders.

Living as an orphan in the streets of Nightshade had caused her to develop a visceral fear of Ferals. If caught in the streets by Ferals, it was death; if the Ferals hadn't managed to pick up a scent, silence and stillness could sometimes preserve life. She felt like that child now.

Ferals in the fiefs no longer terrified her. These creatures did. She wondered how much better—or worse—it would have been had Ferals been intelligent enough to speak. And she wondered why, in speaking, they'd chosen Elantran; it was the human mother tongue in the Empire. Orders from the Barrani Lords traveled up and down the line; twice, lightning flashed in the trees nearest the carriages.

Those trees then disgorged angry Shadows.

Evarrim, much as she loathed him, was there in an instant. Iberrienne held the other side of the road. Whatever else he'd planned, whatever he'd done, he was risking his life on the front lines. Two men not graced with the tiara of the Arcanum joined them, although they didn't sheathe their swords. The small dragon stopped its circling flight above her head; he darted toward the nearest pack of Shadows. And they were a pack, to Kaylin's eye; they worked in concert.

Severn joined the group nearest Kaylin, standing to one side.

Kaylin looked at her daggers and swore that she'd master a sword if it killed her. Then she just swore. It helped. It burned through some of the terror that kept her nearly immobile. She caught sight of the small dragon as he flew above the three beasts who had formed a front line with which to attack the Barrani; three were all they could fit, given the placement of trees they hadn't bothered to overturn in their rush.

Teela was in the front rank. The Consort was not; she stood behind, her arms by her side. When the borders of Tiamaris had been heavily contested, the army of Shadows had stayed on the right side of the boundary. Here, nothing kept them in check.

Some of them died. They died in number, but the Barrani Lords were injured; the miracle was that they weren't corpses. Sheathing daggers, and knowing just how little Barrani liked healing, she ran, keeping low to ground, to reach the first man's side. Someone had already stepped into the space he'd vacated. She dragged the Barrani Lord out of the immediate range of jaws or friendly swords, he was so heavy that she stopped well before she'd reached a carriage.

Placing her hands against his cheeks, she concentrated. The marks on her arms—the few that were visible in the long sleeves of the dress she'd been gifted by the Hallionne—began to glow. In the moonlight, they were warm and golden. The Barrani Lord was conscious, but in a way that suggested this was a bad thing; his eyes were open, unblinking, his stare glassy.

He grimaced, focusing on her face; it clearly wasn't a face he wanted to see, and he caught her hands—or rather, her wrists—in both of his to pull them away.

She said, "The Shadow will kill you. I'll let you die if you fight me; even mostly dead, you'd probably win. Your choice."

He was going to choose death; she knew it. But Evarrim's voice, sharp and cold, drifted into that resolve. "The Consort is on the field. How many can we afford to lose before she has no defense at all?"

The words were enough, but only barely; the Barrani Lord's hands trembled as he released hers.

At her back, the creatures were snarling and barking orders; in front of her, a dying Barrani Lord was struggling not to curse her existence. She would get no thanks for this night's work, but at the moment, it didn't matter. Something was wrong with his wounds.

Kaylin pulled her hands back, fumbling with the studs on the bracer that contained her unpredictable magic. It snapped open and she tossed it over her shoulder; she couldn't work with it on. She hoped whatever magic caused it to return to its keeper—generally Severn—worked outside of Elantra, because there was no way she was going to find it again tonight.

Remembering the sudden dissolution of a newly felled tree and the physical chaos that had once been road, she could guess. Healing wasn't magic in the Sanabalis sense of the word. It was less about forcing a body to conform to her will by dumping power into it until it was too stupefied to disobey, and more about channeling power into the places it needed to be for the body to naturally heal itself. It was about holding enough of the body together so that the person didn't die while the healing began—and continued.

Bodies had a natural shape, a natural form. Shadow, in Kaylin's experience, did not—it changed shape and form on the fly. She knew Shadow by touch, although for obvious reasons she had had as little physical contact with it as she possibly could; touching Shadow in general was a good way to shorten life span precipitously. This felt different. More solid, somehow; less amorphous and pervasive.

No, she thought, as she explored the damage done. It felt almost alive, distinct. It was growing and rearranging parts of Barrani blood and body as it spread. And it was doing so by changing the natural order of the physical form.

She pushed it back, which was hard. The Barrani Lord grunted in pain, his whole body stiffening as she worked. Whatever it was she was doing to save his life wasn't gentle and couldn't be painless. The saliva of the beast had worked its way into flesh, and the flesh needed to be uprooted to remove it.

She did the uprooting. She made no apology. She couldn't—it would have taken too much time to draw breath and offer the words. The rest of the Barrani body knew its own healthy shape, its own natural form; she was going to have to trust it to channel and guide the healing.

She tried very hard not to hear Barrani thoughts. He tried harder not to share them, but some spillover was impossible to avoid. Everything about him was a unified whole: the sound of his heart, the motion of his lungs as they struggled to inhale and exhale, the way his ribs snapped as she uprooted the last of the foreign substance, the sound of his anger at his injuries, his self-loathing at the idea that survival might depend on a mortal—an upstart Lord of the High Court, and the Consort's personal pet.

It didn't even feel harsh to her as she guided his body into the right shape; it felt natural. He had endured his father's brief anger as he declared his intent to take the test of name and join the High Court—or be lost to the race forever. He had endured his sister's pleas, and worse, her abiding envy and resentment when he had failed to fail. He had endured the derision of Lords who had been members of the Court for so long they had seen the rise and fall of not one High Lord but three. Everything about him spoke of his ability to endure.

He would endure this, and if the mortal dared to breathe a word about him thereafter, he would see her dead; he would not allow her the handful of years remaining in her insignificant, animal life span.

When he was at the outer edge of an endurance that meant survival, he grabbed both her wrists and yanked them away from his face, and she cried out at the shock of the loss of contact. He was still bleeding; he was still injured. But he could judge the state of his health for himself—in a way that most humans injured that badly could not—and he would not accept her pity for one second longer than absolutely necessary.

He knew what she'd seen and felt, but regardless, he composed his expression instantly. "You have done enough, Lord Kaylin." His voice was soft; it conveyed none of his fury. She didn't bother to tell him to sit down when he rose. Sergeant Moran might have been able to do it—she'd had years of verbal combat in the confines of her infirmary—but Kaylin couldn't bring herself to try. He retrieved his sword, looked to the fighting, and walked away.

She sat for a moment in all kinds of dark and then shook

herself free of the worst of it. There were other injured here. They were going to have to let her do something.

At the end of her third such ordeal, one of the things she considered—briefly—was suicide. The feelings of rage, self-loathing, and resentment felt entirely natural, as if they were part of her thoughts rather than Barrani spillover, and she had no easy way to shunt them aside. Severn found her; he was bleeding, and she leaned into his chest anyway.

"Kaylin—"

She shook her head. "Let me do this," she whispered. "I can't—"

"I'm hardly injured."

"I know, but you're you. The Barrani healing—I—"

"You're shaking."

She nodded.

"You'll exhaust yourself."

"They won't heal if they can't get rid of—of whatever it is in their wounds." She touched Severn's cheek. He hadn't lied; the wound—across his left forearm—wasn't bad. More important, it was clean. Not all of the injured Barrani had been contaminated, either; those that hadn't she didn't approach. It wasn't hard; they went out of their way to avoid her as word of her healing spread.

But right now, she healed Severn's wound instead. She felt his concern like a balm, although it was followed by unwelcome guilt; he feared to tax the power she had because neither of them really understood it. No one did. But he saw some part of what the Barrani had felt, and struggled with his sudden surge of anger—he knew anger wasn't helpful. As a child, Kaylin had hated it. Now? It felt normal. It felt clean. She wanted to cling to it.

"I'm sorry," she said to his chest, because she was still leaning against him.

"You could have let them die."

"I'm not sure they would. Die, I mean."

He pulled back, but only far enough to see her face. He didn't ask her what she meant; he seemed to be able—for the moment—to absorb meaning from her expression. Exhaling, he said, "Would you let them die if they'd stay dead?"

She laughed. The sound surprised her. "I'd try harder."

"And probably fail." He pulled away. "I'm heading to the back of the caravan; there's still fighting there."

"And the front?"

"Everything's dead."

She frowned and turned as the hair on the back of her neck suddenly sprang to attention. "No," she said softly, "it's not."

Trees had been partially uprooted by the time the attackers had been dispatched, and the ground in which the roots were sunk had been transformed into something vaguely metallic. The bodies of the creatures lay in an uneven circle, blocking the road; Evarrim and Iberrienne hadn't yet emerged to dispose of them. The sound of fighting drifted up the road as Kaylin walked toward Teela.

Teela stood in the curve of the circle of corpses, standing on one of them; she faced the road beyond the bodies. Her hair was caught by night breeze in strands. Her arms were by her sides; in her right hand, she still gripped her sword. She had chosen—they'd all chosen, with the exception of Kaylin—to forgo Court dress for light armor, but she fought without helm.

The Consort cut Kaylin off before she could reach Teela. "Lord Kaylin."

Kaylin did have clothing more suitable for an out-and-out fight in the dark, but the Consort had deemed the dress better protection. In this fight, she thought it better than the full armor Swords wore when wading into riot territory. "The heart of the green," she said, "is proof against simple Shadow."

There was, as far as Kaylin was concerned, nothing simple about these Shadows. Ferals? Yes. Ferals now seemed simple. And she hated that, because for citizens of Nightshade, they weren't. They were nightmare and, in the worst case, inevitable, painful death. They just weren't her death anymore.

"What is Teela doing?" Kaylin asked the Consort.

"Teela." There was no way to mistake the voice for anything Barrani or mortal; it was as if a dragon had chosen to speak Barrani in its native form. But he'd used a name the Barrani never used.

"Terrano," Teela replied. She lifted her chin. "I thought it must be you."

"Oh? What gave it away?" Out of the darkness something approached. Kaylin expected a creature; she knew they could talk.

It wasn't. It was…a man. Barrani, by looks and the arrogance of his posture. The Consort's eyes were so dark a blue they were indistinguishable from black; she was rigid, although the rigidity was reminiscent of a perfect sculpture.

"You always liked dogs," she replied. Her stance didn't change at all, but Kaylin thought her knuckles were white. It was hard to tell from this distance, and the Consort didn't allow her to get any closer. "Most of yours, that I recall, didn't speak much."

"No. It was a failing of their physique, not their will." As he approached, he glanced at the bodies beneath her feet. "Did you kill them?"

"Not all of them," she replied. "They were trying to kill me."

"How unfortunate. I didn't realize that you were traveling with the Court. They are here in number, this year." He looked past Teela to the Consort. "Lady?"

The Consort failed to reply.

"It must be significant. A significant telling. The Hallionne are waking, and they have not woken since the end of the wars with the Dragon flights."

"Terrano…"

He smiled. It was a Barrani smile in shape and form, but it was not a mask; it was lit, almost incandescent. "I am. I was. Terrano. It is not all that I am, Teela. You were not happy; I remember. I remember your father—"

Teela lifted a hand. In a cool voice, she said, "He is dead."

Terrano clapped. "I am pleased for you. But if you are done, you should leave all this behind. You heard the words, Teela. I am certain you can still hear them."

Teela said nothing.

"If you will leave the Lady, I will grant the rest of the Court passage."

"Why?"

"I am not concerned with the rest of the Court at this time."

"Terrano."

"…And I am not interested in seeing the Hallionne fully awakened; they are troublesome."

Kaylin took a step forward; the Consort grabbed her left arm.

"As you are," he continued, "you can't stop me. I offer you the compromise because you are—you should be—one of us, one with us. You are lost. But she, at least, must be silenced."

"She is the guardian of the Lake," Teela said evenly.

"Yes. That is unfortunate. But they will call others to take the test, and one will be found eventually who can fulfill her role. The children will not die; they will simply fail to wake.

You, Teela, have failed to wake. Do you remember what the Court intended for us?"

"They intended," Teela said stiffly, "to empower us."

"Then they succeeded admirably. But I believe they thought we would be under their control, bound as they are bound. They would have killed us all before we had fully been reborn; you saw that."

She said nothing.

"I do not desire your death, Teela; do not—" He frowned as a third entity entered their conversation.

It was the small dragon.

"What is this?"

The dragon hissed, flapping in place some three yards from the Barrani that Teela had called Terrano.

"Let me go," Kaylin told the Consort.

"Do not engage him," the Consort replied, not noticeably easing her grip. "You do not understand what he is."

"He's not Barrani."

"No, not now. But he remembers."

"He wants to kill you." Kaylin stopped trying to free her arm. "You intend to stay here and let the others go."

"We cannot spend more than a day in a fight of this nature," the Consort spoke. "And it will be more than a day. We will perish on this road. If that is the case, I will perish, regardless."

"You're the only person—"

Her finger's tightened. "No, Lord Kaylin, I am not."

Kaylin's eyes widened.

"Yes," the Consort said evenly—and coldly. "What I have seen, you have seen, and, Lord Kaylin, what I do for the newly born, you have done."

The small dragon squawked; the Consort and Kaylin both turned. He was glowing. He was glowing the way a lamp does when someone's lit the wick; there was a bright light that radiated from his center, through all the contours and ridges of his body. Terrano's eyes widened as the small dragon did its pathetic imitation of a roar—and exhaled.

"Kitling," Teela said, the word sharp and fast.

"I'm not in control of him," Kaylin replied. "You know that." The Consort let her go then, and she walked over to Teela's side.

The stranger glanced, briefly, at this second interloper, and his eyes rounded again. He had a much broader range of expression than the Barrani with whom Kaylin worked. "Teela!" he said, sounding shocked. "What is this, what is this?"

Teela's face had the usual range of expression: almost none.

"Look at her arms, Teela! They're marked!"

"Yes."

"Is she— But she looks mortal. She can't be Chosen, can she?"

"I wouldn't be the first mortal to be Chosen," Kaylin informed him. "I am also a Lord of the High Court."

His eyes narrowed. "Impossible."

"Tell the High Lord that; I don't argue with his rules."

"You're mortal."

She nodded.

"A Lord of the High Court is one who has taken—and survived—the test of name."

"Rules haven't changed much."

He frowned, and she realized he didn't understand the Elantran that was her automatic fallback. In High Barrani, she said more or less the same thing; it had more words.

He folded his arms across his chest. His face, which was like a Barrani face in shape with its higher cheekbones, finer chin, and perfect skin, was nonetheless far more expressive than the norm. He was annoyed. If it weren't for the obvious marks on her arms, he wouldn't have believed her. "Go away."

She felt her mouth open as her jaw dropped. Go away? What the hells kind of Barrani comment was that? Was he ten?

"Kitling," Teela said almost under her breath. "Please, leave us."

Kaylin, Nightshade said at almost the same moment.

She took a step back; it wasn't a large one. *Kind of busy right now.*

Yes, I understand that. I cannot see where you are without effort, and the effort at this time would be costly. What are you doing? No, that was the wrong question. What are you facing?

Something that looks a lot like a Barrani male. Same hair color, same skin, same height.

You do not think he's Barrani.

I don't know what to think—but he knows Teela and the Consort, and the Consort doesn't believe he's Barrani anymore.

The silence that followed was not good. *How many are dead?*

None. There are a half-dozen Barrani Lords who would happily see me dead because they aren't.

More silence of the same quality; it was like punctuation. *I am almost moved to regret my offer to the Halls of Law at this point.*

Stand in line. I think Teela would kill you herself if you were actually present.

She would not make the attempt. Remove yourself from your current situation if at all possible.

I can't. Terrano has offered to let everyone but the Consort leave. The Consort's willing to stay, and I'm not ready to leave her.

Did you say Terrano?

Since it was impossible to mishear the internal voice—although misinterpretation of the words happened frequently, at least on her part—Kaylin knew Nightshade was shocked. *Yes. You know him.*

Kaylin—leave. Leave now.

The small dragon belched.

This did interrupt all conversation, not that there was much of it, given Teela's tense silence. Terrano's eyes widened. He was facing the small flying lamp, so he could see first the stream of smoke that the little creature started to exhale.

In the light he cast—because otherwise, there wasn't enough light in the body-strewn clearing—his breath looked the same as it had before: murky and cloudlike. Terrano threw his arms up in front of his face.

The small dragon followed him as Teela shifted her grip on her sword. "Kitling, I'm not certain your pet will survive."

"He's not my pet, and you'll notice it's Terrano who's running."

"I do, but when cornered, we have always been dangerous, and that has never been more true of one born Barrani than of Terrano. Call him back, if you can. Lady," she continued without looking back, "assemble the Court, retrieve the carriages. We will not have time to purify the roads if we are to have any hope of survival."

The Consort hesitated for one long moment and then turned to do as Teela had all but commanded.

CHAPTER 22

The small dragon pursued Terrano for some distance. Kaylin attempted to call him back—to shout him back, really, which caused Severn to draw a breath so sharp it should have cut his tongue. She stopped.

"We don't know how many more of those creatures are in the woods," he said by way of explanation. "You're not a Hawk here. If the small dragon won't come back, we're going to have to leave him."

"And Teela?"

"Teela is not a fool."

Kaylin nodded, stopped, stared at the side of his face. She couldn't quite decide if he meant to imply that Kaylin was one.

"Terrano clearly had no intention of harming Teela; I believe he made the offer to spare the Court because of her presence. She may intend to threaten him; she may not. Neither you nor I are Teela." Severn caught her arm.

Be very still, he told her.

She obeyed. She obeyed as if she were once again living in the fiefs and it was night in the streets of Nightshade. Because she was now squinting to make out details, she closed her eyes and listened.

She could hear Severn's breathing as if it were her own; they were breathing in time, as one person. She could hear no other signs of movement, no cracking of small, dry branches, no squawking of small dragon.

No, wait; she could hear squawking. It was attenuated, soft, and it was followed by, accompanied by, a wild keening that she thought was meant to be song or speech. It wasn't the usual strangely familiar but utterly foreign language; it was simply foreign. She didn't recognize the voice at all, but the pain and the rage and desolation in it were unmistakable. It wasn't until Severn once again grabbed her arm that she realized she'd been unconsciously moving toward it.

He pulled her back, toward where the caravan was now assembling.

"Teela—"

"She'll follow. Trust her."

"It's not her I don't trust. It's Terrano, or whatever he is."

"Kaylin, your small dragon took down one of the creatures by breathing. Between the two of them, Teela will survive. If Terrano summons more of his Shadows, we won't, and that is not going to help Teela."

Because he was right, she followed.

Moving the carriages proved difficult because large patches of the road weren't packed dirt anymore, and no one liked the idea of attempting to cross them. In the end, the Consort chose to take the horses and abandon the carriages for the time being, for later retrieval. They therefore walked down the road. The various bags, packs, and outdoor gear that were strapped to the carriages were transferred to the horses, but the Barrani *moved.* Gone was the indolent look of arrogant tolerance that usually adorned their faces; they were alert, here, and on edge.

Gone, too, was the subtle bickering that posed as Court etiquette. They weren't concerned with their position in regard to the Consort—although they were all aware of where the Consort was. They watched her not as a ladder up the invisible ranks that divided the High Court but as the only woman who could currently approach the waters of the Lake of Life.

She wondered if this was what the Barrani had been like during the wars, and then wondered why it was that threat of death by external enemies was the only thing that seemed to draw them together. Then again, most mortals were like that, as well.

The walk was brisk. Given their greater stride, it should have been hard to keep up—but they were cautious, and they often signaled a halt while a small party of armed Lords, accompanied by Evarrim, went ahead. This stop-and-start continued until the forest suddenly stopped.

What was left as the Court emerged from beneath the darkened bowers of tall-standing trees was the bright, silver light cast by the two moons across an open expanse of grass—or at least what appeared to be grass. It looked, to Kaylin's eye, like slightly overgrown lawn, absent fences and slightly rundown homes in its center.

The Consort exhaled about three inches of height.

There were no creatures in the field, and creatures of that size couldn't hunker down in this grass; it was far too short.

"There," the Consort told Kaylin, lifting a slender arm and pointing at nothing.

Kaylin squinted harder. She also slapped her arm when she felt something bite it—what, at this point, she couldn't tell. She tried not to care. The city streets on whose patrol her job depended had insects; flies, mosquitoes at the wrong time of year, the occasional wasp. She promised she would never complain about them again.

"I'm sorry," she told the Consort, rubbing her arm, "I can't see anything. What are you looking at?"

"The Hallionne Bertolle," she replied.

Kaylin didn't understand what the Ancients had against normal buildings. There was enough variation in size, design, and architectural execution that they should have been able to achieve what they wanted without making it so difficult to find the damn door. Castle Nightshade and the Tower of Tiamaris at least presented themselves as residences and occupied street space.

Hallionne Bertolle appeared to be dirt with a bit of grass thrown on top. Hallionne Kariastos had been the river. Hallionne-whatever-it-was-named had been a tree.

The horses, however, were more sensitive than Kaylin, because they started to whicker as they approached the center of the very large, empty plain.

Evarrim stopped the party three times; Iberrienne joined him twice. Every time Iberrienne moved, she tensed, looking for Severn. Severn, however, stayed close to the Consort. They appeared to be looking for evidence of Shadow or its contaminants. Kaylin had, until this journey, subconsciously equated Shadow with civilization. In the light of the two moons, no trace of obvious Shadow was found; Evarrim remained unconvinced of the safety of this ground.

Kaylin remained unconvinced for better reasons but chose not to share them. She didn't need to remind the Court—three of whom had already tried to kill Nightshade—of her connection with the fieflord.

The Consort had reached the center of the field. The Lady lifted her arms; they were pale and silver in the moonlight, and as the minutes passed, they began to glow softly, as if she were a vessel into which that moonlight was being slowly poured. As she had done by the riverside, she began to sing.

Nightshade did not arrive to take the harmony to her melody; no one did.

But Kaylin felt the marks on her arms begin their slow, itchy tingle as the syllables passed by. Kaylin's voice was only remarkable for what it lacked. She liked singing but tended to avoid it as a kindness to anyone around her who had functional ears. She walked toward the Consort's side anyway, because in the moonlight, the dress—dyed in the blood of the green—also began to glow.

No one stopped her or barred her way; Evarrim and Iberrienne retreated. This was not a vote of confidence. The Consort didn't appear to notice Kaylin; she didn't appear to notice anything except the words of her song. Her eyes were wide and unblinking, but in the soft glow that surrounded her, they were a pale, pale blue. It wasn't the blue of anger; it was untouched entirely by the green of happiness. But it suited the silver cast of her face and skin.

As she sang, the earth at her feet began to tremble. It didn't break; it wasn't an earthquake. But it moved almost in time to the beats of the strange melody the Consort carried alone. And *carry* was the right word; she seemed to be straining under the sheer weight of the words that left her. It made no sense, but magic made no sense, either.

Kaylin, who could barely use her power to light a candle, couldn't carry a tune and didn't try. Instead, she watched the ground as it continued its odd rumble. In the domain of Hallionne Kariastos, the river's water had risen out of its bed to become a great, flying Dragon in shape and form; she expected that something would rise out of the earth in a similar fashion. Standing on top of it while it formed was probably extremely stupid—but she knew the Consort wouldn't move, and the only support she could offer was to remain by her side.

Sing, Kaylin.

I can't.

This is not the time for petty mortal embarrassment. This is not a song to entertain; it is not a song designed to part money from an audience. It is an invocation, not more, not less. Sing.

I can't. I don't know the words.

He fell silent, but she wasn't fooled; she could feel his frustration, and nothing about it spoke of retreat. Her arms were glowing, each stroke and line the soft silver that the unmarked Consort also shed. It was an unusual color for the marks, but she'd never managed to figure out how the color of the marks was significant.

Nightshade began to sing. Kaylin heard it instantly—felt it as a sudden, inexplicable warmth in her own chest. She understood that he meant her to follow his lead, because as she stood absorbing the feel of a voice that wasn't a sound, she became aware of his presence; both his voice and the sense of him strengthened as the seconds passed. Her cheek grew unpleasantly warm, and she knew the mark he had placed there in the fief of Nightshade was now glowing, as well.

It wasn't what she wanted, but it didn't matter. The Consort's arms were visibly shaking, as were her lips, and sweat now beaded her forehead, although the night air was cool. Kaylin drew a shallow breath, because that's what she had the nerves for, and then she joined the Consort's song, carrying Nightshade's harmony into the external world, where it could be heard by anyone who wasn't marked the way she was.

She tried to ignore the sound of her own voice, which was thin and reedy to her ears. The Consort's was rich, deep, its range so far above Kaylin's she couldn't hope to match it by squeaking, let alone singing. She tried to sing louder, tried to concentrate on only Nightshade's part of the song—which was easier because at the moment it filled most of her conscious thought.

She drew deeper breaths as she struggled with syllables and words that made no sense to her. She lost the fear of exposing her voice to an audience—especially one as unfriendly as the Barrani—and concentrated on increasing her volume. If she didn't understand the words, she felt the emotion with which they were conveyed: there was longing in these words that she hadn't heard in the duet of Nightshade and the Consort by the river's side.

It was a longing she herself had never felt. It was not the song she would have sung after her mother's death, not the song she would have chosen for Steffi and Jade. It was like a visceral, terrible need—there was no guilt, no regret, no confusion, just a universe full of loneliness, isolation, pain. There was only one way to end that, and she sang a plea, a tirade, a demand. She laid bare the whole of her desire.

But it wasn't her desire. She almost stopped singing, stumbled on two words, and righted herself with effort. The Consort continued without her. So, if it came to that, did Nightshade, and she once again slipped into the stream of his voiceless voice, pulling harmony that matched melody in a blending of two voices. Of three.

The earth rose. At first it appeared to Kaylin that something that lay beneath it must be slowly crawling its way out of the dirt, but as the song continued, she realized it was the earth itself, the way Kariastos-as-Dragon had been the river water. Something about the fluidity and the clarity of the water had added beauty to that transformation of nature; the earth itself was not so kind. The dirt that rose, rose in dark clumps and only slowly took the form and shape of a man. In the dark,

Kaylin thought she could see the confused struggle of worms much happier below the earth's surface.

She closed her eyes and then forced herself to open them again. She regularly washed blood and birth fluids off newborn infants who had looked just as disturbing the first time. She could think of this as a birth. She could force herself to do that. Even with the worms and the million-legged unknown insects that also reared up from the sculpted earth.

The dirt condensed as it rose; a misshapen pillar that was tall and slender formed as invisible hands—or words—packed and pressed it into shape. The fact that parts of it almost fell off only became disturbing when the body, in the light of two moons and two singers, looked more or less complete. At a distance, she would have mistaken it for a Barrani Lord. That Lord turned toward the two singers; only one of them seemed to be aware of his presence.

He walked, and as he took his first step, breaking free in some ways from the bindings of the earth itself, a cascade of brilliant light passed through him, and the color and texture of packed dirt, small stones, and moving, living creatures vanished in that instant. What was left was a Barrani man. The light began to expand and dim. It left him clothed in robes that were very similar in color and texture to the dress Kaylin was wearing—at least in the moons' light.

He did not speak. But he approached the Consort as she held a sustained, attenuated note, lifting both hands to cup her face in his palms.

Without thought, Kaylin reached out and pushed his hands away.

A murmur went up in a semicircle that happened to coincide with the Lords of the Court. Even the Consort's eyes widened as her voice dipped. Kaylin, however, hadn't given up the harmony to silence, and the Consort, stepping back, drew breath and once again shouldered the weight of the song. She didn't ask—as the other Lords did—what Kaylin was doing. It was clear from the width and color of her eyes—they'd shifted to the usual darker blue—what she was thinking, but she only had voice for one set of words and chose the song instead.

Kaylin's hands encircled the wrists of the Hallionne's Avatar. They felt like warm rock. He swiveled to look down at her and then raised his hands, dragging her onto her toes. She sang, but her voice rose into a squeak at the sudden shift of movement. The marks on her arms, which had been glowing a steady, soft silver, shifted color; they became a bright, burning gold. Sadly, burning felt literal; over half her body suddenly felt as if it was on fire.

But she knew what she was looking for, because the Hallionne had opened his eyes—and his eyes looked like patches of chaos, encased in sockets. She knew that the Avatars weren't flesh and blood, that the rules of physical form didn't bind them the same way they did the rest of the living, breathing denizens of the world. Even given that, his eyes were wrong.

And Nightshade had told her there would be some difficulty with his awakening.

What he hadn't told her—probably because it seemed so bloody obvious—was that healers never attempted to heal a building. Healing for Kaylin was intuitive. She could only detail the effects of what she did because she'd spent a long time at Red's elbow in the morgue. The body had its own energy, its own sense of its best and truest self, none of which generally involved injuries or diseases.

The Hallionne had a body; touching wrists that felt like warm stone was almost like touching fingernails. The sense of the rest of its form was there but almost beyond reach. She reached anyway. The Consort sang. Kaylin wasn't certain if she continued the harmony; she had found something very similar to the infection or intrusion that had almost killed the Barrani by altering their essential nature. But in the Hallionne, she found something else as well, and it almost caused her to let go and pull out as quickly as she possibly could.

At the heart of the Hallionne was a name: a True Name.

It was not like the names in the Lake of Life; it was much closer to the density of design and pattern of Bellusdeo's final name. But it was larger than that. She couldn't see the whole of it at once, or couldn't keep the whole of it in mind.

She understood, staring at this word, that she would have to try—because she understood that it, like the Tower of Tiamaris, was under attack. In the Tower the words that comprised the Laws of governance had been physical; she could touch them, could hold them, could brace them with hands or shoulders to keep them from collapsing or falling.

Here, that wasn't the case: there was nothing to hold on to and nothing to brace herself against; there was a word that seemed strangely elongated, as if it were being constricted by something she couldn't see. It was, in some ways, like a normal, living body: she had an instinctive sense of what its shape should be. Unlike a living body, she had no ready way to channel power into it so that the form righted itself.

She opened her eyes and discovered that she could still see the name; it hovered behind and above its Avatar. She released his arms and slid to the ground. He tried to grab her, but he moved far too slowly. She sprinted toward the word that she saw, and when she reached it, she placed her palms against the nearest surface. She touched it as if it were flesh.

This time, she could feel the problem, she could see the effect: something it had absorbed, or something that had invaded its perimeter, was transforming the sigils in its center. It wasn't Shadow as she understood Shadow, but it didn't matter; it had a similar effect, and that was the only thing that counted.

Severn, don't let him touch her. Don't let him interrupt her song.

To Nightshade, she said, *Don't stop singing. He can hear you, even if you're on the inside.*

She began to work. She tried to think of the word as a living form, a body; it helped, but only a little. If she could understand the whole of the word's meaning, she thought it would be easy; she could say the word, reinforce it. But she didn't understand the truth of these words and never really had. In the Tower, it had been Tara who had guided her through the hundreds of syllables each form required. Tara wasn't here, and had she been, the Hallionne would have considered her just another form of attack—and at that, probably a more dangerous one.

What had she done with the Barrani?

She had separated the parts that were foreign from the parts that were original. And it had caused more injury, more bleeding, but not, in the end, death. She wasn't certain if she could perform the same type of healing here, because she didn't know how the parts affected the whole—but she knew if they weren't separated somehow, the whole would become entirely different, entirely other. What was left would not be the Hallionne that the Consort was, even now, attempting to awaken.

The element of the word she was supporting with her palms was vibrating, and as she concentrated, she realized it was almost humming in time—and in tune—to the Consort's song. It wasn't a voice, not precisely, but she felt some of the sense of urgency the Consort's voice contained. Which made no sense; the word wasn't sentient, it wasn't emotive. It couldn't and didn't sing.

But it responded to song, to sound, to the unknown language of the Consort's entreaty.

She let her hand fall away from the word's surface as she reached into its center; her fingertips brushed the first of the three altered marks. It was cold. It was cold and it was silent.

Don't stop singing.

Words were like cages. She'd been trapped by words before—her own, both the ones she'd said in fury or fear and the ones she couldn't force out. She'd been hemmed in by the words of others: their orders, their rules, their commands. They created a maze through which it was almost impossible to navigate on the bad days.

This single word was both like and unlike the host of the daily little ones. She could—with effort and the notable loss of surface skin—maneuver around the rigid bits of its shape, its exterior lines. It wasn't easy and, like orders or commands, was to be circumvented only at need, but this was pretty damn necessary.

She heard the clinking of metal at her back that meant Severn had unleashed his weapon's chain. She knew this meant she had almost run out of time, and if she could have bent the exterior bits of the large, dense rune out of shape to make her passage to its heart faster, she would have. The flexible bits were all attached to her; she was certain the dress would be markedly worse for wear if she managed to writhe her way out again.

But she'd reached the three points of change; she could place her palm flat against their surfaces, and did, braced for cold. They were cold. They were cold like ice was, in dry winter air. Far too thick to be brittle, they couldn't be snapped or broken, and she thought if she pulled her hands back, she'd leave skin behind.

She could afford that; she could heal herself in a pinch. But she couldn't afford to let these go—not yet. Closing her eyes again, she felt the cold travel up her arms, and she pushed warmth back into them and, from there, into the palms of her hands. Here that warmth was like fire, although it shed no flame; she felt the ice beneath her hands begin to melt.

It would have been less jarring if it hadn't also screamed.

The marks on her arms were glowing gold-and-white; she could see them clearly through the tightly closed lids of her eyes. They existed in darkness, they existed when she tried her best to ignore them, and they existed in the same way the Hallionne's name and the Hallionne's invader did. Just…smaller.

They were warm. No—they were hot. They were hot, but they didn't burn the rest of her skin, and before they could, she drew heat from them and sent it, once again, out through her palms. The screaming increased in tenor, and clamping her jaws, she braced herself against the sound. It didn't help.

But the Consort's song did. She sang, and Nightshade sang, and Kaylin tried very hard to hear melody and harmony, not dying screams. Her arms were shaking, she was so tense; her hands melted figurative ice and the literal form of something that wasn't flesh. As it dwindled, the word's natural form began to reassert itself, healing shape and alignment, shifting cohesion.

Only when it stilled did the song come to an end—and even the end was a long, attenuated note.

She had no idea how to get out; she was standing in the word's heart. Lifting her hands, she touched a dot and a slender, undulating line. They were warm, not hot, and they felt very much alive to her. She couldn't remember whether or not similar structures had felt almost like flesh to the touch. She didn't think so and wondered if this was a characteristic of the Hallionne or maybe even the Towers of the fiefs.

"Lord Kaylin."

She turned—with difficulty—in the direction of the Consort's voice.

"Lady. I appear to be stuck."

"Stuck?" The Consort said, repeating the intonation of the Elantran word more or less perfectly.

Kaylin reddened and switched languages. "Is the Hallionne whole?"

"He is. He is now awake."

"Can he do something about this—this—"

"This what?"

Kaylin hesitated and finally said, "His name."

"You…can see his name." It wasn't a question. It also wasn't happy.

"I'm stuck inside his name, Lady."

"This may present a difficulty," she replied at length. "He is content to have you, as you put it, stuck inside his name."

"I'm not inclined to remain here," Kaylin told her.

There was more silence. Into it, Nightshade said, *You should not have spoken those words aloud, Kaylin.*

Clearly. The Hallionne would know anyway, and at the moment, he's my biggest concern.

Think beyond the moment. You understand that the Hallionne were made as defensive structures?

I got the impression they were made as babysitters.

She felt his smile.

To know the name of the Hallionne is a threat.

Kaylin spoke a few heated Leontine phrases. *If I hadn't seen the name, I wouldn't have been able to help him!*

He is aware of that; it is why you are not dead.

I'm not standing in the middle of a word for the rest of my natural existence. You may tell him I said as much, but skip the Leontine.

And I am now your servant, Kaylin? An unmistakable edge crept into the words. This was the fieflord's voice. It chilled her.

And then it angered her. *Fine. Tell him to keep me here. I won't go to the West March and you can handle the damn story on your own.* Had she not been surrounded by so many different forms, she would have found a patch of ground on which to sit, and occupied it like a feral cat. She did have enough room to ball her hands in fists, not that it made much difference.

Kaylin? Severn's voice was quieter and entirely free of ice or edge.

I'm fine. No, I'm really pissed off, but I'm not injured.

The Consort is speaking to Hallionne Bertolle.

Does he look less wormy?

Significantly less, yes. I don't understand the language she's speaking.

Which meant it wasn't any of the languages that were spoken in Elantra. *Is he answering the same way?*

He is.

Are they arguing?

Hard to say. The Consort's eyes are the wrong shade of blue, but she doesn't otherwise appear to be angry or frightened.

Is Teela back yet?

No, I'm sorry.

She closed her eyes. When she opened them again, she could see the night sky, the Consort, and Severn. She could see the less welcome Lords of the High Court, but given the work of the evening, didn't resent them at all. The bars of the cage had evaporated. Stealing a glimpse at her arms, she saw that the marks were once again the dark, dark gray they usually were.

She offered the Consort a very formal bow.

"Might I suggest," the Lady said, approaching Kaylin, "that in future you refrain from even mentioning the fact that the Hallionne has a name?"

"Done," Kaylin replied in hasty Elantran. She would have

said more, but the Avatar of the Hallionne chose that moment to approach. He looked, to her eye, to be made of chiseled stone. His every motion implied a perfect sculpture, every shift in position an act of artistry.

He came to stand in front of her and she closed her mouth, which had fallen open in an unfortunate way while she watched. Teela would have mocked her.

Teela wasn't here.

"You wear the blood of the green," he said. His voice was very low, almost gravelly.

Kaylin nodded.

"It is unfortunate. I am in your debt, and you are now a danger to me." Kaylin was surprised that the Hallionne understood the concept of debt.

"It is the debt and not the danger that concerns you?" he asked, reminding her that he was, for all intents and purposes, a Tower, and she was standing on his ground.

"I can't see the danger," she replied. "I understand what a name means to you—mostly—but I can't see a point at which I could ever use yours. It's too big, it's too complicated. I don't think I could get past the first two syllables before you—"

"Destroyed you?"

"That, yes."

"I would not take the risk if you were not Chosen, in all ways." He turned to the Consort. "The Hallionne, Lady, is at your service." He gestured and the earth cracked beneath his feet.

CHAPTER 23

Although a large crevice opened beneath the Hallionne's feet, he didn't fall. Instead, stairs rose, climbing out of the earth in flat, thick slabs that led down. The Consort bowed to the Hallionne before she took the stairs that led into the ground itself. Here, the Lords chose to take the risk of residence within the Hallionne, rather than upon the plains that surrounded it; they even led the horses. The horses were nervous—understandably so—but the Barrani to whom they'd been entrusted coaxed them down the stairs toward a standing stone arch that appeared to open into dirt.

The horses were not required to offer the Hallionne's entrance their blood; the Barrani, clearly, were. Some passed through without making that offering, a sure sign that they had come this way at least once before. Severn, however, had not. When the Barrani were gone, he made his way down the stairs and stopped at the midway point to make certain Kaylin was following.

During this tired procession, the Hallionne's Avatar kept watch. When Severn cut his hand and pressed it into what looked like softly packed dirt, the Avatar nodded. Severn then handed her the knife, as he had done once before; Kaylin hesitated.

"It is not necessary for the harmoniste to offer herself. I am aware of her now, and she will be aware of the rules of governance. Enter, Lord Severn."

Severn did not appear to have heard the Hallionne. The Hallionne, however, was aware that he had.

"I intend no harm to her," the Hallionne informed him when he failed to move.

Severn nodded stiffly. Kaylin indicated that he should accept the Hallionne's offer of hospitality now, and he failed to see—or hear—that, either.

"Don't bother," a familiar voice interjected.

Kaylin spun in place; Teela was walking down the stairs. She was bleeding from a gash in her left arm that had apparently melted armor, but her sword was sheathed. Her eyes were blue and ringed with the dark circles that spoke of exhaustion; her hair was braided. Floating above her head, in a way that would have been dangerous had he been a pigeon or a seagull, was the small dragon.

"Hallionne Bertolle," she said. She offered him a perfect bow, injuries and the unfortunate state of her clothing notwithstanding.

"An'Teela," he replied. "You are welcome here."

The small dragon darted forward and wrapped himself around Kaylin's head. She reached up, pulled him off, and deposited him on her shoulders instead, as his tail was more or less blocking her vision. Then she approached Teela, who stiffened. It was meant as a warning, and Kaylin heeded it in a way she hadn't when the other Lords of the High Court had been injured.

"You're sure you're all right?"

"I am demonstrably capable of standing, walking, and

speaking," was the tight reply. "But I am in almost desperate need of a bath."

Before Kaylin could ask another question, Teela broke what might have become a deadlock by the simple expedient of grabbing Kaylin's hand and dragging her through the dirt on the other side of the arch.

The interior of the Hallionne was, of course, not dirt. The foyer was of stone, and similar in look and feel to the solid angularity of the cliff station, whose name Kaylin was now very aware she didn't know. The minute they landed, or at least the minute she could see her feet again, she immediately turned to Teela, who still had her hand in a death grip.

"Do not," Teela warned her.

"But the others—"

"If I were in danger of unwanted transformation, kitling, I would allow it. This is just—a wound. It is by no means the worst I've taken."

It was the worst Kaylin remembered seeing.

As if divining the thought, Teela exhaled, sliding into Elantran. "I was a Hawk before you were born. I've taken worse in the line of duty."

Teela started to walk. Given that Kaylin was still holding her hand—with most of the strength of the grip squarely in Teela's hand—Kaylin went with her. She managed to stumble her way into a fast walk, because Teela was in such a foul mood that she might not notice if Kaylin fell flat on her face.

"Teela—the Hallionne—"

"To hells with the Hallionne," was the grim reply.

Kaylin was watching the floor. The telltale light-of-direction, as she thought of the soft glow that pointed the way to the room the Hallionne had chosen, failed to appear.

"And to hells with dinner, if that's what you were going to say next."

"But I—"

Teela came to an abrupt stop and looked down at their joined hands. "Oh." She managed to disentangle her hand; Kaylin's fingers were white and tingling. "Apologies, kitling. I believe your Corporal is now at the entrance. He's not a fool; he knows better than to have a contest of wills with a Hallionne. But for some reason—and I admit I'm short of context—it looked like he was determined to do just that. This would be your fault?"

"No."

"No?"

"Well, yes. But not on purpose."

Teela began to walk more slowly, and Kaylin fell into step beside her, as if they were patrolling. "I saw the Hallionne's name."

Teela stopped dead, inhaled loudly, and looked down. "Remind me not to kill Nightshade when I next lay eyes on him. I've traveled to the West March before, and on only one occasion was it this much of a disaster—and at that, only during the recitation."

"Teela, was Terrano one of the children?"

"The children?"

"The twelve that went with you. Was he one of—"

Teela lifted a hand to her brow. "Yes."

"But I thought they were—"

"Dead? To the race, to the Barrani, they are."

"He recognized you. I don't even think he wanted to kill you."

"No, Kaylin. I will no doubt be questioned at length by the Hallionne and the Consort. There is some possibility that I'll also have to deal with my cousin. Evarrim," she added, before Kaylin could ask. "And I do not wish to do so while I am filthy and obviously injured. I will accept your help with the bath, if you insist."

Kaylin didn't insist, but she followed, trying not to look like an anxious puppy.

The Hallionne appeared to know where Teela wanted to go, or at least where it wanted her to go; the halls opened and turned—at sharp angles—to accommodate her long stride, but they didn't go on for miles; they ended in a hall of closed doors. "You may find the baths primitive," Teela told her as she headed toward the closest door on the left-hand side of the hall. "They are considered restorative."

The door opened into a small hall composed mostly of open arches; through one, there was a bedroom, through another, a conference room, and through the last, something that looked at this distance like a moderately well-lit cave. Teela peeled off in the direction of the cave, leaving Kaylin to shadow her.

The help Kaylin was allowed to offer involved aid removing armor and scabbard. She allowed Kaylin to peel cloth off skin so sticky with blood the fabric had adhered, and during this, she said nothing. Only the fact she was willing to accept the help made it clear she required it. Teela didn't grimace, flinch, or complain, and as her complexion was usually pale, it was hard to gauge whether or not its color was due to blood loss.

"If you won't let me heal it," Kaylin said, folding arms to keep her hands away from an injury that looked worse, not better, when it was uncovered, "at least let me sew it up a bit."

"Fine. I'll take the needle."

Kaylin went to the bedroom, where she found her pack in a closet that was part of the wall. She pulled out the requisite tools and returned to the room. Teela was half-submerged in warm water that had, as far as Kaylin was concerned, far too many large rocks in it to be suitable for bathing. Her arm, on the other hand, was both above the water and dry.

"You hate stitching wounds," Teela said, closing her eyes and leaning her head against a tilted rock.

It was true. Kaylin found something that looked vaguely like soap and did her best to get her hands clean; her fingernails had accumulated enough dirt she could fill a small planter. "I hate writing reports, too. But I do them."

True to her word, Teela let Kaylin clean and stitch the wound on her arm, which was about as bad as it looked.

"Teela—"

"I really do not want to answer questions, kitling."

"Was the small dragon helpful?"

"…Yes."

Kaylin inhaled sharply. "I think you should go home."

Teela swiveled her neck to look at Kaylin, who had joined her in the bath. She sat, legs folded, knees beneath her chin, a few feet away from where Teela lounged.

"You're not the Teller, you're not the harmoniste, and you're not the Lord of the West March."

"If you tell me that you're afraid that the recitation will hurt me, I will strangle you. Or drown you, which might be easier on the arm you've just stitched. Very tidy work, by the way."

Kaylin forced herself to say nothing, but the small dragon squawked.

"I'll strangle you, too," Teela told him.

The dragon now hissed, and Teela stood, shedding more water than strictly necessary as she did it so quickly. Her eyes were blue, but only an idiot would have expected a different color. Kaylin kept her arms wrapped around her knees as Teela grabbed a bathrobe and stormed out of the cave that served as a bath.

The small dragon turned to look reproachfully at Kaylin. "What? What do you want me to say?" She rose, aware that her dress—which should at the very least be bloody, dirty, and probably torn—looked as good as new. The rest of her, not so much, although her hands were clean. "I don't really love it when people worry pointlessly about me, either, and I'm trying to be consistent here."

The dragon snorted.

"Yeah, well. It's easy for you—you don't have any actual words."

Five minutes later, Kaylin found herself outside in the hall. Alone. She turned to look down the hall and wasn't surprised to see that it had expanded in her brief sojourn on the other side of the door. The halls seemed taller and wider, and the doors on either side of its walls had proliferated. She couldn't easily discern which way was out, or at least, which way led to food.

She was almost tired enough that food was less appealing than sleep, although her stomach didn't agree with this assessment. The small dragon sat on her shoulders, chewing her hair.

She looked at her feet and waited for the lights on the floor to start their directional glow. The Hallionne, if not present in Avatar form, obliged. She followed, trying to rescue her hair from a dragon who seemed to be…bored.

But the light did not immediately take her to the dining hall—if there even was one, given the events of the day.

It took her, instead, to a room situated at the end of the hall. This room had double doors instead of the wide single doors, all closed, that characterized the other rooms on the way, but as she approached them, they opened. None of the doors in any Hallionne seemed to have the wards favored by the security conscious everywhere in Elantra.

She was not surprised when the doors opened into an almost palatial room. There was, in fact, a long dining table off to one side on which food was heaped. The food should have been her first concern; it wasn't.

To the left, she saw a sitting room, and in that sitting room, two men she recognized: Lord Andellen and Lord Nightshade. Lord Nightshade had the stem of a conical crystal glass in his left hand, and he raised it—and a brow—as she entered the doors.

Andellen and his lord were seated; she failed to join them, choosing to lean against the stone frame of the entrance instead.

"The Hallionne seems to be whole," Nightshade said.

"For the moment, yes. I don't know how long he'll stay that way, because I have no idea how he was infected." If that was even the word. She drew a sharper breath, folded her arms across her chest, and said, "When did you know you were to be the Teller for this particular recitation?"

His gaze fell to the wine in his glass. "An interesting question." The words were cool.

Her eyes narrowed as she examined him—from a distance. Barrani skin was always exquisitely fair, and his was no exception, but he seemed to her eye to be paler than usual, and not in an entirely good way. Some of the anger and the justified suspicion left her. It had not been a good day for anyone.

"Did you know before you made the deal with the Hawklord?"

"Does it matter?"

"Clearly it matters to me, or I wouldn't be asking."

"Yes, I knew."

"Could you have refused the role? Could you just ignore the crown?"

"I?" He smiled. It was a slender, cold expression, but it was also startling in the way it changed the lines of his face. "No,

Lord Kaylin. It is not in me. Could it be refused? Possibly." He glanced at Lord Andellen.

Andellen rose. He retrieved an empty glass, filled it, and brought it to Kaylin, which made her uncomfortable. Andellen was, in every way—except for his oath to an Outcaste—a proper Lord of the High Court; Kaylin was a base pretender.

"Accept it," Andellen said softly, his smile robbing the words of danger. "I am, as I have said, in your debt, and even your observational skills must make clear to you how little the Barrani appreciate debt. There are two ways to discharge it."

"Kill me or save me from death?"

"You do understand."

Kaylin took the glass, and as she did, she caught Andellen's hand. "You're injured."

"I am. I was not as gravely injured as my Lord, but I will not thank you should you choose to interfere."

She let his hand go. "Are there any Barrani who appreciate a healer?"

"The Lord of the West March was not notably enraged when you saved his life," Andellen pointed out.

It was true. She glanced at the ring around her finger. "No, he wasn't. This clearly makes him very unusual."

"The Lord of the High Court was likewise unruffled by your interference."

"You're telling me you're not either of those men."

"No, Lord Kaylin; nor is Lord Nightshade. The injuries he sustained he expected."

"But—"

"He made his choice. It was never going to be a...popular choice, and there were always going to be repercussions. Iberrienne has more support than either of us expected, but neither of us envisioned the appearance of a female Dragon. The ways in which the two—the Exchequer and the female Dragon—

coincided was very unfortunate. The High Court would have turned a blind eye to Lord Nightshade's interference in the matter of the Exchequer. It was a paltry affair that involved, and harmed, humans for the most part.

"Had Iberrienne been uninvolved with the Dragon, it would have been for the best."

"He wasn't," was her flat reply. "And he incidentally destroyed my home."

"Lord Nightshade is aware that had the Dragon perished, you would have, by default, done the same, and he is not pleased; it is part of the reason—" He cut off the sentence instantly, turned, and offered Nightshade a perfect obeisance.

Nightshade's eyes were narrow and blue. Kaylin wanted the rest of the sentence, but not at the possible expense of Andellen. Andellen wasn't Teela, Tain, or any of the Barrani Hawks Kaylin knew well. He almost never spoke Elantran, and she couldn't imagine him engaging in bar brawls as a way of avoiding boredom. But she had grown fond of him.

"If you are here, Lord Kaylin, I will retire to the dining hall to speak with the Consort. There are matters that involve the Hallionne that must be discussed." Andellen left before she could think of a way to stop him that wasn't awkward.

"Kaylin," Nightshade said as he rose and set his own glass aside on the long, low marble table in front of him.

She met his gaze and held it. The small dragon tensed; his wings knocked hair into her face as he lifted himself to full height, still retaining his shoulder perch.

Nightshade raised a brow, but his eyes shaded toward green as he met the small dragon's intense and ridiculous challenge. "Do you think you own her?" he asked softly.

The small dragon said nothing, but while he wasn't capable of speech, he had ways of making his opinion clear. Kaylin couldn't see the color of the small dragon's eyes; his head was so far forward she could only see his ears and the back of his head.

"I think," she said carefully, "he thinks you don't."

"I…see." His eyes were still more green than blue; the small dragon's act of angry defiance had amused him.

"I wouldn't be amused, if I were you," she said evenly and quietly. "He was responsible for the death of at least two of the creatures who attacked us on the road."

He didn't even raise a brow.

"Did you know that I would be chosen as harmoniste?"

"No."

"But you suspected I might."

"Yes. Given the unusual disposition of the role of Teller, I thought it likely, if you were present at all."

"I don't understand the point of this game."

He did raise a brow then. "The point of any game," he said in a light tone, "is to win, Kaylin. It is not unlike your betting."

"If I make a bet, I know the stakes."

"True. But even if the stakes are not in your favor, you choose to take the bet."

"There are some bets I wouldn't touch." But not, if she were being truthful, many. "You recognized Terrano's name."

He nodded. "There are very few Lords of the High Court who would not. The names of the twelve lost to us are preserved; it is one of the few instances in which failure is marked and regarded with something akin to respect."

She listened to the words; they were polite, distant, formal. They were true, but they weren't the whole of the truth.

"We do not easily expose the whole of the truth," he replied.

"That's not why you recognize the name."

Her thoughts were an open book to Lord Nightshade; his were opaque to her.

"I have told you in the past, there is no reason why they should be. You hold my name, Kaylin; I do not hold yours. If you cannot learn to take what you desire, you will be hindered in all ways."

"I don't want to take what isn't offered."

"That, too, is a limitation. Or perhaps it is human nature; mortals would like something, but they do not fully appreciate desire. Their concept of desire is weak and ephemeral; they wait and hope, but they do not turn their will and their intention toward what they claim to seek."

His words irritated her; she wasn't certain why. She was certain that giving vent to the irritation, even in the Hallionne, wasn't smart. "You're changing the subject."

"Am I?"

"Yes." Her arms tightened.

"And the subject?" He was closer than he had been when he'd started speaking, small dragon notwithstanding.

"How and why did you know Terrano?"

"Was that the subject?"

"Yes. You wanted me to come to the West March because you knew that I'd be harmoniste, and you expected difficulty with Terrano. With the other children." The mark on her cheek was warm. It wasn't hot; it felt like a flush that occupied only half her face.

His eyes were a shade of violet as he lifted a hand to touch her mark-adorned cheek. She forgot to breathe. The small dragon wasn't paralyzed in the same way. He bit Nightshade's wrist. The fieflord's eyes shaded instantly to indigo; he reached for the small dragon's neck with his free hand.

Kaylin caught his wrist as his palm and the translucent

length of the small dragon's neck met. To the small dragon, she said, "Let go right now."

The small creature opened his delicate jaws. There was blood on his teeth.

"Please don't attempt to strangle him," she then said to the injured party.

Nightshade said nothing. He hadn't looked at her once, not even to acknowledge the whitening knuckles of the hand that gripped his wrist.

The small dragon, however, didn't appear to notice Nightshade's grip. Given the color of the fieflord's hands, this said something about his need to breathe.

"Lord Nightshade," she said. "Let him go."

To her surprise, Nightshade relaxed his grip. The color of his eyes was now in the solid blue range; he was angry. "Yes, I knew Terrano before the recitation that destroyed him. Yes, I thought you might be chosen as harmoniste, and yes, there is a risk. But there is a tale that was half-told, broken, ruptured, and we two—we three—might at last finish and understand as much of its meaning as it is given to us, by the Ancients, to understand.

"It is not the only reason; it is one of many. But it is the reason that you will most easily grasp, because it is a reason you are willing to face. I did not expect to return to the West March. For reasons which remain obvious, my chance of survival would be low. It would not be zero, but the possible gain—if any—was vanishingly small. But the Teller is immune, in theory, to the predilections of the High Court."

"Why did you suspect that this telling, this recitation, would somehow finish that tale?"

"I did not suspect, Lord Kaylin." His voice was formal, stilted. "I hoped." He turned away.

She started to follow him, but the small dragon bit her ear.

Not hard enough to draw blood, but hard enough to catch her attention. It was necessary. This was a side of Nightshade she had never seen, and she had instinctively turned to follow him as he retreated. Her hand was raised, as if to catch his arm or shoulder, to turn him around, to offer—to offer what?

She wanted to ask him who, among the lost children, had meaning to him, but she knew he wouldn't answer. He had given her as much explanation as he was willing to give, and even that had been far more than he wanted.

"It is," a new voice said.

She turned to see Hallionne Bertolle.

"Calarnenne, will you not speak plainly?"

"I have spoken plainly, Hallionne."

After a significant pause, the Hallionne nodded. "She holds your name."

"She does."

"And you do not fear her. She has seen mine."

"Yes, Hallionne."

"Should I?"

"I would not presume to give advice to a Hallionne," was the cool—but respectful—reply. "She will not break your rules, and she will make no attempt to harm you, if that is your concern. Left to her own devices, she behaves in a manner that would meet your approval no matter where she chooses to reside."

"And she is Chosen."

Nightshade nodded.

"From within your Castle?"

"Even so."

"Very well. I will speak with the Chosen. Will you join the Lady at her meal? She wishes to converse with you."

"I will."

CHAPTER 24

Nightshade left the long hall. Hallionne Bertolle indicated that Kaylin should leave, as well. She stared, with some longing, at the food on the table, but obeyed his silent command and left the room. He followed.

The small dragon yawned, displaying his very fine teeth. Those teeth were now more solid than she remembered them being. They retained some of the bright red blood. It was, of course, Nightshade's, and she was surprised at how much she regretted it. In all the time she had known him, or even known of him—the latter being longer—she had never heard him express concern that she trusted.

When she'd been in the High Halls and trapped in the dreams of the Lord of the West March, his voice had reached her. It was Nightshade who had saved her from a very long stretch of empty, empty gray; Nightshade who had pulled her out of the literal maw of an almost insensate Devourer. In all those things, she had felt his concern not as concern but as the worry Severn might have for his favorite dagger.

This once, she felt that he had a genuine attachment to—to someone. Not her, of course; not a mortal. But—it was real.

"Why does this matter?" the Hallionne asked as they walked.

"Because the Barrani almost never love anything."

He nodded; she might as well have said "water is wet." "You value it for its rarity?"

"I don't know if 'value' is the right word. I was…surprised. It made him seem almost human. He'd hate that, by the way."

"I will not repeat it. But I do not understand your thought. If you could speak with our tongue," he said softly, and with what sounded like genuine regret, "I would understand the whole of your thought, and I would never need question you again."

She shook her head. "You'd understand the whole of me as I am right now."

"Yes."

"But I'll change. I'm not who I was a year ago. I'm not who I was seven years ago, or thirteen. If I could have spoken to you in your own tongue at any of those ages, you would only know who I was at the time—but nothing in the speaking prevents change."

He stared at her for a long, long moment.

"Lord Kaylin," he whispered in a tone of voice that not even Tara had ever used. "That is exactly what the speaking does." He walked on in silence; the halls seemed to go on forever.

He came to a stop in front of a door. "This room," he said, "is safe."

"Is safety now an issue? We're in the Hallionne."

A smile—a genuine one—transformed his features, adding a depth of warmth that Barrani features generally eschewed.

"I am aware of that. Some of the Lords of the Court are concerned about your presence."

This wasn't new.

"It is; before your arrival, they were merely annoyed. Four covet your companion because they do not understand his nature."

"Neither do I."

The Hallionne smiled. "Not all of them believe this, although two are certain you are ignorant; they are, however, certain they are not. They are wrong. Regardless, all are concerned that your knowledge of my name will grant you control of my abilities, and they feel that you intend them harm."

She snorted. "Every Barrani Lord at some point in his or her miserable existence intends every other Barrani Lord harm."

He nodded pleasantly. "They are seldom in the position to cause the harm they intend, and they fear the consequences of their success enough that they seldom attempt to kill each other within the Hallionne. Not, demonstrably, never. I feel it wise to take precautions."

"Will I like them?"

He opened the door into what was not, by any stretch of the imagination, a room. It was a graveyard.

"And I thought the Hallionne had no sense of humor." The small dragon lifted his head, glanced through the door, and lowered it again. He wasn't worried. Then again, he slept on her shoulders or head most nights; he didn't need a bed.

Every other room she had seen in the Hallionne so far had boasted a bed. A single bed, true, but those single beds were large and relatively comfortable. Here, there was stone—stone markers, stone statues—and trees that looked as old and forbidding as the standing stones themselves. The air was chilly.

She glanced at the small dragon; he opened one eye, snorted, and closed it again.

Fine.

"I think I'd prefer the less safe," she told the Hallionne.

Hallionne Bertolle walked through the door into the graveyard, and she hesitated for a minute before following him. She wasn't certain she wanted the door to close.

"Hallionne are capable of lying," he told her, "but it is seldom required. It would, however, be difficult to lie to you."

"The name?"

"Indeed. I imagine that your Tower—"

"It is so *not* my Tower."

He lifted a perfect brow. "Very well. Your Tara, then. The distinction is necessary?"

"The owner of the Tower is a Dragon."

"The distinction is necessary. Your Tara would have similar difficulty."

"I don't think it's occurred to her to try; she's almost painfully honest."

"The Hallionne have a different concept of truth. I did not, however, lie. This is the safest part of the Hallionne; it cannot be breached unless I fall."

"You live here?"

He nodded and began to walk. Kaylin lifted her skirts to avoid the roots of a tree that defined *gnarled,* and followed. The air was chilly and damp, and the breeze, humid and cold. The irony of possessing the Hallionne's name and finding the heart of his vast domain so dismal and unpleasant wasn't lost on her.

But as she walked between the headstones, she frowned. She had assumed that they would be Barrani graves—why, she wasn't certain. These graves, however, were marked in a language she couldn't read. She knelt by a headstone that stood at two-thirds her height, and looked at the symbols engraved in the stone.

Reaching out, she ran her fingers across the runnels. The small dragon hissed, springing instantly to attention, and she withdrew her hand immediately.

"An interesting choice," Hallionne Bertolle said softly. "Why that one?"

"It was closest." She rose. The word carved in the headstone's center had begun to glow, and she found the light disturbing. Her own marks often shifted in color and intensity—blue, gold, gray—but in a uniform and even way that seemed to imply wholeness. This was a light she had seen in the fief of Tiamaris, after the shadows had transformed the ground; it was a light she had seen in the eyes of walking corpses, and a light she had seen take the forest floor where the transformed had fallen.

"It is not the same," was the Hallionne's quiet reply.

To her eyes, it was. The small dragon's posture and tension lent support to her interpretation. "How is it different, to your eyes?"

He frowned. "To my eyes?"

She nodded.

The eyes that she'd referenced widened. "I think I understand your difficulty."

Her difficulty. Of course, it would be hers—she was limited in all possible ways by birth, ability, and mortality. She drew an irritated breath. "My memory's not perfect. I've had some training, but I acknowledge my own subjectivity. I understand that at some point in prehistory, there were Lords of Law and Lords of Chaos."

He nodded.

"They disagreed about the fundamentals of what life either meant or should mean."

"That is inexact."

"Is it close?"

"It is a gross generalization. There were Lords of Chaos and Lords of Law, yes, although they no longer walk this world in freedom; only their children are left, and we stand sentinel against their return."

"You were created by the Lords of Law."

"I was created," he replied, "by one such Lord. The Lords of Law were not, as the Barrani are not, of one mind or one goal. No more were the Lords of Chaos, unless that goal be the overthrow of the Lords of Law. Law and Chaos," he added, "are also incorrect. They are symbols or motifs, and they have the same relation to the reality as a simple line drawing of a figure has to a living, breathing person. I would not use those terms, were I you."

She was looking at the changing face of the headstone and stepped back as the runes carved in stone began to morph, pulsing and writhing as if seeking release from the constriction of their shape. "Shadows," she finally said, "were the creation of one such Lord?"

"Three," he replied. "You can see the signatures of their creatures like eddies or echoes if you read them carefully."

Given that the Shadows she had met were murderous and intent on her death—or, to be less personal, the death of anything moving or growing in their path—reading them was not high on her list of priorities. But she had seen sigils or signatures in the wake of Shadow magic before, both in Tiamaris and in the Leontine Quarter.

She took another, deeper breath. "So your definition of Shadow is based on the work of three Ancients."

"Yes."

"Mortals are likely to make a broader judgment."

"Oh?"

"Lords of Chaos—or their leftover creations—have caused

a world of problems, literally. Several, actually. The creatures that we fought are Shadows by any definition of interaction with the rest of the solid world."

"Their goals," he said quietly, "are not the same. They are smaller and more discrete."

"How do you know?"

He smiled. It was not a happy expression. He turned toward the gravestone, which was now doing its best to melt; the stone was running in cool rivulets on the left front side of the whole. "Because these," he said, lifting an arm to encompass the gathered gravestones, "are my brothers."

Kaylin was confused, which wasn't her favorite state. The answer to her question, which he'd offered in the same frank way he offered any answer, appeared to be entirely unconnected with what she'd actually asked. Adopting the neutral tone she used during investigations, she said, "Hallionne Bertolle, you were, you said, built by a Lord of Law. Were all of the Hallionne constructed by the same Lords?"

He raised a brow. "No." He appended a silent and definitive *of course not*.

"When you speak of brothers, you aren't speaking of the other Hallionne."

He took a step toward the melting stone and the flashing, grasping light it emitted. Before Kaylin could react, he caught the liquid as it dribbled, like candle wax beneath flame, toward the ground. "That is perceptive, Lord Kaylin. No, I am not."

The stone flowed around his hands, between his fingers; he whispered a word and his hands changed shape to prevent it from reaching the ground.

"They're alive."

He cradled the stone as it flowed around his wrists and waist; the plain gray of its surface took on flecks of marbled color. "They are not dead," he replied. "But in any sense of the word *life* as you understand it, they are not alive. They do not speak. They do not sing. They cannot truly touch me."

The small dragon was hissing, his wings rigid and high. Kaylin stepped back, her arms aching. No, not her arms; her skin. The marks were active, reacting in their own way to the flowing stone.

"Did they ever?"

He didn't have to look at her, but did. "Yes, once."

"Were you—were you like they were?"

"Yes. I was not, however, what they have become. Can you hear them?" His voice was so soft she had to strain to catch the words.

"No."

"No more can I. Come. They cannot transform you if I am with you."

"And if you're not?"

"I will not leave this room until you leave it."

She moved toward him, and the dragon hissed in her ear. "I can't," she told the Hallionne.

"Your companion is afraid?"

This caused a different hiss.

"I think *worried* would be a better word. I don't know." She turned to face the small dragon. He held her gaze with his tiny opal eyes, and then he leapt off her shoulder toward where the stone was pooled in the Hallionne's cupped palms. "The word on the headstone—" She stopped. She wasn't even certain if the word had been a name, or the headstone a true marker.

"It was not; it was a rune of containment."

"And the headstone just a convenient shape?"

"A reminder." The dragon hovered in front of his palms. "What will you do?" he asked it, as if he expected an answer.

His eyes widened, which implied that he'd even received one. "Kaylin, your familiar—"

"I don't know very much about him," she replied quickly. "He can't talk to me."

"Can you not hear his voice? Can he help as he claims?" There was open anxiety in the question. Fear, she thought, but not a fear of the small dragon. "I cannot hear his thoughts unless he desires it."

"I can't hear them—at all."

"Can you not?" His eyes rounded. "But he is yours."

She owned him, she thought, the way most people owned cats. She didn't bother to say this, because she hadn't seen anything like a small pet in any of the Hallionne and didn't relish having to explain the reason for their existence. "What did he say he could do?"

"Speak," he said softly. "Speak with my brothers."

She stared at the hovering small dragon; he reminded her of a gigantic glass hummingbird. "He doesn't completely trust the Hallionne," she said. "But he can interact with them in some way."

He said nothing, staring at the small dragon so intently, Kaylin suspected that if the Barrani attempted to assassinate each other right now, he wouldn't notice. "Does he not trust us?"

"No. He's never let me cut my hand and offer the Hallionne my blood."

This caused him to look away from the small dragon, a brow raised. "But you were granted entry?"

She nodded. "He…bit…the tree."

"Hallionne Sylvanne. He bit the Hallionne, he survived, and you gained entry?"

She nodded. "The Hallionne recognized me thereafter."

"Yes," Bertolle said to the small dragon. "If you will do this, yes, I will take the risk."

She didn't ask him what he was risking. She didn't understand this graveyard, these headstones—one of which was now a cool, moving liquid—or the Hallionne. She understood, however, the strength—and the fear—of his hope.

The small dragon landed on Hallionne Bertolle's wrist, just above where the stone lay pooled. He then inhaled.

Kaylin's eyes widened. "Hallionne Bertolle, there is a danger—"

But the Hallionne said, "He cannot harm me, Lord Kaylin, and I have chosen to take the risk."

The small dragon exhaled. A stream of white smoke left his lips, glinting and sparkling in the dampened light of the graveyard. She had seen what the inhaled smoke had done to the hunting pack that had loped out of the forest. But…liquid stone couldn't inhale or ingest. If it changed, could the change actually be inimical?

It wasn't the stone that was her chief concern—it was the heart of the building in which she was now standing. If something happened to the Hallionne, assuming she survived… Her imagination was not up to the task of offering scenarios for their possible doom. Nor did Bertolle offer any; for the first time since she'd entered the building, so much of his attention was focused on one thing he appeared to have none left for the smallness of her thoughts and worries.

The stream of oddly reflective smoke hit the puddle that had once been carved headstone.

Kaylin watched, breath held, as the two combined. It was a visually striking joining of two disparate elements; the stone absorbed the smoke, but the smoke absorbed the stone as well, gas bleeding into liquid and becoming something other. The other had a texture and a form that was neither stone nor gas;

it expanded, changing shape, as the Hallionne opened his hands and let it spread.

And when it was done, Bertolle's hands were suspended in front of his chest in a loose cup that looked almost like the nerveless plea of a beggar at sundown, hands empty, eyes—oh, his eyes. She had to look away. She looked instead at the emerging form of what had once been the marker over a figurative grave.

Arms grew, and legs; a face emerged, cloud and stone merging to form an alabaster expression. It was, in length of chin, height of cheekbones, and complexion, a Barrani man's face. But his hair was the gray of stone, although in length, it matched Bertolle's or Nightshade's. He had the same full lips of the Barrani, but his eyes were gray, and if they changed in color, the range was not Barrani; gray was Aerian. He grew no wings, although it wouldn't have surprised her to see them. She thought, at this moment, nothing would.

But then he opened those lips and he spoke. His voice was not a Barrani voice. It wasn't a mortal voice in any way. It was…a song. It was, she realized, very like the song that Nightshade and the Consort had sung to wake the Hallionne—but the song came easily to his lips. The Consort had struggled; the construct showed no sign of effort at all. But there was no harmony to carry what sounded like a melody missing a few notes.

The small dragon did a pirouette in the air and then returned to Kaylin's shoulders. She was silent. Bertolle was not. He opened his mouth on a word and a song, and it was the song that took flight. She thought he would sing harmony, but he didn't; he changed the melody, dragging this newly wakened creature with him. Their voices were so much alike, in the end, she couldn't separate them, couldn't tell them apart. She listened. She watched.

Music had substance here. Notes were physical. The form of the stranger solidified; it gained color, texture, and weight. Strands of hair began to move as stone gave way to something softer and more delicate. Even the gray of his eyes deepened into an almost endless night. She thought they might sing forever, and felt a visceral sense of loss when the last attenuated notes faded and they closed their lips in concert.

Hallionne Bertolle was crying. He wasn't sobbing; silent tears trailed the length of his face, unheeded. He spoke a single word—a word of many syllables that somehow sounded to Kaylin's ears like a whole, cohesive sound.

She expected the former gravestone to melt or dissipate or vanish; he didn't. But he spoke as well, softly, syllables blurring as if he had multiple voices, not one. Only when the two fell silent could she speak and feel she wasn't interrupting something so personal she should have fled in embarrassment instead.

"Are they all like that?"

The nameless Barrani—who was not in any way truly Barrani—was examining the palms of his hands. "They are like I was," he said, each word annunciated as if with difficulty, or as if the language itself was utterly foreign.

"It is," Bertolle said softly. "He learns it now from me, but he finds it—"

"Confining," the stranger finished. "Have they returned?"

"No," Bertolle replied. They spoke Barrani now. It was vastly less musical, and for a moment, it sounded as thin to Kaylin's ears as it must have sounded to theirs.

She glanced at the small dragon. He looked exhausted. And smug. He looped his tail around her neck as he yawned.

"He wasn't dead."

"No, Kaylin. He was…asleep. This is the only place that they sleep quietly."

"I don't understand." She frowned. "You called them brothers."

"I did." He hesitated, which was unusual for the Hallionne. "Your familiar, would he be willing to wake them all?"

She glanced at the small dragon, who exhaled heavily. It sounded like a sigh. But he rose again, loosened his tail, and began to flutter toward the next headstone in this hallowed graveyard.

When it was over—and it seemed, to Kaylin, to take a long time—the awakened numbered six, not including the Hallionne. They spoke among themselves, and they did odd things with their hands and legs, as if testing the limitations of their forms. Sadly, their forms weren't as limited as a regular Barrani's, and at least one took about five minutes to readjust the arm he'd elongated to three times its original length.

While she watched, she listened; some of their words were as foreign to Kaylin as Barrani appeared to be to them. The small dragon was flopped across her shoulders and had made it clear he had no intention of moving again in the near future.

Bertolle approached her and offered her a perfect bow. He held it a long time. When he rose his eyes were brown. They looked almost like her eyes. "I am in your debt."

She shrugged. "You're in his debt," she said, indicating the small dragon with her chin. She was by now completely familiar with the Barrani attitude toward debt and wanted no part of it—or as little as she could shoulder. "Were you like them?"

He was silent.

"Before the Lords of Law, were you like them?"

"I...was."

"They weren't created by the Lords of Law."

"They were not created solely by the Lords of Law, no. Understand, harmoniste, that life as you conceive of it did not evolve in the hands of only one creator. They were multiple, and they worked in different fashions; no two, even among the Lords of Law, had the same paradigm of creation. No Lord of Chaos, either, although perhaps that is a given.

"But those of us who were alive—in a fashion you would not understand—knew death. We could be unmade. We could, if pressed, unmake. We understood the need to preserve the form and the shape of the world. I was not forced to assume the role of Hallionne; I accepted the request."

"They couldn't have chosen a Barrani?"

Both of his brows rose toward his hairline in an entirely un-Barrani way. "You have some familiarity with the Barrani. How many of your acquaintance could contain multitudes and rearrange themselves to provide both protection and shelter?"

"Zero."

"Exactly. I admire your tenacity in the face of your limitations, but feel that your ability to assess and observe requires work."

She couldn't help it; she laughed.

"That is amusing?"

"Not intentionally, no. I didn't expect a lecture in a graveyard at the heart of an ancient, wild building." As her laughter faded into a smile, she asked, "What will they do?"

"My brothers?"

She nodded.

"They will accompany you on the portal paths."

That scrubbed the rest of the smile off her face. "Pardon?"

"Was I unclear? They intend to travel to the West March."

The Consort was going to strangle her.

Bertolle raised a brow. "If she does," he said, "she will wait until after the regalia, and she will not attempt it here."

"I wasn't being literal." Mostly.

"Why will she be concerned?"

"Six unknown companions, who look like Barrani but demonstrably are not, are going to accompany us to the West March, passing through the other Hallionne on the way. She has no idea who they are or what they want, and they owe her no fealty or obedience. We've already taken injuries, most of which would have been fatal if not for—" She exhaled. "If not for intervention. You've been compromised, and—"

"Yes. Were it not for you, I might have fallen."

She stared at him. "I didn't do you any favors, did I?" It had never occurred to her that the attack itself might possibly be welcome.

"You did," was his soft reply. "I cannot be what I once was, before my days as Hallionne. I was…reborn."

"And them?"

"They came, after my ascension, to…keep me company?"

In a graveyard.

"Yes, although it has a different meaning for my kin than it does for you; there is no finality."

The small dragon yawned, nudging Kaylin's chin with the underside of his head. "I'm sorry," she told the Hallionne, "but I really need to sleep. And I'm not one of your brothers—I don't want to do it underground."

"No, of course not. You would die. I did not bring you here to wake the sleepers; I did not even guess it could be done. I brought you here because it is here that you are safest. If, however, you prefer, I will ask my brothers to accompany you; they are otherwise unoccupied for the moment."

They looked like children playing with a new toy. Sadly, it was their bodies, and it was very disturbing to watch. Noses and ears shouldn't do that. "No, really, I'm fine."

"Then you will remain within my sanctum. I do not understand your dislike for the decor, but at this point, it is meaningless. I will house you as you desire." He gestured, and the six odd non-Barrani men looked up, as one, toward him, their eyes bright with curiosity.

She knew they could kill her. She even thought she knew how. But they seemed very unlike the Barrani Lords who had lived for centuries within the political mesh of the High Court; they were almost like puppies or kittens.

Bertolle laughed. His laughter was like an earthquake; it shook the ground, causing Kaylin to stagger. "I will," he told her, "keep that to myself. It is interesting. If asked, you would say you are without power, but you see the world in a way that suggests the opposite." He pointed toward a small stone building in the distance. "There," he told her.

She walked quickly toward it, her legs shaking because the tremors beneath her feet hadn't exactly stopped. The door was, to her surprise, a little warped; the doorknob looked as though it had seen better decades, although that might have been a trick of the light, which wasn't good. It was like street light, she thought, after sunset, although there were no streetlamps to cast it, because there were no streets.

She almost reached for a key, and really, that should have been a hint. Shaking her head, she opened the small door and froze in its frame.

Turning to Bertolle she said, "Why?"

"Because," he replied, "it is your home."

And it was. It was the apartment that she had found with Caitlin's help. It was the first home she could truly call her own and the first in which she'd lived on the city side of the Ablayne. She entered the room, with its unimpressive, low ceilings and its creaky floorboards. Even her rug was here, worn and patchy. The small vestibule contained a mirror—her mirror. The one she'd paid for, admittedly with a partial grant from the Hawks. Across the room were the warped shutters that kept rain—mostly—out; she could see the string with which she had to tie them shut.

Her chair was between the door and the bed, and it had clothes strewn over its back. Her bed was tiny compared to every other bed she'd seen in the Hallionne; tiny, with a crappy pillow and sheets that were a little on the threadbare side.

She swallowed. Walked into the small kitchen, with its scratched table. Severn's basket was on the floor. She lifted its lid and saw that the cheese she'd bought was still nestled against its enchanted weave. She closed the lid, lowered her chin, and struggled with tears. She was mostly winning, too, but the Hallionne said, "Why?"

She shook her head, because speaking would have caused the tears to fall.

"You are not in the company of your enemies. You are not surrounded by your rivals. Not even your friends are here to witness."

"It's only a room," she managed. "It's—it's only a room. It's a building; it's not even alive."

He quirked an eyebrow at her, and in spite of herself, she laughed. "It's a building made by men. It'll rot. It doesn't speak and it doesn't read minds and it can't defend itself—it's got no mind, no heart, no—" She swallowed. "Do you mind going to talk to your brothers?"

He understood that she meant him to leave her, and did.

She crawled into her bed, still wearing a dress that had never seen the inside of her apartment. Tucking faded counterpane under her chin, she closed her eyes, and she cried the same tears that the Hallionne had.

CHAPTER 25

In the morning, Hallionne Bertolle knocked at the door. Kaylin rolled out of bed, instinctively glancing at the mirror; it was a safe, clean gray. The light across the edge of the shutters meant she hadn't overslept, and as the rest of her mind caught up with her body, she exhaled. Marcus wasn't growling at the other end of the mirror; she wasn't late for work. She wasn't anywhere near the Halls of Law or any other pressing emergencies of the kind that usually dominated her life.

Nor did she need to change clothes. Lack of laundering hadn't affected the long green dress. Given her usual day, this was useful magic. Unfortunately, it wasn't the only magic that came with the dress.

The small dragon was curled up to the window side of her pillow; he propped up one eyelid as she walked toward the door, well aware that the Hallionne had no need to actually knock.

"No," he said as she opened it. "It is a courtesy."

"In this apartment," she replied, "most of the visitors don't bother."

"The Consort is in the dining hall," he told her, glancing around the apartment, "and my brothers are waiting. We conversed while you slept," he added, "and I think you will find their behavior less unusual. I have made it clear that they are not to distort their faces or bodies beyond the acceptable norm for Barrani.

"Come, Kaylin. It is time to leave."

She took a deep breath, walked over to the bed, and picked up the small dragon. He opened both eyes this time, but only for as long as it took her to rearrange him like an awkward shawl. "What will you do with this—this room?"

"Nothing," he replied.

"Nothing?"

"I understand that it is significant to you, and I understand that it is also lost. This place," he added as he stepped into what was no longer a graveyard but just as elegiac, "is meant for similar things. I will preserve it here, although it is gone in the world you inhabit, and perhaps, should you come this way again, you will visit it.

"But you will know that it is here, even if you do not. Time will no longer change it. It is safe."

She shook her head. "It's not mine."

"Is it not?"

But…it had been her apartment, before both Bellusdeo and the Arcane bomb had arrived. It was home. And maybe, she thought, as she closed the door, home was like that: something you felt and desired, not something you actually owned. "Thank you."

Nightshade was seated to the right of the Consort when Kaylin entered the dining hall; it was more crowded than she'd expected.

"Lord Kaylin," the Lady said as Kaylin attempted to make

her way to the safe end of the table. "Please, sit." It wasn't a request. Kaylin nodded as gracefully as she could manage and joined the Consort's conversation-in-progress, which continued as she turned, once again, to Nightshade.

"You walked the portal road to arrive here."

He nodded. "I did not have the keys to awaken the Hallionne fully; I did what I could, as the Teller. He recognized the crown," Nightshade added softly, "or it is possible we would not have survived. Some of the Shadows had breached the Hallionne."

The silence was so thick it was tangible and oppressive. The Consort, however, nodded and indicated that Lord Nightshade should continue.

"He was not so injured that he could not deal with the Shadows; they are gone."

"Such a breach might explain the unexpected encounter on the road."

Nightshade hesitated. Everyone marked it. "That is my belief. The Hallionne was unclear."

"He didn't know or he didn't volunteer the information?"

"The latter."

The Consort relaxed her grip on the cutlery. "The other Hallionne?"

"Bertolle has been in communication with them. They are—or appear to be—fully operational."

"They are awake?"

"That is my understanding. But, Lady, I would not trust the forest paths at this juncture."

"Or the Hallionne?"

He chuckled. "We are forced to choose between the forest paths and the portal paths."

"It is not a choice I like."

"No, Lady," was his grave reply. "But yesterday's battle implies that we will take casualties—heavier ones—if we continue as we have been traveling. Kariastos has sent the rest of the pilgrims who have chosen to join us in haste through the portal paths; we number a full fifty. It is not a war party," he added, "but it is not insignificant. The choice is therefore still a choice."

"Do I get any say in this?" Kaylin asked quietly.

They both turned to look at her. They weren't the only ones. "Yes, Lord Kaylin. Any member of the High Court is of course given leave to express their opinion."

"I think we should take the portal paths." She almost couldn't believe the words that had just left her mouth. Apparently, neither could anyone else. Forcing her shoulders not to fold into a defensive crouch, she accepted the Lords' shock and cool disdain. "What we faced last night we cannot face every night without incurring losses. If the losses do not concern the Lords of the Court," she continued, her voice chilling to match the Court's general expression, "I will not plead for their survival. I, of course, will survive."

She had expected the rush of mute, distant syllables and was petty enough to enjoy them. But not petty enough to actually want the speakers to die. Not even Evarrim deserved that death, although she wouldn't argue against a strict, clean execution, which she was certain he deserved for something. "The recitation, however, seems tied to a season or a time—and if we're to fight, if we're to spend every night in a running battle between the Lords of the Court and the Shadows, we won't arrive in time. Our rate of progress will be too slow."

"There is a reason the portal paths are seldom taken," the Consort finally said.

Kaylin waited.

"Not all those who walk them arrive at their intended destination." Before Kaylin could gather enough words to form a single question, she continued. "The Hallionne judge and decide, and no one of us has ever understood the whole of that process. If the paths are open, some who walk them will return to Kariastos; some will be sent as far back as Sylvanne or even the High Halls. Only two gathered here are guaranteed to arrive in the West March, should we choose that option: you and the Teller."

Conversation around the table resumed. Although Kaylin couldn't pick out full sentences, the general effrontery at her presumption—apparently mortal Lords of the Court weren't entitled to opinions, the Lady's permission notwithstanding—was nonetheless perfectly clear. Kaylin was silent herself; the thought that some of the Barrani might not make it didn't trouble her. The thought that she could lose Severn just by walking between the Hallionne did.

But if Severn were somehow sent back to the beginning, he wouldn't be hunting here. He wouldn't be killing. Or if Iberrienne failed to arrive, there'd be no target. Not here, not now.

Kaylin.

She froze, her gaze cutting past all the High Court toward the end of the table, where Severn now watched her.

I am committed to this.

But you're not a Wolf—

I am. In this, I am. Understand why the Wolves exist. If they—if we—didn't, the Emperor would kill. The Emperor would fly. It's happened before. It's to prevent the deaths of those who don't deserve it that the Wolves were created. The Emperor was enraged by the assassination attempt on Bellusdeo. He almost destroyed part of the High Hall, and if that had happened, we wouldn't have a City. We'd have a war zone, and anyone caught between Barrani and Dragons would be dead.

Why does it have to be you? She stopped. Closed her eyes. *Can you forget I asked that?*

A ghost of chuckle came to her in the silence. She opened her eyes, because she realized it *was* silent. Lord Evarrim was standing, and beside him, she saw Lord Iberrienne rise, as well. One Lord whose name she didn't know joined them.

"Lady," Lord Evarrim said, bowed, "I believe the portal paths are less risky. If Lord Kaylin is new to the Court and its customs, she is nonetheless correct: we cannot afford the time we will lose in fighting a running battle from the Hallionne Bertolle to the Hallionne Orbaranne. We will therefore support Lord Kaylin's request."

The resultant inspection of Kaylin—furtive glances all around—implied that some of the Lords were now wondering what Evarrim's angle was. Kaylin certainly had thoughts on that herself, but none of them were fit for the dinner table.

The Consort finally lifted a hand, calling for silence with an expression that indicated displeasure at being forced to do so overtly. "Hallionne Bertolle," she said.

Bertolle appeared at the head of the table. He did not appear alone; his brothers, all of whom were kitted out as Barrani Lords, appeared, as well. They stood in a half circle at his back, surveying the table.

Bertolle tendered the Consort a bow that was considered a gesture of respect among equals. Her eyes were a shade of blue that looked almost green. She didn't recognize his companions but made no reference to them at all. "You have made your decision?" the Hallionne asked.

"I have. If you will allow it, and at need, we will risk the portal paths."

"I will allow it on one condition," he replied. That caused a sudden lack of motion to travel down the length of the table, although Teela and Severn both immediately looked to Kaylin, not Bertolle or the Consort. "These," he told the Consort, "are my warriors." He did not use the term *brothers*. "And I would have you take them with you."

"Do you expect difficulty along those paths?"

"Not if they are with you." He'd said he was capable of lying; Kaylin wondered if he was lying now. He glanced at her but didn't otherwise respond.

"Under whose command will they travel?" The Consort's voice was cool, and her eyes were now the blue Kaylin had expected on first sighting.

"They will obey your commands in all matters that involve your Court," he replied. "But in matters that concern the Hallionne, they will obey mine."

Kaylin, having seen them at play, wasn't as certain, but again kept her peace. She knew a losing battle when she saw it.

So did the Consort. "Very well. We will accept their company if you will grant us access to the path."

"Done, Lady." He turned to Kaylin. "Why are you not eating?"

She reddened and immediately retreated to the end of the table that contained Severn and Teela. Teela looked…tired. Tired, but less tense. "Kitling, try not to change the rules of every game you play, hmm? Some people consider it cheating."

"If anyone's cheating here, it's not me."

"No. If it were you, it wouldn't be dangerous."

Kaylin's brows rose.

"You're very easy to read," the Barrani Hawk said. "Who are the six?"

"I don't know their names," she hedged as she pulled out a chair in front of an empty plate. She hadn't had much for dinner, and from the sounds of it, this was going to be the big meal of the day.

"How dangerous are they?"

"If they want you dead? You're probably dead." Kaylin

spoke in quiet Aerian, because she was relatively certain that was a safe language; Leontine would have worked as well, but it was by necessity louder and less subtle.

"You," Teela added, "or me?"

"You. I'd put myself in the 'definitely,' not 'probably' category."

Teela nodded, watching Kaylin eat. "You slept well." It wasn't a question.

"I did. I didn't expect to, but I did. How can you tell?"

"You have an appetite and your color is better. Where did the six come from?" Teela was not about to let this go.

"They came from the heart of the Hallionne," Kaylin replied around a mouthful of very soft bread. "Where they've been more or less sleeping for—actually, I didn't ask. Possibly as long as the Hallionne has existed."

Teela's Court smile froze in place. "Corporal?"

"Oh, she means it," Severn replied with an easy smile that was a complete contrast to Teela's. "She's concerned, but not more than she would be if six Lords of the High Court insisted on joining us without explanation."

"That is not comforting."

He laughed. "No."

After breakfast, the remainder of which was enormously subdued for the Barrani, the Consort left the head of the table and walked toward the empty space behind it. She lifted her arms, as she had done in the first two stations, and the exit—or what had been an exit in those places—appeared. "Lord Kaylin," she said.

Kaylin nodded and approached. She didn't like the arches, but they didn't make her ache the way magic almost always did. The small dragon looked bored. "Don't pick up bad habits from Teela," she whispered in his ear.

Teela coughed loudly.

Kaylin looked through the arch. To her surprise—and discomfort—she saw nothing through the arch. A gray, vast nothing, like the empty space that existed between worlds. It wasn't like mist—mist moved, implying it had substance even if it was otherwise untouchable.

This implied nothing, loudly.

Hallionne Bertolle joined the Consort and the harmoniste. To Kaylin, in a soft voice, he said, "I am in your debt."

The Consort stiffened. Clearly, debt was trouble even if you weren't the one who incurred the obligation.

"It is possible that it is a debt that cannot be discharged," he continued, "but in all the small ways, we will do what we can. Give me your hands."

Can they still be attached to the arms? she considered asking, but decided, given the Court, it would be a bad idea. She placed both her hands, palms down, into the Hallionne's. His hands were warm, but not the way flesh usually was; they felt like fire in winter at the perfect distance. His eyes were opals; they reminded her of the small dragon's.

"And perhaps there is a reason for that," Bertolle said as his hands began to glow. Light, like translucent gloves, covered the length of his long, unblemished hands, and as her hands rested in his—looking absurdly like the hands of a child—it spread to cover hers. She had absorbed the light that had, literally, smacked her head by falling on it; this was different. It felt different.

The Consort did not seem overly concerned, an indication that Kaylin shouldn't be worried.

"No," Bertolle corrected her, "she understands what she can and cannot change; concern is a waste of her time and her energy. But she is less concerned because I am in your debt;

she considers it unlikely that the debt will prove so onerous I will kill you rather than service it."

"The Barrani would probably be a whole lot more comfortable with the wakened Hallionne," she told him, "if you stopped exposing their thoughts when they choose not to speak them out loud."

"It is not in their best interests to be made more comfortable," he replied. "When they are uncomfortable, they are cautious; when they are cautious, we are not forced to end their lives."

She tightened her grip. "Keep us together," she asked him. "If you have the choice—if the choice is yours—send us all to where we have to go." Kaylin lifted her hands. She could still see the light that surrounded them, although she couldn't feel it.

"You are afraid to lose your Corporal."

She didn't answer. Nor did the Hallionne. The six new additions to the Court now joined the Consort, as if at her unspoken command. While they crowded her, the rest of the High Court chose to stand back. All except Kaylin.

"Are you ready?" the Consort asked her.

Kaylin nodded. She didn't enter the portal at the Consort's side, though; she let the Consort lead, and hung back, waiting for Severn. As she waited, the High Court joined the Consort, stepping with their usual confidence through the arch. They vanished.

Nightshade followed, pausing a moment before Bertolle. He didn't speak. Neither did the Hallionne. But the fieflord didn't bow, and Bertolle didn't extend his gratitude for Nightshade's part in the song of awakening, either.

The room emptied until Teela, Severn, and Kaylin remained in the Hallionne, alone.

Teela then said, "You expect difficulty on the portal paths."

"Yes. But my brothers walk the roads. They will keep attackers at bay. If they vanish, they will reappear at the Hallionne Orbaranne when it is safe to do so. Go with grace, An'Teela," he added, voice softening. "You are known to the heart of the green; it speaks your name."

She stiffened, as if the spoken words were a threat. Kaylin was unsettled. Teela was…annoyed. Her eyes were blue. She turned to glare over her shoulder. "Hang on to your Corporal," she said in Elantran as she stepped through the arch into the gray.

When she was gone, Bertolle stepped forward. "Listen well, harmoniste, when the story begins. Nothing will be repeated."

"Will I understand what's said when the recitation starts?" she asked. It was the whole of her worry.

"That is not a promising question."

"No, but it's not a promising situation, either. Why did the heart of the green choose me?" When he failed to answer, she tried a different question. "What do you think the rationale for their choice was?" She spoke in High Barrani.

"You are Chosen," he replied. His eyes were the color of slate, with no pupil, no iris, no whites. "There is danger. Do you understand the nature of story?" the Hallionne asked after a pause to indicate the gravity of the question.

Stories, she thought, were things told to children to scare them into better behavior—or, if she were generous, to give them hope and dreams. Even broken dreams were often better than none.

"Our stories are not like those."

"I know. Your stories are true. But…"

"You feel that there is truth in the tales you tell your… orphans?"

"Yes. And no. No two people will tell a story in the exact

same way, but the children still recognize what they hear as the same story. They only get outraged if you change their favorite bits."

"...Favorite bits." His tone of voice was familiar and oddly comforting, she'd heard it from Tara so often. "There is no truth in the words you speak. Why, then, would small variances matter?"

She exhaled. "There's no truth, according to the Ancients, in any of our words, but people still need to talk to each other. We hear stories when we're young. We don't have immortal memories. If a hundred people hear the same person speak, they'll remember different parts of the speech. When we tell our own children, or our own audience, we've changed parts of the story. Sometimes it's because of our faulty memory. Sometimes," she continued, thinking of the Imperial Playwright, "it's deliberate. We change stories that are familiar to our audience. They listen expecting familiar things, and they're surprised. It changes the meaning. It makes them think."

His eyes darkened. They did not shade to indigo, nor to the obsidian that Tara favored when she was on high alert and couldn't divert enough attention to appearance; they looked, instead, like the depths of a very deep gorge would if a person was terrified of heights.

She reached out to place her palm against the Hallionne's upper arm, aware as she did that the gesture of comfort would mean very little to a building. "It doesn't harm the listeners. It isn't meant to change them; it's meant to make them think about things they haven't thought about before."

"And your thoughts are not inimical to you."

"It depends on your age." She grimaced, thinking about Dock in the Foundling Halls during his want-to-fly stage.

"Your thoughts cannot destroy you."

"No."

"And yet you hide them. You are afraid of their clarity."

She wasn't talking to a child. He didn't understand the things most mortal children understood, but he was a scion of the Ancients. "We're afraid of what they reveal about us," she replied with care.

"Even you, Chosen?"

"Even me, but I'm working on it. We're afraid that if we appear weak, we'll be attacked, ridiculed, or killed."

His frown was Tara's frown; it made her smile as she winced. "And so you lie?"

"I'm a terrible liar, but yes—we lie. We lie because we believe we're protecting ourselves. Sometimes we lie to protect others." This was not the conversation she'd expected to have with a Hallionne. "But when you speak the tongue of the Ancients, there are no lies."

"No." He closed slate eyes. When he opened them again, they were brown. Brown, she thought, and liquid; they looked almost like living eyes.

"Thank you," he told her gravely. "You are Chosen," he said. "And you are mortal. It has happened seldom in the long history of the Ancients. Not all the Ancients consider your kind with care; you are like the animals to us; you live brief and fleeting lives, and you cannot comprehend—cannot speak—true language.

"But you bear it, Lord Kaylin." He appeared hesitant for a moment, after which he spoke a single long, resonant word. The ground shook beneath her feet. "The Barrani require the truth as we know it to speak, to think, to live. But they do not hear the words we hear in the way we hear them, and some are resentful.

"Perhaps it is not unlike your secrets."

"Hallionne Bertolle," she said as the echoes of the vast word faded into silence, and a thought—an uncomfortable one—struck her. "What happens if someone who can speak True Words attempts to tell a lie with them?"

He closed his eyes and turned his face away, releasing her curled hands.

She had expected to walk through the emptiness of the vast gray space that existed between worlds until they reached Hallionne Orbaranne, but when she cleared the arch, she found herself in, of all things, a forest. The forest floor was dappled by shadow that implied branches thin enough at the heights of trees to let sunlight through.

The Consort, around whom the six had formed up like an honor guard, was waiting. "Lord Kaylin. Lord An'Teela. Lord Severn."

"You're sure we're in the right place?" Kaylin asked Teela.

"I am certain, Lord Kaylin," the Consort replied.

Looking at the trees and the road—both of which appeared to be solid, normal landscape—Kaylin noted the absence of carriages and horses. There were two familiar packs leaning against a tree. She passed Severn's to him and shouldered her own.

One of the six turned to her, with his unblinking, oddly colored eyes. "We thought that you would find forest familiar, but maintaining it is not an insignificant expenditure of power."

This did not make her feel any better. "Lady?" she asked the Consort.

"I have never seen the portal paths take this shape," the Consort replied. "It is a shape that everyone present sees; they appear to be forcing the pathways to conform to us." She glanced at Kaylin. "The Hallionne Bertolle must have felt the weight of his obligation keenly."

"This means we can walk to Hallionne Orbaranne without losing anyone?"

"It appears that way at the moment."

Kaylin turned back to the stranger. "I expected there to be a whole lot of nothing," she confessed. "And if it's not, I'm worried it'll attract attention."

He laughed. It was a very human laugh and therefore slightly creepy coming from a Barrani mouth.

"Really?" The laughter slid immediately out of the lines of his face. As the question left him, the rest of the Barrani tensed; Kaylin hadn't put the thought into words, but clearly, her lack of words were no barrier. Kaylin, however, did not react. If the Hallionne Bertolle—and Kariastos—seemed far too sophisticated and intimidating, Bertolle's brothers, for want of a better word, didn't. They really did remind her of Tara in her earliest days.

"It's because you look like the Barrani," she explained as the Consort began to move forward. "The Barrani don't laugh like that."

"You are not Barrani?"

That caused the Consort to miss a step, although she made no comment. Teela, however, snorted. "She is in no way, shape, or form Barrani. She's mortal."

"Ah." Pause. He turned back to his brothers, and they conversed in their almost musical and completely foreign tongue. "You are an…animal? A talking animal?"

Without missing a beat, Teela said, "No, of course not. She's much, much harder to train."

Kaylin had to admit that the trees—which varied in height, placement, and shape, much the same way normal forest trees did—made the walk much less disconcerting than a walk through the featureless gray would have been. This bothered her, because she knew it wasn't real. Taking comfort from something fake set her teeth on edge.

"It is not fake," the Hallionne brother told her. She wasn't even certain he was the same brother who'd spoken to her initially.

"We are all the same," he replied.

"Then why does there have to be six of you?"

He raised both brows. "We are all the same," he repeated, "but also different. We find your language limiting."

She glanced behind her and stopped; the other five had disappeared.

"They are with us," he told her. "But they walk the outer edge of this space. There are things within the passage that are inimical to your kind."

"But not to yours?"

"No. They attempt to harm, but they cannot succeed; we absorb them if they come too close."

The small dragon lifted a lazy head. He had done no flying, and little squawking, since she'd left the heart of the Hallionne. But he nodded before lowering his head again.

She was getting highly tired of referring to her companion by a generic, and not terribly descriptive, noun.

"Does the appellation signify anything?"

"It stops us from getting confused. No, it stops us from getting confused about which of you is which."

"Then you may assign us these appellations and we will attempt to respect their use." He added, in case she was dim, "They are not, you understand, names."

She bit her tongue. "Yes," she said gravely, "I understand the difference."

"I will join my brothers."

* * *

"Do you think Wilson can get lost?" Kaylin asked an hour later.

The Consort raised a white brow. "If you must identify them by name, could you not choose more appropriate ones?"

"He didn't seem to mind."

"No. I admit I find it jarring." She inclined her head toward Nightshade. "Lord Calarnenne."

"Let us continue; if they can, they will join us. I understand the reason for the forest, but it seems to me that the passage between the two Hallionne is longer than necessary."

"Time has always been...subjective on the pathways," the Consort said softly.

"The time, in this instance, is not subjective, Lady," Nightshade replied. He glanced through the trees as the scouting party signaled, his eyes shading into a dark blue.

The small dragon squawked at him, and he lifted a brow, dark to the Consort's white. "One day," he told Kaylin's passenger, "you will need to find words."

"He can make himself understood," Kaylin said because the small dragon couldn't.

"In a broad sense, yes."

"...And at least this way, no one's insulted."

Before Nightshade could reply, something else did. Sadly, it had the same facility with words that the small dragon did, but it also had a much, much louder voice. It was a roar. The Barrani turned in its direction. Kaylin, however, looked down at the small dragon on her shoulder, who had lifted his head. His wings now rose as well, batting the underside of her chin.

"Time to go," Severn said softly in Elantran.

"Probably long past," Kaylin replied just as loudly.

The roaring—and it was roaring—grew louder as they formed up and began to move.

Kaylin asked—once—if anyone was certain they were even going in the right direction. She received two glances and several glares and decided the answer, which was about as verbal as the small dragon's general utterances, was yes.

The Consort gave orders; the Court spread out. Those who carried swords drew them; those who relied on magical defenses also began to cast. Their spells did cause Kaylin's skin to break out in goose bumps in protest. Quick, curt Barrani traveled in all directions as the marching order changed; even Teela armed herself.

A second roar joined the first. The small dragon dug claws into Kaylin's shoulder. "I don't have a sword," she told him. "I have daggers; would you feel better if I drew them?"

He snorted, turning toward Kaylin's left. She kept walking, but turned the brunt of her attention to the left, as well. "Teela."

Teela nodded. Severn began to unwind his weapon chain.

A tree cracked and fell in the distance.

The Barrani didn't pause; they moved faster. Kaylin lengthened her stride to keep up. The skirts of the dress were loose and wide, which helped. Another tree crashed into its surroundings; it was far enough away that it couldn't be easily seen.

Kaylin continued to jog until she ran into Nightshade's back. She didn't even need to ask why the Barrani had stopped their silent forward movement; she could see. The flattened dirt path unexpectedly forked.

The roaring grew louder, which made a decision necessary; sadly, it provided no other clues. Kaylin, who never particularly yearned for command, was glad the decision was not in her hands. Left to her, she would have flipped a coin, which would hardly improve morale. Then again, the Barrani didn't seem to require it. They were grim, silent, they waited on the word of the Consort but shifted to the left, fanning out as they faced the forest and the sound of the occasional falling tree.

"Nightshade?"

No, he replied in silence, indicating that she should do the same. *Understand that we very seldom choose to risk the portal paths. This is not the first time I have taken them; it is, however, the first time they have presented such a distinct paradigm.*

The forest?

Yes. What I encountered on those paths the first time was almost formless; it was like a tunnel of glass. The path between Kariastos and Bertolle did not fork.

You think something created the fork? No, sorry, that was a stupid question.

It was, rather. There was genuine amusement in the response, although it underlay worry. *I do not know. If the path has been broken or altered, we can assume that neither branch is safe, inasmuch as the paths here are ever truly safe.*

Kaylin turned to the small dragon. He was sitting on her shoulders, his claws once again almost piercing her dress. "Right or left?"

He stared straight between the two paths, which was the answer she didn't want. To Nightshade, she said, "I don't think it's safe to take either."

It was the Consort, however, who replied. "Why, Chosen?"

The Consort never called her by that title—and she gave the title weight by the way she intoned the word.

Kaylin glanced at the small dragon; he didn't appear to notice. She considered the folly of attributing the decision to him and decided against it.

But the Consort had seen the direction of her brief gaze.

Her eyes were Barrani-blue, but at the moment, everyone's—whose eyes could change color—were.

"Teela?" Kaylin asked.

Teela joined Kaylin at the fork of the path. Like the small dragon, she stared between them, as if attempting to see through the trees that stood in the way. "It would be safer," Teela finally said, "to return to the Hallionne."

"I do not think," the Consort replied, "that is possible."

"Why?" Kaylin asked.

Teela gave her a look.

"Perhaps your sense of direction in this place has been impaired," the Consort said. "But if mine has not, the falling trees you hear are in the direction from which we came."

"They're to the left," Kaylin pointed out.

This got her rather more Barrani attention than she wanted, given its nature.

"They are to the left of where we stand, yes, but they come from behind. The path here has not been straight."

"Why the hells not?"

More stares. Kaylin winced and repeated the question in High Barrani, adding, "The Hallionne, in theory, built this path. Why wouldn't they make it a straight path between point A and point B? A winding path makes no sense."

"Lord Calarnenne?"

"She is remarkably straightforward." He smiled, and Kaylin felt the mark on her cheek warm slightly. "And it is perhaps a flaw in her training as an Imperial Hawk that she expects both logic and sense. There is a reason that the portal paths are seldom taken and only at need; it is not merely because not all those who take them are guaranteed to arrive at the destination of their choice.

"This is the other. It is my guess—and where the Hallionne are concerned, we are reduced to such guesswork—that the

Hallionne created these paths in order to transport the Court, whole, to the West March."

"And without the paths?"

"We would wander, Lord Kaylin. We would not see the same things; some would see the elementary gray of the space between portals. Some," he said softly, "would see other elements, and they would pick a path between them. It is very difficult to progress as a group of any composition in that case; my obstacles might not be your obstacles; my path might be a chasm in your eyes. At the moment, however, we all see the same forest; it was not a small expenditure of effort on the part of at least Hallionne Bertolle, and the difficulty may now reside within the domain of Hallionne Orbaranne."

The next sentence was lost to the sound of roaring and the accompaniment of falling trees. The ground shook beneath Kaylin's feet.

"Lady." Lord Nightshade bowed. "Your decision?"

"Lord Evarrim," the Consort said, turning to the Lord Kaylin most disliked. "We will attempt to carve out a path of our own."

CHAPTER 26

The why of Evarrim became almost instantly clear: he summoned fire. It was not the fire that lit candle wicks and of which Kaylin had felt so justifiably proud what felt like months ago. Her fire, small and flickering, had had no voice, no presence; it was an echo of the essence of flame.

Evarrim's fire was not. As Evarrim met her gaze, she understood that he had, without hesitation, revealed some part of his mastery of the element—to her. It surprised her. He knew it. Although it was hard for Evarrim to keep his predatory gaze away from the small dragon that currently adorned Kaylin's shoulder, he managed. "We are cautious," he said in his condescending voice, "where caution is wise; where it hampers us, we cast it aside. Remember this."

She nodded, or thought she nodded; it was hard to keep her attention on the Arcanist when the fire appeared in front of him. It was an elemental, not a flame, and it emerged in the space between them fully formed. She had seen a similar elemental only once, in the heart of the Tha'alani Quarter, and at that time, she'd seen a bonfire, absent the wood generally required.

Today, she saw a man of fire: arms, legs, the general shape of a face seen from behind a sheet of orange-red. He had no hair, although flames leapt and twisted above his head. She didn't expect him to be happy to be here; he was chained to Evarrim, as all summoned elementals were chained to their summoners.

But it wasn't to Evarrim that he turned. It wasn't to Evarrim that he bowed. It was, of course, to Kaylin. *Tell me,* he said, his voice crackling and sizzling, *a story.*

Evarrim's eyes were the blue Kaylin identified as surprise in Barrani. Given the Barrani, it was also a color she seldom saw. "Lord Kaylin," he said in a winter voice—but colder.

She immediately lifted both her hands. "I'm not doing anything." This wasn't entirely true; she was attracting a lot of attention—or at least the attention that wasn't being given to the approaching sounds of destruction.

"You are not attempting to exert any influence over the element?"

"No!"

The fire turned as she spoke, and then turned again; Evarrim was pale, and his eyes had gone the indigo of anger, which was more common—and less welcome.

Tell me a story, the fire said again, and she heard, in its thin voice, a hint of the fire at the heart of the Keeper's garden, hundreds of miles from where she now stood. Or would stand if she were actually in the world.

She cleared her throat. "We need," she told the fire carefully, "to clear a path through the forest. Without burning to death while it's being done."

The fire blazed in silence.

"...But I will tell you a story, while you work."

Surprise colored Evarrim's eyes again. It was strong enough that he spoke through it. "You will tell the fire a story?"

"It's what he wants."

"And how, exactly, are you aware of this?"

Evarrim couldn't hear the fire's voice. Kaylin closed her eyes briefly. "Does it matter?"

"If I do not maintain control of the element here, Lord Kaylin, it will."

"He asked."

Silence.

"It's not the first time I've told stories to the elements." She considered her options with care. "I spend time," she told the Court, "in the Keeper's garden."

The silence developed a different texture.

"In the Keeper's garden, I speak to the elements. Sometimes I tell them stories. They consider it their due and my function." Lifting her arms so that the drape of the sleeves fell away from her wrist, she exposed the marks that adorned her skin. They were glowing faintly. "Maybe it is. The Keeper's control in the elemental garden is absolute. When the elements speak to me there, they don't fight him to do so."

Without waiting for Evarrim's response, she held out a hand to the fire.

The fire didn't hesitate; he took what was offered. Kaylin tensed as warmth became heat, and relaxed when heat failed to become pain. He did not speak her name, but she spoke his: the name of fire.

It came to her naturally, easily; had it come that way on command, she wouldn't have spent months glaring at the unlit wick of a candle. The conceit of form fell away from the flame, as if consumed. Even so, he still held her hand.

"We're clearing straight ahead?" she asked the Consort.

"If it is possible, yes."

★★★

The good thing about elemental, sentient fire was that it could, if pressed, choose what to burn. It didn't spread, consuming anything flammable in its path. It wanted to, of course, but you expected that from fire. Unconstrained, it was death. But it was also warmth in the winter; it was at the heart of the forge and the heart of the stove, and in both cases, it transformed what it touched. It was compelling, almost hypnotic, to watch, a fact Kaylin quickly became reacquainted with as she walked.

The one time the fire had carried her across the elemental gardens at their most wild, it had burned nothing in its path. She began her small story from that moment, as trees cracked, split, and fell at his touch. Fire was not complicated; what it wanted from narrative, Kaylin didn't understand. The story she told the elemental fire would have seemed pointless—and boring—to the foundlings under Marrin's care. It was not boring to the fire. It liked to hear the stories about itself and the interactions—the necessity—of flame's presence in the lives of mortals.

She didn't speak of death, although fire caused death; she spoke of the ways in which it granted and illuminated life. She gave it, she realized, as more trees slowly vanished, a sense of its own place in the world. She did slip in a few words about the candle, as well, because it had taken her so long to get the damn thing lit.

This last part interested him enough that he forgot to burn anything else for a minute while he listened.

Kaylin, please. Concentrate.

Reddening, which she would blame on the heat if anyone asked, she let her grievance with the candle go.

The small dragon was wide-awake. His head swiveled back and forth between his perch and the elemental in her company.

He didn't seem frightened to Kaylin; he seemed excited. When the elemental deigned to notice him, he puffed up his translucent chest and squawked. He really did sound like a bird.

He is not a bird, the fire said.

"You—you know what he is?"

He is yours. When the small dragon squawked, the fire stopped. Heat rose, treading the dangerous line between uncomfortable and deadly. *If you do not understand this, you are in danger,* the fire whispered as he brought his flames back under his control. *You must see him, and you must name him.*

"Why?"

The fire continued to burn its way through trees and undergrowth. *When you try to light a candle,* he finally said, *you call my name.*

She nodded.

When you call fire, you must contain it, or you will die.

She nodded again, waiting for the conclusion. The fire, however, seemed to feel he had said enough. "And?"

You do not wish to chain or contain him, the fire replied. *But if you do not contain me, I will destroy.*

"I don't contain you now."

No. Lord Evarrim does. But I am contained. I do not desire your destruction; I desire the burning. You will die if you are not cautious, and in the same way.

She glanced at the small dragon. He was not, in any way, shape, or form, elemental.

He is, the fire told her. *He is not fire, earth, air; he contains himself—but he cannot continue to do so. You should not have brought him here.*

The small dragon met her gaze. His eyes, wide and dark, reflected a landscape that had nothing to do with trees, ash, and fire. She knew it as reflection only because she could see her own face staring back at her. For a moment, the small dragon seemed ancient to her—the way the Keeper's garden was ancient, the way the Hallionne were ancient. She knew this was wrong, because she'd seen him hatch.

She had no name to give him, because she knew that calling him Wilson, or the closest thing that came to mind, was not what the fire meant. She had delivered a part of one name to the High Lord of the Barrani Court. She had taken a name for herself, although it hadn't changed anything as far as she could tell. She suspected—strongly—that taking a stroll down to the Barrani Lake of Life wouldn't help her here.

It would not.

"He has a name of his own."

He has, just as I have. But you have found my name. Find his. Find it quickly.

What else did she know about names? She thought of Bellusdeo then. And, inexplicably, of Tara. But…the small dragon was the size of a mangy cat. It couldn't contain what a Dragon or a Tower with constantly shifting geography could. It couldn't require it. But the fire…the name of fire was the name of fire. Lighting a candle or burning down a building complex required the same name.

It's just that she understood water, fire, earth, and air on an instinctive level. She knew what they were capable of, for good or ill. What did a small, translucent dragon want? To sit on her shoulders and complain a lot? To breathe dangerous but small clouds when threatened? How was that elemental?

The dragon's claws tensed and she stopped staring at herself in his eyes, mostly because his neck swiveled. A distinctly loud, rumbling growl had taken the place of the distant roars. It was hard to tell whether or not it was because the roaring creature was closer or a new, giant enemy had joined the first one.

The Barrani Court didn't have this difficulty. The swordsmen split evenly down the middle, one group skirting the edge of the clearing to the left and one moving to the right. Severn had the blades of his chain in hand; this was not the best place to start it really spinning. He joined Kaylin, and Kaylin said, "No, keep an eye on Teela."

A lift of dark brow asked the question he didn't put into words.

"I'm worried about her, that's all. I should never have brought her here."

"I heard that," Teela said more loudly than strictly necessary. "Frankly, I'm astonished you think you had any choice."

Kaylin would have cringed her way through an apology, given the chill in the words, but before she could start, something came crashing through the trees up ahead and to the left. It was Wilson.

He was bleeding. It was not a small amount of blood. At a distance, it looked like the normal red that fell from injured Barrani, not that that happened often in Kaylin's daily life. The Barrani closed ranks as he approached, and Kaylin headed for the very small gap between two of them. Nightshade caught her arm. He said nothing; she made no attempt to break free.

Wilson slowed before he crashed into the Barrani Lords; they didn't move. He met Kaylin's eyes over what had become a living wall. Blood ran down the left side of his face, his chest, and his left thigh. "Lord Kaylin," he said, which was ridiculous. "There has been some difficulty."

"Where are your brothers?"

Wilson didn't answer. Instead he said, "You have chosen to create your own path, where the terrain is solid."

She nodded.

"Orbaranne is under siege. I do not know how long the forest facade will hold. Two of my brothers have chosen to secure a very narrow gap of land. It will not be Orbaranne's facade; it will not be forest."

The Consort had reached Kaylin's side, and at a gesture, she parted the Barrani defenders. The forest growled again, at Wilson's back. "Yes," he said to Kaylin. "The nature of the forest is changing. The trees will impede your progress."

Kaylin glanced at the blackened ash that remained to mark the path they had taken so far.

Wilson's brows rose. He bowed to the fire. "My apologies, eldest," he said. "But you are not present enough to guard against what must follow."

The fire rippled.

"Lady?" Kaylin deferred to the Consort.

The Consort, however, said, "Is he as he appears, Lord Kaylin?"

"...Yes. Wilson and his brothers—can change their shapes and forms, so we can't really judge by appearance, but...yes, I'd bet on it."

"And his brothers?"

"If I had to guess, I'd say they just offered to turn themselves into a road."

"Yes," Wilson said. "You must not leave it."

With the Consort's permission, Wilson was allowed past the perimeter of swords. He seemed fascinated by the fire; the fire seemed pleased by the acknowledgment. Kaylin, however, was focused on his injuries. Or rather, on the blood; when Wilson drew closer, she couldn't see any actual wounds.

"The blood?" she asked.

"It is mine. But not all of it." She might as well have asked him about his hair.

"You're injured?"

"Yes." It was, again, so tonally wrong she was nonplussed. "Do you want someone to look at you?"

His head tilted to the side, as if he needed to shift his view to understand the question she'd just asked. "Everyone already is," he finally said.

"I meant, look at your injuries. Possibly treat them."

"Ah. You mean a healer."

She nodded.

"I do not require a healer at this time."

"If you do require a healer, will you ask?"

"I will ask."

She surrendered. She knew that the form he had taken was not his native form, and had no idea whether or not blood was even part of that. "Where did the paths to left and right lead?"

"To the West March," Wilson replied.

"But that's where we want to—"

"No," Teela said sharply. "It is not. Not that way. Wilson, is Hallionne Orbaranne compromised?"

"We are uncertain," he replied. "Bertolle is not, but it would be difficult to return to Bertolle by these paths now. It is our supposition that Orbaranne holds fast; otherwise, there would be no reason to divert the existing path. It is almost certainly not Orbaranne's doing." He tilted his head to the side again, as if listening to something at foot level. "We must depart." He turned toward the forest that had not yet been cleared. "Lady?"

"You have my permission," the Consort replied. She did not, however, call him Wilson.

"My apologies, eldest," he then said to the fire. He reached for the closest tree that happened to be standing in their path. He forgot that the length of his arms were supposed to stay fixed, and they traveled a good three feet farther than they would have had he actually been Barrani. "These forms are very confining."

Kaylin didn't bother to point out that he wasn't in form at the moment, because what he did next was vastly more dis-turning: he grabbed the tree by wrapping his arms around it twice, as if they were rope, and then proceeded to consume it. He didn't eat it, not in the way Barrani usually ate food, but it was being devoured nonetheless. It took him less time than it had taken the fire.

"Lord Evarrim—"

"I will retain the fire for the moment."

The Consort nodded and stepped back while Wilson brought down a few more trees. It was vastly more disturbing than watching the fire consume them, although, given the end effect was the same, Kaylin realized this made no sense.

She fell in beside Severn, who seemed less repelled. "It's a reminder," he said quietly.

"Of what?"

"Wilson is not Barrani." Severn watched in silence. "In combat, he would be like facing Shadows. Unique Shadows, not Ferals. He's more dangerous."

"Because he looks Barrani?"

"Because he can. I suspect he could also conform to mortal norms, as well."

"I think he's doing it because—"

"It doesn't matter why."

When the sixth tree vanished, the forest opened up. What lay beyond it, however, was not a beaten dirt path. It was a mosaic of corruption that extended as far as Kaylin's squint could follow it. Her arms began to itch, and as she scratched them, Severn caught her hand.

The Barrani Court did not immediately avail themselves of the path. What Kaylin saw, they also saw, and they turned to the Consort. Kaylin turned to the small dragon perched on her shoulder. He was alert, his eyes wider and larger than they often were when he flopped. "Well?" she asked him softly.

He turned his gaze upon her. Once again she saw her reflection. To one side, she saw flames. To the other, shadow. It was the shadow that disturbed her.

"Is it safe?"

He had no obvious eyebrows to lift, and his shoulders were slender and translucent, but he seemed to shrug them. Or maybe that was just the movement of his wings. He had not relaxed once since they had begun this woodland trek, but he was capable of his version of a definitive no when he felt it necessary.

"I'll take that as a yes."

She then turned to the Consort, who seemed to be waiting for her.

"I'm willing to go first." This was, judging from the darkening of the Consort's eyes, not the appropriate response. It was the only one Kaylin had, so she tried anyway. "I can't say it's safe; my arms are starting to hurt. But I don't think we have much choice, and I'm willing to take the risk."

"You," was the glacial response, "are mortal and the youngest member of the High Court ever. It is not the custom of my kin to push children into the path of danger while we cower behind them." She spoke High Barrani as if it were a language composed entirely of instantly lethal curses.

Nightshade stepped forward and bowed—quite low—in the face of the Consort's anger. "Lady," he said in the smoothest and softest of tones, "forgive my companion. She means no offense. What she is willing to risk, I will risk. I am no child," he added as he rose. "And no newcomer to the High Court."

"Calarnenne—"

He smiled at the Consort. It was a lazy movement of lips and the corners of his eyes. He almost called her by her name; Kaylin felt it and wondered, again, what their story was. "Do you fear for me? I am Outcaste, Lady." His smile deepened.

"Allow me this; you have never been able to protect us from ourselves."

Her eyes had shaded from the near-indigo of anger to a paler blue, her expression softening in response to his. "I would almost think you planned this were I not so certain such planning were impossible. If you are not careful, it will devour you."

"Many, many things have tried," he replied, sweeping again into a bow that was not perfunctory. "And yet, I am here." He turned to Kaylin as the affection faded from his expression, leaving it perfect, flawless, and almost lifeless in comparison.

But he smiled again. It was a different expression. "I ask that you wait until I call you. I do not command it." He made no attempt to speak softly.

She nodded, but as Nightshade stepped beyond the boundary of discernible forest, she took a step forward. Severn caught her arm and shook his head. "He's made it clear that the choice is yours, yes." Before she could reply, he added, "That was—or would have been, were he not already Outcaste—costly. Honor the request, if you can."

She wanted to tell Severn she didn't care if Nightshade died. Ten years ago, she would have been grateful. Joyful, even. But something had happened to him in the past, in the West March and in the High Halls. Something that implied he had once had a heart.

Does it matter? Nightshade asked. He didn't run; every step he took was deliberate. But he didn't slow, didn't hesitate, either.

No.

He laughed in the silence that joined them, one to the other. *You are a child, Kaylin. That is how you survived. You had hope, and you protected it, nurturing it in the face of every new despair.*

You came close to death only when the strength to protect it had all but guttered. You fight, always, to keep hope alive. Yours. Others'.

And you? she asked.

I am not you. Hope is not required, and over the centuries, it becomes a bitter, bitter companion; it is bright, but it is bright the way blades are: it has an edge that cuts, and cuts, and cuts if you but attempt to grasp it.

But you grasp it anyway.

He failed to answer for a long moment. *The path is stable. It is texturally unpleasant, but it is solid.*

She turned to the Consort. "Lord Calarnenne believes the path to be stable. Will you allow me to risk it?"

"Yes. I will allow you the same risk that the Court itself will now take."

"Kitling."

Kaylin was staring at her feet. The soft, supple boots seemed to weather the passage across ten yards of blistered matter without any significant transformation.

"You're holding your breath."

"Sorry." Her arms had gone from itchy to a throbbing, painful ache, and she was certain that the runes that covered more than half her body were glowing. Wilson had sprinted across the terrain to join Nightshade, who was still on point.

"Do not expect humanity from Nightshade."

Kaylin said nothing.

"It is a weakness to desire to see humanity in everyone with whom you interact."

"I don't care for Evarrim."

"No. But were he to reveal his vulnerabilities to you, it would disarm you. Not immediately; he is not a fool. His general contempt for the animal races prevents even the attempt, which serves your cause. Nightshade is not Evarrim;

he is subtle and unpredictable. But in my opinion, his is the greater danger."

"Do you know what he wants here?" Kaylin asked, lowering her voice and switching to Aerian.

Teela did not reply.

"Teela?"

"If he will not answer that question, I will not, although I do not owe him that consideration."

"And you?"

"What I wanted—when I set out from the city—was to bring you back in more or less one piece."

"And now?"

Teela was, once again, silent. It was the introspective silence that was dangerous. It led to taverns, brawls, dirty fights on the banks of the Ablayne with really stupid drug dealers. Teela didn't particularly like introspection. "I want to believe that we cannot go back; we cannot relive or revive the past. Enough; if you feel it necessary to badger someone unwisely about the events in the distant past, badger your Corporal."

"My Corporal wasn't—"

"He has clearly traveled to the West March before. If he arrived—and left—in safety, as he obviously did, he traveled in the company of a Lord." She fell silent in the blue-eyed way that signaled an end to the conversation.

The ground was not ground in any meaningful way, except one: it lay beneath their feet. It did not, however, lie still, which was unsettling. Patches of the path resembled dirt, patches resembled sand. Puddles of something that wasn't quite water occasionally exposed themselves to the sky and the passing Barrani. Kaylin had seen similar landscapes only on the edge of the border of Tiamaris, and there, they'd been cause for panic.

Walking across a cause for panic was distinctly uncomfortable. Continuing to walk across it made everything else distinctly uncomfortable; her legs, arms, and back were aching, and every movement of the very fine, very soft dress felt as if it were sandpaper against burned skin. The small dragon's claws didn't help.

Wilson spoke a few times, but not in words that Kaylin—or apparently most of the Barrani Lords—could understand; he made them nervous. Given the casual way he'd demolished whole trees, that was understandable. She glanced at her feet and wondered which one of his brothers—or which two—she was walking across now. It did not help morale when the ground a yard ahead shifted to eject half a face. The front half.

"It's me," the face said. It was, of course, one of Wilson's brothers. Kaylin found it hard to fear them. In the Foundling Halls, any of the children who could transform themselves into a nightmare path would have done the same thing.

"That's only one of you," she pointed out.

"Yes, sorry. He's busy."

That was so not what Kaylin wanted to hear. "And the other three?"

"Fighting."

"Are they hurt?"

"Yes."

She almost stumbled.

"We are not you," he added. "If you lose a leg, you cannot walk. If you lose an arm, you cannot fight. If you lose your eyes, you cannot see. This does not apply to us; we are not constrained."

"But you can die?"

"We do not die. We are. We sleep," he added as his face once again melted into the ground, leaving only his lips behind. "It is like death, maybe. It is like the lakes and the harbors of Life, the words of Life?"

"That's not death."

"Even when the words return to the Lake?"

She was silent, then, and the lips disappeared—which was good, because she didn't relish stepping on them. To the fire, she said, "Do you understand what he is?"

Yes.

"I don't suppose you could explain it?"

How? You might. You explain me to myself. Not the heart of me, not the essence of what I am—but all of the ways in which what I am can touch what you are. It is only in those ways that I exist, for you, at all. They are the same. They exist to you only in the ways you perceive. Perhaps you could explain them to yourself? You understood the Devourer.

"He's not what you are."

No.

"And I didn't understand him. I understood one of the things that he wanted. It's not the same."

Is it not?

"No."

She looked down the length of the path; it continued on for as far as the eye could see. Unfortunately, that wasn't as far as it had been. When the forest had opened up, the trees had fallen in line to either side of this uneven mishmash of colors and textures. Trees had girded it as if it were a natural road. They were gone.

"Wilson?"

Wilson nodded without turning back. Nightshade had slowed, an effect that rippled slowly backward and left the Court more tightly bunched together than it had been. As Kaylin caught up with them, the fog roared, and the path beneath their feet buckled.

CHAPTER 27

Barrani were far better at regaining their balance than most people, Kaylin among them. She'd stiffened at the sound of the roar, had started to turn in what felt like the right direction, and had been knocked off her feet by the sudden appearance of a swell in the ground beneath them. It was Wilson who caught her before she stumbled off the narrow path. She tried not to notice the elongation of his arms as he…pulled them back in, still attached to her.

"I do not think you will be in the same danger your companions face," he said softly. "But I urge you to be as cautious as they are."

She didn't bother to point out that her nearly falling had been entirely due to the fact that the road wasn't standing still, because none of the Barrani had done more than stumble. The buckling had calmed to an even rumble, which was not a comfort. "What happened to the forest?"

"Bertolle's hold on the outlands was broken. We must assume Orbaranne's was likewise severed. It is why I told you that you must stay on this path."

Kaylin froze as a single word pierced the rest of the worry and strangeness. "Wilson, you called these the outlands?"

"Yes."

Kaylin turned to stare at Teela's back. Teela, if she heard—and given her hearing, she must have—didn't turn to meet her gaze. "Teela." She spoke in sharp Aerian.

Teela turned then. "Yes," she replied in the same tongue. "The portal paths exist in the outlands."

"And this is where—"

"It is an Imperial matter," Teela told her before Kaylin could finish the sentence. "Not a matter for the High Court."

Kaylin swallowed words and bile. She couldn't see Iberrienne. "This is where he sent them."

Voice low, Teela said, "The outlands are not one place. They're not fixed. It's possible—"

Kaylin lifted a hand, cutting off the words. It was a rare day when the gesture worked; here it did. She knew she now had the attention of the Lords of the Court—as much of it as they could spare. "Where is Iberrienne?"

When Teela failed to answer, when the Lord himself failed to step forward, she wheeled, hands in fists, toward the Consort. Even the fact that the Lady had become both still and pale didn't dim her sudden fury. "Lady, where is Iberrienne?" It was a totally inappropriate way to address the Consort. She knew it, but she couldn't hold on to her tone. These lands were trying to kill the Barrani High Court. Wilson and his brothers had somehow kept them safe. If normal people had been brought here, what chance did they stand?

"Lord Kaylin." It was Nightshade who spoke. The mark on her cheek flared to life; she could see it by the blur at the edge of her vision. It burned. The small dragon rose, elongating his neck and opening his delicate jaws. "Now is not the time."

"Now is exactly the time," was her grim reply. "Lord Iberrienne had some way of reaching the outlands from the fiefs, and it's too much of a coincidence that we're here, everything has gone to hells, and he's nowhere in sight."

"You cannot possibly imagine," Nightshade replied, his voice pure ice, "that Lord Iberrienne intends the Lady any harm. It is therefore highly unlikely that Lord Iberrienne is involved."

"Where is he?"

"The nature of the portal paths often causes unexplained absences. Not all those who set out upon those paths will reach the destination they intended."

"So I've heard." She turned to Wilson. "Where is Lord Iberrienne?"

Wilson's brows gathered. They bunched. "Lord Iberrienne. He is your kin?"

"He's Barrani. In appearance—to my eyes—he's very similar to Lord Evarrim."

Wilson's gaze immediately went to Evarrim, which meant he understood the use of names. "Do you know who Lord Nightshade is?"

Wilson nodded. "Calarnenne."

"And Teela?"

He frowned this time, but his glance went instantly to where Teela stood. "Severn."

"Yes. Should I name all your companions?"

"No; I wanted to make a point. Wilson, do you know Iberrienne?"

"Yes."

"Was he here with us?"

"He did not leave Hallionne Bertolle with the Court."

"You are mistaken," Lord Evarrim said into the silence that followed. He spoke with certainty, but the fact he spoke at all said much.

"Lord Iberrienne was with us," a man she did not recognize added, speaking in support of Lord Evarrim.

Wilson frowned. "He was not."

"Wilson, is everyone who set foot upon the portal path to Hallionne Orbaranne present now?"

"No."

"How many are missing?"

He frowned. "One. Or two. Two?"

Part of the path grew lips again and said, "Two."

"Two. But they were not Barrani," the brother's mostly disembodied voice added. "They had no names."

The ground bucked twice, breaking all conversation and shifting the tension. But when it was stable again—or as stable as it was likely to get—the Consort turned to Evarrim. "Lord Evarrim, where is Lord Iberrienne?"

"It is a question that is now much on my mind," was the cool reply. "He was at my side until we broke through the last of the forest."

"What game is he playing?" The question was far too direct for Court conversation.

It is, Nightshade said. His momentary anger had already vanished. *She now reminds Lord Evarrim—and the rest of her audience—that she has no equals, here. She is angry,* he added. *But so, too, Evarrim.*

And you? Kaylin asked, the sharpness in the question impossible to hide. *Did you know this would happen?*

No. I would never endanger the Lady.

He was lying. Barrani did; she didn't expect better. But this time, she pushed him. She spoke his name with force. To her surprise, he smiled; there was no strain in the expression. *Very good, Kaylin. It is not enough to force me to surrender information. Will you go that far now?*

The answer, given the circumstance, was no.

I would never, he said, *deliberately endanger the Lady. Whatever my status at Court may be, I have no wish to see the slow annihilation of my kind.*

Did you know—

Did I know all of Iberrienne's intent? No, of course not; nor would I expect it. We each play our own games, for our own purposes.

What did you think he would do?

That information, Kaylin, comes at a cost to both of us. What I will offer freely is this: I did not expect what now occurs. I did not expect to be driven to the outlands to gain access to the West March, and I now fear what we will find there, if we arrive at all.

"Lord Kaylin," the Consort said in a softer tone than she'd reserved for Evarrim.

Kaylin blinked.

"Lord Iberrienne is not to be found on the stretch of road now deemed safe. Lord Evarrim?" Her tone chilled instantly.

Evarrim avoided meeting Kaylin's gaze by ignoring her presence. "I cannot discern his presence in the outlands through which the path is carved. It is possible the Outcaste—"

"Is it?" the Consort said in a voice that made ice seem warm. "I am not an Arcanist of any note. I would appreciate plausible explanations for how Lord Calarnenne might be responsible for Iberrienne's disappearance."

Evarrim bowed instantly. When he rose, he was pale. What he might have said next was lost to the roar of something too throaty to be wind; the ground once again dipped and buckled. Wilson steadied Kaylin.

"What did you know of Iberrienne's intentions?"

"I would discuss the matter in private, Lady."

"You will not waste your power and effort on such a containment at this time." After a more pointed silence, she said, "Very well. We will speak of this in a less contested venue."

He bowed again, aware of the whispers that passed among the courtiers. When he rose, he said, "The portal paths seem less fortuitous now."

"I do not think the normal roads would have been to your advantage," Wilson interjected. "The forces assembled there are greater in number, and the forest barrier is altered in shape. What exists on the portal paths is a fraction of that gathered force. Lady, we must move. The path will not remain stable for long."

The Consort gave brief orders, and the Barrani, some now watching Evarrim at least as intently as the loud geography to either side of the road, once again formed up around her.

Kaylin began to walk as Wilson did; Severn walked to her left. As loud, low growling once again filled the air, she asked, "Are they like you?"

"What do you mean?"

She glanced toward the gray space that contained the loudest of the growls.

He was silent for a few yards. "The answer is no, they are not like us, or of us. But I am not certain that answers the question you thought you were asking. They can exist in your world as readily as they can the portal paths."

"How did they reach these paths?"

"From the Hallionne of the West March."

"But—"

"The Hallionne of the West March has long been lost to us," Wilson said, gazing into the gray.

The path narrowed until it was the width of two men, but only barely and only if they were careful. It also jogged to the left in a wide arc, for no reason at all that Kaylin could see;

there was nothing immediately visible to explain the deviation—just gray, formless fog. The roaring seemed to come from the left, as well; it was almost as if the path was heading toward it.

Teela ran behind Kaylin; Severn ran by her side. Nightshade and Wilson were still at the front of the loose pack until Wilson called a halt—in a voice as loud and fully textured as the ominous, invisible roars but with comprehensible syllables thrown in. The entire line staggered, because even as Wilson roared, the ground buckled and tilted. Kaylin, given Wilson's tone, was prepared for this shift, and this time, she managed to more or less keep her feet directly beneath the rest of her. She did not manage this with any notable grace.

The small dragon bit her ear, and she wheeled instinctively in his direction—which didn't have the effect of bringing her any closer to the dragon, given he was attached, but did give her enough time to reach out and grab Severn's forearm to steady him. It took a second, maybe two. Since the rest of the group were Barrani, she didn't worry about their footing; they wouldn't lose it here. Teela could drink the contents of an entire keg without threatening her balance.

"Kaylin," Wilson said as she approached. His face was white. Not pale—pale skin was a Barrani racial characteristic and, as such, not noteworthy—but white. His eyes were black, flecked with color, and moving independently of each other, which almost made her look away. She didn't.

"What do you need me to do?" she asked, voice low.

"Hold them."

The answer didn't make sense, and given the tremors beneath her feet, they didn't have time for confusion. "Hold who? Your brothers?"

He frowned. "No, of course not. Your own people. There

is a grave danger that my brothers will be unable to maintain their current form, and if they cannot, you will be scattered."

"How do I hold them? I can't turn myself into a long, flat road."

"Nonetheless, I leave them in your hands. If we can meet you on the other side, we will." He began to lose the texture and consistency of flesh. "This is not your war," he said, his body fading and lengthening at the same time. "It is not a war that any of your people have fought or faced; not even your Barrani Lords.

"I did not expect to see even the echoes of it. Do not let the Hallionne sleep until it is done. If they sleep, wake them."

He was taller by half and now resembled white Shadow. "I will fight. You will flee. Go." As he spoke the last word, he stepped out of her way and into the looming gray. She wanted to help, to watch, to do something, but Severn caught her arm.

She ran.

The path beneath their feet continued into the distance; it didn't narrow any further, but it was now in motion half the time, and those movements became more extreme. Twice, the ground tilted sharply, as if someone had grabbed its edge and attempted to upend it.

They lost the first of the Barrani Lords to this. They almost lost Kaylin, and would have, had it not been for Teela. Kaylin waited until the ground—a patch of green-gray metal, at least where she was standing—had settled before turning to the Consort.

"Lady," she said, dropping into Elantran, "we're going to lose each other. Even if the path remains solid."

"What would you have us do?"

"Use ropes."

"Ropes?"

"Yes. We can either hold them or loop them around a wrist, but we need something solid as mooring if this happens again." She tried very hard not to think of the foundlings on a day trip. "I brought rope; Severn brought rope. I don't know if anyone else did, but we're going to use them."

If the Barrani Lords had problems being treated like five-year-olds on a day trip, they kept it to themselves. The loss, without bloodshed or visible assailants, of one of their own made it clear the threat was real. That, and the Consort commanded acquiescence. The ropes available weren't long enough to allow for any knots; they were long enough to extend from the front of the group to the back, on either side. The people in front and back did get terminating knots, and the group was compressed.

This meant an end to running.

If something physical attacked them here, it wasn't going to be pretty—but it wasn't going to be pretty, regardless. Kaylin and Severn had both had training; they could fight in enclosed spaces, and the path wasn't that much narrower than the average City hallway. But the City halls had the advantage of walls to either side; here, without walls, misstepping into nothing while in combat wasn't just easy; it was practically inevitable.

When the road was once again almost yanked—to the side—from under their feet, the rope held; Kaylin lost her footing, but not her handhold. For half a minute, her feet slid off the shining, slightly liquid surface of the patch over which she'd been walking. She expected the ground beyond it to have the gray, formless give of the space between worlds; it didn't. It was so hard beneath the soles of her supple boots that she thought it was stone—natural stone. She pushed off and leapt back onto the path, letting the rope bear some part of her weight as she regained her footing.

They continued to move.

There was no sunlight here, because there was no sky. Nothing cast shadows, short or long; it was hard to gauge the passage of time. Kaylin's arms and legs ached in a bone-deep way, but she couldn't tell how much of that was due to the marks and how much to physical exertion over an extended period. She knew that if she'd been chasing a runner in the streets of the City for as long as she felt they'd been on the move, the runner would have been free and clear.

Her stomach made noise. She ignored it, or tried. There was no place to stop for either food or rest.

Wilson did not return. Neither did the faceless roar. The ground was the only difficulty they faced, but it was more than enough. The path jogged to the right so sharply it wasn't a curve but an angle. That was bad.

What was worse lay yards ahead.

The path simply stopped. Beyond its border, on all sides, was the thick, mistlike gray of the outlands. If the path led to the Hallionne, Orbaranne hadn't opened any doors or left any signposts to indicate they'd reached the checkpoint.

Nightshade, at the head of the line, said something in Barrani that was just that little bit too soft to catch.

"Is the Hallionne here?" Kaylin asked without much hope.

Nightshade hesitated. "I cannot sense the Hallionne," he finally replied. "But I cannot definitively say we are not close. Lady."

The Consort made her way to his side; it was awkward—even for a Barrani—because the rope was still a necessity, and much of the shift of position occurred at the same time as the physical swaying of the path.

"This is what we would have faced had the Hallionne not exerted themselves," she finally said. "I do not sense Orbaranne's presence."

Kaylin hesitated. Since Kaylin's hesitations were never subtle, the Consort and Nightshade turned to her.

"Lord Kaylin?"

"I think you should try."

"Try?"

"To wake Orbaranne."

"Orbaranne, according to Bertolle, is awake."

"That was the wrong word, then. Try to call Orbaranne."

The Consort and the fieflord exchanged a brief glance. It was Nightshade who said, "I do not think it possible. The song of awakening is taxing even when all other conditions are neutral. The ground, such as it is, is unstable that we risk loss merely by standing or walking."

To underscore this, the chaos ribbon, as Kaylin privately thought of the path, once again bucked, as if trying to throw off a rider. "It's that or walk," she told him. "We can't stand here—"

Roaring.

Kaylin turned to the small dragon. "I don't know if you can do anything," she told him softly, "but…we need this patch of ground—this patch, the one the Consort is standing on—to remain stable for as long as it takes."

To Nightshade, she said, "Do you recognize the sound at all?"

"I?"

"To me it's just generic angry-monster-or-animal sound. It's not Draconian. It's nothing specific. If it's anything like the beasts we met in the real forest, Severn can stand against them. If it's not—"

"I would not assume that it is," Nightshade replied. "Nor would I assume there is only one."

The small dragon pushed himself off Kaylin's shoulder, hovered for a moment over her head, and then landed, more or less lazily, on the ground between too many boots. He was translucent, as he'd always been—like an empty glass or a ghost—but Kaylin, who had opened her mouth to reply, forgot what she was going to say as she looked through his body.

He tilted his head as he returned her stare.

"Lord Kaylin?"

Through the thin layer of wings, the stretched, slender length of body, even the slight bend of his raised neck, she could see bodies, parts of bodies; the brief glimpse was like a window onto a battlefield. Something might be alive, but if it was, it would have to struggle its own way out—no one would see it.

"Kaylin?"

The small dragon nodded, as if he knew and understood what she was seeing.

"What is this place?" she asked, kneeling, bringing her face closer to the small dragon's so that she could see his eyes. His eyes and his open mouth appeared to be the only two things about him that weren't transparent. His eyes widened, his head at a tilt that was almost a right angle to the rest of his neck.

"Yes," she said as if he'd asked an actual question—as if he could. "I want the answer."

Small wings rose. He turned his head, glanced at the rippling ground beneath the Consort's feet, and sucked in air.

"He's going to breathe," Kaylin said, voice rising in panic.

The small dragon exhaled. He exhaled pale, opalescent smoke in a steady stream that hit the path directly in front of the Consort's feet. It spread from there, blanketing the surface of the tenuous road. What had moments before been a sickly, reflective mass of something glass, metal, or oil began to shift in texture and color. Greens, blues, purples, and obsidians folded into each other to become a solid, almost nondescript gray. It was stone. Flat, thick stone.

Nightshade did not speak a word.

The Consort, however, bowed briefly to the small dragon. Turning to face the gray fog, she lifted her arms, her shoulders, and her head. She sang.

Kaylin looked back to the small dragon, who had not moved. Where the ground nearest his tail had become solid stone, she saw stone; beyond that edge of solidity, she saw corpses. "What have you done?" she whispered. "What happened here? What is this place?"

"Kaylin," Severn said above her left shoulder. "Don't let go of the rope."

She glanced up and saw that she had. She raised her hand to grasp it, and the dragon squawked. The hesitation lasted a few seconds. "Your show," she told him, lowering her hand into her lap.

That is unwise, Nightshade said.

Being here at all, at the moment, trumps it. She hesitated. *Can you see them?*

See what?

That would be no. When I look through him, I see corpses.

Nightshade turned immediately; the small dragon met his gaze, tilting his head. *Kaylin, I do not mean to question either your perception or your sanity, but how, exactly, are you looking through him?*

He's transparent.

He is not.

It was her turn to shift gaze; she looked at Nightshade. His eyes were blue, his expression intent. Barrani were often accused of having no sense of humor, which was unfair. Mortals, on the other hand, seldom found Barrani humor amusing—which was fair, in Kaylin's experience.

"Severn? What do you see when you look at the small dragon?"

Severn immediately understood that the question wasn't trivial. "He hasn't changed size. His wings are high, his neck is extended, his tail—"

"Does he look transparent to you?"

"His skin is vaguely translucent."

"Can you see through him?"

"Through him?"

"As if he were a window, but all the wrong shape."

"No. I see the hint of veins, vessels, possibly even a heart or lungs. But he's not completely transparent."

She exhaled. "He is to me."

Severn's brows rose slightly. "You're looking through him now."

She nodded.

"You don't like what you see."

"I don't understand what I see. And no, I don't like it."

Looking at her expression, Severn hazarded a guess. "Dead people?"

She nodded.

"When you say 'people,' is that a general term or can you differentiate race?" Nightshade's voice was sharp and cutting. He couldn't speak quietly because the Consort's voice was now louder. Louder, stronger, clearer.

"Does it matter?"

"It may. This is not a matter of Immortal arrogance," he added. "If the corpses you see are mortal corpses, there is something very wrong."

"More wrong than corpses no one else can see? They're

corpses, Nightshade—not skeletons, not desiccated husks. They're recently dead."

"If they are mortal corpses—and I think you would recognize Leontines instantly, so we may discard that possibility—think: how did they arrive in this place? These paths connect the Hallionne."

"They connect more than just the Hallionnes, or we wouldn't be under attack!"

Teela placed a hand on Kaylin's shoulder. "Kitling," she said, "think like a Hawk."

"I am. I know there's something wrong with the Hallionne in the West March. Whatever is attacking us here had to originate from there, if everything you've said is true. But we met some of these non-Shadow Shadows in the actual forest. They weren't mortal."

"No."

"The Hallionne aren't mortal. Anyone who stays in a Hallionne isn't mortal."

"You are."

"And I'm a Lord of the High Court, as is Severn. How many other mortals can say the same?"

"None at all, as you well know."

"If these are— If what I'm seeing is—"

Teela inhaled. Exhaled sharply. The tremulous song of the Consort rose, and Nightshade rose with it. Kaylin knew why. He joined the consort, and as he did, he, too began to sing. For just a moment, the sound of their voices was so perfect it was all she wanted to hear.

But when she opened her eyes—and she had closed them almost instinctively—she once again saw corpses.

"You don't think they're Barrani," Teela said. It wasn't a question. "I know you, kitling. Please tell me they aren't children."

Kaylin said nothing for a long moment. "I don't think they're only children. But no, Teela. I don't think they're Barrani. They're too—too dead."

The Barrani Hawk raised a brow.

"I mean, I know what it takes to kill a Barrani. It takes a lot less to kill…me."

Teela knelt in a crouch in front of the dragon. She didn't bother with the rope, and Severn didn't remind her that she needed it. "Yes," she said as she rose. "I concur."

Severn became utterly still. "You see what Kaylin sees."

"I do. They are corpses. The window is not large; I can't estimate numbers. There are more than six. There is some possibility that not all the bodies are dead, but they appear—to my eye—to be very recent deaths."

"Mortal."

"Human." There wasn't even the hint of a doubt. "There isn't a Barrani among them, although the window, as I said, is very small." She looked down at the small dragon but continued to speak to Kaylin. "We need to see more."

Nightshade turned but did not drop the harmony he had shouldered. His eyes were indigo.

"You don't need to do it now," Severn told the two Hawks. "I think Hallionne Orbaranne has finally arrived."

The air—or mist, or miasma—directly in front of the flat, heavy stone began to twist, gaining both momentum and size as it moved. It had, for the first half a minute, no form. The flat, thick stone had not notably increased in width, and as the Consort and Nightshade occupied its edge, there was no way for the Lords of the Court to interpose themselves between it and their Lady.

Not that one Lord didn't try; Evarrim raised a hand, no more, and the man froze.

Kaylin's arms, legs, and back already ached so intensely the Arcanist's use of magic didn't actually make it worse. The fire that she'd lost track of during the very brisk walk appeared from the left, emerging out of the mist as if evaporating it. She recognized the fire's size and shape, and the lack of a path beneath his figurative feet seemed to cause no difficulty, but he stopped short of the gathering storm at the path's edge, waiting.

"What do you see?" She spoke softly, and had he relied on the normal variant of hearing, her words wouldn't have carried over the Consort's song.

The fire crackled in response and drew closer to where she knelt, the small dragon at her knees. She rose in a panic. "Don't burn them!"

I will burn nothing that you do not wish burned. I see a door opening, he added. He was gazing at the standing storm, which seemed, as she watched, to be condensing.

"What do you see here, where I'm standing?"

A path, he replied. *It is both living and dead. I will not burn it, in whole or in part. You must leave this place soon,* he added. She heard roaring; it was the only sound in the immediate vicinity that was louder than the song, and it sounded closer than it had been—if that meant anything in the wilds beyond the twisting path.

It meant something to the dense, roiling cloud. She bent and lifted the small dragon; he squawked in feeble outrage as she more or less dumped him back on her shoulder. The cloud took on both size and shape: it was not Barrani.

It was, just as the first wakened Hallionne had been, a Dragon—a Dragon of storm whose wings shot out to either side of its growing body as a neck and head at last emerged.

CHAPTER 28

The small dragon stirred, raised its comparatively tiny head, and squawked. The Consort's final note—and Nightshade's accompanying harmony—faded, and as it did, the Dragon roared. The path beneath their feet began to shudder. Kaylin reached out with a nerveless hand and once again caught the rope.

She is angry, the fire said.

"Lady, could you ask the Hallionne to destroy everything after she opens her doors?"

The Consort, however, now listed to the side; Nightshade threw out an arm to catch her before the ground did. Kaylin sucked in one sharp breath. To the small dragon, she said, "All right, never mind. You tell her."

Squawking, the small dragon rose. His tail whacked the top of Kaylin's head.

The small dragon flew up toward the maw of the large one as the large one roared again. She half expected the smaller one to suffer blowback, but he managed to cling to his small bit of what passed for sky in these parts. When he reached the level of the larger Dragon's eyes, the large Dragon paused.

She heard her own dragon's squawk; it sounded pretty pathetic. It certainly contained no words. But the large Dragon looked down, as if seeing the path and its occupants for the first time. It lifted its head again, roaring so loudly Kaylin had to choose between her ears and the rope; she chose the rope, but it was close.

The Dragon then folded its wings, and as it did, it diminished in size, although its lack of solid, physical form made it harder to track the transformation. In the end, however, a Barrani woman stood a yard beyond the edge of the stone. She was the gray and white of perfect, distant clouds.

"Lady," she said. She stood at the heart of rolling mist, wings of pale gray rising above the height of her shoulders.

The Consort nodded, her eyes blue and darkening.

"The way is closed."

"How, Hallionne?" was the urgent reply.

The Hallionne said, "I do not know. The outlands are held against us. Even the path upon which you now stand will not exist for long."

"Who fights against us?" Kaylin asked as the small dragon returned to her. "Who are our enemies? Are they your enemies?" Kaylin knew they were not necessarily the same. The Barrani generally brought their enemies with them; the Hallionne provided a safe space in which enmity must—and therefore could—be held at bay. This was clearly different.

The Hallionne swiveled; around her, the mist began to rise, turning in on itself as if it were trying, for a moment, to take form. "I do not know. Our enemies are here, and if they seek to prevent you from reaching your destination, they may be your enemies as well, although you are too young and too slight in all ways to bear the burden of that enmity for long."

Kaylin didn't argue. She turned to the Consort, who had pulled herself to her feet, releasing Nightshade. "Lady," she said, voice low, "where do we go from here? We can't go back."

The Consort reached out and caught Kaylin's hand; hers was cold and trembling. "When you look at the Hallionne, what do you see, Chosen?"

"She's like Kariastos, but made of mist, not water."

"When you looked at Bertolle—" She broke off, but her grip tightened. Kaylin understood the question then. She turned to the Hallionne, but as she did, she reached up to place one palm against the small dragon's body. He was warm.

She was in pain. It was a constant, throbbing pain; it had grown deeper and sharper as they'd stumbled, at speed, along the path held by two of Wilson's brothers—a path that had ended at the foot of an Avatar. The stone upon which she was standing, however, was solid; only its edges were fraying. The pain made little sense. The dress was demonstrably magic, if subtle. The illuminations were magic. The Hallionne themselves, magic, all. But none of those three had caused her the usual pain. Evarrim's magic—his elemental—did. But if he was summoning or casting now, he was utterly silent, utterly still.

Iberrienne, the only other Barrani Lord to reveal his mastery of the Arcane, had vanished. She didn't believe it was accidental. Yes, the path purportedly sent those who walked it in entirely different directions, but it was just too convenient. Someone was casting. Someone was using a magic that set off Kaylin-style alarms. Someone neither she, nor any of the Barrani present, could see.

She turned to face the Hallionne, her hand still cupped around the body of the small dragon. As she did, the Consort drew breath and began, once again, to sing.

* * *

The Hallionne's wings rose as the notes grew louder and fuller. Nightshade hesitated before he added his voice to the Consort's. Kaylin watched the Hallionne, even when the small dragon bit her fingers, forcing her to release him. He pushed himself off her shoulder, moving so slowly he might have been underwater, his wings spread and stiff, as if he were gliding. He paused in midair a foot away from Kaylin's face, wings spread like windows before her eyes.

And they *were* windows. They cut through the rolling folds of gray that surrounded Kaylin on all sides.

The first thing she saw was the Hallionne's Avatar. What the wings of the small dragon revealed bore no physical resemblance to the Barrani. It was both taller and wider; it had no obvious limbs, no chest, no neck. It wasn't the gray of rolling mist; it wasn't a single color or texture. It had something that trailed to its sides, miming the lifted wings she could see if she looked above or below where the small dragon hovered. The mass—and it was a mass, there was no other word for it—appeared to be quivering.

"Teela."

The Barrani Hawk was beside her almost before the last syllable of her name faded into silence. "Yes," she said, grim now. "I see what you see." She drew her sword and shouted a single word that rippled through the line of Barrani at their backs. Severn unwound his chain, but he didn't set it spinning. Not yet, not packed as they were, the only solid ground beneath their feet the stone the small dragon's breath had created.

The Consort fell silent. As she did, the form captured in the window of wings that were too small began to move toward them, and the strands that resembled hovering wings became far too much like Shadow tentacles for Kaylin's liking.

"The Hallionne," Teela said, "is lost."

At her back, the silence of held breath. No one spoke at the enormity of the two simple words.

No one spoke, but Nightshade began to sing; his voice was the stronger of the two singers', and he took up the melody the Consort had dropped. As he did, the mass once again came to a halt, quivering in place.

Kaylin stepped forward and ran into the small dragon. He hissed. "The Hallionne isn't lost yet," she said.

Teela caught her shoulder. "You don't understand what you see."

"Some part of the Hallionne is responding to the song, Teela. The song wouldn't have any effect if the Hallionne was truly lost. It's holding itself back somehow."

Teela hesitated, seeing what Kaylin saw. "Look at it. If there is something at its core, it is not strong. Kitling—"

"Let her go," the Consort said. "An'Teela, let her go."

Teela slowly released a shoulder that was growing numb. Kaylin met the small dragon's eyes. "I need your help," she said. Reaching up, she caught his body and touched his wing; it was soft, fine, thin. She held it before her eyes like a mask as he settled awkwardly on one shoulder, digging claws into the front of her dress. Taking one deep breath, Kaylin took a step off the only solid piece of landscape in sight.

She didn't go alone. Severn came with her. He caught her elbow in a gentler grip than Teela's, and he held on.

"Go back," she told him.

His silence was denial. He held one blade in his right hand; in his left, her arm. "You can't see what I see," she hissed.

He glanced over his shoulder. "At the moment, all I see is you and something that looks like cloud."

"I can see Shadow," she replied. "And I'm walking toward it. I don't want you in range of a Shadow you can't even see."

He said nothing. Kaylin approached, and as she did, she realized two things: it was farther away than the Avatar appeared to be, and it was therefore much, much larger. Hints of solidity seemed to exist within its folds, but its edges were in constant motion as forms attempted to assert themselves and crumbled within seconds, pulled back into the density at its heart. Only the tendrils that had traced the line of wings retained form and shape, and it was not a comforting one.

The small dragon warbled. It was a sound distinct from his usual squawk or hiss. Kaylin, Nightshade's voice clear and resonant at her back, looked at the ground on which she was now standing, and froze.

There were bodies on the ground. With a mask of dragon wing across her eyes, she could see them clearly; the small window had implied multiple corpses. The larger view confirmed it. Scattered across the ground around her feet, and continuing into the distance, the dead lay in awkward, fallen positions. Beyond them, gray folds of mist seemed to roil; above them, that mist took on the appearance of clouds. There was no sun, but there was light nonetheless; it was harsh and gray, like the light in the morgue.

"Severn, can you—"

"I can see them," was his stiff reply.

"You couldn't before."

"No. But neither of us are on the path created by Wilson's brothers."

She let the dragon's wing fall from her nerveless fingers. The bodies did not disappear. The Avatar, however, did, and she forced both arm—and wing—up again. "Can you see the Avatar?"

"No." He sheathed his blade for a moment and wrapped a section of rope loosely around Kaylin's waist; he did the same for his own, giving the rope a large amount of play. That done, he released her entirely and once again drew blade; the weapon chain was loosely looped around his waist.

"Can you see a large mass of Shadow in the distance ahead?"

"No." He knelt as he spoke, reaching down to place fingers against the neck of a middle-aged man in threadbare clothing that might once have been gray or brown; it was so faded it was hard to tell. He withdrew his hand, his expression unchanged, and moved on to the next body, an elderly woman in a dress that was clearly torn across the sleeves and shoulder. Her eyes were wide and foggy with death.

"These are ours." Although it was obvious, she felt the need to say the words.

When Severn reached the third body he stopped. "Kaylin," he said, voice low.

She glanced at the Shadow giant in the distance and then knelt by Severn's side, understanding what her name, in that tone, meant: this one was alive. Severn carefully rolled him over. He was not quite sixteen years of age, in Kaylin's estimate, although the actual number could be lower, and he—like the previous two—wore the mismatched and poorly sized clothing of the streets. He wore no shoes, which wasn't uncommon, but his feet were bleeding in a way that suggested they weren't callused enough.

"I don't think any of them were wearing shoes," Severn said when he noticed the direction of the glance. He made room for her as she knelt and placed a hand on the boy's neck. She could feel what Severn felt: a pulse. It was slow; the boy wasn't conscious. And maybe, she thought, as she released the dragon's wing and placed her other hand on the boy's face, that was a mercy.

"What is it?" Severn asked, voice sharpening. "What's wrong?"

She had no words. For a long moment, no words. The boy was like, very like, the Barrani who'd been injured by the foreign Ferals: something had infected him. His body had no real sense of itself, no sense of what it meant to be whole or healthy. He was alive, but she had no idea what that really meant for him now. She could only barely reach him. Lifting a hand, she very carefully opened his eyes. They were brown, mortal brown; similar in color and depth to her own.

She let his eyelids fall. Her arms hurt, and the hair brushing the back of her neck felt like sandpaper. She thought she could hear someone speaking, but at a great remove. Nightshade's song was the stronger sound, and she tried to derive strength from it; comfort, given the presence of the dead and the dying, was impossible. The people here were his. If they weren't all his, it made no difference. He'd sold them; he couldn't have assumed they would survive.

Bitterness fed anger, and anger grew; her hands were shaking with the need to do something. She felt the marks across her body as they began to burn.

Kaylin. Severn's voice. If Nightshade could hear her at all, he chose not to speak. She drew as deep a breath as she could, holding it as she struggled, for a moment, with raw fury. With guilt. They were here, and she could do nothing.

The small dragon bit her ear as if he was trying to pierce it. She offered him some of her finest Leontine, and he leapt off her shoulder for Severn's instead. Kaylin was surprised when Severn's sharp intake of breath made clear the small dragon had also bitten him. Having made whatever point he'd intended to make, he came and perched on Kaylin's head, hissing in agitation.

"We get it," Kaylin told him. "You don't need to pull out all my hair."

Still on her knees by the side of the boy, she exhaled. At

least one of her angry questions deserved clinical examination. "Severn, why are they here?"

It wasn't a question he could answer, of course. But he understood what she was doing. He examined another body as Kaylin once again attempted to figure out what was wrong with the boy. She lifted his hand; it was limp, and when she released it, it fell heavily to his side. Frowning, she lifted him—not easy, given their comparative sizes—until he was mostly in her lap. And unconscious. He made no noise; he appeared to be breathing. Severn came back. "All shoeless."

"All bleeding?"

"Not from their feet."

She frowned. "Come here and carry him."

He did as she asked, because he could accomplish it more easily; Kaylin was now intent on the ground over which he'd sprawled. "Are they all in physical contact with another body?"

"I haven't looked at all the bodies. All the ones I've examined are. Those I've examined are," he added, "four dead, and four living; the four living, like the boy, are not conscious. In three cases, the bodies are heavily overlapping one another. They are all, however, in contact with at least two others, and they are all touching—"

"The ground."

"The ground."

"Severn, what do you see here?"

He frowned. "Gray. It has no texture; it's a color. You?"

"Stone," she whispered.

"That's not all."

"No. It's not." Pale against the stone, glowing only faintly in the harsh light, Kaylin could see two familiar sigils. She was silent for a long, long moment, and when she spoke, she didn't break the silence.

Nightshade.

Kaylin.

I need you to keep singing. She felt his laughter; it was both genuine and bitter. Her own anger was now under control. *And I need you to send Evarrim to me.* Now she experienced surprise. It was not quite shock, but it was close.

It is not advisable.

Look at what I see, she shot back. *If you can tell me what the hells this is about, keep the bastard there. Iberrienne did this. Whatever it is. It's his sigil. His and one other's. Evarrim is probably the only person here who has a hope of understanding what was done.*

And if he already knows, Kaylin? If he knows and was a willing participant?

Then she'd kill him. Somehow.

I will have to stop the singing.

I think we can survive for a minute. Maybe longer. I don't know. But the song is hemming the Hallionne in, and we need it to stay that way.

For how long?

As long as you can. But send Evarrim.

There is no guarantee that he will be able to reach you.

He will.

She saw the circlet first, because the ruby at its peak was glowing. Evarrim came out of the gray as if parting a curtain; the mist eddied at the edges of his robe. His eyes were a very dark blue, and his expression might have frozen water, if any of it could be found. Kaylin didn't even try to care. "Lord Evarrim."

"Lord Kaylin." He was either angry or alarmed enough that his gaze met hers instead of lingering on the small dragon. "The Consort...requested...that I attend you." He offered her the stiffest of bows; it made him look as if he'd snap in the middle if it went any farther. Kaylin didn't rise to offer the same. Maybe later she'd regret it.

"I need your help."

His eyes rounded, the blue in them shifting slightly to make room for a bit of surprise.

"I'm not an Arcanist. I'm not, by any useful definition, a mage. I have an extreme sensitivity to magic, and to magical signatures. You are an Arcanist. So is Lord Iberrienne."

"I have no knowledge of his—"

"I don't care if you know where he is. My guess is he's not far. But he's done something here. You see the bodies."

Evarrim's expression didn't change at all. "I do."

"Not all of them are dead. Maybe half. We haven't examined them all, because we don't have time. But that one," she continued, nodding in the direction of the boy in Severn's arms, "has been infected."

"Infected?"

"Yes. In a similar way to the Barrani that were bitten—and wounded—by the Ferals we fought on the road to Bertolle."

"They were not Ferals."

"I don't care what they're called. It's not the point. The point is, I wasn't here when they were bitten—if they were—and I couldn't do what I did for the Barrani, even though they would have appreciated it a lot more. It's my suspicion that all of them are infected; some didn't survive it. I don't understand why. They weren't eaten; they weren't otherwise savaged. They were stripped of shoes and left here."

"How many?" Evarrim's question was sharp.

"We don't know. Possibly hundreds, in the worst case."

"And the best?"

"Fifty. Sixty."

"They are all mortal?"

"They're all human. I think." She drew a deeper breath and

added, "And if they aren't, you would know. A building you own the leasehold for had something to do with the Exchequer and Iberrienne." He started to speak, and she swatted the words away as if they were flies. "It's not an accusation. It's a fact. Iberrienne was with you on the road. He appeared to be helping, in some fashion. I know that lying and subterfuge are highly prized arts. But I also know that the second sigil isn't yours. Tell me: Do you think the Consort will survive this?"

His silence was brittle, and it lasted too long. But so had Kaylin's words. "What," he finally said, "are you now kneeling on?"

"Stone. Gray, flat stone. It has no markings that I can see, but it bears two sigils. One of them is Iberrienne's." He didn't insult her. He didn't ask her if she was certain. "You can't see them?"

"I cannot see the stone. Lord Severn?"

Severn shook his head.

"How far does the stone extend?"

Kaylin frowned. She approached the first two bodies with far less care than she had the boy; they were dead, and the dead didn't care. She didn't bother to lift them gently; she rolled them out of the way.

"Be cautious," Evarrim said sharply.

He was not a man who would offer any respect for the dead. "Why?"

"Anything can become a weapon, Lord Kaylin." He spoke with reluctance; every syllable sounded grudging. "Let me handle them."

Before she could reply, she felt the telltale signs of casting—but her arms and legs were already so damn sore, he didn't make much difference. The bodies moved farther out of the way; she didn't touch them again.

Beneath each of the corpses was more stone; it was a continuous piece. It wasn't cut or marked in any way that implied slabs, although farther down, it might be. She shuffled across the stone, scraping knees as she moved. Here, too, she saw evidence of both sigils, but she saw something else: there was a mark in the stone, an engraving; it was the color of dark blood, and it glistened. It wasn't wet to the touch; rather, it felt like cool glass.

"What," Evarrim said, "are you doing?"

"Examining a mark." She described it quickly and looked over her shoulder to see his expression. It was a study in outrage and disgust. This felt oddly comforting. She moved to the place where the last body had been, and found a similar mark, in the same color, engraved in the stone. This one, however, she didn't touch.

"There's a mark here, as well." She looked to Severn. "I think we need to—"

"Move the living bodies."

Kaylin rose to help and stopped, because the mark she'd been impulsive enough to touch was no longer engraved in stone. It rose, pulling itself out of the gray, flat surface, becoming, as it did, fully dimensional. It was like, and unlike, the marks on her arm; the components were similar, but not exact. The weight of the strokes was uneven, but not in the way of a hurried, artistic brush; they were too solid for that, too malformed. They rose until they rested at the height of her chest, the longest lines elongated and anchored to the stone.

Kaylin felt magic again, Evarrim's magic. "You can see that?" she asked.

"I can see something, Lord Kaylin. What do you see?"

"A word. An attempt at a word. It's distorted, but I think the distortion is deliberate. You?"

"That is not what I see."

Gods damn it. "Severn?"

"I see a heart," he replied, and his tone of voice made clear it was a morgue heart. "It's beating."

"Is it bleeding?"

"Yes."

Kaylin rose quickly. "The only unmarked stone was the boy's. We need to move the living bodies off the damn stone." Severn very gently set the boy down. "Lord Evarrim, what is the stone meant to do?"

"I am uncertain," he replied. He was staring at the floating word. "I would have said, before the emergence of the… word…that the mortals were being used to fix or enclose a space."

"And the stone?"

"That would be part of the enclosure. It is not stone; people do not carry stone to the outlands in any great quantity. If they did, it would be lost."

"You think the stone was created by the victims."

"Yes. I would have said that would be the whole of their purpose."

"What purpose would it serve?"

"I think you will find the bodies form the perimeter of a loose circle. It will not be small. It cannot have been meant to last."

"It must have been meant to last—this wasn't a small endeavor!"

"Believe that I am aware of that, Lord Kaylin," was the chilly reply. "Come, we waste time we do not have. Lord Calarnenne will not be able to maintain his song for long. We must move the bodies—alive or dead—off what you perceive as stone, and we must do it quickly."

"The living—"

"All. What you see as a word is not a word. If we do not

move the corpses, they will rise, and they will not be under our control."

"Will they be able to reach the Consort?"

"Soon," he replied, gesturing. Bodies rolled away from their stone beds at the motion. Severn had sheathed his blade; he walked as far as the rope that bound them would allow, and she followed, leaving Evarrim at her back. She didn't count the dead as she moved; she didn't, which was worse, count the living. She wasn't careful about how she moved them, and if she started out by offering apologies to people that probably couldn't hear them, she ended in grim silence. Evarrim had been right; the stone took the shape of a flat circle, and it wasn't small.

But the words in the stone that the dead left caught and held too much of her attention; they were deep and glittering. She didn't touch them again, and absent her touch, they didn't rise—but she knew they could now, and she was afraid of what they meant. They were not all the same word; that much was obvious, although they looked like perturbations and variations on a theme. She wondered if dying on the stone was an essential part of a plan she didn't understand or if dying was the only way to somehow release the word itself.

And then she stopped her frenzied rush and knelt by the body of an elderly man. He was half-bald, and his jaw was bruised; his forearms were bruised, as well. His feet were bare and bleeding. "Was physical contact with the ground here necessary?"

"Demonstrably. They were left to stand in place, while alive."

She touched the man's face. He was, as the boy had been, alive; as the boy, he was infected. But this time, instead of withdrawing, she moved inward, toward the old man's heart. The heart was there; she had no trouble finding it. But she would have had the same ease had he been a corpse she was intent on dissecting; it was almost irrelevant to the body's sense of self.

Almost.

But not quite, not yet. She knew she couldn't do what she'd done to the Barrani; there, she'd all but cut off parts of their flesh in a mad race to stop whatever it was from spreading. Here, it had spread. It had done whatever it was intended to do. The small dragon warbled in her ear, and she reached up and pushed his head gently to the side. "Not now," she whispered. "I have to listen."

She did. She let go of her sense of body and listened to the body's almost nonexistent sense of self, because she realized, as she did, that it was telling a story. It was much like the story she told to the fire: it had no obvious narrative, no elements, no easily found beginning, no end; it was all middle. All of it. It had no easy meaning, and it was a meaning she required. She listened, stitching together the story of blood and bone and injury; of bruising, of scars, of teeth, their loss, of breath, the odd growth of hair, the slow descent of flesh. Mortality, writ small, made both personal and larger than the life that contained and defined it.

Healing deep injuries had never been only about the physical; had it, the Barrani and the Dragons would raise no objections to being the healed.

"Lord Kaylin," Evarrim said. His voice had an edge, but it was distant, attenuated. "What do you think you are doing?"

"I'm trying," she said, her own voice oddly quiet, "to find him."

"To find who?"

She shut him out, closed her eyes, and then realized they were already closed, which was disturbing, because she could see her hands against the man's face, could see the almost minute movements that meant he was still breathing, could see the small dragon. He hovered above the man's chest, his wings like glass, like windows, spreading as he landed.

He didn't fold them; he kept them wide as he rose on his delicate, sharp claws; they pierced the man's chest. Blood was slow to respond, but it did—and Kaylin, holding the man, could only barely feel the injury. She had healed for years—it had been the only advantage to the marks that had changed her life—and nothing in that time had prepared her for this.

She almost jumped back when the man suddenly opened his eyes, blinking rapidly. He started to push himself up off the ground, met Kaylin's eyes, and stopped. "Where am I?"

His eyes were an unremarkable shade of brown. She had seen the citizens of Tiamaris taken by Shadow before but their eyes looked like black opals, and when they spoke at all, it wasn't in ordinary Elantran. They looked dead to her. This man, at this moment, did not. She swallowed, and when he looked down at her hands, flushed and removed them.

"Where am I?" He asked again, and this time, he did push himself, weakly, to his feet. Kaylin rose, supporting his weight as he teetered. He brushed the front of his tunic down, but the motion didn't dislodge the small dragon. His hands passed through the creature, as if he weren't there at all, although he continued to cling to the front of the man's clothing.

Kaylin stiffened. She turned, slowly, to look at the ground and the landscape, and exhaled when the rest of the bodies were still visible. The relief didn't last; Severn and Evarrim were not. Wherever she was at the moment, she didn't occupy the same space. She turned slowly toward the center of what had been shadow, and saw, in its stead, a building.

"I don't understand," she said, looking at the small dragon. He flew back to her shoulder and perched there, wings tensed for flight.

"I don't, either," the man replied, assuming she meant the comment for him.

"I'm Private Kaylin Neya, of the Imperial Hawks. You?"

He looked nervous, but given they were standing in the middle of what could only barely be called fog, he said, "Brent." No family name.

"Are you okay to walk?"

He nodded, shook himself, and straightened.

She glanced at the stone circle. The marks engraved in the surface were still visible; they were not, however, red or glistening. They were gray, a much darker gray than the formless, featureless clouds. Alongside the marks were the sigils that graced every part of the stone, but even these were transformed: Iberrienne's sigil was pale and amorphous, a thing of smoke and shadow, and the second sigil was a livid, pulsing green. It was the first time she had seen a sigil take that color. She hoped it would be the last.

Turning to the old man, she said, "I need you to help me wake the rest of the people here up."

"That," a new—and familiar—voice said, "will not be necessary."

CHAPTER 29

Kaylin turned slowly in the direction of the voice. "Lord Iberrienne."

He inclined his head; it was—almost—a gesture of respect. "Lord Kaylin. You are far from your protectors."

The small dragon hissed.

"Go," she told him softly. "Help Brent wake the others." He hissed again. "I'm not afraid of him here."

"And that is singularly unwise." Lord Iberrienne stepped through folds of fog; it didn't part so much as evaporate. At his back, the sky was a shade of blue-green. It was the same color as his eyes. Kaylin had seen the slow fold of emerald-green into blue many times; his eyes were not that color. They were paler, harder, and—as he approached—without whites. She took a step back as he lifted an arm. "You do not understand where we are," he said, smiling. "You do not understand what we are when we are here."

She held her ground. The air around her was dry, although it looked like the densest of fog, and as Iberrienne walked toward her, it changed color, becoming a pale, bright gold; flecks of light glittered, as if the air were crystallizing.

Iberrienne's eyes narrowed as they began to shift in color, losing the appearance of pale turquoise shell to a livid bright green. She recognized the color: it imbued the second sigil evenly spaced upon sections of the stone ring. She realized, then, that both sigils were his.

Or that he was not Iberrienne.

What had Wilson's brother said? There were two extra travelers but they couldn't be Iberrienne, because neither had a name. Yet Iberrienne had entered the Hallionne, had eaten at the table, and had been housed within its confines. Iberrienne was Barrani; he had a name.

Two travelers.

She glanced over her shoulder, at the people who were gathered behind her.

It was a mistake; she realized it instantly when mists burned away in a flash of incandescent purple light; she was at its heart. But the fire—and it was fire, a fire she recognized from her brief walk through the border zone in the fiefs—failed to burn or destroy. Encircling her as she stood was a shimmering globe of pale light; the fire burned beyond its edge, obscuring sight of everything: Iberrienne himself, the people she had turned, without thought, to look at.

"Go back!" Iberrienne shouted.

The small dragon warbled and butted her cheek with his head.

"I have given you my word that you will leave this place when your work here is done. Go back!"

But Kaylin had been trained to speak—and speak loudly—over the voices of a crowd; to speak as if she was speaking, not shouting. The Swords were better at it, but the Hawks had all received some of their training, and she put those lessons to work. "Do not return to the circle. If you must move at all, head for the Tower." As she spoke, the purple flame banked.

Iberrienne's eyes rounded. And, predictably, narrowed. "You interfere in things you do not understand."

She shook her head. "I interfere in things I do. You are killing these people."

"They are mine to kill."

She refused to engage in an argument about commerce and ownership, although her nails bit into her palms as they tightened into fists.

"They will die, regardless. They were born to die. It is the fate of the animals."

Tighter, trembling fists.

"But I have offered them a brief glory, Lord Kaylin. I have offered them a glimpse of grandeur and a window into a world that they would otherwise never see."

"An offer," she replied, voice as tight as her fists, "implies choice. An offer implies negotiation. You needed these people, and you offered them nothing at all for their service." She hesitated and then said, "You don't belong here."

His brows rose. "I? I do not belong here? And what of you? You are mortal, you are only barely sentient, you are barely out of infancy, and you stand upon this hallowed ground."

Keep him talking, she thought, aware that it bought time—but time for what? The people who stood at her back in a disturbingly uniform crowd had been altered. There was no other word for it. The alteration had killed maybe half of them already; she'd bet the others were destined to follow, and soon. No one with half a thought would touch that bet.

But they weren't dead yet—and clearly, they were meant to die while standing on the circle. While they were alive, there was some hope that they could remain that way.

"You don't belong here," she said again. "Or rather, Iberrienne doesn't."

* * *

"What did you just say?"

"Lord Iberrienne does not belong here. None of the Barrani do. None of the mortals do," she continued.

"And you absent yourself from that number?" He was angry. He was angry, but something else invaded his tone.

"I," she replied, "wear the heart of the green. I bear the illuminations of the Hallionne. I," she continued, raising her arms to half height, although her hands were still fists, "am Chosen. I can stand here without making any of the compromises you have made." It was a guess. She spoke in High Barrani; the edge in her voice was less obvious in that language. "You are merely a Lord of the High Court."

Purple flames rose again, searing away more of the mist. Kaylin flinched, but the fire was so thick it hid her expression. She wasn't afraid of the fire; not yet—the small dragon's shield had been proof against an Arcane bomb. But she wasn't certain what that fire would do to the people who waited, upon either her word or his. She had told them to go to the Tower if they must move at all—but clearly, they didn't feel flight was necessary.

The small dragon batted her head, harder. It wasn't a slap, and there wasn't enough force that it could be considered a punch, but it made clear that he had his opinions. When the curtain of fire lowered again, Iberrienne was much closer. His face was shorn of expression, his eyes still livid-green.

"Magic, it appears, is not enough to dispose of you—but I now understand how you survived the attempt to destroy the Dragon." He almost spit out the last word, as if having it in his mouth at any point was poisonous. She rarely saw such vehemence in the Barrani. Even in fury—no, especially then—they were cold and colder. He reached for her throat with his hands.

This time, she moved, ducking beneath those outstretched hands, rolling across a ground she couldn't see, and coming, in that motion, to her feet. She ran toward the crowd and through them; she couldn't hear his steps at her back. She risked a glance over her shoulder. Sound or no, he was running; he hadn't drawn weapon. Kaylin drew both of hers.

"Stop her!" Iberrienne shouted.

Kaylin cursed. There were more Barrani here?

It wasn't Barrani that stepped from the mists to block her way. To her surprise, her enemies were people, and they wore the familiar clothing of the fiefs. Only their eyes made clear that they weren't entirely human—they were the dark opalescence of Shadow.

She skidded to a halt, daggers in left and right hand, as they moved toward her in silence. They were unarmed, unarmored; in other circumstances, they wouldn't have been a threat. But they numbered three, and as she watched them, that number doubled, and doubled again. Between six and twelve, she knew that none of these were the people she'd helped to their feet here, because she recognized one of them: the first corpse she'd examined. The first of the dead.

She cursed in loud Leontine, but she moved, jogging to the right and avoiding this unexpected blockade. She stubbed her toes, saw the stone circle beside her feet, and leapt up to its surface; it was the only clearly visible path in sight. They paused at its edge and began to walk along the inside of the perimeter. Maybe they couldn't cross it?

She took a step off the circular path and ran into something invisible. It was not, however, inaudible. "No, Lord Kaylin," a familiar voice told her. "You can't leave this circle. It's not safe." It was either Wilson or one of his brothers. She couldn't tell; she couldn't see anything but gray and had found them hard to distinguish even when she could.

"I'm kind of having trouble staying inside it," she said, gritting her teeth to prevent a second outpouring of less quiet Leontine.

"Yes," Wilson's brother replied. "But the circle prevents all from entering it. It is the perimeter of the Hallionne's domain."

"The Hallionne isn't here."

"She is," he replied. "But she will not last. We would help you, but we cannot breach the circle without the Hallionne's permission—and that permission takes effort. We attempt to preserve the Consort and the Teller in your absence."

"Wait. Tell me what I'm supposed to be doing here." She was jogging along the circle's perimeter as the dozen not-quite-dead people followed. "Tell me where I am."

"You are in Orbaranne's domain in the outlands," he replied after a pause. "The circle is not as you see it. It is not anchored in ground, but in life."

"The people chasing me—can you see them?"

"Yes, Chosen."

"Are they dead?"

The answer was so long in coming, Kaylin wondered if Wilson or his brothers even understood the word. "Yes, Chosen. To you, they are dead."

"To you?"

"They are part of this space; they cannot leave it. They are like your parchment, like your reports; they lay unread upon your desk."

They were *so* not like her reports.

"You are overwhelmed by your reports, yes? And they are written? And you dislike them because you feel they express, poorly, the truth of your experience, even if it is your experience that forces the choice of the words?"

Gods damn it all.

"They're reports, Wilson."

"I am not—"

"Fine. Robert. They're reports. Reports. No one cares about them and they serve no purpose! They are so not the same!"

"There is nothing else similar in your experience," he replied. "That was all I could find."

"How can you even read my mind when I'm here and you're on the other side?"

"It is the gift," he replied, "of your companion. Did you not know? We cannot do it with anyone else."

She wouldn't have asked had she known, and didn't consider it a gift to her. But as she jogged, aware that her stamina would give out even if theirs didn't, she considered what he'd said. "Robert?"

"Lord Kaylin."

"When these mortals died—and they're dead—they left words on the stone. Some of the words are still here. Can you read them?"

Pause. "No, I am sorry. They do not look like words to me."

"What do they look like to you? They're engraved and they appear to be similar to the words on my skin. But when they separate from the stone, they look like very poorly crafted words; everything is slightly off shape, or so roughly carved they look distorted." She took as deep a breath as she could. "Can you read them at all?"

"They do not look like words to me," he repeated. "They are as much words as your alphabet, randomly concatenated, would be."

Kaylin frowned. "Are they?"

"Are they what, Chosen?"

"Are they like an alphabet? If you look at all the nonwords on the perimeter, do they spell something to you?" It was not the way the runes worked, in her mind; they were composed of parts—of strokes, straight or curved, squiggles, dots, things that intersected to form a distinct whole. Some of these were very simple and some so complex it was hard to see them all. It was like trying to describe the shape of the Imperial Palace if you'd only ever seen the public face of its Library. But regardless of complexity, she had a sense when looking at them that they were complete.

But…there were two exceptions, and both were significant: the High Lord and Bellusdeo. In the High Lord's case, Kaylin had retrieved and carried what she knew was a word, a True Name. It was complete in and of itself—but in giving it to the High Lord she understood that it was also a component; it was half the name he was meant to bear. Neither the name that had given him life nor the name that had renewed it were incomplete on their own; had they been, he would never have opened his eyes.

Bellusdeo's was similar and at the same time entirely different. Like the High Lord, she had had some variant of a name, but unlike the High Lord, it had been, in the end, not half the name she would encompass, but a ninth. The first name hadn't been taken from the Barrani Lake of Life; Bellusdeo was a Dragon, and the Dragons didn't require a name to waken. They just required a name to be Dragons. She had found a word for herself, with the help of an ancient enemy, and it had both transformed and sustained her. But it was only in the combination of that single word and the eight she absorbed from her dead sisters that she emerged as she was meant to be.

Yet incomplete, her first name had been a name, a word, something that had meaning in and of itself.

Robert was silent for so long Kaylin thought he'd run off. And he had, apparently; he'd run the perimeter of the circle he couldn't cross, to wind up at her side behind a wall of gray mist. "I will ask Wilson."

"Lord Kaylin."

"Wilson?"

"Yes." She could almost see him, although he was indistinct; a gray, shadow outline of a Barrani male. She knew this was bad. "It is. The Hallionne is retreating; she may collapse."

"What will happen if—"

"You will die," he replied.

"And the others?"

"We may be able to defend them if we retreat to Bertolle; we will not be able to reach the West March."

"Can anyone hear the Hallionne?"

"You can," he replied.

She couldn't. She could hear Wilson and her own breathing.

"I did not say you do; I said you can. Robert has asked me your question; he has relayed the information you offer."

"Can you see Severn?" she asked.

"Yes."

"Can you see me? I mean, is there another unconscious me where he is?"

"No, Lord Kaylin. You do not require the anchor. Everything else in this space does, save the Hallionne—but if the Hallionne shifts position, she is lost."

"She won't be under attack—"

"She is under attack on all planes, Lord Kaylin. She is under attack on the forest road, she is under attack on the portal roads, and she is under attack in the heart of her domain."

"I'm in the heart of her domain."

"Yes. You, the mortals, and Lord Iberrienne. Lord Severn

and Lord Evarrim cannot reach you. Lord Severn is upset," he added. "Lord Evarrim is angry."

"And water is wet."

"I do not understand how," Wilson continued, ignoring her observation. "But you may be correct. The writing you see—the writing we do not see as writing—may be the components of a word."

"Why would it even be written this way?"

She could feel his confusion. "Written what way?"

"When I write words—" She let the sentence trail off.

"Yes," he replied. "You have never written a word. None of you have ever written a word. You have heard words, Lord Kaylin; you have read them. I believe you have even spoken them. But you have not written them; you have always come to the language that is already extant.

"If what you suspect is true, Lord Iberrienne is attempting to write a word."

"Why?"

"Words," he replied, "have power. The Hallionne are the sum of their words; each Hallionne is bound by the word that gives them life."

She looked at the stone beneath her feet and understood why it was where it was. It was the boundary of the Hallionne's domain. The end of the space transcribed—in ways that made no sense to mortals—by a word.

"Yes," he replied. "This can only be attempted at the heart of a Hallionne. Bertolle is alarmed. He says this should be impossible. Humans do not require words; they cannot contain them. If Iberrienne had attempted this with Barrani—"

She lifted her arms. There, the runes glowed.

"He considers your counterargument, Chosen, and he asks that you attempt to..."

"Attempt to what?"

"There are no words in your language. In any of your languages. Save the Hallionne."

"I want to save the people."

"Your only hope of that is to save the Hallionne." His tone made clear that he thought it scant hope, regardless. But Kaylin had experience living on next to no hope.

She nodded. "How?"

"I am sorry," Wilson replied, "but Bertolle does not know. He asks you to consider what you did to aid him."

"That's not the same!"

"And what you did to waken us." Wilson paused. "Lord Kaylin," he said, his voice rising as if in question, "what do you see?"

"Here? People, walking undead, a Barrani who isn't Barrani, and a large Tower. And the circle."

"That is not what we would see, were we there. You did not see Bertolle that way, when you first approached the Hallionne."

"You're telling me I choose what I see."

"No. But it is chosen."

"Great. How do I deal with the Shadows?"

"They are not Shadows," he replied. "You see their eyes and you make assumptions. Those assumptions are not correct. They cannot exist as they do outside the confines of this circle. Everything about them is contained here. I ask you to think of your Leontines.

"I must leave you now. The Consort faces the reborn."

Think about Leontines. Kaylin felt this gave permission to vent her frustration—and yes, to take the edge off her fear—in her language of choice. The walking dead, for want of a better description, continued to follow her, but they moved slowly. They had also increased in number. They didn't speak, shout, or move in any way other than to pursue, and she was far enough ahead of where they walked that she wasn't in immediate danger.

She wasn't certain the same could be said of the people who were not yet dead. How, she thought, were words written? The Barrani Lake of Life existed. The Consort didn't add names to its very metaphorical water: she extracted them, delivering them to their bearers. Kaylin slowed to a brisk walk.

When she had first seen the Lake of Life, it hadn't been a lake. Not even in the abstract. It had looked to her eyes like the surface of a very fine-grained desk. Only when she traveled by the side of the Consort—please let the Consort forgive her before she died—did she experience it as a lake. It had never occurred to her to ask what the Consort or Nightshade had seen when they looked at Bertolle on the night she'd wandered into the cage of his name, cutting herself against its components.

And it had never, ever occurred to her to ask how words were created. She knew the Lake of Life was a gift from the Ancients. She'd never considered how more words might be added—if that was even possible.

But…words were the source of Barrani life. They were the source of Draconic life. They were the entirety of the Hallionne. The small dragon bit her ear. "Yes," she said, "probably you, too."

We're alive without True Names. We're alive without words. But we're alive. Biting her lip, she came to an abrupt halt before one of the graven marks. Kneeling, she touched it.

The rune in this place was a dark gray; it didn't look like shed blood. But when she touched it, it was warm. It was warm the way flesh was; it was also soft, as if the stone itself were a carapace, beneath which the rest of the body lay protected.

As she withdrew her hand, the rune began to rise, in shape and form no different from the red mark Severn and Evarrim had seen as a beating heart. Her fingers were stained, as if she'd touched wet ink. Given that it wasn't ink, she felt uneasy, but she didn't try to wipe it off; the only cloth she had she was wearing, and if the ink itself was something inimical, she'd rather not commit treason by damaging or destroying it.

Instead, she rose and headed toward the next mark. She touched this one as well, and it rose to the level of her chest, pulsing faintly as if it were the heart that Severn and Evarrim had seen. She had no idea why she was doing this, not to start; Evarrim had been appalled by the casual way in which she'd touched the first bloodred marks.

But it wasn't spite. She was, she realized, trying to understand the alphabet, the syllabus, of language. She approached it by touch because it was dimensional; it had texture, shape, color. She couldn't speak it, couldn't—in any real sense—read it. She had no other way of coming to an understanding of what it was, because she certainly wasn't going to bite it. She did listen.

She heard Iberrienne shouting commands, and she wanted to countermand them—but as the walking dead continued to pursue her, one of the words she'd pulled up from its casement of stone began to stretch, to elongate. Kaylin didn't hold it; it slid easily beyond the reach of her fingers, unanchored, and traveled toward one of the dead men. He stopped as it hit him. Tendrils that might have been part of the letter form reached into his heart center, as if seeking anchor there. They took root, and as they did, the word buried itself in the man's chest.

It drew no blood, but as it disappeared from view, the man's eyelids began to blink like insane shutters, and when they stopped, his eyes were normal eyes. She couldn't tell what color they were at this distance. But she noticed one thing: her pursuers moved past the man. They moved with less cohesion; it was almost as if they could sense what had just happened to one of their number, and they wanted it for themselves.

Iberrienne screamed in what sounded like rage. Within the circle, purple flares went up. When she paused to watch where they landed, the small dragon bit her ear again. "We are going to have words when this is over," Kaylin told him. But she moved, touching each of the graven runes; by the end, she didn't even pause to watch them emerge.

She saw Iberrienne only once, and it was clear from the way he moved that he didn't see her. That he couldn't. It made no sense, but nothing did at the moment, and at least this was a good crazy. It was a gift.

When she had pulled the last of the runes from the stone circle, the entire circle began to rise, to form a wall that literally stretched up, beyond her view. This was either very good or very bad, and judging by Iberrienne's cry, he considered it the latter.

What had he been trying to do here?

What could be gained by trying to write new words? New truths? She leaned against the wall, catching her breath. Trying to sort out what she knew about True Words. They were whole; their meaning, if you could converse in true language, was complete. There were no shades, no subtleties, and no misinterpretations; context didn't matter. Single words were necessary for the Immortals to live, but the Immortals didn't speak the tongue, or if they did, they didn't speak it the same way the Ancients had.

She frowned, pulling herself away from the wall. The Tower still dominated the area enclosed by the new walls.

The Arkon could tell ancient tales. Some of them were true. Sanabalis could recite the story of the Leontines—and that, too, was true. What *truth* meant, in the case of the dragons, was simply that she could see the words emerge. She couldn't speak them, couldn't understand them as language; she could see them as structures. But hearing them didn't change her; speaking them hadn't noticeably changed Sanabalis. Hearing them had, in the age of the Ancients, changed the Leontines. It had birthed their race. It had given them speech, awareness, a community that was rooted in whatever it was they'd been before the tale had started.

The story, recounted, had resonance for the Leontines, but it did not have the power to alter them again. It had no power to alter Kaylin or Sanabalis. Nor did it apparently grant the Leontines True Words of their own. Kaylin wondered if such a story had been told at the birth of her own race, or the race of the Aerians; if the Tha'alani had likewise emerged from an entirely different race; if there was some creature, somewhere, who could retell the story in a way that she could touch and examine.

She walked toward the people she had gathered into a group. Iberrienne had told them to return to the stone circle; she had told them to head to the Tower. They remained standing between the two. Unlike Iberrienne, however, they saw her as she approached.

"Kaylin," Brent said. "We're waiting."

"For what?"

"For the others," he replied. He paused as a young woman jostled her way into the crowd. "They are gathering." He glanced at her hands; they were black.

"What will you do when they're all here?"

He smiled. There was something very odd about his smile. The confusion—and the fear—he'd experienced on waking was gone. "Brent, did Iberrienne tell a story when you arrived here?"

"Yes."

"Did you understand it?"

"No. Not then."

"And you understand it now?"

He frowned. "Not all of it," he finally replied, as if he was struggling with the same concepts that now plagued her. "We have no True Names. We do not live forever."

As he said it, she stilled. "Do we need True Names to live forever?"

"We need True Names," he replied, "if we are not to change. Growth is change. Age is change."

"The Barrani age. They're not born full-grown," Kaylin pointed out.

Brent glanced at the child who stood beside him, and without dropping a beat, the child continued the conversation. "They grow into their name and become it; it holds them, it holds their shape."

"Is that what Iberrienne was trying to do? Give you words? Make you immortal?"

The old man chuckled, but so did the child. It was truly disturbing. "It is what he has promised the Caste Court: immortality."

"In return for the money he used to bribe the fieflords."

"To buy us, yes."

Iberrienne came to stand to one side of the boy; he was shouting, which was all kinds of wrong coming from a Barrani. The livid-green light had leaked from his eyes, changing his pallor; he did not look healthy. Maybe, she thought, he would die here.

"He cannot die here."

"I can't kill him?"

"You can. But he cannot die here." He turned once again, as the edge of the crowd rippled, growing in size. "Mortals cannot be made immortal, Lord Kaylin." The man frowned as he regarded her. "You carry the cage within yourself. I do not know what it will make of you." She realized, as she listened, that Brent was no longer speaking Elantran. She also realized, as she struggled to identify the language he was speaking, that she didn't actually know it.

"What did he do to you?" she whispered.

"It is done. It cannot be undone; we listened, and we are now here." He raised a hand to his chest. Every other person mirrored the movement.

"What did you hear?" Her voice was lower, softer; her hands felt cold. The marks on her arms, however, were bright and almost hot.

"Did you know," he asked, turning once again to face the Tower, "that we were once told a great and complicated story? It was the story of a world," he continued, "vast and almost endless."

"Iberrienne told you that story?"

He frowned. "No. Not Iberrienne." And he spoke a word that registered as a cacophony of sound; musical notes, the harsh crack of thunder, the crackle of branch in flame, the wail of wind, and more, much more than that. "It was the story of a world. It had a beginning, but we have not yet arrived at its end. We cannot contain it; we contain only its echoes, and the echoes are broken and fractured."

The words, she thought, her hands falling slowly to her sides. The words engraved in stone, the words that Severn had seen as hearts. They weren't words; they were the echo of words, the shadow of something told them in a language they would never, ever master but nonetheless understood on some level. Understood, she thought, in the way she had understood Sanabalis's story of, and to, the Leontines. When the Leontines heard it, they heard it in a way that she didn't, because she was not, no matter how much she adored some of them, Leontine; she was not of them.

"The Arcanists have a theory," the child continued. He turned to a woman a few years older than Kaylin, and the woman continued the story, her voice softer than his. "The Ancients created all life, in all its many forms, but they did not create the mortal races from nothing. They told a different tale to those they had selected, transforming them in the process into something other, something different. At the dawn of the many worlds, the Ancients at play did not understand how to create people like us.

"They understood Dragons, Barrani; they understood how to create a race that was an echo of their own, diminished and dwindling. They did not understand how to create animals that could think, reason, argue. Only later, much later, did they develop the subtlety to do so. Lord Iberrienne does not subscribe to this theory; he prefers to think that their power had dwindled so significantly they could not create something as impressive as his own race."

Now Kaylin was worried. All the people here looked as if they'd lived in the fiefs for the whole of their lives—but no fiefling spoke like this. Whatever Iberrienne had intended, it couldn't be what she was witnessing now.

The woman smiled. "No," she agreed. "That was not his intent. You interrupted his endeavor. It was too late for the people who are your concern, but too early for them."

"Them?"

"Iberrienne," she replied. "Iberrienne and the reborn." She lifted her arms, and in silence, the young boy to one side and the old woman to the other took her hand. Hands stretched out immediately, from all quarters. Only Kaylin remained separate; no one offered a hand to her.

"What—what are you going to do?"

The woman closed her eyes. "You will have to oppose Iberrienne," she said, which wasn't exactly a comforting response.

"But the Hallionne—" An ominous, very real crack interrupted her. She turned—was the only one who turned—in the direction of the sound, in time to see a very large section of the wall tumble. Framed in the large, gaping hole it left behind were the forest Ferals.

CHAPTER 30

"They heard a different story," the woman said, although in theory neither she nor any of the other people had bothered to look in the direction of the sound. "They will kill you if they can."

No kidding. Kaylin didn't bother with weapons now; there was almost no point. She could see the Feral as it walked through the yawning hole in the wall; it was joined by a second such creature. The third didn't make it. The opening in the wall snapped shut, crushing its midsection. Half of it toppled forward, howling. No, screaming. The scream was mercifully brief.

To her surprise, the two turned at the sound, their heads lifting as they examined the smooth, unbroken wall. Clearly, the Hallionne was not yet defeated. They padded back to nudge the body, murmuring to each other. Kaylin wondered whether they'd been dogs that had been transformed and empowered by Shadow. By what Wilson wouldn't call Shadow.

She didn't ask out loud, because there was no need. As the third of the Ferals died, blood seeping into the mist-covered ground, the answer was made clear: it wasn't dogs. The black, large claws of a predator began to dwindle in shape and size until they were hands, attached to arms. Not human arms. Barrani arms.

As she watched, almost frozen in place, the Barrani form—half a body, bisected very messily at the hips—began to shimmer. The two Ferals stepped back as the body started to glow. There was no other word for it, but Kaylin held her breath because she almost recognized the light: it was golden. The livid-green that appeared to characterize magic in this space was entirely absent.

She began to walk toward the body, frowning. The Ferals were still there, and they should have been the greatest danger present; in case her insanity wasn't clear, Iberrienne finally joined them. Nor did he attempt—as he had done on the forest road—to kill them. He approached them as if they were no threat at all.

The body continued its shift into incandescence. As she watched, as she moved, it melted, the light coalescing into a shape that was instantly recognizable: it was, of course, a word. A name. A Barrani True Name. Kaylin had seen Barrani corpses before—but not often and not so immediately after death. She understood that the Barrani believed that their names, upon death, returned to the Lake of Life. She'd never really examined her own beliefs, because until very recently, there'd been no reason. If something she was fighting could kill a Barrani, she had bigger, better worries, none of which involved a close study of corpses unless she wanted to become one herself.

The small dragon bit her ear, which was getting tiresome. "Forward or back?" She favored back, because she was sane, but felt compelled, in spite of that sanity, to walk toward the word itself. If Barrani names returned to the Lake of Life, this one didn't appear to be able to make it there on its own. It wasn't anchored to the body; it didn't appear to be in search of a host, the way the gray not-quite-words were. It hovered, as if waiting to be read.

Iberrienne raised his arms. They were trailing green light, and she realized as she watched that the hearts were not the only things to be anchored in this space; there were thin lines, like webbing, that ran from his hands to the gray murk that passed for ground. Purple flames didn't emerge from those hands; nothing did. But the name that she saw suspended in the air very close to the former breach in the wall began to move, slowly and evenly, toward his outstretched palms.

The Ferals watched him in silence; one of the two growled. Whatever it was Iberrienne was doing did not merit instant approval. The small dragon bit her ear harder; when she failed to move—either forward or back—he began to squawk, and his small claws bit through green fabric so sharply Kaylin was pretty sure she'd see blood. She was surprised that he remained on her shoulders at all. She began to walk toward Iberrienne, and the dragon subsided.

"I wish you could talk," she told him. "I'm certain I'd regret it later, but it would be really helpful at the moment."

The growling grew louder. Kaylin instinctively understood why: the name of their fallen companion had finally come to rest before Iberrienne. He reached out to touch it. Kaylin had touched words before, with no ill effects—that she knew of—to either herself or the words. But Kaylin was clearly not Iberrienne.

As she watched, as she picked up her pace, the golden light that illuminated the word began to diminish, as if the word itself were a glass container that had developed a large crack. The small dragon's frenzied noise wasn't necessary; she understood exactly what was upsetting him. She felt the same visceral fear, revulsion, and—yes—anger she would have felt had Iberrienne been strangling a young child in front of her eyes. She could stop him, but stopping him too late would be pointless. He could be brought to justice, he could be arrested, but the child would still be dead.

If asked, she would have said she had no attachment to True Names. Clearly, she would have been wrong. She threw herself into him as soon as she was close enough to safely make that leap. She did not, however, hit him first. One of the Ferals did, and when she landed, she got a face full of unexpectedly soft fur for her trouble. That, and the attention of the Feral and the Lord.

Iberrienne's hand fell away from the rune as he gestured; purple flame engulfed the Feral. She wasn't clear on where she was, on who the Ferals were, or on how much of their presence here was tangible and physical—but her nostrils filled with the smell of singeing fur, burning flesh. The Feral, burning, was slowed, but not so much that his jaws couldn't snap shut on part of Iberrienne's arm. The Barrani Lord's bone snapped. Kaylin could hear it.

Could hear it, but didn't care. What Iberrienne had done, she now did: she reached up to touch the rune. She was surprised by its texture; it was soft, the way flesh beneath skin was; it was warm in the same fashion. As she held it in place, the marks on her arms, golden, all began to dim; in response, the rune brightened.

Iberrienne didn't give the other Feral orders; the other Feral seemed content, for the moment, to observe. He didn't attempt to attack Kaylin; he didn't appear to see her at all. She turned to the small dragon and said, "Help the furry one." But he tightened his claws, shaking his head in the universal gesture of refusal. He was silent, now that the word was in her hands, and she even thought she understood why: she had no intention of releasing it; she certainly had no intention of handing it over to Iberrienne.

On the other hand, her hands were now full of something that felt too much like a body organ. Whatever Iberrienne had intended for the word, it wasn't good, but carting it around—if it would even move—was going to be bloody difficult. The dragon eyed it, and without thinking she said, "Don't you dare try to eat it." Remembering, as she said it, that he'd done exactly that with one of the marks that was no longer on her skin.

He warbled.

"I mean it." She instinctively pulled the rune in so she could cover it with both her arms, and as she did, it shrunk, dwindling in size until it was no bigger than any of the visible marks on her arms. It did not, however, join the marks on her arms—or her hidden legs or back; that would have been too easy. It floated up, while she tried to maintain her grip on it, and flew at her face, where it landed—if the brief shock of heat was any indication—on her bloody forehead.

The small dragon made a coughing noise that sounded suspiciously like laughter as she turned her attention to Iberrienne and his opponent. The Feral was smoldering; Iberrienne was bleeding. There was now distance between them, covered by growling and Iberrienne's harsh, low words. "What do you think you protect here? We are not what we were—would you return to that cage? We have finally found what we've been seeking. The Hallionne is not yet without resource, and the mortals will not last long enough.

"We have sacrificed none of our own—not willingly. But we need power, and there is power here." He looked up, his green, hard eyes widening. The word over which they were fighting was not where it had been, and as he searched the area frantically with gaze alone, Kaylin was once again invisible.

"Are you doing that?" she asked the small dragon.

He nodded.

Iberrienne snarled in rage, and the Feral that had stayed out of the combat said, "She is there, Iberrienne." His voice was cool, elegant, and very Barrani. "She retrieved Karian's name."

"We need that name," was Iberrienne's tense reply.

"I do not think you will have it, if I understand what I saw."

"She did not—"

"No. She did not. There were rumors in Court that the Chosen had seen the Lake of Life. I did not give them credence." If Ferals could smile, this one was doing so. In spite of the two rows of teeth in an obscenely large set of jaws, it was a typical Barrani smile. "She has preserved the name, I believe."

"Where is she now?"

"If she has not moved?"

Kaylin moved. She didn't stay to hear the rest of the conversation. She ran. She stopped once—only once—when she heard the cracking of stone at her back. She didn't wait to see what emerged from the breach. The sound came again as she worked her way around a crowd that was now a series of human walls, and again as she finally settled on a spot near the front of the gathering.

She turned to the crowd. "The Hallionne is failing."

No one answered. Their eyes were mortal eyes; their bodies were mortal bodies. The story that Iberrienne had told them, if it was a story with any truth in it at all, had not given them the freedom to choose their form—if the Barrani Ferals even had that. No, she thought. It wasn't that. But what? What had he hoped to gain? What was he struggling to preserve, in this space, and why, damn it, this space? How could mortals destroy a Hallionne?

"Not destroy," they said, speaking as one, but speaking

softly. "We were not to speak to the Hallionne at all. And we cannot."

The small dragon moved and she turned to face him before he could bite her ear. "Yes," she said. "We'll go to the Hallionne."

Thunder roared again; this time the ground shook. She glanced once at the people who would never return to the fiefs. Their lack of terror, their lack of pain, eased her. It allowed her to leave them behind.

What the walls suffered, the Tower did not. It was, in shape and form, whole and impregnable. Which was a pity if you were actually trying to find a way in. There were no doors, no windows, no arrow slits; there were no stairs. The ground that surrounded it was the same formless gray that existed wherever Iberrienne wasn't standing. She stopped running in circles around it, because she could see Ferals begin to pace through the crowd. Or to pace around its edge; they didn't have much luck in mowing down a chain made of bodies and arms—proof, if it was needed, that they weren't in the real world anymore.

Instead she placed both hands firmly against the Tower's walls and pushed. She shouldn't have been surprised when she fell through, but she was. The Tower's walls felt, in the brief second of contact, like hewn stone. What she landed on felt like grass. The small dragon warbled, jumping off her shoulder as she fell. Her hands and knees took the brunt of the impact, and she rose, automatically dusting off her dress.

Sadly, her hands were still black from their contact with too many dark runes, and apparently, unlike ink, it didn't completely dry; it left marks on her dress—they looked like long smudges of handprints. The dress, which was so obligingly dirtproof, did not immediately clean itself. While she examined the skirt in growing dismay, the small dragon reclaimed his perch.

"All right, now what?"

The ground that had felt like grass over dirt appeared to be grass over dirt. The apparently permeable stone walls had opened into what she assumed was a courtyard; the assumption lasted until she turned around to look at the entrance. It was gone. She stood on a plain of grass, beneath an azure sky that, while beautiful, looked natural. There were clouds in the distance, but they didn't appear to be rain clouds, and the breeze was mild.

Given that Bertolle had pretty much looked like a field of grass, Kaylin began to walk. Her passenger squawked. She stopped. After a moment, she sat down and lifted a hand. "This is what we know. The Ferals are Barrani." She folded one finger. "They weren't on the road to kill the Consort. They were on the road to find her; they want the Lake of Life." The small dragon was silent. "They clearly still have their names—and the name I rescued looks like a word. It's not the same as the gray runes." She folded two fingers.

"They clearly value the names. I don't think the Feral would have attacked Iberrienne otherwise. Whatever Iberrienne hoped to do by somehow extracting the echoes of ancient words from us he could do far more easily with words that already exist. But even transformed, the Barrani won't allow it.

"In their current state, the humans here remember being told two stories: Iberrienne's and…someone…else's." She stopped. Stared at her hands, which were still mostly blackened. "They remember…" What the Leontines remembered. None of the Leontines could possibly have heard the story that Sanabalis told them before. None of them had been alive. It had happened centuries, at best guess, prior to the birth of the oldest member of the audience. But if asked, she was certain—given the Leontines of her acquaintance—that they wouldn't remember it on their own. Sanabalis had to have presented it.

"Iberrienne couldn't tell the second story, could he?"

The small dragon shook his head.

"Something he told them here allowed them to remember it. And now they remember it, but Iberrienne, of course, doesn't—and can't. Do you think he intended to have them reconstruct that tale somehow? They said it was the story of a world." She shook her head. "But I saw the story that Sanabalis told the Leontines—it wasn't nearly complicated enough. I don't understand."

It frustrated her. "Thc names," she said, forehead creasing, "looked like words. Bertolle's name was the same. Like the words of the Leontine story, or the Arkon's story. They were solid, they were real. Could Iberrienne use those words? Could he gain power from simple retelling?" He couldn't. There was no possible way Sanabalis or the Arkon would expose those stories to witnesses if they could be somehow used or twisted.

"You are wrong."

Kaylin looked up as clouds passed over the sun. Standing before her, in a pale white gown reminiscent of the Consort's dress, was a woman. Kaylin had expected a Barrani.

"No," the Hallionne said. "That is not my truth."

She seemed young, to Kaylin. Her taking a seat in the grass beside the Imperial Hawk didn't do anything to change that perception. She folded her knees beneath her chin and wrapped her arms around her legs, gazing into the distance as the clouds moved in. The breeze had matured into wind.

"You're Orbaranne?"

"That is what I was called."

"You don't look like a Barrani. The rest of the Hallionne do."

"They take the form that most closely resembles their guests' forms."

"So if there were Barrani here, you would be Barrani?"

"I would. Perhaps I would. I was not like Bertolle when I was created," she added softly. "I was one of the last of the Hallionne."

"You couldn't have been mortal."

"Could I not? You make one mistake in your assumptions." She curled her arms more tightly around her legs. "The story you heard the Dragon tell the Leontines was the story of their beginning. It was not the entire story of their creation. It required subtlety and finesse, not because consciousness is difficult—I believe it more difficult in experience than in observation."

"What did I hear, then?"

"The revision," was her soft reply. "The Leontines were not created from nothing. They were elevated from an existing race of creatures."

"I know."

"What you do not understand is that the creatures themselves were part of one long, vast story. You think that the truth of a name is the defining characteristic of the Barrani; it is but one. The other is more difficult. Words are alive. But they are not alive as you are. They do not know change, or age, or decay; their meaning does not drift. There are no colloquialisms; they are absolutes. Once written, they persist."

"They can be destroyed."

The Hallionne said nothing for a long moment. "You dislike rats."

It was so not the comment Kaylin had been expecting. "Do we have time for this?" she asked, gazing at the clouds.

"You dislike…cockroaches?"

It was, however, the conversation she was going to have. "I hate them both."

"Understand that their stories began at almost the same time the story of the Barrani did. It is not a story that your Dragons could tell. Nor is it a story that I could. It is long, complex, and in seeing one rat, you do not see the beginning—or end—of their story; you see one rat. You will never see the beginning or the end, but there was a beginning, and writ in those words, there is an end."

"What happens when the end is reached?"

The Hallionne's smile was bitter. "There will be no more rats." She rose, unfolding slowly and hesitantly as the sky continued to darken. "Your Dragons did not speak the whole of the story—how could they? They spoke the affirmation of the smallest part of its vast middle."

Kaylin froze. "The story that the people remember—"

"Yes, Kaylin. You feel that recounting the story of the Leontines did not open the race to the possibility of tampering, and in that, you are correct. In your world, on your plane, in the place where life gathers, it cannot be done. Even the most powerful in that modality of existence can at most change what they touch."

"And that's not true here." Kaylin hesitated. "Where is here?"

"Here is the heart of the Hallionne. My heart," she added as lightning, followed by the first crack of thunder, rolled across distant sky. "It exists in all modalities. It exists in all planes. But this is a place where people such as you cannot go."

"Others of my kind were brought here."

"Yes. A wrong was done," she added softly.

"Why are they attacking you?"

"Because I am sentinel. Your worlds, your war, are an echo of the war we once fought, and we fought it in these spaces:

wars, of words. Can the Barrani be destroyed in your world? No. They can be killed. But the essential truth of who they have been cannot be destroyed. It cannot be trapped, and it cannot be changed; it can be freed. You would call that death."

"Here it can be destroyed."

"Yes," she replied.

Thunder. Kaylin turned to the Hallionne, who stood and watched, hands loosely clasped behind her back. "If they recall the story of their origin, if they can recite it—"

"Yes. They will alter all and may well destroy it. What your race is and what it will—or can—become, if it exists at all, will be different."

"That wasn't Iberrienne's intent."

"It was, in part. If they alter that story, in some small way, they alter mine." She raised her chin.

"But you're—you're a Hallionne."

"Yes. But my word, my truth, was not created, as Bertolle was not, from nothing. It is why they attack me and none of the others, save one. I am not what I was; I will never be that again. But what I am has roots in what I was, and those roots cannot be disentangled."

"Why didn't the Ancients just create you from scratch?"

"They could not," she replied. "And so, they revised, they elevated, they transformed. What was done for the Leontines, was done—in more complexity—for me."

"Iberrienne brought almost two hundred people here to attempt to break—you?"

"That is a question I cannot answer, Kaylin." The lightning was harsher and closer; there was almost no space between it and the thunder. "But I do not believe that is his intent: he wishes to create, in a small way, a language of his own."

"What will he do with that?"

"Anything. Anything at all that he desires. In this modality, he would become a Lord of Chaos."

"And you can't stop him."

She said nothing. Kaylin lifted a hand to touch her, and stopped; her hands were black, wet. Ink streamed like liquid from her palms, down her sleeve, and into the grass. The Hallionne frowned, brows drawing together over the bridge of an entirely nondescript nose. Her eyes, the only thing about her that didn't look ordinary, widened. Without a word, she reached out and clasped Kaylin's hand in one of her own. Kaylin, aware of the fact that the Hallionne was wearing white, flinched. She didn't pull back. The Hallionne's hand felt like a normal, callused hand.

"I'm sorry," she said, because the Hallionne's hand was now black, and ink dripped across the skirt of her white dress. Hallionne Orbaranne shook her head; her eyes widened. For the first time since she'd approached Kaylin, she smiled. Her eyes faded to a shade of emerald-green that was the color of the grass itself.

"He is here," she whispered.

Kaylin glanced around the wide and empty plain. Lightning struck ground maybe a mile away—if they were lucky. "Who?"

The Hallionne pointed with her free hand. Standing in the middle of the grass, at the height of the encroaching storm, stood the Lord of the West March.

Beneath gray clouds, to the dubious applause of thunder, the Lord of the West March approached them. His eyes rounded slightly as he recognized Kaylin; they were a shade of indigo that made night seem bright. His lips, a compressed, tight line, didn't open to let words escape. Before Kaylin could speak—or bow, which was appropriate etiquette—he swept the Hallionne into his arms, lifting her off the ground. Her hand still clutched Kaylin's, which made what was almost an embrace a bit awkward, as she turned her face into his chest.

His chin rested, briefly, above her head. "Lord Kaylin."

She swallowed. "Lord of the West March."

"So formal." A brief smile softened his expression.

"Lirienne."

"And still unwise. I confess I did not expect to see you here, of all places. You wear the blood of the green." He bent his head. "Hallionne Orbaranne, the forest road is secure. The portal roads are not, but Calarnenne holds the road with the aid of Bertolle's forces; we have sent what reinforcements we could spare. The Consort is safe."

She seemed to shrink in his arms; lightning struck ground, narrowly passing behind the Lord of the West March. "They are here," she whispered.

Kaylin expected rain. Or worse. "Hallionne, let go of my hand." She exhaled, squaring her shoulders. "Let go of my hand and open the door."

The Hallionne shook her head. "There is no door to open. They are almost upon us. I have failed."

The Lord of the West March met Kaylin's gaze and held it. "What will you do, Chosen?"

Kaylin raised a hand, palm up. It was dark, wet, and as she exposed it, rain began to fall. It was a summer storm's rain, instantly drenching. The blood of the green appeared to be waterproof; Kaylin herself was not. She felt like a bedraggled urchin in a stolen dress. The rain didn't appear to care for the small dragon; it avoided him. Literally. Water bent in its downward trajectory to either side of where he sat. She considered dumping him on the top of her head and telling him to open his wings.

She didn't, because the rain was, in fact, melting the grass.

As if it had never been solid, green bled into what lay beneath: gray, dark. As dark, she thought, as the runes engraved in an anchoring circle of stone. Kaylin said, "Hallionne, let me go."

The Hallionne tightened her grip. Her knuckles were white, and her hand felt so entirely normal it was disturbing. She didn't speak. The Lord of the West March said, "Hallionne, you must choose. Lord Kaylin may stand with you, or I may—but not both. They are almost upon us now."

The rain was so heavy, visibility wasn't an issue; there wasn't any. The Hallionne's grip eased. Kaylin started to massage blood back into her hand but stopped. Her hand—the hand that the Hallionne had held so tightly—was clean. No ink, no black, remained on it. The other hand? Black and wet; the rain couldn't wash what she thought of as ink away.

"Kaylin," the Lord of the West March said, "be cautious."

She almost laughed, but his expression was so grave. Turning to the small dragon, she said, "Protect the humans. I know they're not alive, not really—but protect them."

"I cannot protect the mortals, if there are other mortals here," the Lord of the West March replied.

"I wasn't talking to you. I was—" She glanced at the small dragon and realized then that no one could see him. The Barrani hadn't, the humans hadn't, and the Hallionne had made no mention of him at all. She shook her head. Her arms had shed a soft golden light the entire time she'd been within the confines of the circle. "Go and save them," she told the dragon. "If you can." She turned. "Lord of the West March."

"Lord Kaylin."

Ugh, there was water in her mouth. She wanted the rain to stop. "You said the forest paths are safe?"

"Yes."

"And the portal roads aren't. How do you know, if you're here?"

"I am the Lord of the West March," he replied, as if that was any kind of answer. Maybe it was. She was the harmoniste, and she wore the blood of the green, but she had no clue what was happening anywhere she wasn't standing. Hells, she had no clue what was happening here. "Can you get word to Lord Severn and Lord—Lord Calarnenne? Can you give them a message for me?"

"I can. It is not without cost."

"Tell them to find Iberrienne. He's on the portal roads. He's here, but I think he's there, as well. Tell them they need to find him."

"Alive?"

She laughed. It was not a happy sound. But she was spared the stress of answering, as the Ferals had finally arrived.

CHAPTER 31

They were drenched. As drenched, as bedraggled, as Kaylin herself. Their eyes were the color of their fur, but they shone anyway. The small dragon squawked, and Kaylin began to walk—quickly and stupidly—toward the nearest Feral. She drew one dagger, aware that she was still invisible to the Feral; it had eyes for the Hallionne and the Lord of the West March.

She walked quietly; the rain helped. But as she approached the Feral, jogging slightly toward its side, it stopped, swiveling to face her, sniffing at the air. She moved in, leading with her weapon. Its eyes narrowed. She knew she needed to slit its throat as quickly as possible. She'd done it before, although never with Barrani. Never with Ferals, either, if it came to that. Just with people too stupid or greedy to avoid pissing off a fieflord.

This is different. This is survival.

But was it? She wasn't in the streets of the fief. She wasn't in the real world. What she saw here, all of it, was a weird sort of make-believe that took what was there and made sense of it. She wasn't even certain that the dagger could actually cut anything.

Thinking that, she cut her palm. It bled. The small dragon squawked and hissed and jumped up and down, but she didn't care. What he'd refused to allow her to give to any other Hallionne, she now gave to Orbaranne: she bled. She bled freely, because her dagger hand had not been terribly steady. The small dragon didn't like it, but it didn't matter; what was done was done, and he didn't fly down to intercept her blood as it landed, at last, in the dark, gray mud.

But when it landed, the world changed.

Where there had been grass, and then green-gray mud, there was now stone. Stone, in a Hallionne, wasn't rare—but the floor that was suddenly under Kaylin's feet wasn't grand, architectural, magical stone—it was worn from the tread of too many feet, some pretty heavy. It was smooth, gray, ordinary stone. Familiar stone. Walls rose in the distance, and they were curved, as the Hallionne's had been curved, but they were familiar walls, and they ended not in clouds that vision couldn't pierce but in the lip of an aperture that was, at the moment, open to the sky.

At the center of the tower—and it was a tower, the Hawklord's Tower—the Lord of the West March cradled the Avatar of the Hallionne. Kaylin looked down. She was still wearing the dress, but in the center of its chest, as if it were a tabard, was a familiar symbol. The Hawk. She wanted to weep. Instead, she sheathed the dagger. The Feral was in the room. It was not the only Feral, but the Hallionne no longer commanded the whole of its attention; the change in scenery did. Kaylin walked over to the wall, touched the panel there, and closed the aperture.

With it went the rain.

The Lord of the West March set the Avatar on her feet; she was gazing around the room in wonder. Wonder, Kaylin thought, when a Hallionne could take on any form it chose, no matter how architecturally unsound. Sloughing water, she turned toward the closest Feral, and reaching out, she touched the back of its neck.

He froze. Even his breath stilled. She saw the rune at the heart of his form, and it was almost, in its entirety, a name. But beneath it, like smoke or shadow, was the ghost image of that word. It was transparent and, given the light it shed, almost insubstantial. But she could see it. She couldn't touch it, but because it was simple enough, she could say it. She could speak the name, both names.

Closing her eyes to shut out the scenery, Kaylin concentrated on the name, because once she could see a name, it didn't vanish when she shut her eyes. Never had. The small dragon warbled as she gathered disparate syllables and attempted to concatenate them; to speak them as if they were parts of a whole and, simultaneously, all of it. The sound was simple; the saying was hard.

Ynpharion.

The Feral reared like a slender pony, dislodging her hand, its great jaws whipping toward where she stood revealed. It was going to kill her if it could; she could feel its fear.

No, she could feel his fear. *Ynpharion,* she said again, but this time she grabbed the visible name and she pulled it. She'd spoken the truth of a name before—but on every other occasion, the owner of the name had been willing to trust her. This Barrani was not—and that was smart. And it didn't matter. What she wasn't willing to do to Nightshade or Maggaron she was more than willing to do to the Feral, because she trusted herself here. There was no second-guessing.

And it hurt. It felt as if someone was driving a hot needle

into the top of her spine; she went rigid with the force of it. But she held on, because it was cleaner. Because it was her life or his. And she could see him clearly as she tightened her hold on the name: he was Barrani. Barrani but other. It was the other she didn't want. Having taken hold of the name and its structure so completely, she could see the way the shadow was entwined around the rune; she could see the way its light cast and fed its second form.

But she had light of her own; her arms were glowing so brightly, the marks were so hot. She forced some of that heat into her grip, and as she did, the Shadow began to burn.

The Barrani shouted a warning, and as one, all the Ferals in the room turned. But what he could now see, they couldn't. They didn't need to see her. They could see their companion: he was Barrani now. His hair was the color his fur had been, but everything else was different. And as the last of the Shadow burned away, he stilled.

The burning had not killed him.

She turned, stepped away from him, began to walk toward the next Feral. But the next Feral faded from view. He became transparent as she reached out to touch him, and she caught the brief hint of the word at his core before he vanished completely. With less caution and more speed, she ran toward the next Feral, but it, too, simply melted way, as if it had never been here at all.

The small dragon squawked, and Kaylin nodded, because the doors to the Hawklord's Tower—the doors to this imaginary but blessedly solid version of it—were slowly rolling open. Lord Iberrienne stood beneath the peaked frame; behind him was a small, weaponless army: the people he'd spent so much of the Imperial treasury buying.

"I guess Severn and Nightshade didn't get the message."

"They did," the Hallionne said. She was no longer huddled

against the Lord of the West March's chest. "But the portal paths are treacherous now; they are not entirely within my control. They are not," she added, staring beyond Iberrienne, her eyes rounding, "entirely beyond it, either."

Kaylin turned to the Barrani who now stood almost at attention to one side. He was rigid, but it was a different type of rigidity; he was both shocked and—for a Barrani—confused. He knew—how could he not?—that she knew his name, but he didn't appear to remember anything else. That lasted until Iberrienne entered the room.

Iberrienne was bleeding. The wounds were obvious; they were deep. His eyes were still a livid-green, but the pallor of his skin was now a corpse's. All of the marks on her arms flared as he lifted his. "I will kill you for this."

It wasn't what she'd expected—and why not? Because he was injured and she wasn't? He was Barrani.

"He is not," Ynpharion said, speaking for the first time, his voice low and intense with hatred. It was not hatred of her.

Iberrienne's eyes rounded at the sound of Ynpharion's voice. He stared in a type of enraged horror, as if he were a caricature of a Barrani and not a Barrani Lord. Snarling, he turned to the mortals who were filing into the room. They walked to his right and left, spreading out against the walls in, yes, a circle. It was a much smaller circle; the Tower had not been built to contain hundreds.

The Lord of the West March drew blade. Kaylin, who had seen many swords in her life, had seen only one to rival it: *Meliannos,* the Dragonslayer. It should have been a comfort; it wasn't. The man who had called her near-kin in the High Court made no attempt to engage Lord Iberrienne, the architect of the threat: he turned his blade on the mortals.

She cried out in terror and pain as the blade fell.

It was sharp, solid; it bisected the three people—two women

and an older man—standing closest to the Hallionne's Avatar. And they were close; there just wasn't enough room otherwise. They didn't move. They didn't scream. No one did. No one except Kaylin. She stumbled as Ynpharion pushed against her control, taking advantage of her fear and confusion to attempt to disentangle himself. Snarling, she pushed back, hard. It hurt, but it was a bracing slap; she needed it.

Because his was not the only name she knew. She had drawn the Lord of the West March out of a sleep that would end in death, and to do it, she had had to call his name. She knew what it was, and she knew she could stop him. It would break things. But his blade, rising again, would break more. She inhaled, found his name, and started to speak it.

The Avatar moved first, because truly speaking names took time. She moved so quickly Kaylin didn't see her run; one moment, she stood in the dubious safety of the room's center, and the next, in the path of the sword's arc, her arms outstretched in denial. In protection.

"Lord of the West March," she said, her voice clear and resonant.

He did not lower his blade. "Hallionne Orbaranne, you do not understand the danger."

"They are my guests," she replied.

His eyes widened, their blue paling to the color of surprise. They darkened as he sheathed his sword and turned, unarmed, to face Iberrienne.

"Lord Kaylin," the Hallionne said softly, "take my hand."

"You do not understand what you do," Iberrienne told the Lord of the West March. "You do not understand!" Fire erupted around Kaylin, bathing the gray stone in purple, lambent flame. She walked through it, the dragon girding her shoulder, as she reached for the Hallionne's outstretched hand. It was blackened and wet.

"Yes," the Avatar told her, smiling. Her eyes were the color of Kaylin's marks. "I could not touch what you have touched. But you did. And you brought it—and them—to me."

"Lady, do not let them form a circle here!" the Lord of the West March said as the whole of the room filled with poorly dressed mortals. It was too late; they formed it and they filled it. Even Iberrienne was surrounded.

The Avatar smiled in response. It was a heartbreaking smile; young, open, tinged with fear and with a strange hope. She had accepted death and destruction—her own—but that was not what she now saw.

Iberrienne lifted his arms again, and this time, every hair on Kaylin's body that wasn't somehow tied down stood on end. He spoke. His voice was thunder. Literally. Lightning followed; people fell as it illuminated—and consumed—them. Kaylin started to move, but the Hallionne tightened her grip. "They are my guests."

Was she trying to tell Kaylin—as lightning fell again and again—to trust her?

"Yes. Watch," she continued. "He is speaking."

"I can hear that!" It seemed unfair that she had to shout to be heard; the Hallionne didn't. Her words were clear; the thunder of Iberrienne's voice couldn't obliterate them. Lightning struck Kaylin and fizzled; the small dragon hissed. Iberrienne didn't seem to be directing the bolts; they were the aftershocks of the words he now spoke.

And they were words. They were words, but the form and shape they took were foreign. They, like the words engraved in stone, were the wrong shape, the wrong texture; they weren't solid enough to touch. They were solid enough to see, and Kaylin watched as they emerged. Thunder, she thought. Thunder, lightning, and cloud. It was a storm.

It looked like the heart of a storm, and she felt a sickening lurch as she realized, suddenly, that that was exactly what it was.

Ynpharion stiffened. He stopped struggling against her imperative; he searched for, and found, no exit, no means of escape. She felt what he would never express: fear. And he knew she knew it. That it was dangerous to know it, and that right now, it didn't matter. She watched the words form in their amorphous, dark shades; she watched them compress and congeal as their individual forms converged.

And she knew, suddenly, that they would all die—or worse—if that was allowed to happen. She reached out with the hand the Hallionne wasn't holding, lifting it. It was the hand that was ink-dark and still, after everything that had happened, wet. When it came into contact with the dark, dense cloud, she felt something solid beneath her hand. Solid but rough. It did not, thank gods, feel like a living organ.

She pulled it out of the growing mass and it came. It was small and distinct in shape, as unlike True Words as the Elantran alphabet. The runes that had been engraved in stone had been larger, their shapes poor mimicry of truth. This word—if it even was that—was not. It was small, compact, entirely what it was. And what it was, as she withdrew it, was…a stick. A dark gray stick. She stared at it, and as she did, the Hallionne smiled and took it from her hands, examining it as Kaylin reached out again.

She wasn't surprised to find that the next word in her hand was a stone; the one after that, also stone, but smoother and flatter. She found a bell, and also a basket, and although each was dark, dark gray, the textures and shapes were otherwise right. She paused when she pulled a patched, threadbare blanket out of the mire. These were not words.

But the Hallionne was passing them to people in the silent crowd, and as they accepted what she offered, their whole mien changed. A boy took the stick, and a girl, the two stones. An older man accepted the basket, and an elderly woman, the blanket. They stood examining them as if they were precious, personal items.

And why wouldn't they be? These people were all from the fiefs. In the fiefs, sticks and stones were often the only toys you had.

Kaylin shook herself and continued to pull these small words from the looming cloud. They couldn't be what they appeared to be—that made no sense at all. But it didn't matter. She found a ribbon. She found a pendant hanging on thick string. She found a pipe, bowl cracked. She found almost nothing that looked like a weapon and almost nothing of monetary value. But she examined each as it coalesced in her hand, and she passed each to the Hallionne, who, unperturbed, was waiting to pass it on. She seemed to know who should receive each item, and although she never let go of Kaylin's hand, she didn't seem to be inconvenienced by physical distance. Nor did the lightning and the thunder of Iberrienne's voice disturb her.

Were these words?

"No," the Hallionne replied. "And yes. They tell a story. There is the echo of story in each mortal life, but never the whole. But this, this is different. It is not that."

"What," Kaylin asked as she handed the Hallionne a wooden spoon, "am I really doing?"

"What you desire to do. You are giving them back the little that remains of their lives. They are," she added, "dead to you. They will never return home. Do not stop." As she spoke, the floor beneath Kaylin's feet began to lose the texture of familiar stone. It buckled, changing texture every few inches and changing color, as well. This was the ground in the Shadowlands.

"I am Hallionne," she continued as the ground began to slant toward the center of a Tower whose walls were no longer solid. "I understand the majesty of words, I understand their power. So, too, Iberrienne.

"But, Kaylin, you understand their smallness. You understand that in the slight, there is truth and a quiet, almost inaudible dignity. Look: he does not hear it. He cannot understand what you are doing. He believes that mortals have strength only in numbers, and so he has gathered them in number. They do not belong here; to bring them here at all took power—but he himself does not belong here, and the price he pays in order to stand here, where all words have truth, is high. Do not stop," she added more sharply.

"You could help me."

"No," was the soft—and inexplicably sad—response. "I cannot. But I see the small syllabus you return to them, and it moves me. I can almost remember. You work against him," she continued, "because he cannot see the small—but if you do not work, he will create as he intended. I am...interfering now."

"But how?"

"You do not understand what your blood in this place meant." She glanced at Kaylin's hand. "And what you yourself touched; it clings to you. You hold strands of their history in your hands; he holds the rest. But he cannot see clearly, and while he cannot, you must find those stories, those small, insignificant words. They do not speak to him. They speak to you because they are, in part, yours."

Because, Kaylin thought, she was of the fiefs and mortal, two things that were beneath Iberrienne's notice. Two things in combination that often felt as though they were beneath almost anyone's notice—maybe even her own. What had she wanted while living in those streets? Escape. Freedom.

But as she pulled another stick from the cloud, she lifted it to her eyes, and she remembered playing in those streets, just before her mother's death. Not everything had been dark. Not everything had been deadly. There was a ring, a plain band that felt metallic; its color made it impossible to judge the quality of the metal. She frowned when she picked up the slingshot and considered tossing it over her shoulder. The Hallionne took it before she could make that decision. When she found a doll, she smiled. It was old and worn, and it had clearly been patched a time or three. She had no idea if it belonged to a child or if it would at some point, and it didn't matter. She'd brought so little from the fiefs when she'd left them.

So little that she could hold in her hands, as she was holding these. She pulled her hand out of the Hallionne's grip, and the Hallionne allowed it. The floor was slippery where she now stood, and she moved slowly as she tried to find a different place to stand, passing through the edges of cloud and into the center, where Iberrienne stood. She hadn't come to confront him, though. This was where she needed to be.

He looked through her, as if she were already one of the dead.

And she reached both hands into his coalescing maelstrom, and she pulled. What came this time had no physical component. It couldn't be held. So many of her early memories were the same. She'd had oversized clothing, which, over the years, had become undersized; she usually had shoes, but not always. She'd never particularly valued the mismatched dishes and cutlery in her home, although the food had always been welcome, when it was there. But she'd loved her mother. She couldn't remember—as Teela could—what her mother looked like.

But she could remember the comfort of her mother's arms.

She could remember her mother's voice. She could almost hear it.

No. She *could* hear it. She could hear it now, and it was stronger than Iberrienne's voice, stronger than the cracking of stone, stronger than Ynpharion's fear. It had never been solid. If someone had asked her to prove that her mother had loved her, she had nothing to give them. But it was here. The proof of it was here. She could make it solid, whole; she could hold it in her hands. She gripped it as tightly as she possibly could, eyes closed; it wasn't something that could be seen, anyway.

I will always love you.

Had it been a lie? Yes. There was no *always* for mortals. All their forevers were planted in memory; it was the only place strong enough to shelter them. It was what their lives from start to finish built, and those memories were here, at the heart of the storm, where all words were true and Iberrienne was attempting to tell a lie.

There were bad memories. There was no way to avoid that; what was built was built by everything. But Kaylin was making the choices here. Kaylin was building a different narrative, working from the same building blocks.

I will never leave.

A lie, yes. But she could hear the truth at the heart of the words she hadn't heard so clearly since she was five years old. And maybe that's why mortals had no True Names of their own: because their truths and their lies were so often the same damn thing. Her mother had meant every word, every time.

And her mother was not the only one.

She had no toys, no physical mementos, to form tent pegs for the important things, because she realized that that's what they were. People loved dolls or toys because of what they meant; they held on to them because it was a guide to memories, a touchstone. She couldn't draw familiar and sentimental items as touchstones of the love she'd been given and still desperately wanted—from Caitlin, from Marcus's wives, she could admit that here—from the whirlwind.

But she didn't need them. Because in this place, the memory itself was tangible.

She saw her mother's corpse, and that was harsh, as hard, in the wake of her mother's words, as the death itself had been. Harsher, really, because she now understood the endless silence of fifteen years. She accepted it and reached beyond it, because if it was true, it was one truth, and every life accumulated many.

It was the largest thing she pulled from the whirlwind. It was the heart of the storm. And as it came to her, she understood that it wasn't just her memories of her mother that she had released: it was all of their memories.

Iberrienne's voice hardened, but it was a voice now; the syllables didn't disappear into rolling thunder. Kaylin spoke, was surprised to hear herself speaking. That had happened to her before, though. What she hadn't expected was that everyone else was speaking now, too. They weren't speaking—or moving—in concert, and they stumbled when the ground broke and congealed beneath their feet, but they were speaking the way a crowd at an office social function might: as themselves, as individuals. Their voices, their unadorned, mundane voices, were louder than Iberrienne's. They weren't magical. They weren't individually impressive.

It didn't matter.

The Barrani Lord's voice grew hoarse; his arms trembled. He was injured and exhausted. While he teetered, his hands falling to his side, the Lord of the West March approached, sword drawn.

Iberrienne coughed blood. "Not here, Lord of the West March," he said, falling to his knees. "Not here."

Kaylin reached for him, as she could finally see his name. His two names, so similar to Ynpharion's she was certain she could somehow purify him. But to do that, she had to catch him, and as she leapt—and she did—he began to fade.

She added Leontine cursing into what was an already overly chatty room.

The Lord of the West March sheathed his sword. "Hallionne Orbaranne."

She shook herself and glanced across the room. "Lord of the West March. We are secure."

The Barrani man who remained in the room knelt instantly, the gesture skirting the outer edge of total abasement. "Lord Ynpharion."

"Lord of the West March."

"Lord Iberrienne is Outcaste."

It was not a decision that the Lord of the West March could make, in theory. Ynpharion, however, understood how tenuous theory was.

"Were it not for Lord Kaylin, you would join him for your presence here." He turned to the Hallionne. "Is Ynpharion now trapped in this place?"

"No, Lord of the West March. He will leave when Lord Kaylin leaves, and he will not return. He is not what he was when he entered this space; I do not now believe him to be a danger." She glanced down as someone—a boy who was on the edge of childhood—tugged her arm. "If you will show Lord Kaylin and Lord Ynpharion out, I would remain with my guests." She frowned, and as she did, the whole of the geography shifted in place in an instant, and they stood, not in a Tower and not upon a grassy plain, but rather, in the streets of a familiar City.

It was Elantra, but on the right side of the bridge.

"They are my guests, Lord Kaylin." The boy continued to tug at her hand, something no other visitor would have dared to do. "I need to say goodbye, Ger. I'll be there in a minute." She turned, once again, to Kaylin, her eyes, for the moment, mortal eyes. "They cannot leave here. They are dead in any sense of the word—in your world.

"I do not know how long they will stay. I do not know how long I can keep them. But…for now, Lord Kaylin, they are my guests, and I would play host to them. It…reminds me. It has long been quiet in this place."

"But—"

"Kyuthe," the Lord of the West March said, offering Kaylin his arm. She stared at it for a long moment. "Come."

EPILOGUE

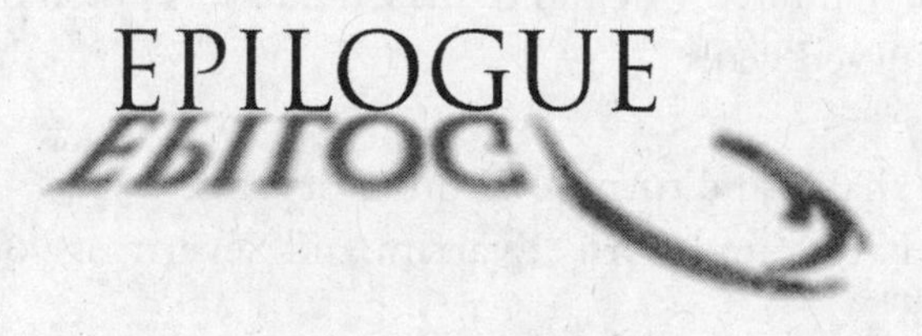

Her hands were red and wet as they fell, at last, to her side. Her hair—a white, pale gift of her mother's ancient lineage—was dusted with dirt, small splinters, pieces of what might, in the City, pass for glass. That she could still see at all was due in large part to Calarnenne's intervention; he had shielded her, at some cost to himself.

He was not the only one. Not since the war of the Flights had the Consort seen so much death, so much carnage, among her own people. And she had not been Consort then. She had been warrior—as devoted to the preservation of her mother as the fallen had been, in their turn, to hers.

The earth formed a gigantic basin around the Hallionne. The Hallionne had taken a form and shape that the Consort had never seen on the forest roads: a Tower. It was simple, unadorned stone. A Tower such as this might be planned and constructed by mortals who had no recourse to magery; it was squat, flat-topped, and heavy. The only nobility of feature was its continued existence. Nothing that had stood here—

not trees, plants, or forest animals—had survived. Nothing but the Hallionne itself.

The Consort's throat was raw; too raw for song. Speech eluded her, but for a different reason. The sunlight was harsh, the sky clear; birds flew in lazy, wide circles, their shadows large across the ground. The dirt and rock were unremarkable, but splintered wood and unearthed roots jutted from the basin's curved walls.

"Lady."

She exhaled and turned. "Lord Corvallis."

"We have found Lords Evarrim and Severn, as you commanded."

"They were alone?" The words came too quickly; she forced a pause. "Lord Kaylin?"

"I am sorry, Lady. No sign of Lord Kaylin could be found. Lord An'Teela is still searching; she sent me to report."

Of course. An'Teela, she thought with only a trace of bitterness. *This is why our Lady warned us all against developing affection for mortals; they die. But the Barrani had died here as well, giving lie to the warning and no lie whatever to the fear.* She turned—as so many of her kin did—to anger instead, clutching it and wrapping it tightly above things that must remain unsaid and unexposed.

"And Iberrienne?"

He shook his head.

"Are Lords Evarrim and Severn mobile?"

"They are walking," Corvallis replied. "Aid was offered, and aid was refused."

Of course it was. The Consort inhaled heavily. Evarrim, legless, would drag himself across molten lava before he accepted the aid of lesser Lords. Lord Severn, however, was pragmatic; if he walked, he was not near death. More than that, she could not yet say.

"They will be here ahead of the scouts. Landaran has taken the liberty of creating stairs for their use."

"They were not found within the basin."

"No, Lady."

"And Bertolle's kin?"

"If they are present, we cannot detect them."

She nodded again. "You did well," she added softly. "All of you."

He bowed; he offered no reply. Only the dead did, and it was silent and wordless.

It took the Lords Evarrim and Severn fifteen minutes to reach the Consort; she did not insult them by walking past the perimeter of her guards to meet them. Instead, she waited, watching as they walked. To her shock, she discovered that she had been wrong: Evarrim had accepted Lord Severn's aid, and to her eye, Lord Severn now supported the greater burden of Evarrim's weight. They were both wounded, although at this distance, she could not discern how. Their robes were red with blood, and given their rate of progress, some of it was their own.

As they drew closer, she saw that the ruby at the peak of Lord Evarrim's tiara had cracked; it was black now, the husk of a jewel. Lord Severn's blades were sheathed, but the chain itself was as blackened as the ruby.

The guards opened up to allow them passage; they approached, and when they were barely a yard away, they knelt. She wanted to tell them that this gesture was unnecessary and unwanted here, but she knew that etiquette was its own cage, and they had all accepted its bars; she held her peace. Their obeisances were awkward, but they were not without a peculiar, specific grace, and she accepted them with gratitude and bid them rise.

Lord Severn said, "Kaylin?" forgetting forms and titles.

She shook her head. "An'Teela is still searching; she has taken the best of my men."

"You were correct," Lord Evarrim said. "Iberrienne was in the outlands."

"You found him."

He nodded, glancing at Severn. "The credit is not mine alone; it is not, in truth, mine at all."

Lord Severn offered her nothing.

"Is he dead?"

"He was severely injured in our encounter, but he was not alone."

"He escaped you."

Evarrim's eyes were blue; he was weary. "Yes." He straightened his shoulders, retrieving the bulk of his weight. "The Hallionne survived."

"Yes. It was…very close. Not even the war of the Flights touched the Hallionne."

"No, of course not." He did not say that only treachery could; it wasn't necessary.

"Lord Severn, if Lord Kaylin was dead, we would know. Lord Calarnenne would inform us."

"Would he?"

"At my request, yes." She glanced at Evarrim; he grimaced. He said nothing, offered nothing; he was angry. But the anger would work in favor of the High Lord here. If the Court had been resistant to the casting out of Iberrienne, none of that resistance would remain. "Rest here, both of you. The danger, for the moment, has passed."

"The Lord of the West March, Lady?"

"His forces have retreated; they are to the west of the basin. We will not encounter difficulty on the road to the West March, and if we do, it will be scant; he has fully two hundred men beneath his banner." Or he had. She was uncertain what toll the battle had taken on their numbers; of the Lords who had chosen to accompany her, a full dozen were dead.

And another ten might join them, but of this, she did not speak. Five of the Lords who had ventured forth from the High Halls were still unaccounted for, and given the extent of the damage done to the immediate environs of the Hallionne, that accounting might never be made; they were lost in the outlands.

"Lady," Evarrim said, "the Lord of the West March has arrived."

She turned instantly in time to see the Tower shift in place, losing some of its drab physicality as it fashioned a door. Stone became momentarily amorphous along the west-facing curve of the wall, and when it hardened again, there was a strong rectangular shape, and in it, a drawbridge. That bridge now lowered, exposing, for a moment, some part of the interior of the Hallionne; that was not the Consort's concern.

She began to walk as Lord Kaylin and the Lord of the West March emerged from the Tower. They were followed by Lord Ynpharion, which narrowed the number of the missing to four. Lord Severn joined her as escort, or perhaps as coconspirator. It was impossible to maintain a stately, distant grace—although it was true that her brother managed it. He saw her, he was aware of her, but he remained poised, diffident, a reminder to her that comportment mattered.

She understood and accepted the implied criticism—she deserved it—but didn't slow; instead, she moved faster, and faster still, throwing off the weight of exhaustion and dread and guilt. She threw her arms wide, running now like a child. She saw his lips compress and thin as he stopped walking, folding his arms across his chest and lowering his chin.

Lord Kaylin glanced up at that chin and then across at the

Consort and Lord Severn; he was not moving with any more restraint than the Lady. He had the longer stride, but he was mortal; any deficiency in his Court etiquette would be laid at the feet of his race. The Consort lacked that excuse, and found she didn't care.

Her brother's eyes were green, an emerald-green, a forest-green. They were, at this moment, the color of the blood of the green. His expression and his posture implied disapproval; his eyes, none at all. Their color dimmed as she drew close enough that he could see her face, and she faltered.

What he didn't say, Lord Kaylin did: "Lady—you're injured—"

"It was not the transformed," she said quickly, slowing to a walk and lifting a hand to cover the deep gash in her cheek. It was vanity, really, a foolish, childish gesture; she forced her hand down, although it trembled. "There was some difficulty of a more magical nature." She came to stand before her brother and Lord Kaylin. "And no," she added, "you cannot heal me here. It is not a terrible wound, and with care, it will heal with little scarring."

The Lord of the West March reached out and caught her by the chin, a gesture not at home in the High Court. Or any Barrani Court. "You did well. You are alive."

"Many of my companions are not."

"Then they fulfilled their highest duty." He caught her in his arms before she could say another word, lifting her off her feet. "Come, we must return to the West March; the High Lord awaits my report, and he has never been patient."

"You told him?"

"Yes. I considered it wise, as I was forced by circumstance to mobilize four of the war bands."

"You are aware that he was not pleased by my attendance of the regalia?"

Her brother laughed. "I am perhaps far more acquainted with that fact than you, Lady. There are things he might safely say to me that would be unwise in the extreme to say to you. If these," he added, encompassing the devastation of the basin in one brief sweep of hand, "are the trappings of freedom, you must find what meager entertainment they might provide; I do not think he will grant permission for another such excursion for the next century. Or three."

His smile dwindled. "It was not my interference that preserved the Hallionne."

She sighed. "No, I somehow doubted it would be; I thought your interference might serve to save her life, not the Hallionne's existence." She turned to Lord Kaylin and frowned. "Your forehead."

The youngest Lord of the High Court grimaced. "There's another mark?"

"There is. It is quite…distinct."

"A Barrani died in the heart of the Hallionne."

All curiosity fled; what remained in its wake was a visceral, icy anger. "And you could…take…his name?"

Kaylin's eyes widened. "No!" She grimaced again, and the small dragon, hidden behind the fall of her unrestricted hair, raised his head. "No, that's not why…" She glanced at her companion, and he warbled.

"I—I only meant to save it. The name," she added. "His name. Iberrienne was somehow draining it. I grabbed it instead. I knew if I didn't, the word would be irrevocably lost—and I couldn't let that happen." She spoke in her inelegant and rushed Elantran. And she believed every word that she spoke.

The Lady's anger did not desert her; it slid to the side, aimed now at a target that was not in reach. Exhaling, the Consort said, "Lord Kaylin, if we survive the nightmare of the coming regalia, and we return to the High Halls alive, all debt between us is forgiven."

She felt a twinge of conscience at the open hope that transformed the young woman's expression, and turned away. It was very difficult for her to nurse a grudge against a child.

And it was also very difficult to stand back and let that child careen, with her terrifying, unknown power, through the hidden, wild places of the world without guidance, even if such guidance was both imperfect and frequently disregarded.

She is a danger, she thought, but wondered as she did whether the Ancients had chosen more wisely than any of the Immortals were willing to credit: Kaylin would live only a handful of years, and perhaps the weight of that handful was not enough to destroy her optimism and her palpable desire to believe that the world—and the people in it—was a far better place than it actually was.

Perhaps it was contagious, this hope, this odd openness. Perhaps it was dangerous—but as the Consort watched Lord Severn carefully put his arm around Lord Kaylin's shoulder, the Consort thought that she might allow herself this indulgence: to believe in Lord Kaylin while she lived. It was such a short period of time.

★★★★★

And still the recitation awaits!
CAST IN SORROW

ACKNOWLEDGMENTS

For the most part, I go about my writing in relative silence, with the occasional bout of hair-pulling during the difficult parts of the book. This book was mostly difficult parts with a few smooth, normal writing sessions holding it together, so there was rather a lot of hair-pulling and kvetching. Which means that my friends don't really have to read this book—they know it inside and out. I probably used more words in my "discussions" than I wrote in the actual book. Thanks, then, to Tanya Huff, Alis Rasmussen and Chris Szego (who is fast becoming the real reason I can't ever leave my part-time job), and also to Thomas and Terry, who are expected, when things are difficult, to offer useful feedback while reading the book a chapter at a time, even when the chapters get thrown out and new ones inserted at a later point.

My thanks go to to Mary-Theresa Hussey at LUNA for being a superhero editor, because when a book is difficult for me, there's usually some fallout for her, and she's been wonderful.

Also, thanks to my mother and father, who keep the house around me running, and keep my kids fed when I am so deep in the book I forget little things like laundry and grocery shopping and eating.